MIRROR SOUND

Also by Monica Sanz

SEVENTH BORN

MIRROR BOUND

THE WITCHLING ACADEMY SERIES

monica sanz

Entangled Publishing, LLC
2614 South Timberline Road
Suite 105, PMB 159
Fort Collins, CO 80525
rights@entangledpublishing.com

Entangled Teen is an imprint of Entangled Publishing, LLC.

Visit our website at www.entangledpublishing.com.

Edited by Stacy Abrams
Cover design by LJ Anderson, Mayhem Cover Creations
And Bree Archer
Cover images by
CoffeeAndMilk/Gettyimages
liqwer20.gmail.com/DepositPhotos
Memento/DeviantArt
solarseven/Gettyimages
IlyaShapovalov/Gettyimages
Interior design by Toni Kerr

ISBN 978-1-64063-721-4
Ebook ISBN 978-1-64063-722-1

Manufactured in the United States of America

First Edition September 2019

10 9 8 7 6 5 4 3 2 1

entangled teen
an imprint of Entangled Publishing LLC

Be strong, darlings.
You will change the world.

deadly things to come

Seraphina Dovetail closed the *Ethics of Binding Spells* grimoire on her lap and pressed her hands on the marbled leather cover to steady their tremble. She had much left to study, but how could she possibly read on when nerves knotted her stomach and made the words invisible to her eyes?

Relax, Sera. You must relax.

Hauling in a deep breath through her nose, she released it measuredly out of her mouth and rolled her shoulders. Her gray muslin dress stuck to her sweat-dampened skin, but she ignored this discomfort. She'd been through worse than a mere doctor's appointment, a feat given her horrid treatment by physicians in the past. But surely she would survive this one. She had to if she ever wished to take the School of Continuing Magic entrance exam and, in time, become an inspector.

She held fast to this thought, repeated it in her mind like a mantra until dread no longer spurred the magic in her belly and her frantic heartbeat ceased to overpower all sound. Yes, not even near death or expulsion from the Aetherium's Witchling Academy had kept her dream at bay. Neither would this doctor.

The office door groaned open. Magic rushed from Sera's stomach and filled her veins with heat, and sweat sprouted like liquid fire from her pores. A stout man with a blunt nose and pockmarked skin walked in, thin strands of his gray hair combed over the bald patch atop his head. He wore a hard-set expression and a white, ankle-length robe with the name *Samson* stitched below the Aetherium crest on the upper-left breast.

He moved to a wood desk mastering the back of the exam room and never once looked at her.

"Why are you here?" he asked by way of a greeting—a rather harsh, cold, and bestial one. "Speak quickly. I've other appointments."

He thrust down her medical file, and Sera's mouth bowed at the reason for his unkindness. The thick, brown dossier was marked with a dark stripe along the length, akin to the seventh-born tattoo wrapped around her wrist. The thin black line telling the world she was the seventh-born daughter to a witch, her birth the cause of her mother losing her powers and, in turn, her life.

Though used to the hostility impelled by her birth order, anger still prickled the underside of her skin, but she stifled the urge to set his paperwork on fire. At least not while her file remained on his desk. "Yes, sir, I know. I have waited four hours to be seen."

"Then perhaps you should have made an appointment." He set her file aside, plucked up another patient's record, and, flipping open the cover, reviewed its contents.

She folded her fingers into her palm, their tips itching with suppressed magic. "I *had* an appointment." And she'd paid half of her wages to the secretary outside to attain it.

He continued to scribble notes on the other file and never once spared her a glance. "Yes, well, be grateful I'm even here."

As grateful as I would be if I were trampled by a horse, she mused bitterly but cleared her throat. The faster she finished with this wretched brute, the quicker she could get back home to study. "I require a physical examination for the Aetherium entrance exam."

He paused mid-script and finally looked at her from over his glasses, close-set brown eyes narrowed under a thick, reddened brow. "But you're a *seventhborn*."

A blush gathered in her cheeks, but she held her chin a touch higher. "Yes, sir, I am. But the exam is open to anyone and everyone, should they meet the necessary qualifications. Given my extensive education during my time at the Witchling Academy, I will not be denied." At least she hoped this was the case. Her approval letter had yet to arrive, though it was only two weeks until the exam. This didn't matter. It would come, and when it did, she would be ready.

He scoffed. "And you need a recommendation from an Academy instructor to take it." He rose to his feet, snatched up her file, and thrust it out to her. "Settle your payment with the secretary in the front, and next time, spare us your delusions. There are others here in need of real medical care."

Sera bolted to her feet, and the lamps flared. She snatched the file from his hand, pulled out her sealed referral, and slammed the folder down before him, the recommendation on top with its gold Aetherium crest prominently displayed. "Professor Nikolai Barrington has provided me with a referral."

Lips pursed, he plucked up the envelope and surveyed Barrington's information on the front, from the emblem of his Invocation ring burned onto the page, to his signature beside it, to his school address, should anyone wish to inquire about its validity.

Sighing heavily, he stuffed the referral inside and perused her medical history quickly. With each moment of silence, Sera's pulse quickened. So far, all other doctors authorized to approve Aetherium potentials had declined her appointment query. This beast of a man was the last one with an availability so close to the exam, and if he refused to see her, she'd have to ask Professor Barrington for help. He'd never deny her, this she knew.

Yet, her soul wrenched. He'd welcomed her into his home after she'd been expelled and taught her magic beyond what she'd ever learned at the Academy. He took her on as his assistant for his private detective work, with generous wages certainly unlike those seen by a seventhborn. After learning of her horrible past, he taught her how to defend herself. Above all, he worked tirelessly to find her family.

And he'd never asked for anything in return, except for her trust. Heat roared up her body, and she pressed a hand over her stomach, which fluttered madly at the memory of him so close, his pale gray eyes fixed on hers when he said, *Be a little mad and trust me, Miss Dovetail. I swear on my magic—I mean you no harm.*

Her blush deepened, and her heart seemed to forget its function, at once falling off rhythm. Through kindness and gentleness, he'd gained her confidence that day, and, shortly after, her heart, but she drew in a deep breath and tipped her chin.

He'd done enough. She would deal with things on her own and wouldn't burden him with her problems again.

He turned the page, and his face contorted in disgust as he beheld the photographs of Sera's scarred body, taken three years prior by cold and heartless doctors like him.

She'd been forced to stand there as they poked and prodded her, looking at her flesh as though she were an animal at the zoo. No, even animals were afforded more courtesy than a seventhborn. To them, she had been nothing, and though able to heal her, they didn't even try. Regardless of the fact that she'd been drained of her magic for nearly a year by a warlock. Uncaring that she had just fought for her life.

Doctor Samson closed her file. His frown deepened. "Very well."

Sera sat down, relief weakening her knees.

"Is there anything I should know before we begin? Anything of concern?"

Sera shifted in her chair. There were her constant headaches and nausea, and her reserves were taking a tad longer to fill, but then again, her best friend had betrayed her. The boy who claimed to love her had died proving just that. And she'd killed a man using a power she didn't know she had. Surely this was bound to destabilize even the strongest of magicians. "No, nothing. I've never felt better."

He moved around his desk, and Sera gulped. He unsheathed his wand, and she flinched, her hands yearning to snatch out her own wand. But she curled her fingers to fists and forced herself to settle. This was simply a health assessment, a requirement. Whatever her fear, she needed this done. Without it, her imminent approval letter was useless.

I will be an inspector.

I will find my family.

Though she didn't remember them, she held fast to the phantom faces she imagined as those of her father and siblings as Doctor Samson clamped a hand on her shoulder and shoved his wand against her temple with the other.

His cold magic rushed into her and wrapped around her bones. Sera hissed in discomfort at his manic approach. He was supposed to ease into her psyche slowly and travel her lifeline, seeking anything that might hinder her powers and ability to defend the Aetherium. Yet, he jammed his wand tip deeper against her skull as though seeking to exhume her brain and searched her lifeline quickly until a sour bitterness filled her head and throat.

Sera's powers roared within, a starved beast rattling the bars of a rusted cage as the doctor's frantic inspection burned the underside of her skin. Wedged through her muscles. Searched every part of her with a careless brutishness, similar to the warlock whose savagery left her body riddled with scars.

His inspection now filled her head with a droning hum that stabbed into her mind like a web of lightning. Wild flames shot to her fingertips, ravenous for release. She struggled to hold them back but grimaced as intense pain radiated across her skull, akin to jagged knives serrating her brain in two. Still, she had to endure. If she wished to become an inspector and find her family, she could not break.

Doctor Samson drew his magic back so fast, Sera was thrust sideways and slipped from her chair, down onto the dingy gray floor. She gasped wildly and skittered back against the wall despite the soreness in her bones.

Back at his desk, Doctor Samson filled out her form in a few quick strokes, punched it with a stamp, and tossed it down at her feet. He walked out and slammed the door closed behind him. Breathless and hurting, Sera glanced down at her paperwork. He'd deemed her fit to take the Aetherium exam, and yet, she clambered to the nearest basin. Her stomach twisted, and she retched into the ceramic bowl, over and over, until dry heaves wrung her insides and nothing else came out.

Winded, she reached blindly for a towel and wiped her mouth, then ran a hand along her forehead and brushed away the chestnut strands that had clung to her face with sweat. Her fingers trembled, and she shivered, her skin so very cold, no doubt the effects of Doctor Samson's cruel examination. But despite this, she thrust down the towel. She had survived him and was now one step closer to her dream.

Sera stumbled back and, snatching up her file, drew her wand and aimed it down at the floor. Transferring required concentration, and a smooth landing demanded a precise amount of magic, both of which were now a struggle with the pain of Doctor Samson's vicious exam alive in her veins. Still, she closed her eyes and forced herself to think beyond the ache. She was going home now. To the peace of Barrington's home on the moors. To him.

Warmth spread through her in a wave at the thought of him, and her powers churned quicker. At his side, she would relish in their investigations and conversations and comforting quiet. He would never shun her or insult her. With him, she was safe, and at his side, she would meet no harm.

Her magic sloshed within her like lava, fast and burning. With the coordinate ciphers to Barrington's home fixed in her mind, she gripped her wand tighter and called on her powers. Raw heat rose through her veins, to her fingertips, and filled the fibers of her wand in red. One flick of the rod and the ground beneath her vanished. Moments later, she crashed down into her apartment in Barrington's manor, a chamber much larger than her old Academy room. There, she'd been relegated to a cramped space within the school's tower, a clear desire to pretend she didn't exist. Her room and furniture had been equally abandoned. But here, a gorgeous dark mahogany bedroom set was spread about, coupled with a burgundy carpet over the hardwood floors. There was a writing table and, above it, a shelf lined with books. She had never been allowed to read for leisure before, save for one dreaded tome, *The Unmitigated Truths of Seventhborns*.

It was nowhere to be found now. She'd torn it apart page by page and burned it.

Stalking to her window, she gripped the brass handles and shoved the panels open, the hinges' loud squeals disturbing the quiet evening. Muted sunlight streamed across the rocky terrain, patches of heather and gorse shading the moors in brilliant hues of yellow and purple. She dragged in a deep breath scented of vegetation and faint traces of brine, and a gentle breeze rustled the tall grass and cooled the sweat on her brow. Though a heat wave engulfed the Aetherium mainland, the northern provinces of the island nation had been relatively spared. And with Barrington's home on the northmost isle, the moors had remained cool and damp.

The relief was short-lived. Still able to detect the sterile stench of Doctor Samson's office on her person and the feel of his magic in her veins, Sera peeled off her gray dress where she stood, kicked it aside, and rushed to her wardrobe. She dressed quickly, though with some difficulty; each step throbbed in her head, and her bones still ached.

Nevertheless, she fastened her kit belt on her waist, slid her wand into the designated holder, and strode to the door. There was work to do and studies to pursue. And now, with her physical examination complete, there was soon an exam to take, and nothing would stop her. Not a headache or aching bones. Not a cursed birthright or the unending cruelty of men.

She pulled the door open. The quiet hallway was swathed in shadows, the sun set for the day. Faint bluish light cut through the darkness beneath the recurrent exposed beams along the corridor. Countless protection spells were etched onto the wood and glittered, telling of their power. The bars ran all along the house like veins, infusing the manor with magic. Some of the spells were for protection, others to conceal the house and the surrounding lands, but it was the newer ones that gripped Sera's heart.

Between the older beams were crossbars fashioned out of wood and milled black tourmaline—a repellant for ghosts. Ever since she summoned the dead to defeat the horrible warlock and maker of her scars, ghosts had taken to appear uninvited, something that happened more and more each day. Upon learning of her phantoms and the nausea, headaches, and dizziness they left in their wake, Barrington had worked diligently to create repellants and installed them in and around his home, but the phantoms quickly proved his expensive endeavor pointless.

She reached the workroom and, with the snap of her fingers, turned on the lamps. Golden light streamed across the chamber, warm and comforting. A long workbench mastered the middle of the space, its exterior marked with various burns, nicks, and pigments from the many experiments she and Barrington conducted on its surface. Shelves crowded the walls, some stacked with books and grimoires, others with tools necessary for their investigative work.

A rhythmic rumble resounded from the back of the room. Sera walked around the workbench to find the Barghest asleep before the open window. In the months since she'd rescued the hellhound from his evil owners, his fur had grown out from under his scales and now covered him in a thick black coat. Tar no longer dripped from his fangs, and a patch of blond hair crowned his bear head, but he still had no name, and not for lack of trying. So far, he'd refused all of Sera's suggestions, and she was forced to simply call him Barghest.

Sera took a step, and a floorboard creaked. The mountainous creature roused from his sleep. At seeing Sera, his amber eyes brightened, and she swore his jowls widened into something of a smile, though she knew it was probably because she was the only one with a weak will and fed him magic more than anyone else.

She held her hand up, and a warm orb of smoke gathered in her palm. She flicked it in his direction, and, with a lick of his forked tongue, he caught it in his mouth.

"Go on, then. I'm only doing paperwork, so no experiments right now."

The Barghest huffed, clearly underwhelmed. Dissolving into a cloud of black smoke, he swept out the window to wherever he could get some undisturbed rest.

Sera turned. Noting the day's mail on her leather-top mahogany desk, she snatched up the correspondence and greedily shuffled through it. With each passed message, pressure gathered in her chest and her throat thickened. It would come. With only two weeks to go, her exam approval would be there. And with her health assessment now complete, she would have all the required paperwork for her test. Yet, upon reaching the last of the post, heat flushed through her and the air grew thinner and harder to breathe. The mail was all addressed to Barrington, her letter yet to arrive.

Breathless, she thrust the envelopes onto the table and squeezed her eyes shut. She found no comfort in the dark, just an endless black that whirled the nothingness around her. Her stomach in knots, she gripped the edge of the table and lowered down into her chair. Clutching her knees, she inhaled deeply and emptied her lungs for some minutes. She hadn't received it today, but it would come. She was a talented witch, and perhaps there was a reason for the delay.

There was still time.

She meditated on this for long minutes, until the heaviness over her heart lessened and her pulse normalized. With one final and lengthy exhale, she wiped her palms on her skirt and moved to a neighboring oak file cabinet. She couldn't break. She had to keep moving, working. So long as she did, panic and grief couldn't find her.

Opening the uppermost drawer, she thumbed through the records. *Camden, Cardale, Carlisle...* She pursed her lips. The one case file she sought—*Carlson*—was missing. There was only one reason why.

"Barrington," she muttered and pushed the drawer shut. She had implemented a system of cataloguing evidence for easier retrieval, but no power on earth could keep *him* organized.

Picking up his correspondence, she walked to his office. As usual, spell books, notes, crime scene photographs, and old newspapers were scattered along the surface of his cherrywood desk and every other space that could support the chaos of his mind. But she neared his bureau and paused. The note she'd written to let him know of her appointment remained unmoved. He still wasn't home.

Her heart dimmed. He'd left the previous night to attend to something personal, and no doubt by *personal* he meant with his informant, Gummy, who was certainly much more than that. Whose crimson lip salve stained his shirts when he came back in the early hours. Whose perfume of rose and spice still clung to him in the morning. As of late, his visits to her had grown more frequent, but Sera pushed the thoughts away. It was no concern of hers where he was, what he did, and who warmed his bed. He was her employer and nothing more, and his kindness during the last six months was something she would always treasure, despite the protests of her heart.

She crumpled up the note and tossed it in the bin, then, shifting aside a few books and papers, she located the case file and snatched it up. Setting his mail on top, she spun and yelped at Professor Barrington standing at the door.

Tall and slim, he leaned against the frame, handsome in a black frockcoat, black pants, white shirt, and burgundy brocade vest. A small smile touched his thin lips. "Good evening, Miss Dovetail," he said, his voice a soothing baritone.

Despite the fact they lived together, Sera's heart took to a strange rhythm, as it often did whenever he fixed his eyes on her. But she cleared her throat and straightened. She would master her reactions to him, even if she had to pin her heart to the ground and strangle it.

"Good evening, Professor. You scared me."

He clicked his teeth. "Yes, I think that was the point."

Sera scowled, at which his grin widened.

He pushed off the doorway and walked across the room, radiating confidence like an aura, not that she could blame him. At five-and-twenty, he was the youngest professor at the Witchling Academy. More, the owner of the Aetherium's most prestigious endowment: an Invocation ring. The sign of a true magician, able to manipulate magic without a wand, and a requirement to becoming an inspector.

As he passed her, Sera searched for signs of his evening on his person. His unruly black hair was rather tame, if a bit long. He kept it short during the school term but let it grow throughout the summer to where the bottoms took on a slight curl. No makeup residue stained his collar, and there were no marks along his neck, bites or scratches or otherwise. All in all, he was rather presentable. She took in a deep breath and only found his comforting scent.

Satisfied, she abandoned her scrutiny and sat in the armchair before his desk. "I couldn't find Lord Carlson's file in the cabinet and figured it would be in here."

He unsheathed his wand and set it down on his mess. Sera shook her head. How he ever managed to find anything was beyond her. "Ah, yes, the Carlson file. I meant to put it back."

She pursed her lips. Of course he had.

Sitting, he picked up the correspondence she'd left for him. "Did your approval letter come yet?"

Panic wormed into her chest and rattled her heart again, but she swallowed it down. "Nothing yet, but I got my medical paperwork verified, so I will be ready when it comes."

"Grand. And speaking of doctors…" He set the mail down and, leaning forward, laced his long fingers together. "I met with the magician we queried about your memories."

Sera's heartbeat quickened. With her every memory prior to two years ago locked in her mind, Barrington collected the names of conjurers able to create complex spells confining a magician's abilities and memories. These spells often manifested as a hallway or a tunnel of doors in their mind. Sera's stomach twisted as she recalled her binding spell chamber: an endless hallway of myriad gates closed with a black padlock. Behind those doors was the truth of who she was. More, the identities of her father and siblings and the events that led to their separation. And in breaking the binding spell chamber once and for all, she would discover where she belonged and whether or not she'd ever been loved.

She shifted to the edge of her chair and swallowed around the knot in her throat. "Did he know anything about how to recover my memories?"

He met her stare levelly, the dim look there answering

her question before he spoke. "He didn't. I'm sorry."

"Oh." Pain gathered in her chest, and the word was a little above a whisper. She turned her head down. Though she would one day become an inspector and use all she'd learned to find her father and siblings, this blow didn't hurt any less.

Standing, Barrington came around his desk and leaned back on the edge. A moment later, he slid a cool finger under her chin and tilted her head up just as her first tear fell. "Surely you don't think I'll give up so easily? If I'm not mistaken, just yesterday you called me a stubborn buffoon."

Despite her pain, Sera's stomach fluttered wildly at his touch, and she managed the beginnings of a smile. "I still think you are."

He mirrored her expression, and, stroking a thumb across her cheek gently, he brushed her tear away and lowered his hand. "Good. And I'm not just the bearer of bad news. I may have overheard some talk about the topics covered during the Aether portion of the entrance examination."

Sera's brow furrowed. "Isn't that cheating?" she asked, the ghost of his touch still alive on her skin.

"I didn't seek out this information, surely, but"—he shrugged a shoulder—"I suppose I'll just keep it to myself and not tell you scrying for an assigned subject will be addressed."

Sera frowned, for which he rewarded her with a quick smile. "You're—"

"Charming? Resourceful? Brilliant?"

Her frown deepened. "Impossible."

He tapped a finger on his thin lips and hummed. "I suppose that's better than, what did you say I was last week? Ah, yes. A wild boar."

Disappointment marred her heart, but Sera laughed.

"Yes, you're still that, too."

Their gazes met, and his smile faded slowly, the mischief in his stare replaced by something warmer that wrapped around her bones. For a moment, that horrible appointment and the dead end with her family ceased to exist. There was just Barrington, his stolen touch, and the heavy silence warming the space between them.

Sera cleared her throat and stood, the Carlson file tight in her hands. "I should get to work on this." Whatever her and Barrington's uncertainty was, whatever her ardent desire to uncover what lay beyond it, it was best to leave it alone. Feelings for a man like Barrington were madness. And with her exam so close, it was a recklessness she couldn't afford. Besides, he was probably just being kind, seeking to ease her disappointment, and she would do well to remember this.

"Yes, right, indeed," Barrington said, all previous warmth gone from his voice and now-shuttered stare. "I went to the Aetherium this morning, and while there, I collected the magic samples we require for the case. Hopefully they can lead us to whoever hexed Lady Carlson's brush."

Ever since Lady Carlson—the Aetherium director of Transfer Travel and Coordinate Affairs—received the beautiful silver-plated ornate brush as a gift during her birthday party, her hair had started to fall out. Sadly, the present had been set on the gift table, the box bore no name, and there had been hundreds of guests at the affair. It was short work to figure out the brush was cursed, and it was also no mystery Lady Carlson wasn't the Lord's only lover. But she was willing to pay for a discreet investigation, and that's just what they would do, however surprising it was that Barrington would consider a case so frivolous in nature compared to their other inquiries.

They walked to the workroom together. At the work-bench was a small wooden box. Sera flipped the lid open to find dozens of small vials, a smoky substance within each narrow ampoule—the samples of magic belonging to their suspects.

She opened her notebook and turned to the page where she'd deciphered the spell used on the brush and uncovered the culprit's spell signature, their magical fingerprint. Now all she had to do was transcribe the signatures on the magic samples and match them to the one used on the brush, something she hadn't yet learned to do.

"Let us begin," Barrington said, clasping his hands together. His aura changed instantly to the serious, ferocious air that consumed him whenever he taught her. As she drew a protection circle on the table, he walked to the back of the room and entered the pantry on the left. On the right was his private workroom, behind a black door. Not even his maid, Rosie, had set foot inside.

Sera scribbled a containment spell within her protection circle to enclose the samples of magic in place, then poured a vial of salt inside the invocation in order to preserve the specimen lest it vanish.

Barrington met her at the table. He approved her work with a nod, then reached into the cloth bag in his hands with a pair of tweezers and drew a plant out by its stalk. Three leaflets branched from a single, thorn-less stem. The leaves formed a triangular pattern, and there were no other leaves on the shoot.

"Poison oak," Sera offered before he asked.

"The great imitator. Poison oak tends to emulate the leaves surrounding it, and it's this characteristic we seek. We never use our samples in their entirety, not without creating a spare in case our original specimen is damaged or corrupted somehow. This is the process of replication. As its leaves burn, it will release its imitative properties and duplicate our sample. The oil the leaves produce, however, causes inflammation and blistering, even from the smoke when you burn them. Therefore, our containment spell has a dual purpose; it keeps both our specimen and the poison oak confined."

He arranged them within the salt circle, creating a bed of leaves. Finished, he twirled his index finger. At the table, the containment spell was powered, and a cool dome of mist appeared over their workspace.

He took one of the vials from the box of samples and opened it within the dome. The smoky purple substance whirled up and bounced against the barrier. "You may ignite the leaves, slow and steady."

Sera unsheathed her wand and aimed it down at the leaves. The magic specimen floated within the dome — a tendril of smoke determined on escape. She touched on the fire she held tightly secured in her core. Wild flames shot to her fingertips, ravenous for release, but she seized them and clutched her wand tighter to lessen the shaking of her hands from the strain. Her wand glowed red, the wood fibers filled with her magic. She guided her powers, a slow stream of red smoke, down toward the leaves.

"Good," Barrington said, his voice low as to not disturb her concentration. "Now keep this intensity. If it becomes too much to gather the magic in your wand, focus it here…"

He touched her pulse at her wrist, his fingertips soft and cool. Sera's magic spiked at the sensation, but, biting her nails into her wand's metal encasement, she wrestled it steady. Her magic settled down on the leaves, and a sheer blanket of flames consumed the glossy plants.

"Magnificent," Barrington said and rewarded her with a smile that made his eyes a little lighter. "And an exemplary display of control."

A furious blush pricked Sera's cheeks from within, but she chastised her heart, that swooned much too easily.

Barrington moved to the table, closest to the dome. "Now, it will take some days for the duplicates to develop. Oftentimes…"

He went on, but Sera winced as intense pain radiated across her skull. His voice sounded far away, to where she couldn't discern his words. The temperatures in the room plummeted, and goose bumps sprouted along her skin, replacing the warmth elicited by Barrington's nearness.

The outlines of ghosts appeared all around her. She cast Barrington a frantic gaze, but, consumed by his lecture, he didn't notice her panic. But even if he did, he wouldn't see the phantoms moments away from materializing, their presence lingering about the room like fog. Only seventhborns were burdened with the cursed second sight.

Go away, Sera thought to herself desperately. The dead had no say in the realm of the living. They had to listen to her. Yet a spirit emerged in a burst of mist, a girl with pale skin and dark circles under her eyes. Her gray dress and once-white apron were both drenched in dirt and blood.

Barrington gestured to something on the brush, and his hand moved near the protection dome.

The ghosts reached for Sera. *Show you…*

Cold fingers wrapped around Sera's forearm, and she screamed. Wild flames shot to her fingertips in a manic gust, and savage flames roared from her wand, consuming the dome and Barrington's hand.

He cursed and jerked back, clasping his burned hand in the other. The dome over their experiment vanished, and plumes of toxic smoke twisted into the air. Barrington gripped Sera's wrist with his good hand and hurried them out into the hall. With a wave of his arm, he forced the windows open, and the poisonous smoke was sucked out into the moors.

He gave her a once-over, as though to ascertain her well-being with a single look. "Are you all right?"

She nodded, though her pulse thundered within. Not only had she seen a ghost, but it had touched her…or at least she'd felt frigid fingers on her skin, a cold sensation that lingered painfully on her arm. But the dead existed on an entirely different plane; it was impossible for them to touch the living.

Had she been mistaken somehow? Perhaps, but she would have to think on it later.

Moving to Barrington's side, she sought to inspect his injury, but it was already enveloped in a thin coating of his magic. Within moments, the burn lessened, until only a slight pink tinge remained. His sleeves, however, were charred.

"I'm fine. It was nothing," he assured her, though the thin sheen of sweat over his brow told her it was anything but. "I must have miscalculated the amount of poison oak."

Sera shifted back against the wall. She knew as well as he did that she'd been the reason for the accident. "I'm sorry—"

She winced and squeezed her eyes shut. A headache throbbed with each pulse, the pain a constant scream drowning out all sound.

Barrington's hands came upon her shoulders, and he brought her closer. "Ghosts?"

Sera nodded, unable to lie. Not here in his arms.

He weaved his hands into her hair. Their nearness was dangerous, but the moment his musk of sandalwood filled her nose and his cold hands found the nape of her neck, she rested her head against his chest, lost to him.

"Don't move," he said softly, though Sera wasn't sure

she could even if she wanted to; her legs were completely unreliable. Slowly, he trailed his hands to the base of her jaw and pressed down a little harder. Sera sucked in a breath. The candles above flared and extinguished, leaving them to the soft blue hues of a dying day.

He kneaded slowly, each squeeze pulsing a new wave of his magic across her skull until she felt she could float away in it. But the stink of rot and decay met Sera's nose, and she stiffened. Opening her eyes, she looked over her shoulder and gasped. An emaciated ghost stood close, his hungry gaze fixed on her. Not all spirits sought to share their pain with the hopes of finding peace in the afterlife, and the malice in this phantom's eyes promised pain for pain's sake.

He grabbed for her with a bony, shackled hand.

Sera pushed Barrington aside and moved out of the ghost's reach. "Go away!"

Her magic spiked, and a wild wind whooshed down the hall. The candelabras flared, illuminating the hall in blinding white light. The sconces exploded. They both flinched and ducked at the shards of glass propelled across the corridor.

Sera's magic plummeted, and the violent breeze died. The ghost was also gone.

Barrington straightened and looked at her, a dip forming over his brow. "Sera…"

He reached for her, but she swatted his fingers away and held a staying hand between them. "Please, just…stay away."

Shock flashed across his eyes, but Sera didn't stay to watch it settle into offense or hurt. She rushed down the hall and up the stairs, the portraits along the walls and recurrent exposed beams a blur to her watery eyes.

In her room, she closed the door behind her and paused. The fringes of a bruise peeked out from under her sleeve.

She pulled up the gray fabric, and stark cold rushed down her spine. The contusion was exactly where the phantom girl had grabbed her, and her skin there was sore as though she'd been singed.

Whereas her various encounters with phantoms over the months had been harmless, this one hadn't simply lingered. It *had* touched her. But...how? It was impossible to consider it, yet if so, why did a painful bruise now mark her skin?

She moved to the window seat. Sitting, she brought her bruised hand to her chest and gazed outside. Barrington cut through the tendrils of sea mist rolling over the moorlands, his figure growing smaller with distance as he walked toward the iron gate surrounding his home, no doubt where he'd affixed the latest deterrents and protections. Her soul churned. He wouldn't give up on solving the mystery of her uninvited ghosts, no matter the cost or consequence.

Though she was certain he only did this out of a gentlemanly duty, that of a man determined to keep his word that she was safe with him, his loyalty in that moment both warmed and broke her heart, and she hugged herself. As much as she wished not to be, she would always be a burden to him, and eventually he would come to regret taking her on as his assistant and asking for her trust.

Worse, remembering his burned hand and the bruise on her arm, she shivered. And as he vanished into the fog, a sinking feeling settled in her stomach. Clairvoyance hadn't ever been her forte, but perhaps it was time to accept the ghosts were not just her second sight but the grim premonitions of deadly things to come.

2

business of the worst sort

Sera and Barrington landed neatly on the platinum transfer wheels of the Aetherium's Imperial Palace. They were greeted by an attendant and the loud hum of the crowd that pulsed before them, visitors from all over the island nation, excited for the Feast of Edification. The holiday commemorated the official end of Purism as the dominant Aetherium religion a century before and celebrated the advancements made after its fall, when magic was no longer considered a divine right, but rather accessible to all through sweeping education and government reform. But though the Aetherium government now embraced Pragmatism as their religion, favoring reason over myth, Sera pursed her lips—Purist or Pragmatic, they were all the same nonsense, and the role of seventhborns would never change.

Arm in arm, they stepped out of the transfer wheel platform and into the hall fashioned out of glass and steel. Intermittent hanging metal candelabras illuminated the domed halls with a warm, amber hue. Throngs of guests bustled about just outside of the stall, their amalgamation of voices underscored by a harp played nearby. The air was electrified, a buzz of excitement swelling the night.

But Sera stared out to the ocean of unfamiliar persons and bristled at the many costumes and faces hidden behind disguises. Some wore the traditional sackcloth of mourning to commemorate those lost during the battles that ravaged the Aetherium during the Pragmatic crusades. Others opted for the glittering opulence once donned by Purist officials who, instead of teaching their parishioners how to use their magic, sold indulgences in exchange for protection or any other magical need.

A couple whisked past in raven masks similar to those worn by the Brotherhood, the extremist warlock sect that had nearly killed Sera months before. Sera bristled, her nightmare on full display. How many of these hidden faces were those of Brotherhood members pretending to enjoy a night of magic when all they wanted was to drain it, thirsty and wholly insatiate? One of them could stand mere inches from her and she would never know.

Panic pricked the back of her neck, and her heart quickened. Spurred by the sudden dread, her magic churned at her core, sloshing wildly and hot to her fingertips. But she stifled it. This was no time for fear; she was here to assist Barrington should the Brotherhood decide to attack the celebrations. And if they did, she would make them all burn.

Barrington's silver eyes fixed on hers through her black tulle veil. Never one to miss anything, he tightened his hold on her arm as though to remind her that she was safe with him and guided them out of the vaulted stall.

Steel beams along the wide atrium were shaped into the symbols of magic, seven arcs for every element. The domed ceiling was fashioned out of glass panels, and from outside, Sera imagined the hilltop exhibition hall was a beacon. But while the palace was a vision of light in the darkness, Barrington claimed the night as his own.

Dressed in the traditional Pragmatic black robe of double-bell sleeves and velvet panels along the neck and front enclosure, he was the definition of authority and male beauty, all fine lines and a brooding air and countless secrets lingering behind those steel-gray eyes that dissected everyone he met, as though he sought to look straight to their truths and intentions. This evening, however, his gaze was distant, his mind someplace far.

And Sera suspected where.

He hadn't mentioned a word about the incident and her subsequent outburst the previous day, but she knew it played readily in the back of his mind, a problem he sought to dissect, understand, and solve. She, too, had mulled over the events and followed the web of hauntings to its inception: the night she used the power of the dead to defeat Noah Sinclair, her savior-turned-monster and maker of her scars.

Sera tensed, still able to feel the phantom hands of dead seventhborns on her body, imbuing her with their power and pain. Able to hear Noah's screams as his body burned in black flames. *Death magic*, Barrington had called it, the darkest of black magic and severest of necromancy. He'd suspected the ghosts were a lingering result of this and, after some time, they would go away. They hadn't.

Worse, in all their research, never once was it mentioned that ghosts could touch a conjurer of death magic thereafter. Was this her own personal punishment—that after using their power to kill Noah, the dead now required something of Sera's in return?

And if so, what would it take to consider the debt paid?

Silent, Barrington steered them along the exhibition

hall, seven wondrous galleries, one representative of each element. Demonstrations were being performed within the accompanying corridors that were segmented by province. Before each main entranceway was a statue of one of the seven goddesses, the mythical sisters believed to be the guardians of magic. They cupped their namesake element in their hands, held up in sacrifice. At their feet were smaller representations of their power.

Barrington guided them past the Water guardian surrounded by curling waves and the Fire goddess encircled by a wreath of flames at her feet and stopped at the statue of the seventh sister, goddess of Aether. Unlike the others, who held their elements up toward the sky, the seventh sister was encircled by bars. She held her hands crossed over her chest, a black line on her wrist for everyone to see. Given Aether was concerned with the study of light and darkness and matters of the soul, at the goddess's feet were the sun and the moon, and they were surrounded by skeletal hands emerging from the Underworld and tugging at her gown. The bruise on Sera's arm throbbed, and she shivered at the memories of her ghosts reaching for her. Touching her.

Beyond the statue, the Aether hall was crowded with art exhibits, culinary displays, and musical offerings, a rich array of colors, sounds, and smells to lift the spirit and evoke emotion. Various aromas filled Sera's nose, from the fish and vegetable dishes of the temperate north to the spiced meats and bolder flavors found in the southern regions, but she swallowed tightly. Between studying for exams and the stress of waiting for her approval letter, the thought of food only made her stomach want to crawl out of her mouth.

Thankfully, Barrington didn't take them inside, rather admired the statue of the Aether goddess in silence for a few moments.

"The Fall of the Seventh Sister was my mother's favorite myth," he said suddenly. Sera was enthralled by his words at once. He rarely spoke about his family, save for the few instances he mentioned his dead twin brother, Filip, and their deceased father. "Whereas everyone always focuses on how the six sisters were forced to lock the seventh away in the Underworld for seeking the power over time, or how her actions led to all seventhborns being cursed, my mother instead questioned why the seventh sister would have felt compelled to seek the power over time at all. So much that she would risk her family and her life. She always felt there was more to the story, that the seventh sister was perhaps misunderstood or maybe she was fearful that no one would understand her power." He paused. "It's a sad thought, that surrounded by those who cared for her, she had felt so alone."

Sera's heart dimmed, and she looked at him, their conversation clearly shifted. His stare was open and honest, holding no judgment. But that was now. What of when she told him the truth that edged on her lips? That a ghost had touched her? He loved a mystery, and her phantoms were a formidable one indeed, but even a man as unorthodox as him had limits. There was no way he would keep her on as his assistant, not when he couldn't trust her magic… When she couldn't trust it herself. And with seventhborns considered harbingers of death and their abilities shrouded in fear and disgust, he would think her repugnant. An abomination. Dangerous.

And then he would loathe her like everyone else.

More, he would revoke his recommendation, and her dream would truly be over.

She turned her face away. No, she wouldn't ruin them with a confession. Once the truth staked its claim, not even friendship could save them.

Applause and cheers behind them stole at her attention before she could pursue it further. They turned to the corridor pertaining to the element of Wood, the Aetherium branch for law. Guests hurried inside to partake in the excitement. Barrington guided them toward the entryway, but their steps slowed to a stop as Mr. Delacort walked up onto a stage in the atrium.

Barrington bristled beside her; his mien darkened as he beheld the man who ruined his father's and brother's names. Sera could hardly comfort him. Not when the same man was responsible for her expulsion and the near-death of her dream.

Around him, guests offered him condolences over the death of his son, Timothy, and a knot formed in Sera's throat. Had it not been for Mr. Delacort's involvement with the Brotherhood, Timothy would never have died in her arms, forfeiting his life to save her. Currents of guilt lashed her with a ferocity she hadn't experienced in months, and the stone in her chest grew heavier.

Also dressed in the official Pragmatic garb, Mr. Delacort greeted a few guests closest to the stage, then moved behind a podium. Applause echoed again, and disgust swathed Sera's skin, worse than the summer's humidity. If they only knew the man they celebrated and the crimes he was responsible for.

"Ladies and gentlemen," Mr. Delacort started. "Happy Feast of Edification. Knowledge and magic to all."

Those holding goblets raised them. Others lifted their wands. "Knowledge and magic to all."

"Quite a saying, isn't it?" Mr. Delacort chuckled humorlessly, his blue eyes sparkling as his icy gaze toured along the crowd. "That motto is something my ancestors fought and died to protect, alongside many Pragmatic greats. It is the creed I have defended my entire life, a plight my son would have continued had he not been so viciously taken from us."

Murmurs of sentiment resounded all around them, but he held up a hand and everyone silenced. "Thank you all for your support and outpouring of love during this difficult time. Margaret and I have grieved and will always mourn Timothy, but we will not let that sadness deter us from a truth we can no longer ignore, lest your children suffer like mine. My brothers and sisters in magic, I regret to inform you that we have been too comfortable, too blind in our peace to see the evil brewing right before our eyes.

"Over recent years, Chancellor York has allowed an evil to grow unchecked, letting the tendrils of Purism creep over our borders. He is a kind man, a just patriarch worthy of every measure of respect, but he is a strong leader no more. Where once he was merciless against those who broke our beloved Aetherium's laws, he has grown lenient in his illness. His failure to persecute those who pervert magic has left us weakened. Now our foes seek to break down our doors, to drain us of our magic, to plunder all we've created, and to kill our children. They killed my son!"

Rumbles of anger and disbelief rose from the crowd in support of his words, and the room swelled with violence. And while she hated the man, viciously so, her blood boiled in agreement. Only hers was a real anger with claws that dug deep into the dark parts of her soul and helped ugliness climb out. If Mr. Delacort truly sought to pursue the Brotherhood, she would pledge her wand to help, and once the Brotherhood burned for their crimes, she would turn her monstrous rage against him.

Mr. Delacort went on, saying, "Right now, warlocks and necromancers and the like build up in silence, waiting for the perfect moment to strike. Are we going to let them?"

"No!" the crowd shouted. The candelabras around them flared like a heartbeat, the air electrified with magic.

"Will we let them come and take this magic that flows in our blood?"

"No!"

"Will we denounce Pragmatism, or will we fight?"

"Fight!"

"Then as of now, my brothers and sisters in magic, I officially declare that I challenge Chancellor York for the title of chancellor, and, with your support, our beloved Aetherium will rise! We will protect our government and our people. We will remember that magic is not to be bought or bartered. It is not meant to be stolen and hoarded. Magic is a gift, today and forevermore. Whosoever rejects this is a traitor to the Aetherium. And those who will pervert it forfeit their lives!"

A deafening roar of cheers boomed above the boisterous applause. Barrington touched Sera's arm, and she flinched, unaware she'd been so entranced by Delacort's speech, the air beneath her veil hot and stagnant. Barrington drew them away readily, struggling to get past the masses who moved to Delacort, already pledging him their votes.

"Are you all right?" he asked, once outside. Sera looked at him. An undercurrent of anger simmered beneath his usually collected composure, and now, away from the miasma of Delacort's fierce poise and declarations, the truth dropped on her like a stack of bricks. Though she had no intent of using death magic again, Barrington was a supplier of blood magic. A war against black magic was a war against him.

Sera didn't answer him, unsure of how to feel. The powerfully addictive tonics made of blood imprinted with black magic were used to increase strength, knowledge, and beauty, and were just as forbidden as necromancy. And though he sold it in exchange for information to solve his father's and brother's murders, in the past, he had succumbed to it as well.

She hated blood magic with a passion and had suffered with him through his withdrawals from the heinous poison. However much it pained her to admit it, if Delacort wanted it finished, he had her full support.

"Professor Barrington," someone spoke from behind them. They turned to Inspector Lewis, personal guard to the chancellor's wife, Mrs. York. In his thirties at most, the green-eyed detective looked handsome, his red hair and fair skin accentuated by his maroon double-breasted coat and cape, the official Aetherium inspectorial uniform. Sera's gaze lingered on his attire a moment longer, the fierce desire to one day wear it clenching her soul.

He greeted them both. "Mrs. York requests your presence. She awaits you in the chancellor's pavilion out in the gardens."

Barrington's gaze swept over Inspector Lewis's shoulder, to the chancellor's tent visible through the glass. No doubt it teemed with dignitaries. Barrington hated formal affairs, often declining an invitation before Sera finished reading it. This time, however, he frowned but nodded, and a smile tipped Sera's lips. Mrs. York was like a mother to him, and he never denied her.

They followed Inspector Lewis out into the gardens.

With visitors enraptured by the exhibits inside and the banquet not yet started, the commons were relatively desolate, save for a few patrons enjoying a glass of champagne in the balmy night and the junior guards patrolling the grounds, their dark maroon attire camouflaging them with the shadows. Webbed lights hung over the sprawling field, fashioned into constellations.

A walkway from each of the seven exhibition halls led to a white pavilion at the center where the chancellor and Mrs. York entertained Aetherium dignitaries, their importance increasing the closer they were to the throne. Sera recognized four of six province leaders from their photographs in the newspapers and their towering headdresses crowned with their province stones. Missing, however, were the Archdeacons for the two non-magic provinces, Fairmount and Halivaar. But Sera shook her head, unsurprised at their lack of attendance.

Just as seventhborns were an abomination, non-magicism was considered a shame.

Sitting in his throne, the chancellor looked to be drowning in the traditional royal blue robes, his frail frame hunched to the right. His wispy white hair was covered by an opulent headdress of seven jeweled levels, one for each element. Surely much too heavy, given his state. He stared out into the distance, though Sera was certain he saw none of it. Over the past few months, his health had worsened, no matter how talented a healer Mrs. York was.

Mrs. York smiled upon seeing them in the distance and met them up the path. She wore a beautiful burgundy gown with small crystals that made her shimmer with each step, her brown skin exuding a glow under the lamplights. Popular opinion had dwindled for the chancellor and his wife in the past months, but it was as though the more they hated her, the more radiant she became.

She stopped before them, took one look at Barrington, and laughed. "Oh my, I take it I missed Mr. Delacort's speech?" she said, her absence from the affair clearly not an oversight. "Forgive me, I should have warned you."

"He's all but called for war against black magic," Barrington muttered.

She sighed. "Mr. Delacort has always had a flair for the dramatic, but at heart he is a coward. These impassioned speeches will not get him very far."

Remembering the energy in the room during his speech, Sera couldn't agree.

After pleasantries were exchanged, they broke off into pairs; Mrs. York walked alongside Sera as Inspector Lewis drew Barrington into a conversation behind them. "Talk to me, dear. I long to clear my head with meaningful conversation."

"You've a tentful of people more qualified than I."

She patted Sera's arm. "Nonsense. With all that's happening in our empire, they argue about whose corridor is wider and whose banners are bigger. I'm sure that wouldn't be the case if the room were filled with those of our gender. But alas, here we are. Not for long, however. Times are changing; you're changing them."

Sera's brow furrowed. "Me?"

A warm, conspiratorial smile curved her lips. "Yes, but I get ahead of myself. First, tell me. How have you been? Nikolai says business is good and that you've been studying, but how are *you*? And please forgive my comment earlier. It was insensitive. It must have been hard to watch Mr. Delacort use his son's memory as a chess piece while you still mourn him."

Pain crawled across her heart, and the weight in her chest grew, but she swallowed through it. So long as she bristled her heart against those useless feelings of grief, they couldn't master her and fill her with weakness. She needed to be strong. For the sake of her dream and her family, she couldn't break. "I am well."

Mrs. York looked to her, something of pity over her eyes. "I think people often misunderstand mourning. The tears you shed are as much for those you lost as they are for you, and I say that as a healer…and a friend."

"Thank you."

She nodded once. "On the topic of friends. It has yet to be announced, but with Mr. Delacort officially campaigning for council votes, he had to vacate his seat as chair to the seventh-born program. The chancellor has appointed someone dear to us to the role, and I asked her to look into your application."

Sera's heart quickened.

Mrs. York glanced at Sera, her sly smile returning. "It appears someone *misplaced* it, but that's since been rectified. Congratulations, my dear. You've been approved to take the Aetherium entrance exam, and your letter will arrive tomorrow."

Sera stopped, her legs ready to give way beneath her. Her face grew warm, and the webbed lights above them were like shooting stars behind her tears. "Truly, I can take the exam?" she asked, her voice breaking.

"Indeed. I can supply you with the necessary material for studies, though I'm certain these months under Nikolai's tutelage have left you better prepared than the rest."

Sera pressed her lips together to suppress the cry of elation building in her chest. Finally, *finally* her chance had come! And yet, cold sobered Sera at the sound of Barrington's name. The School of Continuing Magic was much more demanding than her stint at the Academy, and she would have no time for their inspector work. She had known this, had mulled it over repeatedly, but reality was an entirely different beast. A year ago, she would not have minded, would have snatched up the chance blindly as her dream owned her heart and had no rival.

But then Barrington happened and split her heart in two.

"I must get back to help the chancellor," Mrs. York spoke through Sera's brooding. "I suppose I could have sent you a note, but good news is always much better delivered in person. A word of caution, however," she said. Her expression turned grim. "I don't believe the misplacement of your letter was an oversight, as I'm sure you already suspect. Mr. Delacort is determined to blame you for his son's murder and will not take kindly to knowing of your approval after he had you expelled. I know you will do well, but it is crucial you pass. Once you are in, the procedure to dismiss you is difficult and you will be protected. But if he manages to become chancellor before you're admitted... This may be your only chance. And you must take care. Unfortunately, he is still a man of power, and his network of help is vast. Stay vigilant and, above all, be prudent with your trust."

Sera bristled, the gardens seeming to close in around her, but she nodded. "I will. Thank you, Mrs. York."

"No, my dear. Thank you. It seems I am living somewhat vicariously through you. If it were up to me, I would one day call you chancellor. For the time, however, I look forward to calling you Inspector."

She brought them to a stop on the other side of the gardens, closest to the entry for the element of Fire, responsible for all of the Aetherium's defense and law enforcement. Professor Barrington and Inspector Lewis joined them.

"It was lovely to see you both." Yet, she looked at Barrington and her mouth pressed to a tight line, disapproval heavy on her brow. "Not that you ever listen to me, but after today, Mr. Delacort will be looking to solidify his message. I've learned blood magic will be his first initiative, and a prominent arrest will help him immensely. Let's not give him one, shall we?"

A flutter of worry gripped Sera's belly, but Barrington only smiled, a dark challenge glimmering in his stormy eyes. "You're right, I never listen, but I will keep it under consideration."

Mrs. York shook her head. "You're incorrigible, Nikolai."

He glanced at Sera. "Believe me, I've been called worse. Goodnight, Mrs. York. Inspector."

With their goodbyes exchanged, Mrs. York and Inspector Lewis walked away and vanished into the pavilion. But though absent in person, Mrs. York's previous warnings played at the edge of Sera's mind, and she looked at Barrington as he drew out his pocket watch, wholly at ease, and a bud of worry bloomed in her heart. While he was a professor and member of polite society, there was a wildness within him, the reckless part that craved revenge like a mistress he simply couldn't quit. He wouldn't rest until Mr. Delacort and the Brotherhood paid for his brother's and father's deaths…

Even if it resulted in his own.

He hummed and clicked his watch closed. "Would you mind terribly if we detoured down the Water exhibition? Inspector Lewis suggested I meet a physician there."

"No, of course not."

She slid her arm into his and let him guide them into the Water hall, blue banners hanging over the walkway. In passing, they admired the recent advancements in healing and all other restorative techniques of the water art until they entered The Collection of Historical Scientific Instruments exhibit. Barrington was engrossed instantly, leaning close to a stand where a compass of ciphers was on display. More, alchemical ciphers. If there was one thing to enthrall him and rival his love of alchemy, it was cryptography. Memories of their summer brushed through Sera's mind, their days spent learning the minor details of ciphers and their construction. Hours where they sat so close their arms and legs would brush by mistake, until neither of them cared to apologize or move away at all.

Warmth sprouted along her body, the ghost of their every stolen touch awakening along her skin.

An attendant, a short man with a bald head and wired spectacles that struggled to stay perched on his thick nose, drew close. "Good evening, sir. Madam."

"Are you Doctor Figgis?" Barrington asked.

"Indeed, I am. How may I be of service?"

"Inspector Lewis said I should come by."

His bushy brows rose with familiarity of man and topic. "Ah, yes, of course. A friend of the inspector is a friend of mine. Perhaps it's best we talk…alone." He motioned to a door in the back of the room, then started toward it.

Sera pursed her lips; whenever previous clients requested to speak to Barrington privately, he'd made it known that she was his assistant and privy to all information. This time, however, Barrington released her arm, and her suspicions flared. The only discussion he didn't involve her in was business of the worst sort: blood magic.

She glanced at Doctor Figgis waiting at the back door, and her reservations were confirmed. He rubbed his fingers expectantly, a palpable hunger in the way he regarded Barrington. No doubt he was anxious for the vials of magic-laced blood Barrington exchanged for information. But there was something else to his appearance, something in the grayish pallor of his skin and dark circles under his eyes. More, in his stench of decay and sludge. The same traits Barrington displayed after he'd nearly died raising a body from the dead.

"I will only be a minute," Barrington said.

Sera gripped his arm. "Professor, wait. Who is he, really?"

"He's a physician…and a necromancer."

"Professor!" she hissed, aghast.

"Inspector Lewis mentioned he might have some insight into your spell chamber, and I thought it was worth pursuing," he said mildly, which she knew was to ease her. Yet her magic sloshed wildly within, the desire to burn him overwhelming.

"Truly? You think it wise to have that discussion *here*, after Mr. Delacort's speech, with a necromancer of all people?"

His jaw pulsed. "I'm not scared of Mr. Delacort."

"This isn't about being scared. He ruined your father's life simply out of fear his dealings with the Brotherhood would be exposed. Imagine how much more quickly he'd destroy you out of ambition."

He opened his mouth, but shut it at that, and Sera knew he understood the validity of her concern. Still, a flash of defiance washed over his stare.

"Delacort is a fool," he said, his gray eyes dark like the violent storms over the moors and just as ominous. "Besides, I only mean to ask Doctor Figgis a few harmless questions."

She frowned. "Nothing is ever harmless with you."

Meeting her eyes through her veil, his gaze softened. "Will you always worry for me?"

"Someone has to, clearly."

A sad smile touched his lips. Lifting a hand, he trailed a finger along her veil, close to her cheek. The warmth that enveloped them the previous day found them again, and Sera hoped it would be enough to keep him. But, lowering his hand, he spun on his heels and met Doctor Figgis at the door, and together they vanished through the threshold.

Sera shook her head, gladder she hadn't told him of her

recent troubles. If he learned of it and didn't scare away, he'd want to help her. And if he went to such lengths for her spell chamber, no doubt he'd do the same for her predicaments with ghosts.

Her eyes caught on an adjacent exhibit displaying tools used during the persecutions, a time of fear and mass death for seventhborns. When body after body of dead seventhborns were found, people feared it was a seventhborn plague and, unless they eradicated seventhborns, it would spread to other magicians and destroy the Witchling world. Seventhborns were then persecuted for years to come.

She approached a collection of ceramic containers used to store the various tinctures and salves concocted to prevent spread of the plague, mixtures that relied on alchemy as their base. Her attention quickly shifted to a rusted knife with a rounded tip. She read the small plaque beneath the display.

Purists desperate to prevent the plague used this hook knife to gouge out the eyes of seventhborns. They believed if seventhborns could not see ghosts, they were not in danger of spreading the plague.

Frustration and fury churned Sera's magic so fast, she struggled for a breath. She pressed a hand against the glass case to steady herself, her insides at war and desperate for destruction. Only fire would purge this horrid feeling from her skin and scorch these damn artifacts to hell. If only she could burn away the past as well and make it so the thousands of seventhborns who'd lost their lives had never suffered at all, rather lived their lives as they saw fit, not limited by their birth order or the damned tattoo on their wrist.

Goose bumps skimmed Sera's skin, and the distinct sensation of being watched crowded her mind and stoked her peripheral awareness. Various flora and fauna odors overwhelmed her nose, lavender with hints of the floral but earthy waft of heather, and the singular odor of damp earth.

She lifted her lashes, and a frosted breath puffed at her mouth. The ghost of a girl in a muddied dress stood on the other side of the glass, her gaze fixed on the hook knife. Her eye sockets were empty and crusted, dried blood marking her pale cheeks.

Sera gasped, and the girl raised her head. Sera spun away but bumped against a solid frame and lost her footing. Strong arms came around her and held her upright. She lifted her head, expecting Barrington, but instead met the blue eyes of a handsome stranger.

an ideal arrangement

Sera snatched herself away, her pulse quick and magic hot in her fingertips. She cast a frantic glance around them. The ghost was gone.

"Forgive me." The stranger drew his hands away quickly and took a step back. "You looked a bit faint, and I thought perhaps you needed help."

He met her stare and smiled; his hooded blue eyes were rimmed with long black lashes. He was very good-looking. Too handsome, if there were such a thing. His thick black hair reflected a slight amber hue under the lamplights and added a warm glow to his fair skin. Like Barrington, his dark hair made his stare more intense. And, like Barrington, he was young. Surely no older than five-and-twenty. But she shifted away farther, her hand perpendicular to her wand and her mind alert with past abuse and present warnings.

Beauty and youth were false traits of character. Noah had possessed both, and yet she bore the proof of his cruelty on her skin.

"I'm well, thank you," she replied, forcing her voice stable—an arduous feat when the sensation of his hands lingered on her person and her scars prickled as if newly made.

"I am glad to hear it, though I must say, an exhibit such as this is no place for a lady alone, especially around wretched instruments such as these." He glanced about and nodded down the corridor, to a crystal ball displayed prominently behind a tall platform. "For instance, that orbuculum there belonged to an old Purist scryist. The story is she only used this orb since she was a young girl and over time grew bonded to the glass. Their connection was so powerful that, though she passed away ages ago, when used for scrying, the orb shows only images of the Underworld, as that is what its owner sees. Essentially, she and the crystal ball are one. Frightening, isn't it?"

"Thank you for your concern, but I am not easily scared, nor am I here alone. Good evening." With a curt bow of her head, she moved around him just as Barrington exited the doorway.

She walked to him, and his brow dipped. "What's wrong?" he asked, but his gaze swept over her shoulder and he trailed off. His silver eyes hardened, the air suddenly heavy with violence. Sera turned to the stranger stopping before them.

"If it isn't just the man I came here to see."

Barrington's jaw pulsed, his stare a pit of ice and cold fire. "Armitage."

"How the hell are you, Nik?" Armitage's gaze locked on Sera then. "Still forgetting your manners, I see."

"I forget nothing. Miss Dovetail, Mr. Charles Armitage. Charles, my assistant, Miss Dovetail."

"Yes, we've met," Sera said and nodded her hello but never offered her hand. His touch before had been enough.

Not to mention Barrington's chilly reception. She'd seen him angry before, but this coldness and blatant displeasure were unfamiliar.

"I've heard quite a lot about you. Gummy mentioned Nik had gotten himself an assistant. It is my unending pleasure to meet you."

Gummy. Sourness settled in Sera's belly, and beside her, Barrington grew stiff and hot. Magic. He was always in full control of his powers, yet now he held them on a tight leash. For Armitage to unsettle him this way over the mere mention of Gummy…

Sera's heart sunk. She'd always imagined his affair with Gummy to be one of more convenience than sentiment, but given his current jealousy, it seemed she truly did own his heart.

"I went to see her about a situation," Armitage went on, "but she suggested I consult you, seeing as there is something I can help you with in exchange."

Barrington chuckled, a humorless laugh edged with something sinister. "I can assure you, Armitage, there is nothing you could ever help me with. Good night."

He turned them away.

"Not even ghosts?" Armitage said from behind them.

Sera's heart pounded, and her steps grew heavy, halting their retreat. She looked up at Barrington, but he focused straight ahead, his jaw clenched tightly. In the momentary delay, Armitage came around them.

"I mentioned to her I had a delicate situation that needed a discreet inquiry, and she thought it best I speak to you, as you were interested in a spell combination to deter ghosts."

A muscle in Barrington's jaw pulsed. "Then clearly I need to have a word with her."

He started to walk away, but Sera didn't follow. "What

do you know about warding spells?"

"Miss Dovetail," Barrington warned, his voice icier than she'd ever heard it directed at her. "He's a common thief."

"I may be a common thief, but I'm good enough not to have been caught yet. Given my years of experience, I've come across a great number of protection and determent spells, all of which I've documented. Within them, I'm certain you will find a suitable combination for your peculiar situation. They are all yours in exchange for your help in finding my sister. Her orphanage of seventhborns has gone missing."

Sera's eyes widened. "An entire orphanage? Tell us more."

"Orphanage closings happen all the time," Barrington interjected coldly before Armitage could speak. "Lower seventh-born birthrates and survivals lead to many of these institutions being underfunded and subsequently shut down."

"Yes," Armitage conceded, "but I believe it was more than that. She sent me this some days ago." He reached into his inner pocket and drew out a letter. He offered it to them. Barrington made no attempts to take it, and so Sera grabbed it and read.

Dearest Brother,

You must come at once. You requested I not alert the constable, but I was desperate. Something ill is happening. The children are vanishing, and I've no way to explain it. No one will help. The constable and Father Warner believe the children ran away. I think it's far more sinister. I need you, brother. Please don't delay.

With much urgency,

Meredith

"When I went to visit her, she was gone, as were the children. We can be of help to each other," he added. "Find my sister and the children, and I will give you the deterrents."

Dread twisted Sera's belly. Help with her ghosts was enough of a lure, especially now, with her exam once again in her future, but the Brotherhood often targeted seventhborns for their evil spells and experiments. What if they took these children? The mere thought churned her magic, and the rage she buried deep within awakened, all sharp claws and ravenous hunger.

Sera looked at Barrington. This was the perfect agreement. Surely he could set aside his ire and jealousy and accept the case.

Barrington smiled at Armitage, a venomous expression, and the shadows around them deepened. "Thank you for the offer, but I'll have to decline."

Sera blinked. "What?"

A flash of anger crossed Armitage's face. "You're making a mistake, Nik. But in case you change your mind, I'm staying at the Scalar Hotel. You can write to me there."

"It won't be necessary. Good evening, Mr. Armitage."

Mr. Armitage inclined his head to them both and, turning, he walked away and vanished into the crowds. Sera spun to Barrington, intent on an argument, but he met her eyes, a war of fire and murder there, and she knew no matter what she said, he wasn't going to budge.

By the time they made it out of the Imperial Palace and transferred back home, a half moon cast shafts of pale light over the moors, a rival to the darker clouds looming in the distance. Flashes of lightning illuminated them within, followed by the echo of rolling thunder. The summer thunderstorm was yet far, but Sera moved away from Barrington, certain their own tempest had already come.

He walked to his desk, indifferent, and Sera's anger swelled like the scent of rain riding in on the breeze. Arguing when her emotions were so high was a mistake she'd made before, but she couldn't relent. Not when there was a missing woman and children who needed them and a man who could potentially help her.

Still, she clutched her rage tight. There was a chance she could salvage things. The Barrington she knew wasn't heartless. "So, are we going to talk about what happened?"

Barrington slid his hat off, his fingers tight on the brim. "I didn't realize there was anything that needed a discussion."

Warmth waved up her body, her grip on her temper loosening. "A woman is missing, and so are her seventh-born charges. And the man who needs us to find them is a thief. To break into places, surely he must know what these incantations are in order to negate them, which would make him fluent in wards, yes?"

He unsheathed his wand and set it down gently next to his hat. "I would imagine so."

"And given this, you turned down his case?" she said through gritted teeth.

Drawing out his pocket watch, he cradled the fob, then set his watch beside his wand. "We turn down work all the time."

Heat skimmed the underside of her skin, her magic roiling. "Not when the client has something we need. More, when there are children involved!"

Steel-gray eyes met hers, dark and burning. "The man is a liar and a fraud," he said tightly. "And if his story of a missing orphanage is true, it's all the more reason for him to seek the help of a constable, not us."

"You're unbelievable."

"No, Miss Dovetail. I'm practical. Not only is he a scoundrel of the worst sort, cruel and incredibly vicious, but Mr. Armitage has many enemies, a number of whom are our clients. It would be in terrible form for us to be seen associating with him. I'm sorry. I will speak to Mrs. York and have Inspector Lewis follow up on the missing children—if they are indeed gone. As for your wards, all I need is a bit more time to figure out a suitable spell combination. But we will not be working with Mr. Armitage."

The bottles of liquor on the sidebar rattled. Raw fire filled her chest and seared her insides to where she felt breathing flame was a possibility. Remembering the recent ghosts and their ability to touch her, she sensed time would soon be a luxury she couldn't afford.

"So even with the possibility of relief, I'm supposed to suffer now, all because of your damn male pride and pathetic rivalry?"

Barrington slid off his coat and hung it on the back of his chair, then picked up a book and thumbed through it, ignoring the sound of clinking bottles cutting through the silence. He never followed her into rage and was not one to argue, much less raise his voice from his normal baritone, which fueled her fury more.

"I made an oath to someone," he said. "And as such, my reasons must remain my own. For now, you will have to take me at my word."

"Your *word*?" Her voice broke under the weight of hurt and anger and desperation in her chest. "You said you would help me find my family and recover my memories, and I'm still here!"

He looked at her. Hurt flashed across his eyes, and she

knew she'd gone too far, but how could he do this, leave her at the mercy of the dead when solace was one man away?

He closed the book, his knuckles white on the spine. The intent to speak weighed heavily on his brow, and she knew the vow he'd made was what bound the words in his throat. If he pushed through the discomfort to break it, he could lose the ability to speak for years.

But she didn't care about oaths and jealousies. If she waited any longer, Armitage could hire someone else and she'd be left with nothing but ghosts.

Sighing, his stare dimmed, and he shook his head. "I won't change my mind."

Her anger billowed and shaded the fringes of her sight in red. "Then I will take on the case without you."

She stormed to the door and yanked it open.

A violent gust blew past her and slammed it shut. "You don't want to do this."

She turned to him; her gaze widened. He often left when in the midst of a fight, but she stared at him in the middle of the room, the shadows around him deepened, and knew this was not like arguments of the past. Armitage had changed things. No, not Armitage, but Gummy.

Sera's heart twisted. Whatever Barrington felt for Gummy was clearly more important to him than her. But however painful his choosing Gummy was, this was not a fight she would yield. She couldn't.

She curled her hands into tight fists. "Or what?"

He was silent, a simmering hot anger radiating from his person.

Closing the space between them, she stared up at him. "*Or what?*"

His jaw clenched, but he said nothing.

She scoffed and, back at the door, pulled it open again.

"He's not a good man, Sera."

She stopped and glanced at him. "Yes, well, neither are you."

The words were a lie, but now they hung heavy like the pregnant storm clouds in the distance. Worse, she'd insulted him before, but he stared at her now, still and unblinking, and she knew for once she'd truly hurt him. The type of hurt that embedded its venomous roots deeply and wasn't easily forgotten. Every fiber within her told her to take them back. That this was the wrong way to go about things. But she spun on her heels, walked out, and slammed the door closed between them, rage a worthy opponent and reason incapable of winning this war.

Two days later, Sera wrapped her arms tighter about herself, shrouded by the shadows in the Aetherium capital's lower district of Wyndmoor, or Death Alley as it was so often called. Tucked just south of the Imperial Palace and a few streets over from the ports, Wyndmoor was rife with a seventh-born population hoping for safety the closer they were to the capital.

Lamplights flanked the road all the way to the Imperial Palace towering in the distance, the white lights like pearls in the cloudy, black night. Sera flitted a glance to the apartments around her. The buildings had been erected side by side, some pushed farther back and leaning. In all, the street looked like a set of gums crowded with crooked teeth. She hoped that, from somewhere within its ugly jaws, help would come should she need it.

The clap of horse hooves on the cobblestone came to

a slow stop, and the low creak of hinges resounded as an unmarked carriage door opened. Armitage stepped down onto the sidewalk and located her standing in the tunneled entryway of a bakery closed for the night. Adjusting his top hat, he strolled closer with the ease of a man who had engaged in other late-night rendezvous countless times before. Unlike Sera, who tracked every shadow as though they were living things ready to run off and tell her secrets. He looked wonderful in the dark, she conceded. The shadows favored him, like one of their own, which made her like him considerably less. Barrington also clung to the shadows, but never once did he seem to have been born of them.

Armitage stopped before her and inclined his head; the air was consumed with his heady musk of smoke and roses. "Miss Dovetail, to say your note was an unexpected pleasure is an understatement."

She inclined her head in greeting; like hell she would offer him her hand. "Thank you for meeting me."

"The pleasure is all mine, though." A smile flashed across his features, a dangerous sparkle in his blue eyes. "I've concluded you're looking to have me killed."

"Unless you have ill motives, I have no desire to see you dead."

"Yes, well, I know Nik doesn't play nice with others, nor does he like me very much. I don't want any trouble."

Sera resisted the urge to roll her eyes. Armitage exuded trouble like an aura. And if Barrington was right, his role of concerned brother could all be an act and she could be in danger. But becoming an inspector and finding her family was worth any risk. "Your inquiry?"

He reached toward his inner pocket.

Barrington's warning flashed through her mind, and her pulse pounded. She snatched out her wand, and by the time his fingers vanished into his coat, its tip was pressed against the pulse at his throat. "A warning, Mr. Armitage. We're here for business." She gave it a little jab deeper. "Nothing more."

He held his hand up in surrender. "I was only reaching for my cigarettes. May I smoke?"

"By all means." She lowered her wand measuredly and watched him closely, ready should he attempt to unsheathe his own wand. Instead, he drew out a solid silver cigarette case, his initials swirled on the front. He touched a fingertip to the cigarette, and smoke soon wafted past her nose; it smelled of roses.

"Tell me about your sister," she said.

He reached into his outer breast pocket—a space too tiny to keep anything he could use to harm her—and pulled out a small photograph. "This was taken late last year."

The girl in the picture had a slender face and delicate features, her hair swept up into a loose bun at the top of her head. There was a mole beneath her left eye.

"How old is she?"

"Twenty-six. She took over the Saint Aldrich Orphanage of Mercy from my aunt after she passed."

"Did she enjoy her job? Was she prone to violence?"

"Meredith loved those children. She would never hurt them, if that's what you suspect. She was never one to exaggerate. If she believed something sinister took place, I believe her wholeheartedly. And I'd asked her to call on me should she ever meet any trouble. That she went to the constable tells me she was in despair. She's loyal to everyone; she would never cross me."

Sera's eyes narrowed. "Why did you ask her never to contact a constable?"

He paused for a beat. "Sometimes I acquire possessions of exceeding value and I need to store them somewhere until I can find them a new home."

Heat gathered in Sera's cheeks. "You hid your stolen goods at the orphanage until you found a buyer?"

"Meredith was in agreement. For her help in storing my things, I sponsored the home. Funding for seventh-born shelters is at a minimum. It was an ideal arrangement."

Sera pursed her lips. Ideal. Of course. Who cared that it put seventhborns in danger? "Have you considered one of the people you stole from might have captured her and the children as ransom or payback?"

He shook his head. "They would have contacted me by now, if they knew it was me. Despite what Nik says, I am good at what I do, Miss Dovetail. One of the best."

Sera hummed. "Very well. I will take your case, Mr. Armitage. Did you bring what I asked for?"

With the cigarette balanced precariously on his lips, he reached into his inner pocket again. This time, he drew out Meredith's letter and a wand. Sera flinched, but Armitage handed it to her, silver holder first. "Something belonging to her, as requested. This is her wand from when she was younger."

Sera took the wand; it was old and the wood brittle. "It will take me some time to rehydrate the fibers, but I'm certain it still contains some residual magic."

"But I can assure you, I've scryed for her."

"Not like I can." Or her Barghest, rather. He'd proven indispensable at tracking magic and locating culprits who wished not to be found.

"Thank you," he said. "Please, do whatever you must to find my sister."

"And the children," Sera said pointedly.

"Yes, yes, of course," he said through a plume of cigarette smoke.

Sera gave a curt nod to conclude their meeting and watched Armitage retreat back into the safety of his carriage. And as his black coach rolled past, she mulled over his words and shook her head. Barrington said Armitage had many enemies, just as the things he stole had owners. Meredith had been a fool to let him store his *exceedingly valuable things* at the orphanage. Their deal had proven to be a help for her and the orphans, but Sera turned Meredith's wand over in her hands and hoped it hadn't proven deadly as well.

a matter of duty

Sera pulled open her desk drawer, plucked up the apple inside, and smiled at this one bit of luck in an otherwise miserable week. Successfully transferring an object to a given set of coordinates was part of the Air-level portion of the weeklong assessment to evaluate a student's mastery over each element. A placement interview followed, contingent on their score.

Though she often transferred as a part of her work—so much that she no longer had to write down the coordinates, rather hold the ciphers in her mind and spark them with her magic—that morning she'd encountered slight variances in results. But finally, victory…in this, at least.

She looked to the thick study guide that had come with her approval letter and frowned. She had a long way to go.

There were two hundred questions per module, and not all of them would be covered. With each evaluation split into an oral and practical assessment, she had to not only know the answers but how to apply them as well. During her time at the Academy, she'd learned some proctors were satisfied with broad answers while others prodded for specifics.

Sera set the apple down on her desk and pulled her notes closer. Regardless of the instructor, she was a seventhborn. She prepared for the worst.

"Perhaps you should get some rest, dear," Rosie, Barrington's maid, said from Sera's wardrobe, where she finished alterations on Sera's old uniform. "You haven't taken a breather in over a week."

Sera hummed. "I will rest when I'm dead."

"Oh, Miss." Rosie frowned, never fond of Sera's dark humor.

Sera grinned, though, she conceded, her words were a lie. She would have no peace until she found her family, and death would only render her a spirit, determined to find them in the afterlife.

She closed her Air-level book and crossed out *local transferring of inanimate objects* from her list of topics. Now to tackle the different types of alterations that could be applied to a coordinate spell. Sera sighed, certain all this transfer theory was physically melting her brain. Maybe she would take a small break.

Setting aside her book, she reached into the shallow dish where she'd set Meredith's wand, wrapped in a soft cloth damp with lemon oil. After years of going unused, the wood was brittle and dry and had to be treated to be made pliable. As desperate as she was to gather a magic sample to find Meredith and the children, attempting to extract any magic from a wand in its current condition could cause it to snap or burn, so she didn't even try.

Patience might not have been one of her virtues, but she wouldn't risk the wand ruined, not when the children might be in danger and running out of time.

There was a chance they were safe, but memories of the Brotherhood tainted her thoughts. The Brotherhood were monsters who cared little about draining magic or spilling blood. Just the possibility the children might be held hostage by them tightened the knot of dread in Sera's belly.

They would never survive the Brotherhood. She barely had.

But she rubbed a fresh coat of oil along the wand, rewrapped it, and set it back within the dish. Soon, it would be ready. No one else might have cared the children were missing, but she did—and she would find them.

Picking up her own wand, she inspected the fibers for splinters. It was a marvel she had a wand at all, given the numerous times she'd slammed it on the desk, thrown it across the room, or futilely attempted to bend it in frustration. Or that she hadn't filed it to a sliver, given how much she worried it all week, twisting it over and over in her hands continuously like her nerves, especially today.

After receiving her exam approval letter, it had been a whirlwind to secure her supplies and review the study guide. Thankfully, all preparations had kept her mind busy and the phantoms at bay. Sadly, in also reviewing her notes on how to extract magic from a wand in order to find Meredith, the hauntings were replaced with memories of another person she hadn't been able to find: Mary.

Satisfied no strands had lifted from her wand, she wiped it down, unsure how she would ever survive the coming weeks without her friend-turned-traitor. She'd successfully made it through her preparations without crying over Mary, but now the thought of existing in the same space where she had once been happy filled her with inordinate pain. Though she wasn't allowed to know where Mary was being kept hidden from the Brotherhood, Barrington often brought her updates from Mrs. York regarding Mary's well-being. But today words were not enough. Regardless of the fact that her betrayal led to Timothy Delacort's death, she needed her friend.

With each cleansing stroke, a new thought tightened the fist of pain in her throat. Did she remember their times in Sera's tower room and the laughs they'd shared? Their dreams and heartaches? Did Mary think of her at all? Did she miss her, too?

The stone in her chest grew heavier, and Sera's ribs ached under the strain. But she wouldn't cry. Mary didn't deserve it. Their friendship was over, and it was time to move on. And soon she'd have to do the same with Barrington; they hadn't spoken in a week. But this entire affair was all his fault. Had he accepted Armitage's case or at least explained his reasons for declining, then maybe they wouldn't have fought.

Setting her polished wand safely back within its holder, she moved to her vanity. Sitting, she loosened her braid, separating the chestnut strands. Indeed, Barrington could be an ass sometimes, and he'd proven that his heart lay elsewhere, yet the prospect of their arrangement ending so suddenly twisted the rock in her chest, and she heaved a sigh.

"Nervous?" Rosie asked from across the room, where she hung Sera's uniform beside the accompanying cloak, though Sera doubted she would be wearing a cloak any time soon, with the relentless heat in the lower country.

She shrugged. "I've wanted nothing more than to take the Aetherium entrance exam, but going back to the Academy to do so…" Her throat tightened. "How am I supposed to walk down the halls, pretending like nothing happened? Like Mary and Timothy are still here." It had been an eternity since she had spoken their names, and the weight of it made it hard to breathe.

Closing the wardrobe doors, Rosie joined her at the vanity and picked up the hairbrush. She combed Sera's hair, gently tugging at the knots that tended to form from the flyways that slipped from the confines of her braid.

"It's all right to be scared. What you went through is more than any of us should bear. You mourn them at your own pace, for however long it takes. It is your heart; you know it best. And tomorrow, when you walk down those halls, you hold your head high and honor Mr. Delacort's memory by living. And Miss Tenant's friendship, you bestow it on someone else. It's all you can do now. Don't let the past drag you back. It isn't where you're headed, is it?"

She secured Sera's hair into a neat braid. "The professor will also be there, should you run into any trouble. Trust me—though he's proctoring the boys' exam, he will be most vigilant, even if you two are on the outs." She met Sera's reflection in the mirror and smiled.

Sera wished she could return the gesture, but she lowered her eyes. She had no doubt he would watch over her, as he would anyone in his charge. Responsibility was paramount to him, a man of his word. And yet, her soul dimmed. That was all she would ever be to him. A matter of duty, never of the heart. He'd proven it the moment he turned down Armitage's offer and chose Gummy over Sera's sanity.

Still, she nodded. "Thank you, Rosie."

Rosie patted her cheek. "Things between you and the master will right themselves soon enough. Now, get some rest or I'll be forced to use my wand to make sure you do."

Sera winked. "One eye is already shut."

Rosie smiled and exited the room, closing the door behind her.

Standing, Sera forewent the bed, grabbed her notes,

and sat at the window seat. She looked to the silhouetted moors and for a moment wished Rosie would, in fact, use her wand, but instead of helping Sera sleep, perhaps she could bewitch her and make her indifferent to her birth order, to her desire for family.

To broken friendships and dead admirers and the looming loss of love.

Hours and countless pages of notes later, Sera walked to the door. Too fraught over the coming day and unable to study anymore, she went downstairs. Maybe some mindless paperwork would help ease her nerves.

She was turning the corner to walk to the workroom when—

"Bloody hell," Barrington said from inside.

She paused. She could turn around and go back upstairs and Barrington would never know she had been there. Yet, come morning, their days full of discovery and magic would be over.

Sera entered the room. Hard as it was on her pride, in a few months, when she was no longer at his side, she would regret not walking in and forming these last memories, whatever they held.

Barrington didn't notice her approach, engrossed by the stacks of paper he sorted before him. Sera's eyes narrowed. Was he...*cleaning*?

He spun and startled at seeing her. "Miss Dovetail."

She glanced down at the worktable full of papers and arched a brow. "I thought I'd seen everything in our time working together."

"Yes, well, I was finishing the paperwork for Lord

Carlson's case." He held up a stack of notes for her to see, and her heart dimmed. He'd moved on and solved the case without her. But surely she couldn't have expected him to wait until their row had been resolved. This was their work—well, his work, now that he didn't need her anymore.

"I couldn't find the investigative notes," he added, "so I imagined I placed them in the wrong file."

Sera moved to the filing cabinet beside the one he'd ransacked, pulled open the second to last drawer, and plucked out the file reading *Carlson*. "Ongoing investigations are in this cabinet. I move them into this dresser once they've been solved...or closed."

"Oh. Right." He took it from her hands and held it tight between his fingers. "Thank you."

Silence.

Memory of their previous argument crossed Sera's mind, and the long quiet between them told her it plagued his thoughts as well, but she wouldn't let their disagreement ruin their waning time.

"Here, I'll do it." No doubt he'd just stuff the papers inside.

He gave her the closing report, gray eyes fixed on hers. They were lighter than usual, deadened, as if a flame had been snuffed out within him. She yearned to ask if he was all right, but, taking the offered papers, she slid them in the appropriate slot, closed the file, and placed it back within the cabinet. Matters of the heart had no place between them, and now it had no time, either.

"Are there any more to be filed?" she asked.

"No, that was all; I can manage the rest. Thank you." He turned to the table and sorted through another stack, and Sera's gut churned. Had it been so easy for him to get on with life, already preparing for the moment she was no longer around? She closed the drawer, the painful answer to her question glaring in Barrington's subsequent silence and his indifference to her walking to the door.

She crossed the threshold and swallowed tightly. Yes, perhaps it was best her exam started tomorrow. She'd known his heart belonged to another, but now it was clear that not even a small amount had been reserved for her.

She rounded the corner into the hall—

"Miss Dovetail."

She paused mid-step, the sound of her name from his lips a reel drawing her back and into the room. He stood there, a mess of papers and pictures scattered before him, his posture beaten and visage worn. "Perhaps I could trouble you for more of your help?" He met her eyes. "I confess…I'm rather lost without you."

Their stares held for a second where, had she been angry, she wouldn't have been able to hold on to her upset anymore. She nodded and met him at the workbench. Though the width of the table stood between them, an intimacy spread there, warming the space and his stare.

For those seconds where the bells tolled and one day passed the reins to another, it was Sera and Barrington and nothing else.

She turned her eyes down and began sorting the pages by last name and the impressions by case number. Barrington cleared his throat and followed suit. "I seem to have made a mess of things again."

Sera moved to the filing cabinet, one set of impressions already organized. "Not that awful, no. It shouldn't take too long to sort these out."

"I mean I've made a mess…of us."

Sera stopped. Lowering the file, she turned as he leaned back against the side table behind him. There amidst the shadows, he looked so painfully vulnerable that Sera forced herself to sit before she walked to him and did something she couldn't take back.

"I'm sorry," he went on. "It was unfair of me to turn down Mr. Armitage's case without explaining why, especially when it's so important to you. But I'd sworn an oath to someone and needed their permission to break it. I've since obtained it and wanted to share my reasons with you, if you still care to listen."

She nodded, her throat thick and words impossible.

"After Filip and my father passed, I spent a lot of time in some…unsavory places, surrounded by even more unpleasant people. In one of the hovels I frequented, I met a girl who was wanted by no one. You see, she was owned by a man who let other warlocks drain her in exchange for money. She was drained so frequently and severely, she lost her hair, her teeth…and from then on, this vile man took to calling her Gummy."

Sera gasped. "*Miss Mills?*"

A muscle pulsed in his jaw. "Yes. And Mr. Armitage was her owner."

Sera gripped the stool's edge, a sick feeling lurching into her stomach. *No…*

Her hatred for Gummy remained, but now pity was its rival. And Armitage—she gathered her hands to fists. She could have shoved his cigarette in his eye, then set him on fire.

"The only thing that sustained her and kept her strong in his cruelty and constant draining was blood magic. And so…"

Barrington whirled a wrist. The locks upon the black door clicked, and the door swung open. He motioned for her to enter, but Sera hesitated. One of the first things he'd told her when she visited his home was the black door and the room behind it were off-limits. Even Rosie had yet to set foot inside.

Standing, she braced and entered.

The rectangular room was larger than his workroom and office combined. There were various tables throughout, and where his office was in disarray, this room was immaculate. Numerous books lined the walls, their pages edged in black. *Black magic.* A burgundy tome was on a stand before the shelves. Sera shivered, certain it had been fashioned of skin and painted with blood.

Windows governed the wall on the right, though ivy vines had grown wild outside and didn't allow for much light. Yet, staring out into the room, Sera wondered if that was intentional. There were several tables about the chamber, each one containing an elaborate structure of burners, flutes, and retorts. Thin tubes transferred blood through the mechanism and into small vials. It was a slow process; only a drop fell in each container, joining the small amount already in the narrow vessels. But though a minor portion, blood magic was potent and, based on Barrington's dealings with Gummy, rather expensive.

"Here is where I manufacture blood magic." He walked to a flat surface on the wall and pulled on a lever. The wall slid aside, and a waft of cold air brushed out. Within, large ice blocks kept the room cooled. There were crates stacked in the back, and on the adjacent walls, many clay barrels. He gestured to the vats. "I acquire the blood from various morgues and healers. I then imprint it with spells, dependent on what the client requires." He motioned out to the room, to the nearest table. "Beauty." To another desk. "Knowledge." To another. "Strength."

He moved to the back of the room, where there were two doors, one of them reinforced by a black iron gate. He motioned to the wooden one. "Through there is where I keep my father's and brother's research, as much as I was able to salvage after the fire that killed them."

He nodded to the gated doorway. Ciphers were etched into the metal. Some were containment spells and others to ward against ill intent. Barrington pushed aside the gate, and she was unable to read the rest. He opened the door. Light from the laboratory streamed inside the dark room, and where Sera thought to find his store of product, instead there was only a set of shackles on the wall, another pair clasped to the floor. Spells were embedded onto the steel fetters and along the threshold floor.

Sera hugged herself. This room was cold, yet heavy, as though possessing its own aura, one that echoed of torment and regrets. She'd once learned that places where great tragedies and pains had occurred were stained with their sorrow. Empaths were more attuned to feel these emotions in a space, and with empathy being an aether-inclination, all seventhborns were sensitive to it.

She gulped. "What is this place?"

He leaned back against the wall, his arms folded at his chest and his eyes downcast. "Withdrawals are monstrous, and the amount of blood magic I had been using made them more severe. I contained myself here when they were at their worst, lest I hurt Rosie or Lucas…or you."

Sera pressed a hand to her chest, something within her feeling to break. As if a ghost, Barrington's screams and agony while shackled and suffering resonated in the fringes of her consciousness. She spun and hurried out, unable to bear more of the horrid place.

He followed her out of the containment room, stood in the middle of the laboratory, and continued his labor of truth. "Miss Mills needed freedom, and I was desperate for anything that would lead me to my brother's and father's killer, so I manufactured it for her to do as she wished in exchange for secrets and information. Over the years, she made enough from the blood magic to free herself from Armitage and begin her own ventures. I insisted she abandon the name Gummy, but she says that, in embracing it, she has taken back power from Armitage to embarrass her. She has made it into a symbol of strength and pleasure and wealth—all the things he stole from her, and for that he blames me."

Slow steps brought him close to her. "So, you see, you're right. I'm not a good man, and I do hate him, but not for trivial reasons. I know the cruelty he is capable of, and a man like that does not easily change. Perhaps he truly was desperate and required our help, but I also know, given the chance, he will pay me back with ill. And whereas before there was no one he could harm to spite me, I can't say that anymore…"

He turned his head down and shook it to himself as though to banish a morbid thought. "And if he hurts you, Miss Dovetail, I promise you, his and Noah's fates will be the same."

Maybe he spoke out of duty, out of the burden of a gentleman protecting her honor, but his confession twined about her heart and squeezed, and she struggled for a breath. He'd fought with her, weathered her wrath and accusations, and dissolved an oath all to protect her. Surely that meant something.

He might not ever love her, but at least he cared.

Swells of guilt washed over her then. She'd been angry and desperate, yes, but Barrington had never failed her. And now she was trapped working a case for the type of man she vowed never to associate with again.

He reached into his inner coat pocket and drew out a

small box. "I may not know firsthand the burden of your ghosts, but it doesn't mean I won't continue to work my hardest on the wards to give you a reprieve. But in case it ever becomes too much…"

He opened the box to reveal a pendant necklace. The chain was thin, and the pendant was an anchor the size of a small coin, its surface marked by small, hollowed-out coordinates.

"All Aetherium officers are assigned a transfer charm," he explained. "When in danger or hurt badly, it is hard to hold the coordinates of a transfer spell in your mind, much less write one out to then ignite it. In the event of extreme danger, the officers activate their pendants with their magic— only a small amount is needed—and it will transfer them back to the location imprinted upon it. For Aetherium officers, that is usually the infirmary."

Sera touched the pendant, the ciphers rough against her fingertips. "Where does mine lead?"

Barrington met her eyes. "To me."

Their gazes locked for an infinite moment in which she was sure that with a pendant or not, they would always find their way back to each other.

"Thank you," she said. It was all she could manage.

He nodded once, a silent *you're welcome*. "May I?"

She turned around and gulped, closing her eyes in sweet anticipation.

"I suggest you keep it tucked away when outside; only Aetherium officers are assigned coordinates of their own, but Lady Carlson facilitated ours."

A smile touched her lips. Of course. She'd wondered why he'd taken on such a frivolous case as Lady Carlson's in the first place and declined monetary payment.

He had done it for her.

He lowered the necklace onto her collar, the metal cool against her skin. His fingers grazed the nape of her neck as he worked to secure the clasp, and Sera released a shuddering breath. The candles above flared and extinguished, the darkness cut only by a single stream of light coming from the workroom.

"There," he said, his voice low and warm against her neck.

She forced her eyes open and spun to him, their bodies now mere inches apart. Barrington caressed her hair back over her shoulder and hummed, a deep rumble in his chest. "Beautiful."

Spoken in barely a whisper, the word spread through her veins like wildfire, spurred by his cool hand lingering on the slope of her neck and the tenderness in his gaze replaced with something warmer. Reason warned her that emotions were high after their fight and muddled by their looming separation, but Sera leaned into his touch and willed logic away.

Outside, flashes of lightning struggled to cast their light into the dark room as if to warn they'd reached a perilous line, from which there was no return should they cross it. But ivy leaves blocked the storm and aided their journey into this unknown, encouraging them to forget station and reason, to search within the other for home.

His gaze flitted to her lips, his jaw pulsed, and she sensed he heard the call, too. But his hand tensed upon her, and she knew he wouldn't act first, always cognizant of her past and fearful reservations. For this line to be crossed, even if only a mistake made caught in this moment, it was wholly up to her.

Yet, shame flooded her, and she froze. Whereas his kiss would be laced with the honesty of his past and addictions, hers would be a bitter poison that would destroy them when he learned she hadn't been truthful about her ghosts and their ability to touch her. No doubt he'd feel betrayed, disgusted. Then would come rejection. And where his kiss was a dream, his repulsion would be her undoing.

With every desire warming the space between them, Sera lowered her head away. "Thank you. I shall treasure it dearly."

He gave her a sad smile, his gaze still conflicted, and nodded once. He wouldn't push. He wouldn't prod. He would simply accept whatever she wanted, and it broke her heart.

Sera lowered her eyes and walked from the room with Barrington close behind her.

Gazing back at his secret laboratory, she wavered at the threshold, the previous desire replaced by a flicker of worry. "Do you think it's safe, brewing blood magic here with Mr. Delacort using it as his campaign initiative?"

"The mechanisms I use strip my signature from the blood magic. Anyone else who knows of it is held under oath. It can't ever be linked to me. And if somehow it is, there are protections in place, set to safely destroy the room and everything in it should someone try to get in."

She stared at the vats and containment room. "Are you sure? If he finds out you of all people have anything to do with blood magic, he will make it so you never leave jail."

He closed the black door and moved to the worktable still overflowing with case files. "Jail? Do you think so? I'd imagine Delacort would seek a swift trip to the gallows. He would be smart for it."

Sera frowned. "I'm serious, Professor."

"As am I."

He met her eyes, and a shiver curled down Sera's spine. When they'd first met, he'd been refined and elegant, his voice even and smooth as he broke up an argument between her and a brutish boy who lived to see her suffer. But she'd sensed something ominous beneath his cool surface. A dormant darkness. She'd seen glimpses of it, once, after he killed one of the Brotherhood members who had hurt her. He'd asked her not to be present as he *questioned* the man. When he returned, his knuckles and cuffs were bloody and he didn't speak a word, his body stiff with violence.

That Barrington hadn't bothered with magic but had used his bare hands to beat the life out of a monster. For moments after, he'd sat there, silent, locking the beast of him back within its cage. But it peeked through his composure now, that endless void of blood and revenge.

Yes, he was serious, Sera accepted. If Delacort caught him, he'd have to be swift to kill him or else *that* Barrington would devour him.

Glancing down, Barrington secured a folder from the table and held it out to her. On the binder was written *Saint Aldrich Orphanage of Mercy.*

"What is this?"

"The case file for the home. We will find his sister and the children and ascertain their safety, after which your end of the bargain is fulfilled and he must hand over the spell combinations."

She met him opposite the workbench and took the file from him, her heart bursting with equal parts gratitude and pain. "I thought you wanted nothing to do with him?"

Sitting, he leaned forward onto the workbench and smoothed a hand over the surface as though to iron out his thoughts. "I'm not cruel, Miss Dovetail. An orphanage of seventhborns is missing, and they must be found. I inquired of the local constable," he went on. "And it appears, this time, Mr. Armitage tells the truth. The orphanage has been missing for over a week now, with no leads or sightings of the children or the staff. The constable was kind enough to lend me the case file as he's since deemed the case closed."

"Closed? It's only been a week—hardly enough time for a formal investigation."

"Indeed, but they are seventhborns. I'm surprised they even bothered to take any notes at all, but seventh-born orphanages receive a nominal subsidy, and the constable is required to conduct a monthly visit to confirm the institution is open and the children are safe before funds are distributed. If not, he must send proof of the current conditions, at which point the monies are denied, the children distributed to existing orphanages, and the home is closed. Since there were no children, he merely closed the orphanage."

She sat and opened the thin folder to the Constable's Notes. The records were sweeping statements of the home and property. *Dilapidated. Clearly abandoned. Belongings scattered all over the floor. Horrific. Disastrous. Not suitable for dogs. Wholly unfit and should be closed.*

Sera shook her head. "He doesn't even mention that the entire orphanage and its staff are gone." She flipped the page and scoffed at the signature under witness: Father Warner. "Not even a priest cared."

Anger burned her insides until her veins felt sore. Before becoming Barrington's assistant, her sole interest in being an inspector had been to find her family and her memories, but time and time again, monsters crawled from the shadows and men showed their true colors, until family wasn't her only motive anymore.

She handed him back the case file. "My orientation and reserve checks should be done by five tomorrow. It gives us time to visit the orphanage."

"Very well." He closed the case file. "Goodnight, Miss Dovetail."

"Goodnight, Professor." She walked to the door.

"Good luck," he said behind her. "Though I'm certain you don't need it."

She stopped at the threshold and turned to find him leaning back against the workbench, the case file in his arms crossed over his chest. "Let me guess. Because I've had a brilliant instructor?"

"Because you are a brilliant witch. The Aetherium will be lucky to have you." He nodded once. "Goodnight."

She gave him a small smile and walked out and up to her room, his words a balm to her pre-exam anxiety. At her desk, she picked up her notes and the accompanying study guide, the butterflies in her stomach much too agitated for her to sleep.

Yet, as the night wore on and her list of questions grew smaller, it wasn't the imminent tests or the thrill of a new case haunting the fringes of her thoughts, but rather the memory of Barrington's touch. She'd been a fool to imagine they would ever have a clean separation. He proved it the moment he asked Gummy to break his oath so he could tell her about Armitage. The instant he clasped the necklace around her neck, giving her a way back to him whenever she needed it.

No, whether by duty or friendship, they were bound now, and with the pendant tight in her hands, she fell asleep determined not to let ghosts break them apart.

an impromptu lesson

That morning, Sera crashed down into one of the transfer
stalls in the Aetherium's Witchling Academy, her book
nearly toppling from her hands. Her use of transfer magic
had improved immensely over the six months she'd been
away from the school, but smooth travel was impossible with
her nerves tangled as they were. Never did she imagine she'd
return to this place, her dream once again within arm's reach.
Bolstered in this, she moved to the booth's exit to allow for
the next incoming test taker.

Separated by stone walls, each booth contained a large
gold-metallic circle embossed on the floor—a transfer
wheel. A series of ciphers were carved along the gold band,
where magicians merely needed to rotate the rings to their
destination's coordinates and ignite the spell. For arrivals
such as Sera, the wheel spun to reveal the coordinates for
the traveler's point of origin, yet despite her trepidation,
Sera glanced down at her transfer wheel and smiled. With
Barrington's home surrounded by countless concealment

spells, black magic and otherwise, the rings spun and spun and never locked onto a fixed location.

She stepped out of the transferring stall. A wave of hot, humid air slammed into her. Situated in the mid-island province of Demerel, the Witchling Academy succumbed to the heat wave, viciously so. Though, it could be worse. It could have been held at the Aetherium Towers in the capital city farther south, whose temperatures newspapers likened to the fires of the Underworld. Some petitioned to have air-inclined magicians manipulate the wind currents and bring relief, but the Aetherium archdeacons vetoed it, citing the laws preventing the use of magic for personal gain.

Sera pursed her lips. That was unsurprising. With the Aetherium council on break, they spent their time in the cool northernmost provinces on holiday while their constituents burned.

A droning hum filled the space, the chatter of students, professors, and matrons. Welcome banners hung over the hall, each elemental color represented. Red for fire, yellow for air, blue for water, green for earth, gray for metal, brown for wood, and white for aether.

Along the hall, attendants greeted incoming students, yet upon seeing Sera, either their eyes opened in surprise or their mouths bowed in disgust. Sera's cheeks warmed; who knew what rumors had spread regarding her expulsion and involvement in Mary's *disappearance* and Timothy's death?

Still, she held her chin a touch higher. Most of these pupils had been born into privilege, enrolled into the Academy at an early age, and the success of entering the School of Continuing Magic was a natural progression. For her, it had been a war, and now it was time for the final battle.

She had earned her place here, bled for it, and if they didn't like it, they could rot.

She rounded the corner toward the auditorium for the exam commencement speech but stopped short. Timothy Delacort's best friend, Hadden Whittaker, walked toward the auditorium but halted upon seeing Sera. Whereas once he was an arrogant, mountainous boy—as tall as he was wide—now he was much thinner, as though wasting away. His hair was also disheveled, and dark circles dropped from beneath his eyes, accentuated by his pale skin that hinted at an unnatural gray complexion. His uniform sagged on his shoulders, nearly covering his hands with the look of someone unable to retain a tailor and forced to wear clothes that no longer fit. Mary had mentioned his family was poor, but the previous year he had managed to hide it. If it wasn't for people weaving around him, she would have thought him a ghost.

His mien darkened. He clenched his jaw and flexed his hand closest to his wand. Instincts pricked the back of Sera's neck, and her magic roiled in answer. Her fingers cramped with the urge to snatch out her wand and blast him before he dared do it first, if his behavior was any indication. Dragging in a deep breath that flared his nostrils, Whittaker relaxed his hand, yanked open the auditorium doors, and vanished inside.

Sera sagged back, her pulse quick and thrashing, a stoker to her magic, which spun wilder at her core and flooded her veins with heat. *Settle down, Sera. Settle.* The last thing she needed was a run-in with Whittaker now when her dream was so close. Dealing with the ghosts was enough.

After a few calming breaths, she pulled the door open and entered the hall. Thankfully it was dark and she was able to slip inside and sit in the back undetected.

The hum of conversation filled the space. Sera looked about the room, the enormity of it all pressing down on her chest. She located Barrington instantly, in the aisle separating the girls' half of the hall from the boys'. With his hands folded at his back, he focused straight forward, but Sera's brow dipped. His posture was stiffer than normal, in an unsettled way Sera had never seen before. If he bristled any more, she wondered if he would snap in two.

A woman stood beside him; she didn't wear a professorial robe, but a white shirt and a beautiful dark yellow skirt that complemented her brown skin. She had small brown eyes with a bright and youthful expression in them, with just a dash of wickedness. And when she lifted a hand to adjust an errant braid, Sera noted an Invocation ring wreathed on her index finger. She was lovely, and a nudge twisted Sera's belly. Was this mysterious woman the cause of Barrington's behavior?

She forced her gaze away to the room lest she be caught staring. Still, she couldn't help but wonder…

Silence swept over the hall. Headmistress Reed walked onto the stage dressed in a black-and-green-striped gown with a high neck and pagoda sleeves. Sera stifled a scoff; too many times had she suffered at the hands of the horrid woman whose beauty was only matched by her cruelty. She moved to the podium. With her long limbs and elegant nature, she could have floated there, and Sera was certain no one would have known the difference. She cast a serious gaze along the room. Though her lips were pulled into a small smile, her aura was dim and brooding.

"I would like to begin with a moment of silence for one of our brightest students gone much too soon, Mr. Timothy Delacort."

At the sound of Timothy's name, Sera's heart wrenched. She turned her eyes down to her hands clasped tightly together in her lap. No doubt everyone would turn around any second to stare at her, to point their fingers and blame her for Timothy's murder. She braced, prepared for their scorn. Had her conscience not taunted her with the same accusation since his death? Did he not visit her nightmares each night, haunting her with blame in the form of one question: *Why did you let me die?*

A knot gathered in her throat. If only she had fought the Brotherhood a little harder, this moment of silence may not have existed at all. But, pressing her fingertips to Barrington's pendant hidden beneath her collar, she lifted her lashes. Whatever pain and contempt came to her was just desserts. Thankfully, she was camouflaged in the dark and no one looked at her...only Barrington. He gave her something of a fleeting smile, which she knew was to bolster her. Her guilt was only magnified more.

"Welcome to the Aetherium School of Continuing Magic entrance exam," the headmistress started again, too soon for Sera's liking. There would never be a moment of silence long enough to honor Timothy. This is a very important moment in a magician's life, and with reason. These exams will determine whether you will join our government's brightest and strongest mages, to serve the Aetherium and all under its law."

After some words of encouragement and history on the importance of the exam and access to magic for all, she reviewed the four elemental disciplines to be covered: Water, Earth, Air, and Aether, the distribution of schedules, and the strict attendance policy. "After your reserve check, you will obtain your schedules. But keep in mind there are no reexaminations. One missed module and your entire exam is void. Good luck, and remember: whether you keep to one of the fundamental elements or excel in Wood-levels and join our legislative body, embrace the judicial branch of Metal, or defend our Aetherium under the banner of Fire, I speak for myself and the staff when I say I am so very proud of all of you. I know you will make this Academy proud." She nodded once, a stern bow of the head, and walked off stage.

At once, students rose, except for Sera; it was impossible to stand with weakened knees. She'd anticipated these reserve checks, where a proctor would evaluate how vast and deep her magic stores were and how long she could use her powers at full intensity before they depleted.

For the Aetherium exam, a time of three minutes was satisfactory. After her battle with Noah, she had no doubt three minutes was manageable. But it didn't make the affair any less frightening. She took in a calming breath, gripped the armrests tightly, and forced herself up.

Moments later, she reached her examination room and sat at one of the benches that had been pushed against the walls of the third-floor corridor. A group of students down the hall held stagnant orbs of magic in the air in preparation for the reserve check while another kept time. Several others repeated magical facts to themselves, while many were hunched over their books. A girl nearby leaned her head back against a pillar, listing the ingredients needed to purify water as though recounting it to the heavens.

Unfortunately, with the crowd much thinner here, it was harder for Sera to disappear, and she was met with stares and scowls.

A brunette girl sitting in a bench diagonal from Sera's leaned in to her friend. "Look, Eliza, it's the seventhborn. Timothy Delacort danced with her and soon ended up dead. Mary Tenant befriended her and she, too, has vanished."

"How horrid," Eliza whispered back.

Cruel pain and anger jabbed Sera's heart. Losing her temper over rumors was much easier, but to withstand their scorn over the truth was persecution of another kind. Her magic flared in response and rushed to her fingertips, but she opened her book and plucked out her sheath of Water-level notes from inside. She'd prepared for this moment, suffered two years at the Academy in order to sit here. One step closer to becoming an inspector. To finding her family. She wouldn't let them ruin it even if her insides felt ready to break.

"Anne Doughty," called a proctor.

The girl rose, and before she passed Sera, she moved to the other side of the hall as though being a seventhborn was contagious. Sera clenched her jaw. Getting through the week without setting something on fire might prove to be the hardest test of all.

Half an hour later, a door down the hall groaned open. "Miss Seraphina Dovetail."

Sera's heart pounded and muted all thoughts. This was it. Standing, she walked to the room from which her name had been called, and, with her book clutched tightly to her chest, she entered.

A tall, older woman with smoky-gray hair and brown, hooded eyes stood behind a desk, her wrinkled hands clasped before her. Sera stopped at the designated chair, and for moments the woman didn't speak or invite her to sit but merely watched her with a sharp, miserable expression.

"My name is Mrs. Lange," she said finally. "I will be conducting your reserve check." She stalked around the wood desk, stopped in front of Sera, and thrust out her wand. "Your wand."

Sera stared at the offered wand, and instincts churned in her gut, fueled by Mrs. York's warning. "I haven't signed the Privacy and Consent form."

The woman's wrinkled lips curled to a snarl. "Raise your

wand, seventhborn, or it will be my pleasure to fail you for insubordination."

Sera's cheeks flushed, anger a hot pit in her stomach. Anyone intent on ill could use the knowledge gained during the reserve check to purposely tire out an opponent and, when left without magic, disable or kill them. A magician could also tap into another's reserves for information or to possess them. A dangerous endeavor, indeed. But, clenching her jaw shut, Sera hauled in a calming breath. It would be her word against Mrs. Lange's, and it was no mystery who they would believe.

Despite the wrongness settled in her belly, Sera unsheathed her wand and held it up to Mrs. Lange. Without this portion of the test, she couldn't move on to the others and her dream was done.

She hissed; the woman's cold and acrid magic rushed into her wand and veins like clawed nails desperate for her bones. Sera's powers unleashed and rushed up her body in a manic wave, determined to fight off Mrs. Lange's endeavor.

"You must let me through, girl!" The bitterness of her magic pushed against Sera's blockade. Pressure gathered in her temples as Mrs. Lange fought to get through, but Sera's powers spun faster and hotter, a wildfire sloshing in her core.

The door swung open. Mrs. Lange retracted her powers, and Sera cried out, the feeling of the withdrawal like nails scraping the underside of her skin.

"Ah, finally." The woman who had stood by Barrington in the auditorium walked into the room, a file in her hands. She met Sera's stare. "Forgive me for being late. Miss Dovetail, correct?"

Sera rubbed her temples with shaky hands. The revolting sensation of Mrs. Lange's magic lingered in her veins. "Yes?"

"Excuse me," Mrs. Lange clipped. She set her wand on

the desk with a sharp tap. "This is an official Aetherium examination. You can't barge in here in the middle of an assessment."

The woman stopped beside Sera. She had been lovely from afar, but from this close, she was radiant. She was about Barrington's age, if not slightly older. Her hair was in beautiful small braids that she had tied back in a bun, accentuating her delicate features. "Yes, forgive me. I would have been here earlier, but when I inquired as to where Miss Dovetail's exam was, I was escorted to the wrong room." She looked at Sera. "Curious, don't you think?"

Mrs. Lange pursed her lips. "Administrative procedures are no concern of mine. Now, whatever your business, it will have to wait." She snatched up her wand. "I have a test to complete."

"Precisely the reason I'm here." She reached into her folder and held out a letter to Mrs. Lange. The Aetherium emblem was prominently displayed on the top of the page. "My name is Doctor Morgan, and I've been retained to be a neutral party present during Miss Dovetail's examinations, as is stated in this letter from the Aetherium Office of Special Affairs."

Sera blinked. *An observer?*

Mrs. Lange read the note, and a slight snarl curled her upper lip. "I will have you know, *girl*, I have been an Aetherium employee for many years, and there has never been a need to have my work overseen."

"It's Doctor, actually. And this is not a reflection on you, to be sure. I will be shadowing all of Miss Dovetail's exams as a safeguard against any attempts at sabotage or discrimination."

Mrs. Lange pursed her lips and motioned for Sera to lift her wand. "Very well. Now kindly stand back so that I may finish Miss Dovetail's assessment."

"Yes, yes, of course. Once I sign the Privacy and Consent agreement, you can continue."

A moment of terse silence spread about the room, Sera's suspicions now a raging fire. She scowled at the teacher, who touched a hand to her hair and cleared her throat. "I found no consent form in her file and imagined seventhborns weren't privy to that right."

Doctor Morgan smiled, a tight, cold expression and, reaching into her dossier again, drew out the needed form. "Then it's rather fortunate I have a copy." She looked at Sera and winked. "Always a good thing to be prepared."

Color faded from Mrs. Lange's face, and her mouth pressed to a thin line as she beheld the contract. She opened her mouth to speak, but Doctor Morgan turned to Sera. "I'm sure Mrs. Lange has expressed this, but I will repeat it just in case. This test is a general measurement of your reserves. The Aetherium is interested in nothing except for the depth of your abilities, so anything encountered during this check is confidential, and we, as servants to the Aetherium and all under its law, are sworn to secrecy. If you approve, please sign here."

She set the Privacy and Consent form on the table and a quill pen beside it. Sera's gaze caught on the Invocation ring around her finger. Had she been a schoolmate of Barrington's and that's how they knew each other? She shook the thought away and read over the form; the same vow of secrecy was written on the page bordered with a series of ciphers, some of protection and others of silence. Sera picked up the pen and, after rereading the form numerous times, she found nothing of concern and signed it, her signature somewhat askew. Her hands trembled as Mrs. Lange's assault lingered in her veins.

Mrs. Lange signed next, a quick scribble. Doctor Morgan took back the form, clenched her fist, and pressed her Invocation ring onto the page. A small twine of smoke whirled from where she branded the contract with the Aetherium emblem etched into the ring's facing. She signed her name beneath it—*Doctor C. Morgan*—then slid the page back inside her folder.

Doctor Morgan moved aside and motioned a hand for Mrs. Lange to continue. Clearing her throat, the woman raised her wand. Sera did the same until their wand tips touched. Like before, a sticky coolness invaded Sera's veins, and her magic rushed to meet it, but under the safety of the confidentiality agreement, she allowed the tartness to trickle down into her reserves. Minutes later, it retreated as Mrs. Lange drew her magic back, slowly this time. They each lowered their wands, this part of the reserve check complete and less arduous than before, which fueled Sera's anger.

Mrs. Lange walked to her chair and, sitting, jotted down notes in her files, then reached for the pocket watch dangling beside her wand holder.

She clicked it open. "Spark a flame at the tip of your wand and hold it at full intensity, starting…now."

Sera aimed her wand. Hot magic rushed to her fingertips, and a vicious white fire exploded from the tip of her wand like a torch. She fed the flames with the fury she'd felt outside and the pain from Mrs. Lange's horrible examination. For seven minutes, her magic never wavered, a roaring blaze that shaded the room in silver light.

"That's enough," Mrs. Lange said suddenly. "Seven minutes is the maximum time needed."

Sera gritted her teeth and drew her magic back, wincing as the hot flames rushed into her veins. Given her rage, she could have gone for ten minutes.

Marking her score, Mrs. Lange handed Sera her exam schedule. "Your reserves meet the requirement needed for the rest of your exam. Your score will be forwarded to the Aetherium. Good day to the both of you," she said and never once lifted her eyes.

Sera remained still, her magic churning so fast it roared in her ears like a beast starved for destruction. Mrs. Lange's previous behavior had been nothing but prejudice, and with memories, emotions, and magic so tightly wound, had Doctor Morgan not come in, she would have had full access to Sera's mind. Enough to learn about her work with Barrington and his blood magic. About Timothy and the spell the Brotherhood sought to obtain power over time. That Sera had used death magic to kill Noah. The horrible woman would be under no obligation to keep the information private; it wouldn't have taken long for Mr. Delacort to know. And shortly after, her and Barrington's lives would have been over.

Doctor Morgan touched a hand to Sera's arm. "Miss Dovetail?"

Pulled from her brooding, Sera followed her out of the room and into the hall, but her rage was like a rope, binding her to the door, and she stared at it, imagining the woman on the other side wrapped in flames.

Perhaps cognizant of Sera's murderous thoughts, Doctor Morgan moved before the door and blocked the handle. "Are you all right?"

"She had no intention of me signing the Privacy and Consent form," she said through clenched teeth. "She would have ruined me."

"Which is why I'm here." Brown eyes met Sera's, an intense yet kind look there. "Come, let's talk where there are fewer doors and ears."

They walked downstairs and to the gardens. Students lounged in the shade, enraptured by their last-minute studies. Sera paused at the threshold, taking in this place where so many crucial moments of her life had occurred. The enclosed sitting area, where Mary's Wishing Tree had once stood and where Barrington had wished for Sera's forgiveness after their first disastrous fight. The lush forest, where Timothy had first professed his love to her and later helped her fight off the Brotherhood. The woods, where she had almost died.

Swallowing around the knot in her throat, Sera followed Doctor Morgan to a bench closest to the forest, securing them a measure of privacy.

"I've heard a lot about you, Miss Dovetail," she said, sitting.

Sera followed suit. "I'm sure you have," she said, focused on the spaces between the trees.

She laughed, a feathery sound. "Well, yes, I've heard about your temper…and the events from last semester. I'm terribly sorry for your loss. I'm told you were friends with Timothy Delacort."

Sera's pulse quickened, and she stood but pressed her hand against the back of the bench, her head still a bit woozy from Mrs. Lange's first reserve check. "Who are you?"

"Please, Miss Dovetail. You can trust me. I mean you no harm."

A razor-sharp edge of anger sliced through Sera. "I trust no one."

"Yes, I've been told, and with reason." She reached up to a necklace around her neck, two lockets upon it. "But it might make you feel better to know that you are well acquainted with my mama."

She opened one of the lockets to reveal a small photograph of Mrs. York.

"You're lying. Mrs. York doesn't have a daughter."

She laughed, a throaty ripple. "Oh, but she does. She had me when she was very young. My grandparents were against it and had me sent away, but once she married and made a name for herself, she found me. However, we both thought it best that I remain out of the public eye once Duncan decided to run for chancellor. No doubt it would be found unsavory that his wife had a child out of marriage, with a warlock of all things. When Mama learned Mr. Delacort was asking questions about your test, she feared he might try to use his influence and friendships against you. She needed someone she could trust to oversee your exams, and here I am."

Sera gripped the seat's edge to steady herself, but the world felt as if it would close in around her. Being a seventhborn was hard enough without Mr. Delacort to deal with. This was bad. Very, very bad.

If Mr. Delacort was asking questions, it was not so far-fetched to imagine anyone could be a spy for him. Someone like Mrs. Lange or as kind and unassuming as Doctor Morgan. She smoothed down her skirt. Paranoia was not going to help her. She needed to talk to Barrington. "I'm feeling a bit tired. Perhaps we could continue this tomorrow?"

"Of course. Get some rest and replenish your reserves, and we will meet tomorrow for your Water-level module. Goodnight, Miss Dovetail. And remember, you're not alone in this."

Sera bid her goodnight and walked away, certain she was not alone in this. She had Barrington, the only person she could trust.

· · ·

Moments later, Sera landed in her room, the air thick with the lingering fragrance of rain and vegetation. She groaned; her muscles ached, and, after Mrs. Lange's horrid treatment, she wished for nothing more than her bed. But she had to ask Barrington about Doctor Morgan. More, tonight, they were set to visit the orphanage and hopefully learn what happened to Meredith and the children. Rest would have to wait, especially when each day the seventh-born orphans were gone was another day the Brotherhood could hurt them.

After smoothing another coat of oil onto Meredith's brittle wand, she changed into her black dress and black veiled hat she often wore to her investigations and walked downstairs. Barrington's professorial robe hung on the coat tree in the corner of his office, but minutes later, she'd yet to find him anywhere in the house. She thought of his secret laboratory, and her heart churned, but, determined not to think of his blood magic work, she busied herself with her notes for the Water-level module the coming day. Healing had never been her forte, and whenever she'd needed healing, she'd always gone to Mary. But Barrington had challenged her, and now she had a decent handle on the art.

Clatter down the hall stole her attention. Setting down her notes, she followed the noise to the library. The two-story room was one of the largest in the home, with vaulted ceilings and elaborate scenes painted across the span. Books were kept behind steel gates, spells carved along the narrow metal bars. Barrington explained he had enacted the protective measures after many old and expensive texts were destroyed in the fire that killed his father and brother. She hauled in a breath, relishing the scent of the old books comingled with heather riding in on the breeze and moved into the room to find the source of the noise.

Her brow rose.

Rosie was in the back of the room, where they kept their collection of maps, sorted by provinces and year. She was organizing a pile of unfurled atlases scattered across the drafting table, rolling them into tubes and stuffing them back into the map organizer.

Sera frowned. *Barrington.* The man was a tempest, but this particular mess spoke of one thing: he was in a bad mood. Suspicion nudged Sera's stomach. Could Doctor Morgan be the reason?

Rosie spun and, at seeing Sera, she heaved a sigh. "Good evening, dear," she said, her cheeks flushed. "The master awaits you in the stables."

"What happened?" Sera nodded down at the maps.

"Apparently, there is a map missing, but thankfully Lucas has copies."

"Did he mention which?"

"According to him, *the newest map of the blasted mainland,* though he used a lot more expletives."

Sera wrinkled her nose. "Oh dear." The map wasn't missing. She'd needed it to scry a few weeks before and stepped away for a moment to locate a book. When she returned, the Barghest was on the table, the map torn by his claws and saturated with drool as he licked the scrying pendulum for magic.

"Thank you, Rosie. Leave the maps; I will sort through them when we return."

"It's no trouble, dear. But could you take this with you?" She retrieved a basket from the side table and handed it to Sera. "There's a sandwich in there for each of you. The master said he would eat later, but you know how he gets when he's hungry. And would you please tell Lucas not to pluck out the vegetables?"

Sera's stomach twisted at the mention of food, yet a nudge of pain gripped her heart. Should she pass her exams and enter the Aetherium, she would have no one to fuss over her. "Thank you, Rosie. For everything."

Basket in hand, Sera walked downstairs. Once outside, she traveled the dirt path toward the stables in the distance. Gusts of cool ocean breeze whisked past, blowing tendrils of her hair across her face. She would miss this, too, the calm of the ominous moors, the earthy fragrance of gorse and heather and the damp vegetation, though this close to the stalls, it smelled more of hay, leather, and horse.

She entered to find Lucas smoothing a brush down a black stallion's girth, readying him for travel. It must've meant the orphanage was not terribly far. They avoided transferring to crime scenes, lest they leave behind traces of magic Aetherium guards could identify. And if the location was far, they transferred to one of Gummy's brothels and secured a smuggler from there. They opted for the carriage when the scene was within a night's driving distance.

Lucas raked his shaggy brown hair away from his narrow face and smiled. "Evening, Miss. The master is in the back, charting our course."

She reached into the basket and set a sandwich on a nearby table. "Rosie said…"

"Not to pluck out the vegetables," he grumbled. "But she uses so many."

Sera smiled; he was a powerful magician, but she was reminded that he was only sixteen.

She walked past the stables and rounded the corner to find Barrington leaned over a small table, a map spread out before him. He was dressed in all black, and his mood was just as gloomy. Sera shook her head and thanked the heavens for Rosie's basket. The two of them in an enclosed space with her temper and his foul mood was a danger to human, horse, and carriage. Yet, noting the light sheen of sweat over his brow and the slight tremble of his hands, Sera's heart dimmed. This was hunger of another kind. Withdrawals.

She set the basket down on a stool. "Good evening, Professor."

He glanced up at her briefly, and though he was clearly vexed, his eyes softened. Sera's heart fluttered, and warmth crawled into her cheeks, but she stifled the reaction. Surely, she imagined things. He was as happy to see her as he was about rain. Whether or not it was present, he would merely go on about his day.

"How was your exam?" he asked, working out a calculation.

Sera divulged all that had happened, from seeing Whittaker to Mrs. Lange's attempts. Her concerns over Doctor Morgan quickly tumbled from her mouth. "I didn't admit to anything, as I wasn't sure she could be trusted."

He stiffened a slight upon hearing her name but continued on with his work. "You did well, but in this instance, everything she said is true." He reached for a compass and checked it against his calculation. "Mrs. York mentioned she would have Cressida oversee your exam, but I didn't have the time to alert you."

Sera frowned. *Cressida.* She even had a pretty name. More, they were on a first-name basis. Though they'd worked together for nearly a year, Barrington rarely called her by her given name, save when she was hurt or they were in the midst of an argument. "That's a relief, then. She seems nice. Have you known her for a long time?"

"We went to the Academy together."

"Oh, that must be nice, seeing an old friend…"

He paused for a beat where his jaw pulsed. "No, not

particularly. Is that all that happened?" he said, clearly putting an end to the matter.

Sera pursed her lips. He was worse than her spell chamber; it often felt like no magic on earth would make him spill his secrets. But while she wished he would open up about Doctor Morgan—*Cressida*—she abandoned the issue. He hadn't pressed her about her past with Noah, and she wouldn't press him about this. "Yes, that was all."

She moved beside the table as he trailed the length of a road with his finger, then jotted down calculations on a sheet of paper beside him. He was focused on Rotherham, the southernmost province of the Aetherium; she hadn't realized the orphanage was so far. But her brow gathered. By carriage, the journey would take days, yet he still charted their course.

Sera touched the edge of the table, awareness knocking her heart down into her stomach. "Surely we're not transferring with the horses."

"Indeed, we are. The orphanage is in a mountain town. Gummy's nearest brothel would still be a two-day journey, and unfortunately, she had no available smugglers. This is the only way."

Sera lowered down onto the nearest stool, her legs weak and heartbeat quick. Transferring alone or with a companion was easy enough, but to move through the void of space and time with an unpredictable creature such as a horse was exceedingly dangerous. When traveling in pairs or groups, the companions had to hold fast to the magician in charge of the conjuring. If a companion released them at any point, they might be lost forever.

Worse, the travelers had to remain calm. Any drastic shift in movement might alter their course. Horses spooked easily and were prohibited from transferring. Not only were they traveling with three, but also with their bulky black carriage.

"Why can't we transfer there ourselves and call on the Barghest to clear our magic?"

He rolled up the map and, folding the coordinates and calculations of travel, he stuffed them into his inner pocket. "That beast is untrainable. He will devour our magic and all the magic on the scene before we've had a chance to investigate."

Sera scowled. He was right, but she was desperate.

He strode across the room and opened the basket, plucked up a sandwich, and handed it to Sera. The next one, he bit into without ceremony.

She set the sandwich aside and frowned. "How can you eat, given what we're about to do?"

Leaning back against the table, he shrugged a shoulder, plucked a radish from inside, and popped it in his mouth. "Easy. I'm hungry."

He swallowed his last bite and wiped his mouth and fingers, then pushed off the desk and set his napkin in the basket. "My calculations are infallible, Miss Dovetail, and Lucas is a tremendous coachman. He will get us there safely."

She didn't doubt this. Lucas had lived with Rosie and Barrington since his mother had perished in the fire that killed Barrington's father and brother. He had since trained under Barrington in all forms of magic and had grown into a formidable magician, a skilled navigator, and a fierce fighter just as determined as they were to find the Brotherhood and bring them to justice. Sadly, he had no desire to join the Aetherium, despite Rosie's urging.

"There's nothing to worry about," he said, moving out of the small room.

She scoffed behind him. "Besides getting lost in the void between space and time forever?"

He hummed. "Yes, that does sound terrible…but at least we'd be together."

Sera's heart pounded and she looked at him, but he had walked away and she didn't know if he'd been earnest.

She took a few bites of her cucumber and watercress sandwich, more for Rosie's sake than hers, and set the rest of it in the basket. She joined him beside the carriage, where he slid his Gladstone bag inside, then held a hand to her.

Drawing in a deep breath, she slid her fingers into his and climbed onto the first step. Barrington's hold tensed on hers. She stopped and turned to him. Now elevated by the stair, she found their eyes were level and his face so very close.

"If it would make you feel better, I can ride up top with Lucas and oversee the transfer, or would you prefer I stay with you?"

Panic gripped her, and she squeezed his hand, refusing to let him go. "Stay with me."

He nodded once and followed her into the carriage. Sera moved to her corner seat, and Barrington sat diagonal from her. She hugged herself, trembling as though her bones sought to rid themselves of her skin.

"Shall I sit with you?"

She thought to deny him, but the wheels groaned and the carriage jostled forward, and she felt her heart climb into her throat. "Do you mind?"

"Never."

He moved across to her bench and sat beside her. Though his nearness was a dream, she thrust her hat down into the seat in front of them. "I feel ridiculous. I've faced the Brotherhood and a Barghest, and yet a few moments of transferring are my undoing."

"It's all right to be frightened."

She fixed him with a side-eyed glare. "You're never scared."

"Yes, I am rather brave, aren't I?" he said, coolly smoothing a hand down his lapels.

Sera scowled; had she her hat in her hands, she would have hit him with it.

"But I have been scared in the past." His gaze grew distant with memory. "The type of fear that will lead a man to think of magic so dark their soul would be forever banished to the Underworld."

Sera stared at him keenly, wishing she could travel his thoughts to this moment that haunted him. For those seconds, though he was sitting next to her, it was as though he'd disappeared.

Lucas called the horses to trot, and the carriage picked up speed.

"Tell me of that time," she said. Anything to keep her mind from their imminent travel.

He met her eyes and gave her a sad smile. "That, my curious one, is a confession for another time. But I can tell you of what helps me when I'm scared, if you'd like to hear it."

She nodded.

Crossing one leg over the other, he angled himself toward her. Sera faced him as well; she could have stayed here forever, nestled between him and the carriage wall.

"My mother was a non-magic. Unlike other non-magics who lose their abilities over time, she was born with no powers at all."

Sera's heart hurt for the woman. To be born powerless in a world of magic was an aching thought, perhaps as bad as being a seventhborn.

"She said she lived in a state of constant fear, unknowing what the future held for someone like her. And so, in order to defeat this fear, she set out to learn everything she could about magic, even if she didn't possess it herself. She read whatever book she could get her hands on, sat in during her siblings' lessons to understand its workings and parts, its intents and motivations. That way, it became tangible, something she could grasp. Eventually she discovered ways to defend herself using wards and became an exemplary potion maker. She instilled that in Filip and me, though I suspect she didn't intend for it to lead me to black magic." He smiled; his words were tinged with a touch of wistfulness that gripped Sera's soul. "Come to think of it, she would be rather disappointed in many of my life's choices, except for becoming a professor and you. Yes, I think she would have liked you very much."

Sera's breath caught in her chest. She was one of his life's choices...but surely he meant taking her on as his assistant. It was pointless to consider anything beyond that. His heart could never belong to someone like her, despite moments like this, when he looked at her, his gaze softened, and it seemed nothing else existed in the world.

"Thank you," she said finally. "She sounds like a wonder-ful woman."

"She was. She lived her entire life surrounded by the greatest of magicians while having no abilities of her own and yet was the strongest of us all."

"Then I suppose in order to not be afraid, I must learn all there is to know about the spell tonight."

"Indeed." He clicked his teeth. "Fortunately for you, there is a rather brilliant professor who can teach you."

Sera pursed her lips. "Really? Have I met him?"

His mouth flattened. "Or not."

Sera laughed; a measure of her fear was dispelled, but Lucas called the horses to canter, the carriage quickened, and her apprehension reemerged. "Teach me."

Barrington held out a hand; she slid her trembling fingers into his, not knowing what he meant to show her but trusting him wholly. "Horses despise transferring. Though it lasts but a moment, the instability scares them. We must ride with speed into a transfer spell so they will not realize it until we've made it across. You will feel as though we're falling for longer than usual, but this is normal."

He turned her palm upward, nestled within his. "You see, there are myriad bands of magic running from north to south and east to west, each a different element." He touched his index finger to the tip of her middle one and trailed it the length of her hand, slowly, down to her wrist. He then skimmed it across the width, his gaze following the path of his fingers. Sera swallowed thickly, fighting the urge to close her eyes and succumb to his featherlight touch that coiled something within her.

"They aren't straight lines—rather, they bend over material things like mountains and other terrains and constantly shift depending on the moon cycle, the planets, the winds. When we transfer, we travel along a number of these vertical and horizontal bands, moving left and right, up and down, until we reach the point of intersection that is our location. When we attempt large transfer spells such as the one tonight, however, we use a spell that will force us to remain on one band of magic that will leave us close to our destination."

"How?" she asked, her pulse quick and voice trembling.

"By containing our travel to only one element," he explained, his fingers weaving magic against her palm as he skimmed her lifeline. Goose bumps now sprouted along her skin. "It requires expert control; we may all have a dominant inclination, but in essence our magic is composed of a mix of all the elements. By restricting our magic to one element, we restrict ourselves to one band."

He lowered their hands but didn't release her. She didn't draw her fingers away, either, relishing the memory of his previous caress and their present contact.

"At this moment, Lucas is taking us to where this current of magic is calculated to be, and he will spark the transfer spell from there. That way we won't have to risk moving through the web of magic for longer than needed and scaring the horses."

Lucas shouted for the horses to go. Their hoofbeats quickened to a frantic gallop, and the carriage jostled and trembled. A loud hum grew louder, Lucas no doubt sparking the transfer spell in the distance. Sera glanced toward the window frantically, but Barrington slid a finger beneath her chin and coaxed her face back to his.

"We will follow this current until we encounter the horizontal band we seek for our location. This is known as the point of convergence."

The world vanished into complete darkness, and her stomach jammed into her throat as they plunged in the black.

Sera yelped and turned her head, then buried her face into the crook of his neck and her fingers into his nape. Barrington didn't deny her and held her closer as they fell, his steady voice warm against her ear when he whispered, "I'm here."

The frantic hoofbeats resounded once more, this time against the damp countryside of Rotherham.

"We've made it through, sir," Lucas called out from up top as the horses slowed to a canter.

Sera blinked and, realizing where she was, stiffened. Peeling away slowly, she lifted her lashes to find his face so very close, his gray eyes fixed on hers.

"Are you all right?" he asked, his voice low between them.

A furious blush warmed her cheeks. "Yes, sorry."

He shook his head, just barely, and stroked a strand of hair clinging to her lip. "I am your anchor, am I not?"

She nodded; he was that and so much more.

"Good." He gave her a small smile and faced forward.

Sera mirrored him. But though they'd stopped transferring and now moved over solid ground, she settled back and closed her eyes to steady her heart, which kept on falling.

6

an accompaniment and a melody

The carriage stopped soon after, and Lucas opened the door. Despite the humid heat, Sera shivered at the abandoned two-story orphanage towering in front of them, the brick home wreathed in a thick, whirling fog. The windows across its worn facade had been broken, and all Sera could think of were gouged-out eyes watching them, waiting for them to trespass into the mist, where smoky tendrils would twine about their limbs, drag them into the darkness of the house, and devour them.

Barrington stepped down and held his hand out to Sera. She put on her hat and rolled down her veil. Sliding her fingers into his, she descended blindly, her magic and senses heightened in the unnatural silence and stillness that shrouded the home.

As Barrington spoke with Lucas and instructed him to search the perimeter, Sera moved to the hedges surrounding the house. Though desolate, the building was alive with fear and a stifling desperation that skittered down her skin.

"Do you see something…or someone?" Barrington asked gently, coming alongside her.

She inched closer to him, his presence a comfort amid the darkness emitted from the house. "No ghosts, but I sense distress and desperation," she said. Her words echoed in the silence. "Not so much from the forest but from the house."

He nodded and drew his wand, his gaze severe under the brim of his top hat. "The home may be stained with what's happened or what you feel is a premonition of what's to come. There's always the chance whoever is responsible may return to the scene." He met her eyes. "Be careful."

As if confirming his words, a gust of warm wind wheezed past. Despite the pressing humidity, Sera shivered; the breeze sounded like cries. She walked with Barrington to the waist-high entry gate. Two square brick pillars flanked a rusted gateway, a silver plaque upon the right column.

Saint Aldrich Orphanage of Mercy

Mercy? Sera scoffed. Aetherium founder Angus Aldrich was hailed a hero, but she pursed her lips. They'd learned he had been nothing more than a necromancer and maker of the Brotherhood.

Barrington motioned aside with a finger. The latch on the gate lifted, and the gateway creaked open. They walked slowly and quietly along the cobbled pathway toward the house. Abandoned jump ropes and blocks were strewn on the grass, amidst dolls wet and stained with condensation and mud. Sera's eyes narrowed. Closest to the house were shards of glass, from the windows, surely.

She relaxed her shoulders, took in a deep breath, and allowed her second sight to manifest. Magic filled her head until ciphers appeared on every conceivable surface and crowded the air. Hundreds of ciphers glimmered against the grass and the side of the house. Sera narrowed her search to the most recently employed spells, those ciphers that shone the brightest, but none were of any concern.

At the door, Barrington gripped the knob, nodded at her from over his shoulder—a silent *stay vigilant*—and eased the door open. The stench of mildew wafted out, pungent in the heat and dampness. They stepped into a small entry hall. Tables and chairs looked more like waiting monsters in the dark. Barrington held up a hand before him and wriggled his fingers. Tendrils of magic whirled at his palm and joined together until an orb of light floated in his open hand and illuminated the room in silvery light.

White columns and archways lined the area, the paint on them crumbling. A bench was to the left, a rag doll beneath it and, close to that, a spoon. Sera frowned. They moved farther into the home, and her frown deepened. Random belongings were scattered about the wood floors, books and blankets oddly positioned, clearly having been dropped. The same held true for the subsequent nearby rooms they surveyed. Yet it was the walls that gave Sera pause. Various vacant spots were stained with the outlines of previously hung pictures.

They stopped at the dining hall door. The square room was governed by long tables cluttered with plates of half-eaten food. But there were no gnats or rodents. *Maybe they were wise and chose to stay away*, Sera mused, surveying the utensils strewn along the table and floor. Shards of glass on the ground told of tumbled cups. Some chairs were tilted on the floor, others fallen back against the table behind them. Once again using her second sight, she found no signs of any sinister magic.

"This is all rather strange. They obviously ran away from the dining hall."

"Quickly, if the state of the room is any indication,"

Barrington murmured, picking up a napkin with his pen.

"But where could they have gone?"

"Indeed, and what were they running from?"

They jotted down notes and moved along the rooms, their theories and suspicions like an accompaniment and a melody, as one theorized and the other supported their claims with questions and findings of their own. Hours passed for them like this—Rosie always said it was as though once engrossed in their investigations, everything else ceased to exist. Other people. Nourishment. The world.

Once they'd combed through the home together, they separated. Barrington walked upstairs, and Sera searched the ground floor. They would then alternate and, when finished, they'd compare notes.

Sera moved to Meredith's office. She tapped her finger on a candle there; the room was instantly shaded in gold, the shadows quivering in the candlelight. At the filing cabinet beside the door, she carefully thumbed through behavioral files and progress reports but paused, the distinct sensation of being watched pricking her skin with cold.

The floorboards creaked above as Barrington continued his enquiry, and she spun to see Lucas searching the shrubberies outside. Still, remembering the ghosts, she drew her wand. Surely magic did nothing to deter them, but she wouldn't let them touch her without a fight.

She moved to the matron's desk. Trinkets dotted the edge, but the baubles were nothing of importance. Behind the desk was a bookcase, and above it hung pictures of the various wards, innocent faces staring back at her from behind shattered glass. With each passed portrait, Sera's chest tightened, and her magic churned faster and hotter. Given Armitage's past and cruelty, if he had anything to do with the children's disappearances, she would personally see to it that he burned.

She touched her finger to the photograph of a small girl with wide, bright eyes and a gap-toothed, mischievous grin. "Where are you?"

A rush of magic roared up her veins at the question, and she groaned as her brain felt ready to split in two. She leaned forward and clutched the edge of the bookcase, biting her nails into the wood. She tried to assimilate this pain, but screams overwhelmed her senses, the phantom cries of the house now alive in her mind. Discordant and distant shrieks bounced off one another and doubled until there was nothing but their terrible, desperate sound. There must have been hundreds of voices, all with a single plea.

Help.

Sera lowered her hand from the picture but gasped at the reflection of a girl standing behind her. She spun to find it wasn't a girl at all, but a ghost, her skin grayish-purple and her wet hair clinging to the sides of her pale face. She considered perhaps she was one of the orphanage staff, but her fashion was not of this time.

The ghost reached a hand to Sera.

Show you…

"Go away," Sera breathed, her voice shaking and teeth chattering in the now-frigid room, but the ghost billowed forward as though she hadn't spoken at all.

Sera's pulse quickened. This wasn't right. The ghosts had no dominion in this realm; if she ordered them to leave, they had to listen to her. She lifted her wand and called to her magic, prepared to fight back somehow, but the phantom gripped cold fingers around her wrist, ice flooded Sera's veins, and the world faded behind a sheet of dense fog.

Awareness burned her like a brand; the ghost—*Ada,* she knew suddenly—had dragged her into a vision, the way

Barrington had warned her against. *You should never fully immerse yourself in a summoning without an anchor*, he'd warned her the first time she'd summoned. *Some spirits are wicked and will lure you deep into a vision so profound you may never find your way back. You will be lost in your mind forever.*

But this time she hadn't summoned. The ghost had welcomed herself into Sera's thoughts all on her own. Her heart pounded. *A possession.*

She reached for her magic, intending to make something, anything fall. She had to get Barrington's attention; he was her anchor and would pull her from this apparition. But her powers drifted out of reach as if belonging to someone else. How would she ever get out of this?

The smoke slowly thinned and gained shape and form, and a new reality spread before Sera's eyes. She was in a forest, and a thin blanket of snow covered the ground. *The first snow of winter*, she realized, though the knowledge was not her own. Fear, thick and biting, wrapped around her bones as she stared around her, to the dark spaces between shadowy gnarled and skeletal trees. Laughter echoed in the distance, and her pulse quickened. She had to find her way back home. She had to run but, wholly disoriented in the darkness, she spun and spun, unsure which way to go.

"Where are you, seventhborn?" a masculine young voice called from the darkness, underscored by snatches of laughter.

"Yes, why don't you come out? We only want to play," taunted another.

Ada sobbed, though Sera felt the cry come from her lips, could taste the salt of Ada's tears in her mouth. She dashed into the brambles. The forest was a pit of blackness everywhere, and the branches conspired against her, scratching her face and arms and legs with every other step. But she had to move or else they'd catch her. She had to move if she wanted to live.

"Come out, come out, witch!"

Their voices echoed behind her, but she tripped and tumbled, crawled and pulled herself forward until the sound of the river overpowered the hooting and hackles from her tormentors. She glanced behind her; their wand lights were like candles in the surrounding dark, but with each moment, they grew bigger.

She was running out of time.

She eyed a collapsed tree, its top sunken in the flowing water. The broken base formed a small opening where she could hide, and if she held tight, the current couldn't drag her out. They would never look for her there; no one was mad enough to wade in these waters in the winter. But the line between madness and desperation was thin, and so Ada hurried down the muddy bank and into the water.

Cruel and bitter cold dug its fingers into her skin, the water frigid. She winced and cried out, but clamped her mouth shut, determined not to give away her location. She pushed herself through the opening in the bark. Rough wood scraped her fingertips, and splinters stabbed into her palms, but, mastering her pain and the cold, she dug her feet into the frigid, muddy bank and peeked up through a slit.

Four boys jogged down to the riverbank, their wands held up before them like torches, their faces hidden behind raven masks. They spun around, searching for her, and when they were unable to find her, their lanky, shadowy frames ambled closer to the riverbank.

"Do you think she tried to swim across?" one asked, his voice muffled in the mask.

"No," said the tallest one. "No one would be mad enough

to go into the water."

"Maybe that scryist was wrong, then," the one beside him replied.

"No," said the tall one again with damning certainty. "She's never wrong."

The others shrugged it off and walked away while the tall one surveyed the lake a little longer.

Ada considered moving, but her thoughts felt far away and her body grew heavy and numb. Perhaps she would stay here a while and he would forget all about her.

Forget me, she begged. *Please forget.*

She repeated this until the fog of sleep filled her head and her words grew further apart.

Please…

Forget…

For…

…get.

The vision curled into a sheet of smoke that thinned and vanished, revealing a star-speckled sky above. Sera hauled in a desperate gasp but coughed wildly as water splashed into her mouth and nose. There was coldness everywhere and water up to her chest. Her body was weightless, but her wet dress was heavy and dragged her down.

Something taut and warm wrapped around her waist and pulled her closer to the edge. Sera struggled and tried to reach for her magic, but her nerves were splintered and all she managed were small fire bursts above her. She was dragged onto the shore; the bind around her waist loosened and deposited her onto the sodden turf.

She spun wildly; the Barghest stood behind her, his red eyes like glowing rubies in the deep darkness swathing the forest. Sera cupped her mouth and looked around; where on earth was she, and how had she gotten there? More, how did the Barghest know?

The hellhound moaned and lowered his head, then nudged at Sera's foot, as though asking if she was all right.

"I...I don't know," she said through racking coughs. On her hands and knees, she dug her fingers into the mire as realization and panic ripped through her. A ghost hadn't just touched her this time but had possessed her. She'd walked all the way here under its influence and with no recollection of how she'd gotten there, wherever she was.

No, she wasn't fine at all.

The Barghest whirled into a cloud and dashed into the forest.

"No," Sera cried out after him. No doubt he smelled magic somewhere and was driven by his insatiable hunger, but he couldn't leave her alone in this place.

Her chest tightened, fear descending with sharpened claws. Memories merged with reality, and her breaths grew shallow and quick. It had been in woods like these that the Brotherhood had emerged, seeking to hurt her. She searched the shadows among the trees, her wand aimed. Were they there now, waiting to strike? Or would another ghost come first?

A nearby bush rustled. She gasped and spun, her heartbeat thundering in her ears. No one was there. She opened her mouth to call for Barrington or the Barghest, but, breathless, her voice was a weak whisper over the growing heaviness in her chest and panic, panic, panic of imminent death.

She scratched at her chest for Barrington's necklace, but her hands shook and she no longer felt in control of her limbs. And the Brotherhood was coming. As were the ghosts. One would take her magic. The other would own her body and mind and never let her go.

The bushes behind her rustled again. She scrambled around and aimed her wand at Barrington and the Barghest coming through the brush. Upon seeing her state, Barrington held his hands up in surrender, his eyes wide with worry and his chest heaving with ragged breaths. "Miss Dovetail, it's me."

She knew his face, but her mind didn't recognize the person. "Stay away," she yelled, grasping for what infinitesimal magic she could gather.

"Sera—"

"I said stay away!" A flare of fire dashed from the tip of her wand. He reeled a hand and averted its course. It tunneled into the forest and crashed against a tree there with a deafening *boom*. The Barghest whirled into a cloud and sped away after it. But she fixed her gaze on Barrington, his silver eyes nearly transparent in the dark. She found no anger in his stare, only a concern that twined about her chest and made it harder to breathe.

"Stay away from me," she moaned, no longer sure where she was, what was real, and who was the enemy.

"All right, of course. What else do you need?"

"Put down your wand," she said, her breaths quick and tight. A distant part of her mind told her he didn't need a wand. He could manipulate magic with perfect precision and kill her before her next word. But Barrington would never hurt her, and this only made things worse. No doubt he'd revoke his referral and terminate her employment, then he'd throw her out into the streets and let the Brotherhood have her. She would never pass her exam or find her family. She would die, all alone.

He set down his wand, his movements slow and deliberate. "Take a deep breath and look around you, Miss Dovetail. Tell me what you see."

She shook her head frantically, her gaze shifting along the shadows and canopy of leaves.

"Sera, darling, please. Tell me what you see."

She shuddered but, inhaling deeply through her nose, glanced to their surroundings. "Trees and branches. Rocks. The stream. Bushes. You."

"Good. That's brilliant. Now, focus on that. There's no one else here but us. You're safe."

Him. Not the ghosts. Not the Brotherhood. Just Barrington. Alive. Here. Safe.

"I'm moving closer now." He spoke gently and, after a moment where she didn't decline, took a measured step forward, then two more until he reached her. And after another warning, he helped her to her feet and took her into his arms. Assured her that she was safe until her agitated breathing regained its pace and the gentle thrum of his heartbeat coaxed hers to relax.

"It's over now," he said, his nose buried in her hair. But Sera closed her eyes against him, knowing his words were a lie, even if he didn't know it yet. There was no way this was over, now that she had been possessed, both body and mind.

The rest of the night was a blur. One moment, they were on the riverbank, the next Barrington warned her he was transferring her back home. Exhausted, she hadn't the strength to argue that his magic would be close to the scene. She merely buried her face in the crook of his neck and found solace in the thrum of his pulse as he held her tightly against him, the world vanished to a blink of black around them, and the next instant they were in her room.

Intermittent candles ignited, and pulsing shadows filled the chamber. Barrington laid her down gently and draped a quilt over her shoulders. After calling for Rosie, he knelt beside her, stroked her hair, and assured her she was safe. More, that he was there. And then...

She landed in the transfer booth at the Academy the following morning, unsure. Had he left then? Or had he stayed? She hadn't gotten the chance to ask; he was already gone when she'd woken that morning. And though her reserves were somewhat replenished, the haze of fatigue was heavy and she could only grasp fragments from the previous night. All that was certain was she'd been possessed against her will, something that shouldn't have been possible.

Fear prickled the back of her neck, but Sera gripped the doorknob and pushed the cubicle door open. She couldn't fret. Everything would be fine. She'd made it this far, and she couldn't break. For now, her focus was her exam, and after, they would find Meredith and the children, Armitage would hand over the wards, and the ghosts would cease to be a problem.

Strengthened in this, she walked out of the transfer room and down the main hall toward the third floor for her Water-level exams. A twinge of worry tickled her belly. After she had escaped Noah's clutches and was rescued by Aetherium guards three years prior, she'd been admitted to the Witchling Academy due to her impressive reserves and mastery of magic. She had, however, missed the first two years of schooling for pupils her age, and the subjects of Water and Earth became a bane to her existence. But, determined to take the Aetherium entrance exam as soon as possible, she had trained and studied, and under Barrington's tutelage her knowledge of healing had increased. Still, she swallowed tightly. Had there been something she'd missed in those two years that she hadn't yet learned?

Wish as she tried against it, she searched the halls for Barrington. She would see him at home later that day to be sure, but his presence was a balm to her fears and apprehensions, and one glimpse would calm her wrestling nerves. Warmth flooded her veins as she recalled his strong arms around her, his musk commingled with that of the damp earth and sweat from his attempts at finding her. And he'd called her *darling*... Or had that been a figment of her mind? She frowned. Of all the things she couldn't remember...

"I can't believe the Academy allowed a murderer back into its halls."

Sera stopped short at Hadden Whittaker's voice behind her, and her magic quickened at her core, but she pushed her steps forward. She wouldn't engage.

"But once Mr. Delacort wins, he will change that," he said, clearly following. Passing students stared while others whispered and some laughed. Still, she just needed to make it to the grand staircase and walk into the girls' tower, where he couldn't follow.

"Especially after you lured Timothy away to that damned church..."

She wouldn't engage.

"And then you and Mary killed him."

Her anger flared. Her magic churned. She spun round to him towering behind her. "Keep their names from your filthy mouth."

"Where is she?" he asked, ignoring her anger. Given the storm of violence in his eyes, Sera knew he couldn't see anything through it. "Where is Mary? I know you're hiding her. And when I find out where, I won't be the only one to lose a friend."

Sera's skin grew hot, the beast of her magic chomping through the bars of its cage, but after a moment, Whittaker stood there, waiting, and Sera's eyes narrowed. He was livid yet waiting for her to attack first. Then she would be at fault, despite his venomous words. Once the Aetherium found out, they would void her exam. But another, grimmer thought descended upon her, and she stepped away. "How did you know Timothy died in a church? The information was classified and the case file sealed."

Whittaker's eyes widened, and he paled, clearly realizing he'd over spoken. He admitted to nothing, but, given the sheer terror in his eyes in that moment, Sera's suspicion crested.

Delacort.

Surely Whittaker hadn't instigated this argument out of his own malice, but rather Delacort had tasked him with a purpose. To ruin her exam and to find what information he could about Mary. Sera shook her head, realizing just how true Mrs. York's words had been. She could trust no one. Not even the motivations of the enemy.

"I will find her, seventhborn."

Sera scoffed and turned away. "When you do, maybe you can tell me," she said over her shoulder and walked up the main staircase and into the girls' tower.

Moments later, she entered the third floor to find Doctor Morgan waiting by one of the pews lining the hall packed with students waiting to be called inside for the Water-level modules. Today she was dressed in a gorgeous forest green skirt and black blouse with puffed sleeves, her braids tied back in a bun with a few of them curled and framing her face. Sera's mouth bowed; surely Barrington had lost his heart to her at one time and that was the reason for his bitterness. Not that she could blame him. Doctor Morgan was radiant and a far cry from Gummy, which made Sera like her considerably more, despite the protests of her heart.

Doctor Morgan's brow dipped. "I would say good morning, but given your scowl, I'd say it hasn't been very good."

Sera hefted a sigh and, as they walked down the hall to a vacant bench at the end of the corridor, she recounted all that had happened. "But I didn't hurt him, as much as I wanted to shove my wand in his eye."

"The boy does sound like a wonder," she muttered, sitting. "But you did the right thing."

Sera nodded and settled down beside her; if only doing the right thing didn't feel as if her bones were breaking.

"Are you all right? I know it's said *they're just words*, but when in mourning, everything seems to hurt twice as much."

Sera bristled. "I haven't the time to mourn. Timothy is gone, Mary betrayed me, and grieving will not change that."

Doctor Morgan's brow furrowed. "But surely that isn't healthy, Miss Dovetail. Believe me, I know. I'm a thanatologist, after all."

"A thanatologist?"

"In essence, I focus on the emotional, mental, physiological, and magical effects of death, on both victims and those who survive them. It is an interdisciplinary study of forensics, psychology, and magicism."

Sera's heart pounded. "So, you're a…death doctor?"

She laughed, brushing a curled braid away from her temple. Her Invocation ring glimmered in the sunlight streaming in from outside. "I suppose you can say that; at the Aetherium, they refer to it as death lore, and it's all rather taboo. It's much more accepted in Falkirk and Halivaar. Though magic use is forbidden there, our abilities are still studied just as any other discipline."

Sera hummed. Perhaps, like transferring with horses, if she learned more about death lore, she might encounter more information about death magic that would make her affair with ghosts less frightening, at least until she and Barrington solved Armitage's case and obtained her wards. More, that would explain why ghosts were now able to touch her and possess her without her say.

Doctor Morgan's eyes narrowed as though she'd heard Sera's unspoken words. "Is there something you would like to talk about, Miss Dovetail? I know we've only recently met, but I am a doctor, and everything we say is kept under the strictest of privacy. It is a part of my Invocation vows."

The thought of talking to a doctor spurred her pulse, but she rubbed Barrington's pendant hidden beneath her dress. Before, the ghosts were a nuisance, and even when one bruised her, they were an inconvenience at most. But now they could overtake her against her will and lead her to unthinkable madness. This she couldn't ignore.

"I was curious about…death magic," she said, her last words a whisper.

"Ah, well, that's not death lore but black magic." Doctor Morgan spoke for Sera's ears only. "But yes, I've come across some instances of it in my work. Not actual patients, but I knew someone who partook in its study. I can try to answer what questions you have, and if I'm unable to, I can refer to his notes when I get back to Falkirk."

Sera's brows rose. "You live in a non-magic province?"

"Indeed. After a particularly bad heartbreak, I wanted to forget about magic for a while." She was quiet for a moment, echoes of sadness in her eyes. She shook her head then, as though to banish the memories. "I moved to Falkirk after I earned my Invocation ring, and I started my practice there. It's been good for me, and the people are far more accepting, though there is still work to be done in the plight of seventhborns."

Sera's brow dipped; her suspicions flared. Doctor Morgan's discomfort was so similar to Barrington's, as was her reluctance to address it. Could it be he was the reason for her pain?

"I've since dedicated my life to the study of seventh-born mothers and the reasons for their demise. I do earnestly feel seventhborns and their mothers deserve more than fear and prejudice and mythology. We've been taught since a young age that using magic for personal gain is a horrible wrong, yet when a mother embraces the dogma and rejects magic for the sake of saving her child, the offspring is blamed and cast aside. Our government is supposed to embrace logic; instead of blaming the mothers, they should reconsider what they teach. Should find out the reason a mother has to decide at all. Why should both mother and child cross each other on the threshold of life and death and never again?"

Sera glanced down, her heart throbbing. Whenever thoughts of her mother surfaced, she readily stifled them. Like Timothy and Mary, her mother's death during childbirth was yet another path of grief she wasn't ready to travel.

"Forgive me. That was insensitive, but I am so very passionate about my work. So please know I'm here to talk whenever you're ready. I've actually commandeered one of the smaller rooms in the matron hall. Seeing as I'm only here for your exams, it made no sense to secure lodging elsewhere."

"Miss Anne Doughty, Miss Eliza Douglas, and Miss Seraphina Dovetail," a matron called.

"Perhaps we can talk after the exam?" Sera said, standing.

Doctor Morgan's eyes brightened, a genuine joy at Sera's question. She nodded and followed her to the testing-room door, where the girls crowded the matron.

"But surely we can't be expected to test near a seventh-born," Anne said in frantic whispers.

"My mama said they're bad omens," Eliza added.

Ignoring them, the matron moved aside, allowing for the girls to enter. Along the wide room were three worktables, the testing stations for the practical portion of the exam. Countless plants, herbs, flowers, and other flora were spread out upon the benches. Stacked cages of rodents and reptiles were on the adjacent wall, and opposite that, a worktable filled with instruments.

Aides stood beside each table, prepared to monitor progress, assist in mishaps, and prevent cheating of any kind.

The proctor, a tall woman with gorgeous brown skin and reddish-brown hair, approached them. "I'm Mrs. Costas, and I will be your overseer. Welcome to the Water-level portion of your entrance exam."

Without ceremony, she asked each of the girls to scan the lifelines of the caged creatures and offer at least three methods for healing. To test their magic manipulation abilities, they each had to explain how to encourage growth of a lizard's leg while simultaneously employing a continuous flow of magic to alleviate any discomfort so the matter would be painless.

With the oral portion complete, Mrs. Costas nodded to the work stations along the room. "You are to pick a station and review the potion given you, name the ailments and situation it is most commonly used for, and provide a list of side effects, as well as an alternative method of treatment should the first not work. After your explanation, you have twenty minutes to brew said tonic."

Sera hurried to a station and flipped open the file. *Rhodonite Elixir.* She could have fainted from relief.

She'd learned of Rhodonite during her Aether-level courses, its tonic used to extract memories from a patient's mind. During their investigations, Sera used it to aid in her summonings. In healing, however, it was often used to treat stomach ulcers. Confidently, she waited until Mrs. Costas approached her and clearly explained all she knew of the potion, its effects and adverse reactions, and how it was brewed.

Yet, as Mrs. Costas walked away, Sera winced. She'd forgotten to mention that it could also be used for bug bites but collected the ingredients needed for the pink tonic. It was too late now. And as a cloud of green smoke exploded over Eliza Douglas's cauldron and her concoction spilled on the aide's cloak, Sera ignited a flame beneath her cauldron. She might lose some points because of her partial answer, but at least it hadn't been a total disaster.

Sera cleared her worktable as the potion brewed; clean workspaces were part of the grading rubric. She tossed the debris in a waste bin and turned to find her elixir boiled too quickly. She moved toward the table, intending to grab her wand and lessen the fire, but a cold chill spread through her veins at the ghost lingering before her work station.

The spirit, an old woman in a white nightgown and sleep cap, glanced around as though lost. Sera averted her gaze. So far, the ghosts that had attacked her only did so when they knew she could see them.

Remembering the previous night's possession, she swallowed tightly, and panic pricked the back of her neck. She had to lower the cauldron's flame but couldn't use wandless magic. Not with the aide standing right there. More, when it was illegal to perform it without an Invocation ring. She needed her wand, but what if she touched the ghost by mistake? Was that even how it worked? If so, the phantom would then know she could touch Sera and, perhaps, try to possess her. But she couldn't let her potion burn.

Sera's heart thundered. What an impossible situation…

Doctor Morgan sneezed loudly, and the flames all along the room were extinguished.

"Goodness, forgive me," she said and, with the snap of her fingers, ignited them again. Sera's was now at a reasonable intensity.

The aide shook her head and spun back around, never once realizing what had happened. And in the commotion, the ghost had vanished.

Sera hurried to her workstation. Her elixir was safe. She sagged back with a sigh and looked to Doctor Morgan. Her gaze was downcast, but she was smiling, and Sera's heart warmed. Whatever her history with Barrington, she was beginning to like Doctor Morgan very much. But she chastised her heart, which was prepared to soften a little too easily.

Moments later, Sera set her filled vials of Rhodonite elixir on the table and stepped away from the workbench, her heart soaring. Finally, finally, after a night of disasters, a stroke of luck. Or of hard work, rather. She had studied for this. And now she had no doubt she'd aced this portion of the exam.

The proctor marked Sera's file and dismissed her with a nod. Sera followed Doctor Morgan outside, though she felt as if floating. Nothing, not even Whittaker, could dampen her mood. Eliza Douglas, however, ran past her, crying.

"Poor thing," Doctor Morgan said, watching the sobbing girl who vanished around the bend. "The practical portion is always the hardest."

"Indeed. Thank you for your help, by the way."

"Yes, of course. You looked rather distressed. What happened?"

Sera hesitated; was she prepared to share the truth about

her phantoms with Doctor Morgan? The previous night's possession had been a horror, but the last time she'd been careless with her trust, Mary had broken her heart and Noah had tortured her body. That was not a mistake she was keen to make again.

But the ghosts and possessions changed everything. Today she'd been lucky, but what if another decided to overtake her during a future exam or Doctor Morgan wasn't able to help her? Her career would be over before it'd begun.

A school matron stopped beside Dr. Morgan and handed her a note before Sera could decide on a reply. The Aetherium crest was on its front, and three red lines ran along the length of the envelope. Three-banded letters were of the utmost urgency.

Doctor Morgan took the sealed note, tore it open, and read it quickly. Her brow rose, and she looked at Sera with a terror-filled gaze. She handed Sera the missive.

Sera took it from her, her heart suddenly in her stomach.

Dearest Cressida,

Please do not share this with Miss Dovetail until after her exam; I do not wish to upset her at such an important time.

Nikolai has been detained for suspicions of blood magic. Inspector Lewis has been to see him. He is all right and wished for us to tell her not to worry, to focus on her exams, and he will reach out when he can. And, above all, he is sorry.

I will write you once I know more.

Thank you, dearest.

Love,

Mama

Sera's hands trembled. The lights along the hall flickered, and the note burned in her hands, red flames stealing away Mrs. York's words, but Sera's pulse pounded loud in her ears with the memory of them.

Barrington.

Detained.

Crimes of blood magic.

Doctor Morgan touched her arm. "I'm certain he will be fine. It's just a questioning."

It wasn't.

She dropped her hands to her sides; ashes slipped through her fingers. Hot and cold washed through her in dizzying waves, chased by Mrs. York's warning.

He is out for blood.

Surely this was Delacort's doing. And given Barrington's family history, this was all the blood Delacort needed.

"I have to go," she breathed, or maybe she didn't say anything at all. She wasn't sure and didn't care. She had to get home.

The Academy corridors and students were a blur as she dashed to the transferring hall downstairs. With the day's exams over, a line wrapped around the bend; it would take her upwards of an hour to transfer.

Her heart thundered and hands trembled, but she had to think. Transferring had been nullified during exams, save for designated locations, but she would never be allowed to transfer in the Teacher's Hall or downstairs in the servant wing. Not without anyone watching and telling of what she'd done. But there was one more place…

Sera picked up her skirts and dashed to the main stairs. Hurried up, up, up through the vacant dormitory floors and to her old tower room. Back in her time at the Academy, transferring on school grounds wasn't allowed, but Barrington had somehow amended the transferring capabilities in the tower room, making it possible for her to travel to his home for their investigative work. She hoped with every fiber of her being this was still the case.

She pushed the door open, hurried into the dim room, and closed the door behind her. The cracked, paint-chipped, and water-stained walls were still riddled with burn marks from the many times she'd lost her temper. Her amalgamation of mismatched and dated furniture also remained in the room. They hadn't even bothered to clean out her things. Did they even realize she was gone? Sera shook her head; it didn't matter.

Rummaging through her old, abandoned things, she secured a stick of red chalk. There was no way she could hold the coordinates to his home in her mind. Not when morbid thoughts reminded her of the casualties she'd endured so far. She'd lost Mary and Timothy, they told her.

All in magic, please. I can't lose him, too…

Pain scattered across her chest, like a web of needles puncturing her lungs and heart. But, stifling a sob, Sera lowered down onto her knees and wrote out the coordinates to his home, her hands trembling and penmanship just as horrid as his.

She could not break. This was not the time for grief.

With the protection and transfer circles complete, she unsheathed her wand and aimed down. The spin of magic in her belly quickened. When it reached a roil, Sera said, "Ignite," and powered the spell.

A flash of black, and she crashed into Barrington's office. She toppled against the wall but recovered and rushed to the door just as Rosie appeared with Lucas. The stout woman's eyes were rimmed red and her lashes wet, and while attempting to comfort her, Lucas too stared at Sera with a widened expression.

"Oh, thank heavens you're here," Rosie cried. "They've taken him, miss. They've taken the master."

"I'm sure it's nothing," Lucas tried to coax her, but his voice was thinned with nerves. His hair was also disheveled, and he raked a hand through it, tousling it into greater disarray. "He's been questioned before. And it was Inspector Lewis who alerted us and told us not to worry, so he's in good hands."

"Listen to Lucas," Sera said calmly and helped Rosie down into one of the winged armchairs before Barrington's desk, though she too felt just as frantic. "The inspector is a friend."

"I knew this would happen." She wrung her handkerchief in her hands. "Delacort's been wanting to persecute the professor just like he did the master's father and brother."

Sera knelt before her and took her hands. "Get her a glass of water please, Lucas?"

He hurried to the side bar and poured her a cup of water. Back beside them, he handed it to Sera but motioned with his head for her to join him out in the hall. Sera nodded. *Finally, answers.*

She eased the glass into Rosie's hands. "I will be right back. I'll only be a minute."

Rosie settled back, the glass cupped tightly in her hands. They trembled, and her reflection rippled in the surface. Sera hated leaving her but squeezed her shoulder, walked into the hall, and closed the door behind her.

Lucas paced by the staircase, wringing his flat cap in his hands. Sera rushed to him. "Tell me everything."

He hesitated for a moment, but then deflated with a sigh. "He went to Gummy's, ma'am, last night after we brought back the horses, but there was a raid, and Aetherium guards arrested everyone on the premises. Some of the girls who got away said they saw the master being dragged into the detainment carriage, charged with suspicion of blood magic."

No...

Upon searching the brothel, no doubt they would find Gummy's supply, provided by Barrington. Sera pressed a hand to her stomach as though to catch the pieces of her crumbling heart.

If Delacort had his way, Barrington would burn.

"I spoke with the inspector; Mrs. York is doing everything possible to see him released. But is there anything I need to do?" Lucas asked, his eyes wide and unblinking. In all of their time working together, she'd never seen him so afraid. But, though slip-thin and boyish in appearance, he was always ready to do whatever was required of him at a moment's notice, whether it be fight or tamper with a scene. "Shall I clear out his laboratory? If the Aetherium decides to inspect the house..."

Sera shook her head. "Nothing. There are safeties in place should the Aetherium try to get into the lab, but I don't know what they are and I don't want you anywhere near there. For now, stay with Rosie. I don't know how much more of this she can take."

"Yes, Miss." Lucas hurried down the hall and rejoined Rosie in Barrington's office.

Sera lowered onto the stairs, a torrent of worry and hurt roiling within her. Damned Barrington and his stubbornness. She had warned him Delacort should be taken seriously, and now he'd proven it. How could he have been so stupid? Did he not care that there were others who worried for him? Whose lives would be devastated if he were no longer here?

Anger rolled over her fear. No, of course not. They didn't matter. Only Gummy, black magic, and revenge. And she'd been a fool to think otherwise.

But no more.

Just as Barrington had his priorities, so did she. After her exams were complete, she would move on with her life, become an inspector, and find her memories and family. And, like with Timothy and Mary, she would work like mad until her heart was so numb it would no longer feel the pain of him.

And whereas he didn't consider those who needed him, she would never be the same. She would find the orphans and ascertain their safety, and then she would obtain her deterrents to overcome the ghosts and possessions, which made finding Meredith the first order of business.

1

in the here and there

She rushed to her room and secured Meredith's wand. She held it up to the light and inspected the fibers. The wood was more pliable, and the darker strands had a healthy shine. It was ready. All she needed now was a sample of Meredith's magic for the Barghest to trail, and hopefully he would make quick work of finding her.

Moving to the window, she pushed open the glass panes and whistled a high-low melody. Within seconds, an approaching black cloud gathered on the horizon. She moved aside. The Barghest whirled into the room and slowly materialized.

She held her hand up and gathered magic in her palm, a warm orb of smoke that twisted and tangled. His furry ears perked up, and when she flicked it in his direction, he whipped out his snake tongue and caught it into his mouth. She smiled. "Come, then. We have work to do."

With Meredith's wand in hand, she opened the door. The Barghest dissolved into a black mist and slipped through the floorboards. Sera pursed her lips and met him down in the workroom. "Cheater."

He rumbled what she could imagine to be *I know*.

Setting Meredith's wand on the worktable, Sera retrieved a new metal cap to replace the existing tarnished holder that served as a conductor. A dirty or damaged encasement could cause ripples in the incoming magic and variant results to a desired spell.

With the wand properly fitted and primed, she set it down on the workbench and moved to her desk on the adjacent wall. The Barghest trotted near the wand at the table.

"Ah, ah." She held up a finger. "Not yet."

The beast retreated, his ruby eyes fixed on the counter from which Sera often let him devour any lingering magic from her and Barrington's investigations, much to Barrington's dismay.

Sera gathered her notes from when Barrington had taught her the coming experiment and set out the necessary tools on the workbench. The center of the table was a slate board where they tested various cipher combinations to reconstruct spells. On it, Sera wrote out a containment spell, which would hold the recovered magic and keep it from disappearing so that she could then transcribe it. This time, however, she would have the Barghest inhale the collected magic and track its smell to find Meredith, just as Barrington had done to find Sera after she'd been captured by Noah and the Brotherhood.

She set a specimen holder in the middle of the slate platform. The triangular contraption had a cross within it and, at the crux, an opening, where she slid in Meredith's wand and tightened the metal prongs on the casing to hold it in place.

She sat down and patted her thigh. The Barghest

lumbered closer and set its massive head on her lap. She stared at him sternly. "Track this magic as quickly as you can. There are children missing, and this magic is vital to us finding them, so no delays, regardless of how much magic there is elsewhere. Understood?"

He gave a grunt and a rumble that reverberated in his chest.

"Good." She fed him another orb of magic. Back at the worktable, she rechecked the tightness of the prongs and assured the wand was secure. She dusted her hands on her skirt and flexed her fingers, then repeated Barrington's instructions until Meredith's magic filled the vial in her hands.

She should have then attempted to double the sample in case they needed more in the future, but that could take weeks. Every minute that passed was time when Meredith could move out of reach. And heaven only knew where the missing children were and what they were experiencing. No, she had to do this now.

She knelt before the Barghest and petted a patch of blond fur on its head, the stiff strands nearly translucent. "We only have one try at this, so let's not botch it, okay?" She settled back and pinched the cork. "Here it comes."

The Barghest focused amber eyes keenly on the vial as she uncorked it. A cloud of magic whirled out in reedy, twining wisps. The Barghest's wide nostrils flared as he inhaled the sample, and a rumbling sound rolled through him. His eyes illuminated, a fiery red Sera hadn't seen in months. He dissolved into a black funnel and seeped into the floor.

Sera clapped a hand over her nose at the pungent whiff of sulfur. When the Barghest was gone, she snatched up quill pen and paper and watched the floorboards where he'd vanished. As he traveled, following the trail of Meredith's magic, the symbols on the floor changed repeatedly and would continue to adjust until he'd fixed on her exact location.

Sera sat in her stool and kept vigil of the ciphers that shifted and shifted and—

The first set of coordinates locked into place.

She rushed into the library, to the upright storage cabinet where they stored their maps and blueprints. She drew out their largest map of the Aetherium and its districts. Back at the workroom, she pressed it flat on the worktable. The first set of coordinates told of the territory. Matching them to the map, she relaxed a slight; Meredith was not in a non-magic province. Travel to non-magic districts required official paperwork or a smuggler—both of which would take time to obtain. Thankfully, Meredith was still in the immediate vicinity of the Aetherium capital, closer to the ports. But, if she managed to secure passage on one of the ships, things might prove difficult. The most populated port was in Fairmount, a non-magic territory. If she found her way beyond its borders, it would be harder to find her.

The remaining coordinates locked into place. Sera waited a moment. When they didn't change, she stood in the middle of the transfer circle formed by the Barghest, closed her eyes, and aimed her wand to the ground. The floor gave way, and she plunged into darkness.

She landed at the end of a narrow hallway, a tattered brown runner stretching across a dirty wood floor. Behind her was a window also covered in grime, and through one of its cracked panes a dust yard was visible below, a mountainous heap of ashes and cinders and other household waste. The air was sticky and humid, reeking of refuse and burned coal. Nearby smoke stacks spewed thick black clouds into an already-leaden sky. The soot seemed to weigh the heavens down, the tops of the chimneys invisible through the impenetrable fog.

There was a room a few feet away. Murmurs resounded of many voices talking low and in whispers. She paced measuredly toward it, her wand held tightly in her hand and the coordinates for Barrington's home ready in her mind should she need a speedy exit. She stopped beside the open door and peeked inside.

Rows of makeshift cots were lined across the room, some fashioned out of tattered rags and crates, no doubt secured from the waste outside. Girls and women slept beneath threadbare blankets stitched together from dirty remnants while others huddled together, chatting. Two young girls closest to the door played with dolls made of scraps of fabric. The brunette girl saw Sera first and waved; a seventhborn tattoo marked her wrist. The other girl turned and clutched her doll tightly to her chest. She, too, was branded a seventhborn. Sera gazed about the room; there were only seventhborns here.

Worry curled down her spine. Though the ruling government claimed to be Pragmatic, a seventhborn's power remained a thing of fear, with some Purists' beliefs still accepted as truth and taught in schools. Sera remembered the lies she'd been forced to regurgitate of how seventhborns performing death magic was how disease and evil found its way into the realm of the living, which in turn led to the seventhborn plague and mass persecutions thereafter.

And though she and Barrington had since learned the plague had all been the work of a necromancer, society still embraced the lie, and congregating amongst seventhborns was strictly prohibited, unless a permit had been obtained and adequate guardianship was present.

Sera glanced around the room and found no supervision from an Aetherium official or guard or otherwise. A gathering this large was no doubt unlawful and would result in severe punishment.

Swallowing down her apprehension, she peeled her glove off to reveal her own mark and waved back.

"Excuse me, Miss?"

Sera spun to a brunette girl down the hall holding a bundle in her arms. Her hair was parted down the middle and braided in two, which made her appear no older than fifteen. She drew closer, and Sera's heart stuttered. In her arms was a baby wrapped in a ragged blanket. A seventhborn tattoo marked her tiny wrist, the skin still inflamed from where she'd been branded. Sera bristled, anger coursing through her. How could anyone sleep at night knowing they hurt babies like this all because of prejudice and fear?

"The name's Claire. I'm a floor matron of sorts here. All seventhborns are welcome as long as they're not here for trouble. So, coming or going?"

Sera's brow dipped. "Pardon me?"

"Going on one of the ships or coming from one," she clarified and nodded down at Sera's dress. "Coming, I'm guessing. Can't no seventhborn on this side of the sea afford a fancy dress like that," she said, rocking the small child. "But if you're going, the next boats to Fairmount and Halivaar are tomorrow, and there's no more beds left, so you'll have to find a spot on the floor. The paymaster ain't here yet, either. There's no crossing until you pay the fee."

"Oh, I'm not traveling, actually, but thank you. I'm looking for someone and was told I could find her here. But...is everyone here going to a non-magic territory?"

"Of course. With no magic, it'll be harder for the Brotherhood to take us—or haven't you heard? They were snatching up seventhborns some months back, for draining and torturing. One of the girls got away, but the others weren't so lucky. She ran off to Preston in the Fairmount province, said it was safer for us there, and with no magic, we can find honest work."

"Right, yes, I'd heard," Sera said, knowing exactly who this girl was who got away. She and Barrington had traveled to Preston to interview her after she'd escaped from the Brotherhood's clutches, namely Noah's.

"Others are scared about the elections. Delacort promises to fight black magic, but who's to say he won't one day decide a seventhborn's abilities are black magic as well? So, some have decided to go as a precaution. Many have been so desperate, they've just disappeared, even after paying their smuggling fee. Left their belongings behind and everything. I suppose they learned of another way across." She shrugged a shoulder. "Whatever the case, I don't have a good feeling in my gut about this Delacort fellow."

"Neither do I," Sera muttered. The only good about him was Timothy.

"So, who's you looking for? I can't promise they're still here."

She glanced around. "For a woman named Meredith, though she may have given you a false name." She described her using the photograph Armitage showed her as a guide.

Claire's brows rose in awareness. "Yes, I know who you're talking about, though she didn't tell us her name at all. I told her this was the seventhborn floor and everyone else waits downstairs, but she insisted on being near seventhborns. She's not well, that one. Spends her time rambling to herself and pacing the room upstairs whispering that they must *finish the game*." She gazed up as if able to see Meredith through the water-stained and crumbling ceiling. "None of us stay up there. The flooring's not safe, but she insisted. The wee ones were scared of her, so we let her." As if to confirm Claire's words, the baby squirmed in her arms. "Good luck if you're trying to get her to come down. She doesn't eat, doesn't sleep…" she said, bouncing in turn with her words, but the baby roused and cried out.

"Shh, I know it hurts, love. We found her by the river last week," she told Sera over the baby's cries. "The tattoo, it takes some getting used to, and none of us here are much good at healing."

Sera's anger flared. There wasn't ever any getting used to the tattoo forced upon their flesh. Perhaps tolerance, but never acceptance. She neared the baby, took hold of her arm, and moved her magic to her hands in a gentle, warm wave. A cloud soon wrapped around the baby's wrist, and, within moments, the child quieted.

She lowered her hands. "It shouldn't hurt her anymore."

"Thank you." Claire tucked the baby's arm back into the threadbare blanket. "You're her, aren't you?"

"Her?"

"The seventh-born inspector. We've all heard of you." She smiled, her front tooth chipped.

The hopeful look in her eyes stabbed Sera's soul; she was the wrong person for anyone to put their hope in. Like with Timothy, she would eventually let them down. Memory of him dying in her arms twisted in her chest, and the tightness there grew heavier.

"I…I'm not a detective," she said, her voice suddenly hoarse. "Just an assistant to one."

"Well, to us you are, though some said you weren't real. Now I get to tell them you are." Her smile widened, and, stepping away, she motioned to the staircase. "You can reach her through there, second door on the left. But be careful."

Sera proceeded to the stairs down the hall. Seventhborns stared back at her with dirty faces and matted hair, dressed in tattered garbs. But between all the darkness and obvious need, laughter erupted from groups gathered around small-bins-turned-fireplaces. Children played together with makeshift toys and found new mothers who would help them navigate the treacherous road of being a seventhborn. Together, they'd created something of a home and of a family, just as Sera herself had done with Barrington.

She pushed the thought away, the heartache much too strong.

She entered the stairwell and drew her wand. There was no telling what state she would find Meredith in. If what Claire said was any indication, Meredith might be difficult to reason with.

Upstairs, she encountered another hall, only in this one there was no runner and the floor was in ruins. Sidestepping some holes and splintered planks, Sera moved to the door Claire mentioned. It was ajar and missing a doorknob.

The room was dark inside, and Claire was right. Floorboards were missing intermittently, like a perilous puzzle. Meredith stood by a window, her back to Sera and her hands pulled up to her chest. She wore a stained and torn blue gown, thoroughly dirty along the bottom. Her hair was pulled back, revealing narrow shoulders drawn inward.

"One, two, three, four, five. Ready or not, here I come!"

Sera opened the door slowly. "Meredith?"

The woman spun and gasped, her eyes wide and face pale. She scurried back against the wall and closer to the fireplace, where a small flame swayed on dying embers.

Sera sheathed her wand, then held her hands at surrender. "I'm not here to hurt you. Your brother, he's worried for you."

"No! We must finish the game."

Sera sidestepped the rotting planks of damp wood and neared her. "Are you all right?"

"Finish the game. We must finish the game," she whispered to herself. "Then they will come. They will."

"Who will come? The children?"

Meredith pressed a finger to her lips, her eyes large and fearful. "Can't you hear them?" She tilted her head as though listening to a distant call. "They're all here. But it's a trick." She covered her ears. "She lies!"

"Who lies?" Sera asked, hoping to appease and understand the girl, but her words seemed not to reach Meredith, who rocked back and forth, saying, *she lies, she lies, she lies.*

Sera stepped forward. A slat creaked. Meredith startled and held a staying hand between them. Sera winced; her palm was sliced and cut, cruor crusted along the lacerations. Scabbed-over scratches also ran the length of her arms.

Sera gulped. "Meredith, did you…hurt them somehow?"

The girl shook her head, still watching the spaces around them. "She did. She took them here and there. Here and—" She pointed a crusty finger to the window. "There."

What panes remained there were shattered and streaked with blood; she must have punched at the glass and cut her arms on the shards. Beyond the broken windows was the sea, the surface inky black beneath the new moon. At the docks, ships undulated in the water, their fastened sails wafting in sections akin to bound phantoms.

"On a ship? Were they taken away on one of the boats?"

"No, they're still here and there."

Sera took a step closer. "Meredith, your brother is worried about you and the children. Where are they?"

She turned a widened gaze to Sera. "No, he never cared for them, and he can't find me. He will take her, and then they're dead there. But now you're here. I'm so stupid, stupid, stupid." She jabbed her forehead with an open palm upon each repetition of the word. "But no magic, no passage. No magic, no passage. Just magic. Magic. Magic."

Heat flooded Sera's veins, awareness burning through her. Not only were the seventhborns here forced to flee their homes for a semblance of safety, but they had to give their magic to a cunning smuggler to secure their way across. And in using her magic, even a small amount, anyone scrying for her would have been able to find her. Though the Barghest was more accurate, eventually she would be tracked down.

Worse, Sera tried to follow the girl's frantic words, to glean some understanding of where the children were, but they only confirmed she had succumbed to the incoherent madness resulting from countless drained reserves. She'd experienced the same disjointedness and confusion after Noah drained her for weeks straight. He didn't let her reserves refill. Insatiate, he waited until the smallest bit of magic replenished, after which he readily drank.

Once his binge was done, it had taken Sera some days to speak. A few more to finally gather enough strength to move. It seemed Meredith, while somewhat lucid, was suffering the same effects. Soon her thoughts would grow increasingly scattered and distant to where she would be unable to grasp them, and her sense of self would linger so far, she'd become but a shadow of herself, unable to eat or speak. Just sleep.

Sera unclasped the tie to her cloak, intending to drape it around the trembling girl. Meredith grasped her hand and stopped her.

"Go," she hissed frantically, wide eyes scanning the empty room. "She could be watching. She's everywhere."

The floorboards creaked behind them. Meredith's gaze

swept past Sera, and she pressed back tighter against the wall. Sera snatched out her wand and spun to an unshaven man with a thick neck and rough face by the door, his hulking frame blocking the doorway.

"Come, girl, someone's paid the paymaster a pretty penny for you," he said, his voice as gruff as his appearance.

Sera swept before Meredith. "Tell your paymaster she isn't going anywhere."

"And who's going to stop me?" He chuckled. "You're a seventhborn."

"And you're a brute, but we all have our faults."

The man's mouth spread into a slow smile, a silver-capped tooth glinting in the weak firelight. His hand flinched to his wand, but Sera's magic spiked, and an orb of white fire whisked from the tip of her wand and slammed into the man's chest. He flew back, and the sound of snapping planks of wood resounded when he crashed against the wall.

Damn!

"Meredith, we have to go." She grasped for the girl, but Meredith swept out of reach.

"No! We can't leave the children!" She rushed through a large hole in the wall.

Sera's heart pounded. The children were here?

She followed Meredith through the opening. On the other side was a winding metal staircase. Sera peeked up; it led to the roof. The tap of Meredith's muddied boots on the metal stairs drilled dread into Sera's bones, but fear wasn't going to solve this case. Only getting Meredith and the children to safety. And soon, before more of those thugs came.

Meredith pushed open the door and peered outside and up into the night sky pregnant with soot and rainclouds. She rushed to the ledge. Sera's heart stuttered, but Meredith hurried into a pigeon house there. A blanket was spread on the ground where she clearly slept, cold and alone. The cages were empty, and only shed feathers and refuse remained. Though the walls were of wired grating, the thick, mustiness of wet feathers lingered in the dilapidated dovecote. Sera narrowed her eyes; it was dark, and they were barely visible, but protection and containment spells had been scratched into the planks of wood. One surrounded the birdhouse, written in blood.

But there were no children.

"No one can get hurt up here, you see," she said in a stage whisper. She smiled to herself and rocked back and forth with a small, tattered brown carpetbag hugged against her chest. "There's nowhere to go. She's smart, likes to hide, but I'm smarter." She tapped her temple with a grimy finger, her nails black.

Sera placed her hands above Meredith's cold ones. "Why don't we go somewhere warm? We can talk, and you can tell me about the children."

"Lucy, she likes to cheat. Amelia likes to hide in the same place all the time."

Sera forced a smile. "I'll keep that in mind. Come, we will find them together."

Meredith hugged the bag tighter and looked at Sera, her gaze childlike and unfocused. "In the here and there?"

Sera nodded. "In the here and there."

The roof door slammed open.

Another man stood there, a flat cap low over his eyes. He lifted his wand. Sera flicked her wrist and slammed the door shut. She yanked Meredith around the bend, just as the man's magic blew the door open and off its hinges. She pressed a finger to her lips and peeked around the corner. The thug hid within the staircase, and Sera couldn't get a clear shot. She cursed. She could whistle for her Barghest, but there was a chance he was too far, more interested in consuming whatever magic he could find elsewhere. She couldn't risk giving away their hiding spot if he delayed.

Sera aimed her wand to the opposite side of the roof and issued a weak flare of magic toward the dovecote, just enough to rattle its cages. The man fired an orb of magic; planks of wood spilled up into the air. He rushed toward it, probably thinking Sera and Meredith were hurt. In the momentary distraction, Sera thrust a wave of detainment binds from behind him and wrapped him in her magic.

Frightened, Meredith ran for the doorway and vanished inside. Sera cursed and gave chase. She reached her downstairs and dragged her back behind the safety of a wall just as another thug peeked into the adjacent room, but it was dark, and he didn't see Sera and Meredith in the next apartment.

Sera spun to a crack in the wall and watched yet another ruffian enter. *Double damn!* She had to get Meredith out of there, but she wasn't going to allow for them to transfer without a struggle, which was much too risky. If she let go of Sera at any point during the transfer, she could be lost in the void of time and space forever. She could blast these two men, but what then? How many more thugs were downstairs?

The men moved closer to their hiding spot, their figures peeking in and out of the slants of lamplight outside, filtering in through the cracks in the shuttered windows.

Meredith shook her head, the small case tight in her arms. "I have to save them." Frantic, she yanked her arm free and ran out of the hole. One of the thugs speared a cluster of magic at her, but Sera pulled her back to the safety behind the wall.

"Don't kill her, you idiot! We're supposed to take her alive," one of the ruffians yelled to the other.

"Which one?"

"We'll take them both."

Sera flexed her fingers. Like hell they would take them anywhere.

She waved a hand upward. A swell of orange fire blustered across the room. The men dove out of the way, but the old planks ignited.

The room grew hot, plumes of black smoke engulfing them. Sera clapped a hand over her mouth and coughed, the air hot and raw and acrid. A blast dashed above her, and the wall behind her exploded, making Sera scream as she dragged Meredith down. Shards of wood and rubble rained on them. She dove over the girl as the thugs fired orbs and orbs of magic, a cruel and quick attack, to where their blasts filled Sera's ears and thoughts, underscored by her scream and the roar of the flames.

Her magic rattled wildly, a ravenous beast desperate to destroy everything and everyone. But what if the seventhborns downstairs hadn't escaped yet? She would gladly bring the building down around these men, but not with Meredith and innocent people still inside.

Sera blindly thrust out a hand. Shafts of fire whipped across the room and wrapped around the thugs. One was consumed instantly, his screams audible. The other dove out of the way but broke through the rotted and burned floor.

"Come on." Sera reached for Meredith, but the girl slumped against the rubble, unconscious.

"No, no, no." She hadn't made it this far to lose Meredith now. She touched a hand to the girl's temples, and relief flooded her. She was alive and not severely injured. She had to get her to safety. Looping Meredith's bag through her arm, Sera took hold of her hand, intent on transferring.

The door to the roof slammed open, and the thug Sera had immobilized clambered down the stairs, rage and murder in his stare. He aimed his wand at them. A flare of magic whipped from its tip.

Sera lifted her hand to retaliate.

Blackness enveloped her.

She screamed, feeling her soul pushed and pulled, wrung and dragged through hot and cold as if she were being turned inside out in this strange and violent sulfur-scented darkness that engulfed them. A deafening, infinite roar that pierced her eardrums and allowed for no other thought but its terrible, disastrous sound.

Unable to gather her bearings in the clamor and endless dark, she held tighter to Meredith's hand and shrieked as she was thrown right.

Up.

Back.

Left.

Right.

Down.

Down.

Down.

monsters all the same

Sera crashed down onto something soft and feathery. She gasped, a frantic inhale that burned her lungs with the sulfuric tang still lingering on her person. Though Meredith's hand was still firmly within hers, she grasped feverishly at her side, desperate to clutch onto something solid. Damp earth, dew-cooled vegetation, and jagged rocks met her fingers. But where on earth was she? Had she somehow transferred by mistake? If so, then she could be anywhere.

She pried her eyes open and sat up. Meredith lay motionless beside her, but her chest still undulated. Sera lifted her gaze. Tall grass surrounded them, and in the distance was Barrington's home. The Barghest paced before her, licking the ground with its forked tongue. Realization swept through Sera. The blackness and bedlam…

"You transferred us here?" she croaked. She'd never heard of anyone traveling with a Barghest as a smuggler, but then again, there was not much information about the hellhounds, save for the terrifying tall tales their name elicited. "You saved my life…again. Thank you."

The Barghest raised his glistening snout and rumbled what Sera could imagine to be *you're welcome*, then continued devouring the magic he used to transfer her away.

"Can I beg you for a favor? Will you… Can you clean the traces of my magic from the scene? If it is discovered…"

The Barghest lowered his head and extended his front paw in a gesture of agreement. He spun into a vortex of black and disappeared into an opening no bigger than a pinhole in the ground.

Weaving her hands in her hair, Sera curled into herself. The adrenaline that had coursed through her while fighting plummeted, and she trembled violently, the way she did after she'd killed Noah. The desperate desire for survival had bit into her bones and refused to release her for days. She hoped this was not the case now.

She looked to the manor in the distance. She had to get Meredith somewhere safe and tend to any wounds she might have, but there was no way she could bring her into Barrington's home. Not when there was a chance the Aetherium could decide to investigate his residence. It was bad enough Sera lived there—even though she was never his student and had been expelled—but how would she explain Meredith? If any connection arose between the unconscious girl and the missing orphanage, it would be disastrous for Barrington. Whether or not it was true his father and brother were part of the Brotherhood and killed seventhborns as a result, Mr. Delacort would use it for his own evil ends. She wouldn't let him.

But where could she take the girl that no one would find her? Sera glanced to the spire of Barrington's home and chewed her lip as an idea came to mind. One moment they were in the moors, the next they landed neatly within her old Academy room.

Shifting the carpetbag aside, Sera slipped off her boots, moved across the room, and shut the curtains. She touched the tip of her wand to a taper candle, and a flame ignited on the wick. She rushed to the door then and locked it. Kneeling at Meredith's side, she quickly checked for any wounds. Satisfied the girl was merely unconscious, she considered lifting her onto the bed, but Sera's muscles ached, and her magic was now but a weak flame as fatigue rolled down her body from spent reserves. She couldn't carry her if she tried. Instead, she grabbed her old pillow and tucked it beneath Meredith's head, then draped her torn patchwork quilt over the girl's frail body.

Sera picked up the girl's traveling purse and set it on her old workbench. Meredith had been adamant not to leave this behind. *We can't leave the children*, she had claimed. Sera's pulse quickened and hands dampened. Surely it couldn't mean the children—or their ash remains, rather—were in the purse…?

Pulling open the straps, she flipped the latches and opened the bag. She shifted aside a blue muslin dress and other garments. Beneath them was a spell book of rather elementary magic, a book of children's fairy tales, and a shattered scrying mirror with a black glass and a floral pattern on the oxidized handle. Perhaps Meredith scryed for the children? But with the mirror now broken, there was no way Sera could lift a spell from its surface for any clues as to its scrying history.

Sighing, she snapped the bag shut. There was nothing there to even hint at where the children could be. All she had now were the frantic words of a drained witch claiming a woman had taken the children.

She took them here and there.

She could be watching.

She could be anywhere.

She lies.

Yet, glancing down at the sleeping girl, Sera frowned. Could Meredith be trusted in her addled mental state? And if so, who was *she*? Could she have been referring to herself?

Sera caught sight of her shattered image in the black scrying glass, wishing the answer weren't as muddled as her reflection. But, pressing her fingers to the table, she couldn't think of anything much longer. Fatigue rippled down her body in vicious waves, her reserves low. Tomorrow she would question Meredith. For now, she fell face-first onto the dusty mattress, and, gripping Barrington's pendant, she let exhaustion drag her to sleep.

Someone help me!

*   Is anyone here?*

Hissing cries filtered into Sera's mind as the fog of sleep struggled to lift from her consciousness, but spent reserves weighed down her muscles and pulled her back into slumber.

A billowing coolness rolled over her, and goose bumps sprouted along her arms. Awareness cut through her; the room was much too cold for an August night.

I'm so alone.

Who's there?

Help!

Panic jabbed her stomach, and she held her eyes shut as various voices whispered within the room. Exhausted, she could barely move. And with her magic as low as it was, she would never be able to fight off these ghosts should they seek to possess her. There was no telling how deep into a vision they would drag her. With Meredith unconscious, there was no one to pull her out. And with Barrington gone, no one would know where to find her, at least not until it was too late.

A sharp crackle cut through the silence, and the temperature plummeted. Snaps and crunching drew closer like an approaching web of ice. Sera closed her eyes tighter. Bravery lingered far, along with any sensation of her body. There were just spent reserves and the coldness of approaching ghosts.

"Go away," she murmured. "Go away."

Frigidness crawled up her limbs, and her dress grew stiff with frost. A moldy odor enveloped her, and her stomach clenched, but Sera clamped her mouth shut and stifled a heave. The need to scream built in her throat as coolness caressed her cheek and the sensation of someone drawing closer raised the hairs up along her skin.

"Sadness," it hissed, its feminine voice papery thin. "Sorrow."

Stark fear gripped her. Why on top of her cursed birth order did she have to be burdened with this ability?

The ghost moved closer. Its frozen and pungent breath skimmed Sera's hair, chased by what felt like bony fingers brushing a strand aside. Sera grew so rigid she trembled. Panic begged her to use what strength she had to flee, but paralyzed by the cold, spent reserves and all-consuming terror, she couldn't move.

It had been ages since she'd been this afraid, but she wasn't alone. Focusing on Barrington's necklace in her palm, she reached for her magic, now but a miniscule flame at the end of a candle. If the ghost dragged her into a vision, she would quickly transfer away. Whether near or far, he was her anchor. And though he was detained, Sera clutched the pendant tight. Better a cell than a prisoner of her mind.

The ghost seemed to lift and the horrible stench subsided. The billowing coolness also thinned, and the numerous cries for help faded until all was quiet and warmth swathed the room again. Still, Sera refused to open her eyes.

And so, she waded in darkness until sleep found her again.

Sera blinked her eyes open and shielded her face; shafts of light streamed through her carelessly closed curtains. The events of the previous night rolled through her, and she shivered. A ghost had once again touched her, but at least this time it hadn't dragged her into a vision.

She rubbed the sleep from her eyes and pushed up to check on Meredith.

Her heart pounded.

Meredith's makeshift bed was still there, and her luggage, but the girl was gone. Sera glanced frantically to the door. Locked, just as she'd left it. She considered the window, but it too was closed from the inside. Had Meredith been lucid enough to use magic to relock the door once she'd walked out? Or had she simply transferred? Forcing herself to relax, Sera let her magic fill her head until her second sight blurred the edges of everything around her.

All the spells used in the room suddenly illuminated, except for the candle she'd sparked the previous night and the transfer spell Sera used to get to Barrington's the previous day, none of the spells were recent.

She called back her magic. The haziness in the room faded and everything reverted to its crisp edges. She sighed.

Fantastic. She'd secured a lead but had lost her and had no evidence to suggest where she'd gone.

The bells tolled, and Sera gasped. Her exam!

She gathered Meredith's things and pulled open the wardrobe doors. She put the carpetbag inside and started to close the door but caught sight of her reflection on the wardrobe mirror and stopped short. Though the old mirror was spotted, desilvered, and stained with a black film, nothing could hide Sera's unkempt appearance, from her dusty black dress to the wood chips and debris in her hair. And goodness, dried blood clung to her temple, and a droplet had smeared and crusted on her cheek.

Sera lifted her skirt and tore off a piece of her chemise. Holding it tight between her palms, she conjured what small bits of water she could and dampened the fabric, then quickly ran it along her face and neck. Next, she chased her fingers through her hair, combing out the debris, then fastened the chestnut strands in a braid. Bending at the waist, she adjusted her skirt and patted the dirt off her dress.

Straightening, she met her reflection and frowned. She looked just as chaotic as her evening had been. But this didn't matter. Looks weren't going to determine whether or not she passed the exam, anyway, and while her appearance left a lot to be desired, at least she didn't look as though she'd just murdered someone.

She glanced down; one of her buttons had come undone. Sera fastened it quickly then lifted her gaze for one last look —

She gasped and flinched back. An image of Meredith floated in the mirror, wreathed in smoke. Her mouth moved as she called out, but Sera couldn't discern her words. Dread seized Sera.

She only ever saw spirits in a glass when she was scrying,

and all the characteristics of a scrying were there: the subject, the smoke, the lack of sound. Yet, Sera didn't feel herself using any magic. She moved closer to the mirror and tried to sharpen her mind's eye, to discern some identifying feature of where the girl could be, but the mist curled over the glass and Meredith was gone. The smog faded until only Sera's reflection remained.

Moments later, Sera had yet to move. How could she have scryed unintentionally? Conjuring ghosts was one thing, and the possessions were of course far worse. But now her scrying abilities were compromised, something so essential to her future schooling and work. Was this also an effect of her use of death magic? Sera shook her head. She had to talk to Doctor Morgan.

Sheathing her wand, Sera considered transferring, but she needed to save her magic, considering how excessively she had used it the previous night. No, she would walk down. And if anyone saw her, she would simply say she got lost looking for her exam room. They couldn't prove otherwise.

She rushed to the door, pulled it open, and hurried down the tower stairs. She peeked out of the entrance and breathed freer. The hall was empty. She rushed down the corridor and, minutes later, Sera made it downstairs undetected. Rounding the bend onto the grand staircase, she paused. Doctor Morgan waited at the garden doors opposite the landing, but at the foot of the steps was Hadden Whittaker. He spoke with another student, but his brow dipped upon seeing her. Surely her wrinkled dress and haphazardly styled hair were enough reasons to stare, but he glanced up to the doorway Sera had emerged from, and his brow gathered.

"Miss Dovetail." Doctor Morgan waved at her and approached. "Did you just come from upstairs? The Air-level modules are in the gardens."

"Ah, yes. I must have been confused." She forced a smile, but Whittaker glanced back to the stairs from whence she'd come and she knew he didn't believe her. But she had no time to consider a more elaborate lie, so let Doctor Morgan lead them into the garden.

The day was bright under a cloudless sky, and the stagnant heat made the air shimmer. Sera glanced to an unkindness of ravens flying above like black scratches in the expanse. How they could fly in this heat was beyond her. Just mere minutes outside and still in her black dress, she felt as though set to expire.

Students brave enough to weather the temperatures studied in the shady spots beneath trees and close to the forest. Sera noted Anne and Eliza sitting on the grass. Anne prattled on about something, her mouth moving incessantly. Eliza, however, stared absently at the forest, and Sera doubted she heard a word Anne said. Surely she lamented her accident in yesterday's Water-level exam. And if she intended on an occupation in the Water branch of the Aetherium, no doubt her failure ruined her dream and broke her heart.

"I spoke to Mama," Doctor Morgan said. "She said Nikolai is fine. Exhausted, but well. He hasn't been questioned yet, but apparently due to the numerous arrests, it's taking the constables a little longer."

Sera swallowed. The knot in her throat bobbed painfully. "Thank you."

Though happy to know he was all right, the thought of him in a cell around questionable people pressed down on her heart and scattered her magic. She took in a deep breath and pushed all thoughts of him to the back of her mind. She had to focus on her exam.

"But are you all right?" Doctor Morgan asked. "When

you came down, you looked as though you'd seen a ghost."

Sera glanced at the woman. "Something like that."

"Fascinating," she breathed, her brown eyes bright with interest. "You saw one during the Water-level exam, didn't you? I imagined that to be the case but wasn't sure. You know, I've always been in awe of a seventhborn's abilities. Sadly, because so many of you are denied a proper education, the majority never develop their magic adequately to awaken the second sight. A shame, as I'm certain there is a lot we can learn about death and the beyond. Perhaps I can pick your brain one day. There is so much I'm curious about."

"Of course, if you don't mind me asking you a few questions first," Sera ventured. "You mentioned you knew someone who had studied death magic. Could I meet them?"

Sadness filled her stare, and she motioned to a nearby bench. They sat down, and she said, "I'm afraid he passed away some years ago, but perhaps I can help?"

Sera wiped her damp palms on her dress and hesitated. Once these words left her mouth, there was no taking them back, but what was the alternative? The ghosts, possessions, and scrying unwittingly didn't give her a choice anymore. "Yes, I've seen many ghosts…and recently, one possessed me."

On the heels of those words, the rest of her horrible story tumbled from her mouth, from the night she used death magic to kill Noah to the spirit that had commandeered her at the orphanage. "Then this morning, I scryed for someone by mistake, but I'm not sure how. I didn't feel any magic leave me, but she was there in the glass. Clearly it isn't getting better, and hopefully you can help."

Doctor Morgan pressed a hand to her heart, her eyes glinting. "Oh, my dear, I am so, so sorry this happened. Of course I will help. Based on everything you've told me, I have a few theories, but I must first check your reserves before I can diagnose you correctly. I think the deterrents you spoke of might help alleviate your ghosts, but they will mean nothing if we do not address the underlying problem."

"Miss Seraphina Dovetail," the proctor called.

Sera gazed to the gazebo where the test was to take place. Eliza had just finished and walked to Anne, who'd gone before her. If her cries and wracking frame were any indication, she hadn't done well in this exam, either.

"How about we meet first thing after your Aether-levels?" Doctor Morgan said through Sera's thoughts. "Depending on how much magic we use and what we find, I do not want it to be a detriment to your remaining examination," she said, standing. Sera followed. "With that said, I will not be looking at the state of your magic, nor how much of it you can amass like the reserve check you experienced here. I am more interested in the state of your actual reserves, the place in your spirit where your magic is contained. As such, I may have to ask you to empty them so that I can get a better look. If you feel uncomfortable with that at all, we can have someone present."

"No. I don't want anyone to know."

Her brows rose. "You mean you haven't told Nikolai? I can assure you, Miss Dovetail. He will not leave a person in need, and it will help to have someone to talk to—"

"I said no." She sighed. The words were harsher than she'd intended. "Forgive me; I know more than most the extent of his kindness, but he's done enough for my problems as it is. I cannot burden him with another."

"I understand." She nodded then, though wells of sorrow and pity touched her eyes. "Thank you for trusting me."

Sera struggled to return the gesture, but, unable to, she looked away hoping her trust wouldn't be misplaced. It wouldn't be the first time.

They stopped before a small woman standing at the entrance to a large, iron gazebo. She had a heart-shaped face and squared spectacles low on her nose. Her small hands were clasped before her in a rather harmless stance. Sera scrutinized her face and demeanor; she had a kind appearance. With any luck she would be a reasonable proctor, but Mrs. York had warned her not to trust anyone and so she didn't dare hope.

They followed her into the pagoda. Overgrown vines twined about the metal pillars, blanketing the structure in vibrant green leaves. Behind her was a table with various navigation tools and slate boards for spell construction. Smears of chalk told of where other students had demonstrated their transferring capabilities. Where Sera would soon prove hers. Similar chalk marks tarnished the floor. Behind her was a tall bookcase lined with gorgeous glass ornaments. Thin rays of sunlight peeked through the vines and shone on the trinkets, and rainbows were illuminated on the floor.

"My name is Mrs. Hollis, and I will be your proctor for this exam."

She delved into the oral portion of the assessment. With each question asked, Sera's fear lessened; she had many of the answers in her mind before Mrs. Hollis was done speaking, except for the Warner Logarithmic Transfer Model, which, during her studies, she recognized as the equation Barrington used to measure elemental band intensities for travel and their locations on a map.

Sadly, she couldn't remember if the last part of the equation was output of magic per traveler divided by magical inclination, or planetary alignment divided by element then multiplied by traveler. And trying to remember how Barrington had written it made it all worse. Not only was his handwriting atrocious, but thinking of him stirred her worry and anger; her eyes had watered and smeared the formula before her eyes.

With the oral portion complete, Mrs. Hollis plucked a packet from inside of Sera's file. "This is a timed module. In this envelope is a set of coordinates you've been assigned for testing." She motioned to the collection of trinkets in the cabinet. "After choosing an ornament, you must transfer the piece to the designated location, then travel there yourself, collect the item, and bring it back for full marks. Inability to retrieve the given article in the allotted time will result in point deduction. Failure to return the piece at all is an automatic failure. You cannot take any materials with you to write the transfer spell and must make do with what you find at your location. Please choose your item."

Sera moved around the table and considered the palm-sized curios. There were insects and rodents of all sorts, but she stopped short at the statue of a birdcage with a small bird on top and remembered the heinous song Noah sang to her whenever he was done draining her reserves.

Sera, Sera, in a cage
Sera, Sera wants to fly
But her pretty wings are broken
See her fall from the sky...

Her jaw tightened, and her scars prickled to life as though freshly inflicted. But he was dead now, and if using death magic against him had caused her magic to go awry, she would overcome this as well.

She picked up the birdcage and walked back to the transfer table.

Mrs. Hollis handed Sera the sealed envelope and opened her pocket watch. "You have fifteen minutes. Please begin."

Sera opened it and slid out a slip of paper with coordinates. She inhaled deeply and focused on the ciphers to steady her nerves. Securing a stick of red chalk, she copied the coordinates onto the slate board on the table. Set the birdcage trinket inside. Steadied her magic until it rotated smoothly within. Flicked her wand toward the platform. "Ignite."

The ornament was gone in a blink, to whatever location the Aetherium had assigned her. All she had to do now was transfer to the location, gather her item, and return. She could do this.

Sera stepped away from the table and copied the coordinates on the floor. Standing in the middle of the transfer spell, she aimed her wand. The floor vanished beneath her. The next moment, she stood in total darkness.

Sera drew in a breath, but coughed. The air was heavy and dusty here, pungent with traces of dirt and moss and rain. The deafening silence and deep loneliness spurred Sera's pulse. She held up her wand, and a torch flame soon ignited. The reddish hue bounced off the segmented marble walls, each square bearing a name. Sera's pulse quickened. She was in a mausoleum.

Worse, below each corpse's name was the signet of a dove surrounded by the seven elemental signs. Sera's throat dried, her anger cresting. She knew that emblem and the treacherous women it belonged to.

The Sisters of Mercy.

Sera's grip tightened on her wand, and she spun in a circle, looking for the mysterious and elusive order of nuns and sworn enemy to the Brotherhood. For ages, the Brotherhood hunted the Sisters of Mercy, specifically the sisters who had been assigned *Keepers*, protectors to one of the seven spells needed to obtain power over time. With each Keeper guarding one spell, it was harder for the

Brotherhood to obtain them all, but they never stopped trying. And according to Timothy, under the lead of Mr. Delacort and Barrington's father, the Brotherhood killed countless Sisters of Mercy in their frantic campaign to obtain the spells.

Pain webbed over Sera's heart as she recalled Timothy's sorrow when revealing that as payback, when he was a child the Sisters of Mercy tricked him into becoming the keeper of the seventh spell, an incantation that called for a seventhborn to drink the blood of her six sisters, and, after a ritual, a gate would open in the underworld to reveal the power over time. Worse, they then made Timothy swear a blood oath that he would never tell it to anyone or else he would die. If Mr. Delacort wanted the spell, he'd have to watch his son bleed to death to get it.

From that day, Mr. Delacort distanced himself from the Brotherhood and ultimately blamed Barrington's father for the Brotherhood's crimes, though Barrington refused to accept it. And though Sera told him of her conversation with Timothy, he maintained Mr. Delacort couldn't be trusted.

Whatever the case, Sera paced her surroundings carefully so as not to step on the glass ornament. The Sisters of Mercy were just as guilty of Timothy's death as the Brotherhood, and though they shared a common enemy, to Sera they were monsters all the same.

"Are you looking for this?" a feminine voice asked.

Sera spun, her magic hot and quick at her fingertips.

A tall and slender figure robed in white moved from behind a pillar. Her pale hair and lashes paired with her light eyes and white robes made her look like a ghost, but Sera's anger surged. This Sister of Mercy was no phantom, and she held Sera's bird in her palm, the signet of a dove visible on her sleeve.

The sister snapped a finger. Flames sparked along the pole torches beside each tomb, illuminating the space in throbbing amber light. "Hello, Miss Dovetail. It's so lovely to see you again. I take it by the murder in your eyes that you remember me, though I should be the one holding a grudge. The last time we met, your employer tricked me, then left me bound to a chair. Rather harsh, don't you think?"

Sera's jaw clenched. As much as she wished to set the woman on fire, she recognized the sister's baited question. There was no way the sister knew who she was; the night they'd first met, Sera's face had been covered by her veil and Barrington hadn't called her by name. "You must be mistaken; I don't know who you are."

She clicked her teeth. "Then I suppose your friend lied."

"I have no friends," Sera countered.

"Yes, I suppose after what she did, it's hard to consider her a friend, but she meant well."

Sera's heart stuttered. She couldn't possibly mean... Surely she wasn't talking about...

The sister reached into her inner robe. Sera aimed her wand, her magic ready, but the nun drew out a small photograph and showed it to Sera. A torrent of pain rolled up her body, and the pole torches flared as she beheld a picture of Mary. Her brown hair was longer, and coupled with the white Sisters of Mercy robe she wore, she looked rather pale...though life in hiding was a far cry from her pampered upbringings of dresses and boys, perfumes and creams. An ache pressed down on Sera's chest, and despite her best efforts, tears filled her eyes. Mary's smile was the same, only now the light was gone from her eyes. Still, it was Mary. Her dear, dear Mary...

"Is she safe?" Sera asked, her voice a pained whisper. "Did you hurt her?"

"Never. She was placed in our care as a favor. So long as she's with us, she's protected."

Sera met the sister's pale eyes, then glanced to the picture. It was a ruse, surely it was, and yet it made the most sense. After months of scrying for Mary, she'd been wholly unsuccessful. But Mrs. York was smart. If the Brotherhood was after Mary, the wisest thing was to hide her away with their rival, one known for being an enigma and impossible to track down.

"Is that why you've lured me here? To talk about Mary?"

"No, but I do have her to thank. The day Timothy Delacort died, she saw you and the professor embrace and sensed there was more to it than a concerned scholar. She also said you'd previously spoken to her of a budding romance between you and someone of a forbidden station. It didn't take long to deduce his seventhborn companion was you."

Sera pursed her lips, thinking to lie, but what was the use? She scoffed. "Why am I not surprised Mary told? She's a traitor, after all."

"She only spoke because she thought you were in danger. When I disclosed the professor's father's and brother's affiliation with the Brotherhood, she asked me to look into your welfare."

Warmth thorned Sera's cheeks. "The professor is my mentor and employer, nothing more. So, what do you want? Speak quickly. I've an exam to return to."

A fierce defiance glimmered in her eyes, one Sera recognized in herself whenever she was cross. "What is your business with Mr. Armitage?"

Sera's eyes narrowed. "Have you been following me?"

"We've been following him after he met with Vincent Delacort last month. Given Mr. Delacort's ties with the Brotherhood, to see him ascend to power is a frightening thought."

Sera's pulse quickened. Armitage met with Mr. Delacort? "What was their business?"

She hummed. "You want to trade information? Last time, that didn't end so well for me."

"You held the professor hostage, then insulted his father and brother. What did you expect? But you're dealing with me, now, and I would really like to get back to my exam."

She smiled, a slow work of her lips. Her mouth seemed permanently pinched with the look of someone always displeased with something, which made the gesture all the more foreign. "Very well. He asked Armitage to secure something. We want to know what it was."

"Why didn't you question him?" Sera asked. "I'm sure for the right amount, he'd be willing to share information."

"We thought it best to wait until he obtained what Mr. Delacort requested before we took possession of him and the item. If we captured him beforehand, Mr. Delacort would know we're on his trail. So, your business?"

"Mr. Armitage approached the professor and me about looking into a missing seventhborn orphanage. His sister was the matron there, and she's gone, along with the children. I feared it was the Brotherhood, and so we took the case."

"Have you found anything to suggest the Brotherhood was involved and it wasn't just an orphanage closure?"

"The home was closed, yes, but it's as though they ran away from something or someone, then vanished into thin air."

"Armitage gave you a wand that night. Whose was it, and did you manage to locate a trace of magic?"

"It was his sister's, but like I said, she's missing and we've been unable to track her."

Her mouth pressed into a tight line. "We are on the

same side here, Miss Dovetail. If you know where his sister is, it is vital you share that information. We can help find her and the children."

Sera bit her nails into her palms, her magic flaring. "Don't you dare tell me you care about the children. You would use them as a means to an end, the same way the Sisters did Timothy Delacort. Did you know he was five years old when your precious Sisters made him a Keeper? The Brotherhood may have forced him to break his blood oath, but the Sisters of Mercy are just as guilty, and I promise you, one day I will personally see to it that you all burn."

"I look forward to it. But should you ever decide to stop being so stubborn and share information...or should you ever find yourself in need of help, seventhborns are always welcomed here, but leave your traitorous professor at home." She motioned to the back corner, where there was a single torch upon a pillar. "To call on us, transfer here and light this torch. The smoke will warn the sisters, and we will come."

"Aren't you afraid I'll lure you here and kill you?"

She smiled, many secrets in her pale eyes with an undercurrent of sadness. "You can't kill me, Miss Dovetail, and I can't kill you, even if I tried."

"What's that supposed to mean?"

"Good luck on your exam."

"Wait—"

The sister tossed the birdcage bauble in the air. Sera gasped and lunged for it, readily catching it in her palms. Her anger and magic crested, and she spun to the sister, but the woman was gone. Sera gritted her teeth but, aiming her wand to the ground, dropped into darkness.

A moment later, she landed in the gazebo and set the trinket on the table before Mrs. Hollis. She glanced at the mantle clock on the desk and sighed. Right on time.

Mrs. Hollis reached out and took the bird, turning it over in her hands as she searched for an imperfection. All the while, Sera's mind wrought like mad. Armitage was working for Mr. Delacort. What did he need him to steal? Did he have anything to do with the children's disappearance? Armitage said no one had contacted him, and Meredith claimed a woman had taken the children. But then again, Armitage was a liar and Meredith was not in the best mental state. And to make matters more perplexing, how did the Sisters of Mercy manage to intercept Sera's exam transferring location?

"That will conclude today's exam." Mrs. Hollis smiled and set down Sera's ornament.

Sera's eyes widened at the Sisters of Mercy emblem on Mrs. Hollis's sleeve.

9

both love and pain

Sera walked out of the pagoda with Doctor Morgan beside her. Her thoughts were a whirlwind of anger and pain, spurring her magic within. The image of Mary's picture floated through her mind, chased by the knowledge that Armitage was working for Mr. Delacort. And now the Sisters of Mercy were involved. She frowned. All she wanted was to find the children and obtain her deterrents, but it seemed every day they moved further out of reach.

Worse, with Armitage employed by Mr. Delacort, there was a chance the children had been taken as ransom or to settle a debt. Mr. Delacort was running for chancellor, yes, and capturing children was a risk to his campaign. But he was once a prominent Brotherhood member; no doubt the bloodlust and cruelty still flowed through his veins.

Her frown deepened. Damn Armitage and damn Mr. Delacort. And damn Barrington; he'd know what to do. But she was alone now, and so, delaying her discussion with Doctor Morgan and bidding her farewell, she hurried to the transfer hall and soon after stumbled down into Barrington's office.

The void of his presence in the space slammed into her, but, stifling her pain, she focused back on her task. She had to scry for Meredith, and if the girl was more lucid now, perhaps she could disclose who truly took the children and whether Mr. Delacort was involved. Then she would contact Armitage and set up a meeting. It was time for the truth. Now more than ever, the children's lives depended on it.

She walked into the hall. Maybe she would scry for Meredith using an Academy map. She passed the workroom and stopped short, all air caught in her lungs. Barrington stood in front of the bay windows there, staring out at the moors swathed in the late afternoon sun.

She pressed a hand to the doorframe and bit her nails into the wood, the sight of him an invisible hand that clawed through her ribs, gripped her heart, and squeezed out all the worry and dread she'd collected during his absence. The deep-seated fear that he'd be charged with black magic crimes and Delacort would see to it that he burned. That she'd never see him again, hear his voice, or feel his touch… now that she loved him.

Panic flared at the realization, and she flinched back. She couldn't love him; nothing good could come of loving a man as broken as he, governed by black magic and his need for revenge. And yet he'd never once abandoned her, had never once been cruel. Had never asked anything of her… except for her trust.

The last time she'd trusted and loved, it had ended so horribly, and she carried the proof in her scars. But Barrington was not Noah, and with each passing day, he proved this more.

Of course, this only made things worse. Now she was

furious at him and herself. Why had she let him coax her heart open? And he was the scholar and more well-versed at love than she; didn't he know his kindness and caresses would birth this attachment over time?

Perhaps feeling the weight of her inner affliction, Barrington turned. His eyes fixed on hers in an instant, echoes of shame in his stare.

"Sera," he said. Just her name and nothing more. Yet, taking in her rage, he shook his head and said, "Sera," this time in apology.

But to Sera, her name from his lips was a spark to her rage. No magic came to her aid. Only ache. Hurting, she rushed across the room and pushed him. He was taller and stronger than she, and he didn't move. But she pushed him again and punched his chest, over and over, hating him and loving him, needing him closer and farther away. Wanting him to feel both love and pain.

He stood there and endured this tempest of her, allowed her to pour out her pain and frustrations, cognizant of her needs, even in these vicious troughs of indecision.

She pushed him away one last time and then she walked into his arms. She would apologize later, come what may. For now, she hauled in his musk of pine and soap and felt him there, warm and real and safe.

Even if he reprimanded her. Even if he rejected her.

Barrington lifted his arms. Sera braced, ready for him to grip her shoulders, ease her back, and walk away as he often did in the midst of their fights. He wrapped them around her in an embrace, and the rejection never came.

"Some would say you missed me," he murmured against the top of her head. "Or are you disappointed I've come home?"

A hoarse laugh left her, and she dared hold him slightly

tighter. "Of course I missed you, you foolish, stubborn mule. I was so worried. We all were."

He chuckled at this, a warm sound that rumbled in his chest and Sera's ear. He smoothed a hand down her back and up again, a gentle affection that came so naturally. She closed her eyes and relished the tender strokes, conceding that yes, caring for him was dangerous and she would do well to keep far, but in that moment, the only thought in her mind was, *What's one more scar?*

"I'm sorry I worried you," he said, his voice commingled with his heartbeat. "After the night at the orphanage, I went to Gummy and asked her to set up a meeting with Armitage. I thought he might be willing to give me the wards in exchange for an oath that we would finish the assignment. At least it would have given you a reprieve during your exams. Unfortunately, Aetherium guards arrived as I was leaving. I was not in possession of blood magic, however, and they had no choice but to question me and then let me go."

She peeled away slightly and gazed up at him; he made no effort to release her. "You didn't have to do that."

He shook his head and, smoothing his hands down her back one last time, released her and leaned on the edge of the workbench, his fingers clasped together as if to keep from touching her. "You were right. I said I would help you find your family and rid you of the ghosts, and I've failed you on both accounts. This was the least I could do."

"The least?" she echoed. "Your kindness is the greatest I've ever known. You haven't failed me. I don't think you ever could."

He met her stare at this. "Then you think better of me than I do of myself."

The pain in his eyes at that moment cut her to the quick; it went on forever. And whereas once she believed he dabbled in the dark arts to support his quest to avenge his father and brother, in that moment, she wasn't so sure. Rosie once said he manufactured and used blood magic in order to be stronger than his pain. Sera sensed his reason was he didn't think himself strong at all.

He cleared his throat. "When I was released, Gummy's men returned with news that Armitage seems to have gone underground, but Gummy has all of her resources working to find him. He will not be lost for very long. They were even able to track Meredith to a smuggler's den nearest the capital, but there was a fire and she got away. I think she means to find her way across."

Sera bristled. "Those were *Gummy's* men?"

"…Miss Dovetail?" Barrington asked, his eyes narrowed.

She grimaced. "The night you were apprehended, I *may* have used Meredith's wand to track her and found her at a den by the docks." She explained the rest of the events, including the men who came for Meredith.

He regarded her from under a furrowed brow. "That was dangerous. You should have taken Lucas."

"Rosie was in a bad way; I didn't want her to be alone. Besides, had I waited, Meredith might have moved to a non-magic district and we'd have a harder time finding her. I did what had to be done. Thankfully, the Barghest arrived on time."

"Indeed. And where is Miss Armitage now?" Barrington asked.

Sera explained Meredith's disappearance, her encounter with the Sisters of Mercy, and what she'd learned about Armitage's work for Mr. Delacort. "I fear Delacort might have had the children taken. Maybe Mr. Armitage didn't deliver as promised?"

Barrington nodded, his jaw taut and eyes steeled. "I

wouldn't be surprised; Mr. Armitage is a snake. As for Miss Armitage, I will inquire with the staff. Perhaps someone has seen or heard something." Straightening, he led the way to the library. "Did she possess anything of interest on her person to indicate where she planned to go or where she could have come from?"

"Just a few dresses, a book of children's tales, and a scrying glass, but it was broken so I couldn't lift a spell from its surface for its scrying history."

"Indeed. With no more samples of her magic left, we will have to scry for her, though I doubt it will be of any use. Not only is scrying during a new moon much harder, but she was smart not to use her magic before in order to avoid detection. I doubt she will be as careless this time."

At the library, Sera moved to the drafting table. As Barrington searched for a suitable map, Sera reached beneath the desk and drew out a box of crystals. As she stroked the leather cover, her heart thrummed. The crystals had been a present from Barrington after she'd admired them in a catalog during their inventory check. Ever since then, she made sure never to linger on any item for too long, but these scrying gems she would treasure forever.

With her aether-abilities largely governed by moon phases, Sera ran her fingers lightly along the crystals, seeking the one whose pull was strongest during the week's new moon. She settled on an amethyst pendulum and held it over the map of the entire Aetherium Barrington had unrolled. Once she'd managed to trace Meredith to a province, she would know which map to use next to narrow her search.

Yet, various atlases and scrying crystals later, Sera thrust down her obsidian pendulum onto an Academy blueprint. "Another crystal and map and nothing." She sighed and dug her fingers into her hair, dissolving the bun into a mess of chestnut strands.

"Not exactly. In the letter Miss Armitage sent to her brother, she mentioned she had inquired of the local priest. He was also witness to the constable's closure of the home."

"Yes, but whatever she revealed to him is protected by clergy privilege."

"Perhaps, but it's worth a try. I believe he will worry very little about revealing information regarding seventhborns. More, orphaned seventhborns he didn't even care to help."

Sera frowned. He was right. Whether Pragmatics or Purists, the place of a seventhborn would never change.

"I will write him for a visit."

"No need. I've found people are often more forthcoming when they're caught unaware. We will visit him now. I understand if you don't want to go; it's rather short notice, and your exams—"

"I've no problem going, but do you think we should wait until tomorrow? You've just gotten in…"

He rolled up the map and slid it back into the standing holder. "All I did was sit in a small room while being questioned. A normal night of investigations will do me good, even if it involves you calling me a *foolish, stubborn mule*." He smiled, a touch of mischief in his weary stare.

"I called you much worse when you weren't here."

He clicked his tongue. "I'm sorry I missed it. Perhaps an encore?"

She rolled her eyes and walked upstairs to change before he could see the blush warming her cheeks, unsure how on earth she was ever going to survive him.

• • •

Half an hour later, they landed in the square courtyard of a quaint church, its entryway decorated with potted flowers that had wilted in the stagnant heat. The torch flames flanking the door flickered about, the only sound aside from the low whines of a warm summer breeze. Sera eased back from Barrington, and together they walked to the portico.

Barrington rapped upon the two-paneled front door, the Aetherium crest carved into the slats of wood, just beneath the iron speakeasy grille.

Sera's stomach clenched, and she swallowed tightly against a budding nausea. The same hints of terror she'd sensed at the orphanage shrouded the priest's home—only here it was much stronger.

A lock was unbolted within, and the speakeasy door opened. "Hello, how may I help you?" asked a man, his voice frail. From Sera's vantage point, only the man's fluffy white curls were visible through the iron grille.

"We're here to see Father Warner. My name is Professor Nikolai Barrington. I have a few questions about Meredith Armitage and the seventh-born orphanage."

"Ah, yes, yes." The speakeasy closed, and the door swung fully open to reveal a short man in a brown robe, its neckline adorned with the elemental beads, a necklace worn by the clergy, grouped in chains of seven, one for each guardian of magic. He motioned for them to enter. "Please, come in."

Barrington stepped aside and allowed for Sera to enter, then walked in behind her. The entryway was small and cramped, with tapestries along the walls depicting the prominent events from the Aetherium history, namely the Pragmatic Reformation and the fall of Purism.

Father Warner led them from a small foyer, through a narrow entrance hall with a staircase on one side, and into the sitting room. Sera was glad to sit; a sense of dread filled her mind and spurred the magic that now hummed within her, alert and anxious.

After offering them tea, which they declined, he sat at a beaten leather arm chair. A brown spotted cat jumped onto his lap. He attempted to put it down, but the feline issued a screeching protest and stuck its claws into the priest's robes. "Oh, all right." He let the cat settle down. "This is Mr. Oakley. He's been rather clingy lately, never wants to leave my side. How may I help you?"

"We learned recently of a letter Miss Meredith Armitage wrote to her brother asking for help with a number of disappearances. She mentioned she'd inquired with you, too, and we were hoping you could share some of her concerns."

Father Warner stroked the now-sleeping cat. "Ah, Miss Armitage, yes. A good and true heart, but I wouldn't concern myself too much with her claims. She loved those children but refused to acknowledge them for what they were."

"And what were they?" Barrington slipped out his notepad and opened it on his lap.

"Seventhborns, of course. Uneducated, uncivilized, not used to a proper home and care. You can't merely bring in an animal from the wild and expect it to behave. No, eventually, they will rebel and run back from whence they came."

Sera's gloved hands curled to fists, and her magic quickened at her core. This despicable excuse for a magician was the moral authority in this town? It was no wonder Meredith begged Armitage to come. She would never find help here, and neither would her missing wards.

Distant screams and cries for help resounded, and Sera froze. The voices were of children. She looked to Barrington and Father Warner, but, absorbed in their conversation, neither of them seemed to hear the shouts. Sera gulped and glanced around the room discreetly. No ghosts. The voices seemed to come from down the hall, but they faded.

"Are you saying these girls ran away?" Barrington asked.

"A river follows a path, as do seventhborns. You may try to divert its course, but eventually it will falter, fail, and turn to its true route." The cat on his lap purred as though in agreement, and Sera frowned. She never really liked cats.

"Yes, but she distinctly wrote they vanished, and indeed, they have all gone missing. No trace of their whereabouts, and they took none of their belongings. Rather, it looks as though they made a speedy escape."

"Believe me, if I knew anything else that would help, I would have told the constable, but Meredith was given to hysterics. Quite common of her female condition."

Sera stifled a groan. If she had to listen to this man's useless drivel for a second longer, she might empty her stomach all over his floor. She could have stayed at home studying for her upcoming Earth-level exam instead of suffering through this.

"When she came to me, she was frantic. Incoherent. I could hardly make sense of what she said. Gave Mr. Oakley here quite a scare. He dashed straight out of the room with her frantic ravings."

"And what did she say?" Barrington prodded.

"She claimed something was haunting the house and taking the children in the middle of the night. That she heard their screams and, when she ran to their rooms, they were gone." He shook his head and chuckled. "She said it was the Enchantress. Can you believe such a thing?"

Sera's brow dipped. "The Enchantress?"

"It is an old folktale meant to help children overcome their fears, though it really just replaced one horror with another. They were told the Enchantress was always watching and their terror drew her close. If they weren't brave, she would come for their souls," Barrington said. "But that was one of many variances. I'm not entirely sure which is the original, but the tale was adopted throughout the provinces in different ways. In essence, the Enchantress haunts the mirror world for anguished souls to steal away. And though we are a Pragmatic government, fear led many to establish the practice that mirrors should be covered when a person in the household has passed. Non-magic districts believe if you say her name three times while standing in front of a mirror, she will appear and the result is the same. But it's all nonsense."

"Yes, change and true enlightenment are rather slow," Father Warner said. "Here in the mountains and so far from the Aetherium, folklore and superstition are entrenched in the culture. I've requested various times for the Aetherium to allocate more funds to Pragmatic education in these parts so we can eradicate these foolish traditions once and for all. Perhaps once Mr. Delacort is in office we will see an improvement."

Sera frowned. As if she didn't have enough reasons to dislike Father Warner.

"But truly, pay no mind to her ramblings. Like I said, I've known Meredith since she was a little girl, and like her father had his vices, she fell into the same. One of her wards said she'd taken to drinking recently."

Barrington hummed. "Did you meet the children? Do you have any reason to think she might have harmed them, even unintentionally?"

He looked up as if physically searching his thoughts but shook his head. "No, she truly wanted the best for those girls. Perhaps she gave them away in a drunken stupor and ran away herself, trying to escape her doings. But I think it more likely the seventhborns merely ran away. Their sort cannot be trusted. Just as well they're not allowed to attend vespers. Their evil hearts cannot be saved."

Sera ground her teeth together.

Her dissatisfaction waned, once again to the sound of children screaming. Father Warner and Barrington continued their talk, but this time the sleeping cat roused, its ears perked. It jumped from Father Warner's lap and dashed down the hall.

Sera bolted to her feet. "If you will both excuse me. All this talk of the Enchantress and missing children has flustered me." She touched a hand to her forehead for dramatic effect. "Please continue. I saw a garden out back? I think I will be quite safe there. A bit of fresh air and beautiful flowers will do me good."

"Yes, yes. The female condition is much too sensitive for these talks."

Barrington fixed her with a narrowed, steely gaze drenched with suspicion. "Indeed."

"The garden is down the hall and to the left," Father Warner added. "Just beyond the mudroom. I do hope you enjoy my daisies; they were the highlight of last week's botany club."

Sera stifled the urge to roll her eyes and pressed a hand to her heart. "I'm certain they will lift my spirits immensely." She offered him a demure smile and walked from the room. "Bastard," she muttered once out of hearing range.

She traveled down the short corridor and around the corner where, through a mudroom, the back door slammed open and closed, open and closed, colliding against the frame with a *thunk-thunk-thunk*. Sera moved into the cramped room, reached for the handle, and pulled the door closed. She froze; faint screams met her ears again, and the licks of fear and desperation she'd sensed outside wrapped tightly around her bones now.

She exited the mudroom and paused. Father Warner's cat was crouched low before a room, its head tucked into its shoulders and ears turned back. It focused on the closed door, unblinking. Its tail thrashed against the hardwood floor, thumping like an agitated heartbeat.

Sera snatched out her wand, her magic at the ready. There was a reason the same fear she felt at the orphanage was present here, and her mind screamed that whatever it was, it lingered behind that door.

Sera considered the drawing room down the hall. Perhaps she should alert Barrington somehow? But if Father Warner had anything to do with the disappearances, she couldn't raise any suspicion lest they lose their element of surprise.

With her wand held tight in her hand, Sera moved measuredly toward the scared feline, wrapped her hand around the knob, and opened the door.

Books and crates were stacked along the room with other odds and ends, but the chamber was vacant. Behind her, the cat hissed and spat, its tail now curved and stiff.

Sera blew out a breath and glanced at the agitated feline. "Stupid cat."

She turned to close the door.

A scream rose into her chest at the ghost before her, the girl with no eyes. She pressed cold, blue fingers to Sera's cheeks.

Show you…

The world vanished behind a veil of smoke.

10

a crisis of conscience

The fog slowly gained shape and form, and a new reality
spread before Sera's eyes. She was inside a dark room with
a vaulted roof—*an attic*, she realized, though the knowledge
was not her own. Awareness burned her like a brand; the
ghost—*Cassandra*, she knew suddenly—had dragged her
into a vision. Sera reached for her magic, but frigidness bit
into her bones and consumed her veins, the fire in her belly
scattered and waned.

Cassandra looked around this room within the safe
house she'd reached earlier in the night. She'd been traveling
for days, mostly at night, when it was easier to avoid the
Purist officers cleansing the provinces of seventhborns. Her
papa had sold all they possessed to secure safe passage into
the mountains, where an order of nuns offered sanctuary to
however many seventhborns could reach them. *The Sisters
of Mercy*, Sera realized.

Stretching her legs, Cassandra pressed her feet to the
floor. She'd been confined to a crate behind a wagon, and

her only sight for days had been that of her toes pressed against the edge of the box and what streams of sunlight peeked through the cracks in the wooden chest. But finally, they'd arrived at the safe house, and, unlike their previous refuge, there was a window in this room, though shielded by a thick brown canvas tarp.

Desperate for a glimpse of the outside, she eased from the makeshift bed and crawled to the window, sure to remain quiet. The floorboards groaned as if telling of her illicit venture. She winced and looked to her papa. He slept on a chair in the corner of the room, his wand resting on his belly and his sleep fitful, but thankfully deep. This was a risk to be sure, but after weeks of not seeing the night sky, gloriously speckled with stars and governed by the moon, her aether-inclined magic roiled desperately in her veins for a glimpse, a yearning so keen she could already feel the soft moonlight on her skin.

She pushed the tarp aside and angled herself toward the rays of silvery light. A hand clamped over her mouth; she looked to the reflection on the window to see it was her father dragging her away from the glass and into the darkness. She never saw the moon.

The vision exploded to wisps of smoke and rearranged to reveal a new scene: A man with worried brown eyes and a tear-streaked face clutched her shoulders with thick hands. Papa.

"We told you what would happen if you were seen! Why didn't you listen, girl? Why didn't you listen?" Her father brought her close and wept, his warm tears wetting her forehead.

The dream transformed again into a chaotic carousel of misty images as she dragged Sera deeper into the vision: Cassandra being torn away from her papa and forced into the back of a wagon; the wooden doors shut between their stares. The feel of the roughed wood against her bound hands as she dug her nails into the door and begged them to open. Being thrown down onto a slab of cold stone, the surface hard against her back as a group of men in raven masks stood in the gallery above.

Please, don't do this, she screamed, but they watched her shiver, drinking in her torment.

A man in a black robe—the surgeon—drew alongside her. The bald man dabbed at his forehead with a handkerchief, his fingers bloody. He turned away from her, and when he faced her once more, Sera's breath died in her lungs. He held a hooked knife in his hands. "Hold her still."

Heavy, callused hands came upon Sera. She struggled and writhed, but their hold was strong and fixed her to the table. Sera's pulse quickened. Her magic grew wilder, and she reached for it but was unable to grasp it and pull herself out from this dream.

Wake up, wake up now! her mind begged, but she could only watch the horrid curved knife come closer. Feel the weight of the surgeon's hand on her cheekbone as he held her lid open and the cold metal touched the corner of her right eye.

Cassandra's scream filled her head and her mouth. A raw, all-consuming hurt scattered across her body. Her magic crested, raging wildfires bursting from her core and through her veins. She screamed again until emptied of air. She hauled in another breath, but in the space between her cries, she heard him.

"Sera!" Barrington's call sounded far away. "Sera!"

Coolness webbed over her pain, and Cassandra's grip on her mind loosened. Her consciousness grew heavy with the sensation of her own limbs and the cool air now filling her lungs with each breath.

"Miss Dovetail?"

Sera's eyes snapped open to Barrington's worried gaze. She was on the floor, pressed back flush against the wall. He held her face in his cool hands, his magic seeping into her slowly.

"Is she all right?" Father Warner asked, peering at them from out in the hall.

Realizing where she was and how terribly odd this all must look, Sera nodded and forced herself to her feet with Barrington's help. "Yes, forgive me. Your cat sounded distressed. When I opened the door, he jumped and I…I thought it was the Enchantress…"

Father Warner laughed fraily. "Yes, he likes to scare me sometimes, too. I'll put him in the other room so you two can look at the mirrors I told you about," he said to Barrington and pointed to the back of the room. "She brought them with her that day and insisted they were hexed. You can pass through and look at them; I'm going to try to settle him down," he said, petting the vigilant cat. He walked away.

Barrington glanced down the hall to ascertain Father Warner was gone. "What happened?" he asked, his voice low.

She divulged the sensation of dread she couldn't shake and the screams she'd heard but didn't tell him about the possession. "I felt the same agony at the orphanage. But it's much stronger here, and so I thought I'd try to channel that pain and perhaps find the source."

Disapproval weighed his brow. "Miss Dovetail."

She loved when he said her name, but not when it was spoken like a curse. "I know. I…I just wanted to help."

His gaze was icy, but he blew out a sigh and it softened. "We will discuss this later."

He walked into the room, but Sera remained by the door.

Nausea seized her stomach, and when she attempted to follow Barrington, her mouth grew salty and bile squeezed into her throat. She hugged herself and closed her eyes, Cassandra's pain still so very alive in her veins. She'd easily bypassed Sera's command to go away and taken possession of her reason. Was this now the norm and other ghosts were capable of the same?

Barrington stopped by the far wall, where white sheets covered the mirrors. He fisted the cloth coverings and pulled them aside onto the floor. Four mirrors of varying frames and sizes stood side by side, one overlapping the other. They were all freckled with black spots and a sheer film stained the glass.

He knelt before the mirrors; his reflection echoed throughout them in different angles. Sera remembered the outline from the orphanage entrance hall, the missing frame at the top of the stairs. Holding his hand over the first glass in a quatrefoil frame, he conjured a smooth flare of magic. Soon, a thin blue cloud billowed over the mirrors. When Barrington lowered his hand, the glittering mist was sucked into the glass.

"Mirror magic," Sera breathed. She remembered reading about the volatile art during her studies. Where some aspects of mirror magic were beneficial, like scrying, spell casting on the reflective surface was considered far too dangerous, as spells often rebounded off the mirror and caused significant damage to property and persons.

A thought struck her. "Do you think it's possible Mr. Delacort and the Brotherhood have nothing to do with the disappearances, rather Meredith is responsible and whatever spell she attempted on these mirrors led to the children vanishing?"

"Possibly. It keeps with the characteristics of mirror

magic. This Enchantress fixation might be an elaborate ploy, when in reality she is suffering from a crisis of conscience for what she's done to the children. We will only know by lifting the spell from the mirrors."

Barrington whisked the sheets back onto the mirrors. "For now, we must get the mirrors back to the manor and behind protections until we know what spell has been used and if Meredith is indeed our conjurer. It is still absorbing magic, which means it's an active enchantment and very dangerous, considering we don't know what the spell or curse is."

"Have they been of any help?" Father Warner asked, appearing at the door.

"Father, do you mind if we borrow these mirrors?" Barrington asked, straightening. "They are vital to our investigation and, frankly, quite dangerous for you to have in the home."

The man scoffed. "Keep them—I've no use for them."

Barrington readily carried the mirrors outside and, setting them within a protection circle, transferred them to the manor. They bid their goodbyes to Father Warner, and moments later they landed in the workroom.

Thrusting off his coat, Barrington whirled a wrist, his movements sharp and determined. The door to his secret laboratory swung open. He spent the next few moments securing the mirrors within the containment room. Sera watched on from the doorway, the ominous sensation emanating from the mirrors, the lingering feeling of Cassandra's possession, and Barrington's torment staining the room too much to bear.

Barrington raked his hands through his hair. "The mirrors will remain in here until I can determine their enchantment and nullify it. It's extremely dangerous and fickle magic, so I will insist I do it alone. I will call you once I find anything."

"Yes, of course. I have my Earth-levels in the morning; I should review my notes again. Be careful."

He gave her a tilted grin. "Aren't I always?"

She scowled. "Goodnight, Professor." She walked to the door—

"Miss Dovetail?"

Sera stopped and turned to him.

He took in every inch of her face. "Are you sure you're all right?"

Remembering the eyeless ghost, she felt a shiver skitter down her spine, but she nodded and closed the black door between them, unable to lie to him and hating that the truth was something she couldn't give.

The following morning, Sera landed in the Academy transfer booth. She had two hours before her exam and plenty of time to make a stop at the library. After scouring Barrington's books, she hadn't found much about the Enchantress, much less about folktales and mythology, but that was unsurprising. Barrington was a man of facts deduced by math, magic, and science. He breathed and bled Pragmatism. But Sera moved out of the transfer stall and up the stairs toward the main hall. Meredith mentioned the Enchantress. Maybe somewhere within the Enchantress stories, there was a hint as to what Meredith did with her charges. Sera would follow whatever the clue, even if it meant poring over children's stories.

She rounded the bend into the main corridor and paused. The hallway was dim, and though sunlight streamed through the glass, its light was muted as though filtering in through a dark lens. Sera looked to the windows in passing; the panes were clean and yet slightly tinted, like someone had wiped them down with a dirty rag.

"The housekeeping staff will see to this," a matron said to another, both facing a window.

"I heard a few of the maids have already left," the other matron said. "Surely they knew they were going to be fired after this disaster."

Sera entered the library and stopped. Split into two towers, the boys' and girls' wards were joined only by the library. And based on past experience, Sera knew the books she needed were in the boys' half. Maybe now with classes officially over, she could get permission from a matron and not have to wait until late that night to sneak in...

Scanning the library, she noted her old matron, Mrs. James, beside a table of studying pupils. At one time, the red-haired woman had been a tyrant determined on Sera's misery, but she had come around to kindness once she'd learned of Sera's painful past with Noah. Though it didn't excuse her previous behavior, they'd grown to at least tolerate each other, about which Sera was glad. She had enough enemies. Still, Sera hesitated.

A ghost lingered beside Mrs. James, a younger woman with a lace shawl over her brown hair. Sera's eyes narrowed. Mrs. James was dressed in mourning attire.

"Damn," Sera hissed. The last thing she needed was to deal with a ghost, but she needed to find out more about the Enchantress. Every moment they didn't learn where Meredith had gone was another moment without the children and her deterrents.

She could do this. All she had to do was focus on Mrs. James.

Swallowing thickly, Sera fixed her eyes on Mrs. James and neared her.

At seeing Sera's approach, the woman smiled, and Sera's apprehension eased slightly; it was an open and honest expression that temporarily eclipsed a sadness in her eyes. "Miss Dovetail, I'd heard you returned for testing and hoped I'd get a chance to see you."

You must go, Tilda, the ghost hissed. *It isn't safe here.*

Sera forced a smile. "It's lovely to see you, Mrs. James."

Listen to me, Tilda.

"I'm so terribly sorry about Miss Tenant and Mr. Delacort. I know you were all friends."

Sera shivered, the room growing colder as the ghost became more agitated. *If you don't leave now, it will be too late.*

"I wasn't here when it happened," she went on. "I had just gone away to tend to my sister, who was ill. But what horrible news. I hope you've found some comfort in knowing Mr. Delacort's spirit is at rest."

"Thank you," Sera said. "And I couldn't help but notice you're in mourning. I'm sorry for your loss as well."

The ghost huffed a breath and moved closer to Mrs. James's ear. *Will you not listen to me?*

Mrs. James smoothed down her dress, her eyes glinting. "Oh, yes. Thank you. It was my sister, Scarlet. Consumption claimed her, sadly, though she wouldn't want my pity. Headstrong, she was—reminded me a bit of you."

The ghost slung a hand onto her hip, her lips pursed. *So, I die and you compare me to a seventhborn? And a lousy one at that. She can't even see me!*

Sera's cheeks burned, but she held Mrs. James's stare.

"She had a bad experience with doctors when younger and so refused to see a healer. At least she is at peace now."

Blinking the tears away, she smiled. "But you were coming to ask me something?"

"I was wondering if I could fetch a book from the boys' section. My Aether-levels are tomorrow, and I still have some questions to research. Sadly, the book I need is in the mythology section, in the boys' half of the library."

"Oh, yes, of course. I will escort you."

Sera walked with the woman across the dividing tables and to the boys' side. Mrs. James stood by as Sera located a reference book and set it on a stand. Flipping open the heavy tome, she ran her finger down the length of the index page. She stopped on *Enchantress* and followed the dotted lines to its listed location.

Turning to the marked page, she read about the Enchantress terrorizing children, stealing them away into the mirror world. Other books claimed mirrors were her eyes and she could see everything at all times. Though this kept with Meredith's claims, it still didn't explain what she could have done with the children.

Sera closed the last book she found that mentioned the Enchantress and sighed. It was clear she wasn't going to find her answer in this library.

But a thought struck her. There was another library…

Her pulse quickened. Timothy had taken her to the hidden library in the basement, the room and the adjacent dungeons kept concealed with a time-capsule spell that preserved the books and whatever other artifacts were stored inside. If she dared take any of the books out of there, they would be ruined. But her mirth dimmed. There was no getting inside, not without Timothy's magic. Barrington had already tried.

The bells rang. Sera startled. She would have to think of this later. It was time for her Earth-level exam. She set the books back on their shelves, thanked Mrs. James for her help, and left the library. The last she heard was Scarlet warning Mrs. James of *danger*.

Sera hurried down the dim hallway to the voices of students reciting spells and formulas, bemoaning simple mistakes, and between sobs of failure were a few shrieks of celebration from those certain they'd aced an exam. She wished she was that confident. Water-level and Earth-level were first- and second-year courses—years she missed entirely. Having been placed into a higher grade because of vast reserves, she'd simply been told to catch up.

Today would prove if she truly had.

Doctor Morgan waited by the greenhouse. The large, ground-floor conservatory was brimmed with all the necessary flora needed by the school and its classes. Doctor Morgan ran a finger along one of the glass panes, the segmented windows also tainted by dimness.

"The entire school is like this," she told Sera after their greetings. "The teachers blame the maids; the maids blame the cleaning materials. It's all a big mess. Even the mirrors have been affected. They're all being taken down."

Sera glanced down the hall and saw, indeed, the walls were peppered with vacant spots.

The door opened, and Anne Doughty exited. Her brown eyes widened upon seeing Sera, but she didn't hurry away; rather, she approached her slowly. "I…I wanted to say I'm sorry for the way Eliza and I treated you," she said, her words cautious and hesitant.

Sera's brow dipped. "Why?" she asked, used to insults and accusations, not petitions for forgiveness.

"You heard Eliza and me talking about you, then Eliza fails two of her exams. I'd managed to lift her spirits and left her last night studying in the library, yet this morning she didn't show up. I really need to pass this exam. Earth is my inclination, and I wish to become an Aetherium spell maker—you know, the engineers who draft newer spell combinations. Please don't give me bad luck, too. I'm sorry if I offended you."

Sera opened her mouth to speak but could barely form a sentence to address that nonsense or decide whether or not she should be offended. In her silence, Anne curtsied a few times, complimented Sera's dress and hair, then hurried away.

"The lengths some people will go to in order to blame others for their misfortune is alarming," Doctor Morgan said, pulling open the conservatory door. "Don't let it bother you. Every year there are those who simply cannot take the pressure. This year we happen to have a few more."

"What do you mean?" Sera asked, entering.

"Apparently many students have found the exams harder this year, and they've not shown up for the remainder of their modules. Some of their parents say they haven't gone home yet, but that's normal. Many are scared to admit they failed."

Sera followed Doctor Morgan inside, and the entire matter was forgotten as she beheld the greenhouse that befell a similar fate to the mirrors and windows outside, its panes also darkened. And as she walked toward the proctor waiting at the fountain in the middle of the conservatory, her steps slowed.

Nausea clamped down on Sera's stomach with the same unease she'd felt at the orphanage and at Father Warner's home. Suddenly she wasn't so sure a cleaning agent was responsible for this sudden darkness anymore, but rather Meredith. There was a chance she still roamed the school, and whatever spell she had conjured at the orphanage, perhaps she meant to invoke it here? If her suspicions were correct, she had to get to Barrington right away.

"Whatever it is killed the plants as well," the proctor whispered to Doctor Morgan once Sera was done with the oral portion of the examination, during which she'd successfully detailed the history of protection circles and containment domes and their construction and variations. She also spoke on the several theories behind spell building and cipher translations, something Barrington was passionate about.

Sera was certain come morning she would forget half of the facts, but for now, she smiled widely. With tomorrow's test being the last, she was almost done, and she hadn't botched one exam horribly so far.

She turned her attention to the eucalyptus plant in front of her, where she was to display emotional transference, her downfall. Showing emotions as a seventhborn was not something she could indulge in, no matter how unhealthy Doctor Morgan claimed it to be. Still, she touched her wand to the stem of the eucalyptus plant and thought of Timothy and Mary.

She moved her magic to her fingers and filled the fibers of her wand but stiffened. Low whispers echoed all around her like a kaleidoscope of voices, moving about the room like phantoms. Masculine and feminine voices, all crying and afraid.

Her pulse quickened, and she looked around. Meredith was responsible for what was happening to the mirrors, she was sure of it. And reason told her that whether out of malice or mistake, she was responsible for the children's disappearances. Hopefully Barrington found something of interest in Father Warner's mirrors to help them locate the children or learn of their fate from Meredith's mirror magic.

As she thought of the children harmed, Sera's magic

darkened, withering from a roiling flame to a dark and toxic miasma. She guided this up to her fingertips and poured it out over the plant in a rolling fog. The plant, housed beneath a protection circle and enclosed within a dome of magic, was instantly covered in the mist. Its bright green color dimmed, and its branches sagged.

The proctor came up alongside her, held one of the leaves between her fingers, and closed her eyes. After a moment of scanning the shrub for Sera's emotions, she noted her grade and concluded the exam with a nod.

A torrent of emotions flooded Sera, and though desperate to get to Barrington to tell him about her theory, she dragged in a deep breath. She was almost done. One step closer to her family. One step closer to learning who she was.

Hope soared within her, but she clutched it tight and buried it deep. She still had one more test and an interview, not to mention deterrents to obtain and children to find.

She turned to Doctor Morgan. "I'm sorry to leave so suddenly, but—"

"Something has come up," she said, smiling. "Mama told me all about your other work, but tell Nikolai not to work you so hard. Your Aether-levels are in the morning, and after we're to meet to examine your reserves."

Worry fluttered in Sera's belly at the mention of both imminent tests, but she nodded. "Good evening, Doctor Morgan."

Moments later, Sera's feet touched the hardwood floors of Barrington's office, and she instantly wished she could transfer back to the Academy. The pungency of clementine filled the air, and her existing nausea crested. Clapping a hand over her mouth, she followed the stink to the workroom, where she found Barrington standing before an open window, holding a retort outside with a pair of clamps. White smoke billowed out over the moors like an exodus of phantoms. When the strong fumes had subsided, he set the rounded vase on a cooling rack and moved to the washstand. He reeled a hand over the basin. Thin blue tendrils of magic whirled from his palm and funneled into the bowl. Water bubbled into existence and filled the sink.

He proceeded to clean his hands. "Sorry about the smell; I know how much you dislike clementine."

"What were you doing?" she asked, already having an idea of the answer. She often walked in on him concocting one experiment or another, especially in between cases. It was as though he couldn't keep motionless, whether of body or mind. He was either teaching or learning, working or experimenting, but never was he still. Yet, now knowing of his method to combat fear, she sensed these experiments were about nothing more than increasing his knowledge. He would learn all there was about magic, and perhaps then he wouldn't feel weak anymore.

"I'll assume you've seen the mirrors at the school."

"I was just coming to tell you." She explained how she heard voices similar to those at Father Warner's house. "I think Meredith is our culprit."

He scrubbed his nails, rinsed his hands, then ran them through his hair and pushed the long strands back. "Given Miss Armitage vanished within the school and we already suspect her for conducting mirror magic at the orphanage, I believe you are right, but tonight we will know for certain. I've obtained a spell signature from the mirrors Meredith left at Father Warner's. Once we find its match, we find our culprit."

"How will we do that? I used all of the magic in her wand. We don't have a sample to analyze for a match."

"Yes, but I've recently learned that, since she received

funds from the Aetherium for the orphanage, she was required to submit a sample of her magic for official records."

Sera smiled. "Brilliant. Have you written Mrs. York for help securing the sample?"

He sat back on the edge of his desk. "Unfortunately, she is away. And with Mr. Delacort campaigning for chancellor, alliances are shifting and Mrs. York can't trust her previous sources anymore. As such, unless it is for an active case where Inspector Lewis can obtain the files without suspicion, she is unable to help us. We will have to go at it alone and find the samples ourselves."

"But all the samples are kept in…" The words descended on Sera all at once. She gasped. "No."

"It's the only way. Surely I don't expect you to accompany me, but it must be done."

She paced in a circle. "No, no, no. There is no way you're breaking into the Aetherium!"

"I'm not breaking in," he said mildly. "I'm visiting a friend who will escort me into the records room. The only caveat is he only works at night and the main entrance is out of the question. A guard would have to personally escort me to his workroom, and he is not someone I can be seen with, especially not given my recent arrest."

"Why?"

"He's under suspicion for necromancy. But," he said over the beginning of Sera's protests, "Inspector Lewis assured me he isn't due to be arrested until after the elections. The headline *Necromancer in the Aetherium* is not one Mrs. York wants plastered over the news ahead of a vote. She fears it will make the chancellor look incompetent and unable to keep his house in order."

He took the cooled retort and parceled the liquid out into a small vial. "Therefore, I'll have to go through the one place no one will search for the living."

Cognizant of his words and the smell of death now emanating from the retort, Sera stopped. "Oh, blast. Please don't say—"

"I'm going through the morgue."

Her heart shriveled, and she sat down in her chair.

"The potion I've brewed will put me into a deep sleep and slow my heart to where the most advanced of healers will not know I'm alive. The effects last an hour, the time it takes to get through the Aetherium checkpoints and to the morgue. Rowe will play the part of my attendant while Lucas drives the ambulance carriage and waits in the loading dock for our imminent escape."

"And what will I be doing?"

He paused and after a moment had yet to speak.

Sera's mouth gaped. "I wasn't a part of the plan?" she asked archly.

"This is the best and safest way for everyone involved, including you."

"That's nonsense, and you know it. What if you don't wake up on time? Brewed potions have a partial time variance; you say it will be active for an hour, but it could be less or more than that time by some minutes."

"Yes, but I'll have Rowe—"

"Who is a non-magic. No offense, but how on earth is he supposed to help you if you run into any delays or problems of the magic sort?" Rowe was one of Barrington's best friends and informants, but sadly, during his time at the Academy, his magic had waned until now he was a non-magic, his powers but a weak ember where other magicians' were raging flames.

"And before you suggest Lucas, he is our driver so he must remain by the loading dock to facilitate the escape. No, you can't go." She set her chin and squared her shoulders. "I'm the only one who can do this."

Barrington looked at her as though she'd grown a second head. Sera wondered about the state of her head also; she couldn't quite believe what she was saying, either, and yet it made the most sense. "They will not care for a seventhborn and will pass me through without an added thought. You can play the role of ambulance attendant and can delay any and all trouble to keep me from waking early and getting caught."

"But what of your ghosts? I would imagine the number of phantoms in a morgue is inordinate."

He was right, and fear nudged her heart, but she set her chin. If she was to be an inspector, she would have to get comfortable with taking risks. "I will be fine. Besides—" She touched a hand to his hidden pendant flush against her skin. "You're my anchor, are you not?"

He met her eyes at this, a direct and open gaze that moved through her heart and to her soul and left her a little breathless. He nodded.

"Good. Now, let me go and get ready…" *Before I change my mind.*

Rosie walked into the room with the day's correspondence.

"Oh, Rosie. Perfect timing," Sera said. "We're about to leave, and I need your help to prepare. Can you unearth one of my old dresses, a black one? The more distressed the better."

Her brow dipped. "Of course, but why?"

Sera walked past her. "Because tonight, I'm going to die."

magic bound

The carriage rocked back and forth, and the wheels groaned again as they descended a steep hill. Sera bristled, her stomach finding a home in her throat. Wearing a simple brown jacket, white shirt, and pants—a workman's uniform—Barrington sat across from her, deathly quiet and his gaze far away. She had no doubt he rolled the coming events backward and forward in his mind, dissecting it for alternatives, but after transferring with the horses to within an hour's drive to the Aetherium capital borders, he still hadn't found one.

The carriage stopped. Sera peeked out from their window and frowned. Darkness shrouded the forest flanking the sides of the road as far as the eye could see. "We're in the middle of nowhere."

"Precisely." The carriage door opened. Barrington exited, then held a hand out to Sera. She reached for her veiled hat. "You won't need it," he said. "You're amongst friends here."

She set her hat back down, blew out a breath, and

accepted his help. An ambulance carriage was parked on the side of a wide dirt road flanked with overgrown brush.

A smile touched her lips upon seeing Rowe leaned back against the ambulance cart, biting on a thin reed. The blond-haired thief-taker flashed them a wide smile and lifted his cap from over his bright green eyes. "Right on time." Thrusting aside the reed, he met Barrington and Lucas's hands, then bowed over Sera's.

Still miffed, Barrington moved beyond him, toward the ambulance cart with Lucas.

Rowe gave Sera a questioning look.

"There's been a change of plans," she said.

"How's that possible?" Rowe asked. "Nik's as rigid as a brick."

Lucas snorted a laugh, but Barrington simply stared at them, unamused.

"Did you get what we needed?" he clipped.

"Indeed." Rowe gripped the metal handle on the wagon and pulled it open. On one side was a long bench for the ambulance attendant. On the other were two flat beds, one atop the other. A dingy sheet was folded on the bottom one.

After explaining their new plot, Barrington helped Sera into the ambulance carriage, then climbed up behind her. Rowe touched the tip of his hat and closed the doors, thrusting them both into darkness cut only by the streams of the carriage lamps. Sera lay down on the cot and pulled the blanket up over her chest. The metal was cool beneath her, a welcomed relief from the heat, even though her nerves wrestled and body trembled.

Barrington drew the elixir from his inner pocket.

Sera glanced to the vial, her magic racing within. She reached an open palm to him. "I'm ready."

Barrington set the elixir in her hand but didn't release it. He met her stare, his eyes black in the newly settled darkness. "Are you sure about this, Miss Dovetail? We can still turn back."

She gave him a small smile. "Will you always worry for me?"

"Someone has to." He skimmed his knuckles along her cheek. "I will be beside you the entire time."

She leaned into his touch, relishing the feel of his fingers before the unknowns awaiting them that night. "I know."

He released the vial into her hold. Sera wrapped her fingers around it. The liquid was warm, and black particles shifted within. A fitting color for death.

She twisted the cork off, handed it to Barrington, then brought the vial to her lips. With one more calming breath, she tipped the contents back into her mouth. The acrid sweetness burned down her throat and gripped her stomach, which contracted with the need to vomit. But soon it was as if her body had been disconnected and her limbs were now made of air and an independent will.

With the last of her energies, she looked to Barrington, who said, "I'm here," but soon his voice faded, the world grew black, and she fell asleep.

See her fall from the sky…

A dream caught Sera. She knelt in the middle of the abandoned church where she had stood six months prior, the night her life had changed forever. This time, the crushed pews were reconstructed and the tiled nave gleamed white, its gold edging catching the light of the raven chandelier above. The scents of dust and mildew was replaced by frankincense burning in the silver thuribles hanging from chains. Around her, the once-shattered stained-glass window panes were whole, the images of the seven guardians of magic staring down at Sera with pitiful, mournful expressions.

She spun away from them and gasped; the altar was illuminated by hundreds of candles, held up by the bloodied hands of murdered witches—some with their throats severed, others burned—all of them seventhborns.

Behind them stood the maker of her nightmares and the patchwork of scars along her body.

Noah smiled, his angular eyes glittering like onyx stars. But he didn't smile at her; rather, down into her lap. She followed his terrible, cruel gaze to Timothy Delacort in her arms. His eyes were closed, his face void and serene; he looked so devastatingly beautiful, as though wrapped in the sweetest dream. But Sera knew that, while he was indeed resting, he would never again wake up.

Sorrow became an invisible hand, weaving its fingers through the hollows between her ribs. It clenched her lungs and squeezed, and the sob in her throat broke free. Timothy's eyes snapped open at the sound. Sera flinched and sought to release him, but his cold hands gripped her wrist, his nails digging into her seventh-born tattoo.

"My love." He tilted his head, and bloody tears streamed onto his pale cheeks. "Why did you let me die?"

She shook her head, wanting to tell him she hadn't— that she'd fought and killed for him—but cracks appeared along Timothy's face, and the words dried in her throat. The hairline fractures spread down his body. The pieces chipped away like porcelain, revealing a dead Barrington instead.

Sera screamed and released him. He hit the floor and

shattered into shards of jagged glass. They blustered around her in a phantom wind full of the screams and cries of seventhborns…

And all the while, Noah laughed and watched her bleed.

Sera roused with a gasp. Air rushed back into her lungs, hot and searing as it spread like a web of fire through her chest. She clawed at her sides, her limbs twisting and jerking as she regained life. Barrington hovered over her in an instant and held her down, angling himself to meet her eyes.

"Look at me, Miss Dovetail. Focus on me and my voice. You're all right, and I'm here. It'll pass."

Trickles of his magic soon wrapped around her bones and infused her with warmth, chasing out the chill of death. Within moments, she stopped thrashing, once again in control of her appendages. But nothing could tame the hollow pit in her heart left by the horrible dream still staining her mind. Was coming here a mistake and her nightmare an omen of what was to come?

No, she was being foolish. This was dangerous, but she would meet greater perils as an inspector.

Barrington released her shoulders and helped her sit up.

They were in a large room with a row of beds along one wall, various dead bodies covered by blankets laid upon them. The diagonal wall was a door with the word *Holding* on a plaque above the doorframe. But thankfully, though countless bodies surrounded them, there were no ghosts.

Barrington draped something thick and warm over her shoulders and gave them a gentle squeeze. "You did marvelous."

"I don't see how I could have done otherwise," Sera

struggled to say through her chattering teeth. "I was practically dead."

"You could have woken up in front of the guards." He smiled and held a hand to her.

Sera accepted his help and lowered one foot off the cot, then another. She glanced down to see she now wore the brown robe donned by all Wood-inclined employees. Barrington also wore one. She lifted her eyes and gasped. A man in a green robe stood at the door. But she quickly remembered him from the Feast of Edification: Doctor Figgis. He still watched Barrington with a palpable hunger, as though he wished to sink his teeth into Barrington's flesh and drain him of blood.

"Come. Doctor Figgis will take us to the records room now. The sooner you move, the faster your body will metabolize the elixir."

He reached out and fiddled with the enclosure on the neck of her cape, clasping her robe shut, for which Sera was glad. Her fingers were numb and her body still shivered as if to shake off the last of death's fingers clinging to her skin.

They met Doctor Figgis at the Holding Room entrance. Opening the arched wooden door, he peered into the hall. The coast clear, he led them out into the corridor. The dim passageway was narrow, with high, vaulted stone ceilings and numerous doors with no handles. The walls were bare, save for the stained-glass windows. They passed a large opening, and Sera's steps slowed. Though she'd seen pictures of the Aetherium in books and leaflets, nothing could have prepared her for witnessing it with her own eyes.

The group of seven towers gleamed white in the night, wrapped in protective magic. Each one was like a frosted sword, speared into the stone they were built upon. Around each main tower were the newer buildings, like smaller sentinels ready for an attack. Sera's lungs constricted. This was her future, should she pass her exam. Should she find Meredith and the children and obtain Armitage's wards. Should she rid herself of possessions and ghosts. Yearning and determination grew to solid things in her chest, and it felt as if each tower was in fact a sword stabbed right into her heart.

Following behind Doctor Figgis, they weaved along the halls of archways until they made it to a plain wall with a single door. Doctor Figgis touched his hand to the middle of it, an Invocation ring around his index finger. The door groaned open. They entered readily and closed the door behind them.

The rounded chamber within had seven doors, one marked with the symbol for each element. Behind the doors were samples of magic for every student and employee ever in service to the Aetherium. Sera's chest tightened, and she glanced around the endless space. If her mother, father, or siblings had ever been schooled or employed by the Aetherium, samples of their magic would be in this place. She could learn their names. Perhaps see their faces beyond the smears of watercolor she imagined whenever she thought of them. The heaviness in her chest grew a stone heavier. Never had she felt so close to them and yet so very, very far.

As though cognizant of her desires, Barrington drew close to her ear. "Soon." She met his stare, his face so very close, and nodded.

"Come on, then. What's the spell signature?" Doctor Figgis wiped meaty fingers along his bald head, his hands trembling. Whether he was scared or simply in need of a fix, Sera didn't know.

Barrington reached into his inner coat pocket and drew out his notebook. He flipped to the page with the spell signature he'd collected, the identifier preceded by the conjurer's inclination.

"Aether," he said.

Doctor Figgis hurried to the adjacent entryway and pressed his wand to the door. Latches unlocked, and Sera winced, their sound much too loud in the deafening silence. He pulled the door open, and they filed inside. The records room within was dark, lit only by intermittent lamps of weak silver light. The path before them stretched farther than the eye could see, and Sera glanced up to find the shelves also seemed to go on forever. On the shelves were narrow boxes stuffed side by side with a small plaque, bearing the magician's name on its spine.

Flares of silver light billowed from the tip of Doctor Figgis's wand and cast a stronger halo of light around them. Sera's heart crawled into her throat, and she wished he hadn't done that. Otherwise she wouldn't have noticed the ghost just over his shoulder. She lowered her head and fixed her eyes on her feet. In her peripheral vision, she caught sight of a little girl with a stringed ribbon rushing past. Sera cursed. Avoiding the gaze of matured and taller magicians was simple, but damn it all. She hadn't thought about ghostly children.

"What's the next set of ciphers?" he asked. Barrington held the notepad out to him. He nodded. "This way."

They moved down the main vestibule. The mosaic tiles before each row of shelving were fashioned into a symbol. "Like coordinate travel, we first match the first cipher and then work our way down the set until we reach the last cipher and the magic's owner," Barrington explained in low tones as they followed Doctor Figgis, but Sera could hardly hear him. Not through the screams and shrieks of the dead. They were everywhere. She'd imagined they'd linger by their bodies, but it seemed they were drawn to their magic.

They rounded a bend, and Sera shivered, the temperatures much colder here.

Edward? Darling, where are you?

Sera bristled, and her steps slowed.

Barrington paused. "Do you see them?"

She nodded. "And hear them."

Just then, a bride emerged from between the aisles. Her face and veil were burned, and her bridal train was stained with soot and blood. She paused just before Doctor Figgis and glanced up and down the hall. *Edward? We must go. Danger approaches!*

Sera flinched and lowered her head, and Barrington drew her closer. They followed Doctor Figgis along their web of halls, and Sera kept her eyes downcast, lest she make eye contact with one of the many ghosts who roamed the halls...like the barefoot man, his toes edged black with rot. He'd lumbered past, his swollen feet chained in shackles. His ankles were engorged and rolls of gray, bruised skin hung over the rusted fetters.

No one is safe, he hissed, dragging himself forward. *There's nowhere to hide.* And then he laughed, a spluttery gurgle of a snicker that echoed in the hall until the sound diminished to nothingness, the jingle of his chains the last to fade.

"It's here," Doctor Figgis said, holding his wand to a shelf at eye level. Barrington pulled out the brown box, much more faded than the others, and brought it closer to Doctor Figgis's light. But where they'd imagined to see Meredith's name, instead he read, "Serena Shaw."

"Serena Shaw?" Sera echoed. They matched the spell signature Barrington obtained to the one imprinted on the box's spine. It was the same, but it wasn't Meredith's magic.

He opened the file, and their suspicion withered at the picture of Serena Shaw. A girl who was not Meredith. Dressed in a black mourning gown, the girl sat on a high-back winged armchair and looked directly at the camera. Her brown hair was tied up in a loose bun, and on her lap was a plague mask. Barrington turned the picture over, and his mouth bowed at the text written on the back.

Serena Shaw. Scryist, Executed for her participation in the Persecutions. Method of Execution: Buried alive.

"How is this possible?" Sera breathed.

"It's not," Barrington said, sounding troubled, and yet they both stared down at the picture of a dead woman whose magic had been recovered on both the mirrors from the orphanage and the school. "There's nothing else here. What of her academic and employment history?" he asked Doctor Figgis. "Even Purists kept detailed files."

"How am I supposed to know? You asked me to bring you here, and I've done my part. Where is my payment?"

Barrington gritted his teeth, dug into his pocket, and withdrew the velvet bag. "You will get the last third when you get us out—"

A clank echoed as the latches to the door were opened from the outside. Wide-eyed, Doctor Figgis snatched the bag from Barrington's hand. "Find your own way out."

"And which way is that?" Barrington hissed, but Doctor Figgis rushed away and abandoned them in the dark.

Sera's heart quickened, fear emerging from the depths of her soul. Her magic roiled in answer, a rabid wave of heat that rushed up her body and sunk its teeth into her bones.

"Halt! Who goes there?" A light shone brighter in an adjacent hallway as a guard chased after Doctor Figgis. "He spoke to someone! Search the room, there might be more."

A clatter of footsteps rumbled. Approaching.

A bright light sped by them and crashed against the shelf. A thin sheet of vapor glimmered above the bookcase, a protection spell securing the files. "Halt!"

Barrington gripped her hand and met her gaze. "Run!"

They dashed down the neighboring aisle, but in the dark the passageways were indiscernible, and within moments they were lost and without a sense of direction.

Another blast of magic slammed right above them. "Stop, by order of the Aetherium guards!"

In the light of the flare, Sera noted a door on the other side of the corridor. Whether or not it was locked, it was their only option. She tugged Barrington's hand and dashed toward it. Blasts of magic shot over and around them, illuminating them in silvery sparks, but, focused on the door, they ducked and wove around shelving, tables, and chairs to avoid injury. They reached beside them as they ran left and right through this labyrinth of hallways and yanked out boxes blindly, toppled over tables and chairs, leaving behind them a mess of papers, downed furniture, and scattered vials of magic.

They rushed into an intersection; Barrington yanked her down, and she winced, her knee slamming against the marble floor. An orb of magic sizzled past and crashed against the shelf beside them.

At the door, Barrington gripped the knob and pushed. The door was locked, but after a flash, he shoved it open and hurried them inside.

"Why did you do that? You can't use magic," she hissed. "They will find your trace."

Barrington held up the doorknob. "Not if there's no evidence."

A rush of relief rolled down Sera's body, but she turned, and dread instantly replaced it at the brooms, buckets, and cleaning supplies lining the walls of the supply closet. There was no other exit.

No...

Streams of light peeked through the seam. "They're in here!" a guard called from outside. A rumble of footsteps advanced, and the hue of their light intensified. "Come out with your hands up, by order of Aetherium guards!"

Barrington spun in a circle, his calculating gaze taking in their surroundings. Seeming to realize the same thing as she—they were fatally stuck—he turned to her, cupped her face in his hands, and ran his dark gaze along her hair, her nose, her mouth, as though to memorize her.

He met her stare, and, for the first time, she saw his fear. Not of his death, but of hers.

His fingers tightened upon her, his jaw clenched, and his mien darkened. "Stay here," he said, his voice a warm fog against her lips as the room grew colder and the shadows blacker. "And whatever you hear, do not come out."

Sera froze; she knew the damning certainty in his words. More, this spicy, acrid stench of black magic. Driven into a corner, the cage of the beast within him was open.

She pressed her palms to his face and moved closer, bringing their bodies flush together. Needing to feel him safe. Needing to remind him not to lose himself to the intoxicating rush of rage, revenge, and bloodshed. "Stay with me."

With their gazes fixed on each other, a different air swept over him, just as intense and full of ardor. His chest undulated with ragged breaths, and his hands anchored into her back, and she could feel his slipping restraint.

"Come out and surrender your wands or we will shoot! This is the final warning!"

The air electrified, pungent of death and charged with magic.

Barrington pressed his forehead against Sera's, breathless, but she didn't release him, rather, closed her eyes against him. *Bloody bride. Shackled man. Little girl.*

"Three!"

Repeating their names in her mind, Sera focused on the raw heat churning in her belly, faster and stronger and louder. On the feel of Barrington growing colder in her arms as he pooled his magic to protect her. Just as she'd summoned the dead to kill Noah, she would channel them here. Allow them to share their pain with her and use it to immobilize the guards and save her and Barrington.

"Two!"

Outside, the streams of light grew to a blinding white as the guards prepared for their final assault.

Pressure gathered in Sera's skull, and the temperatures plummeted. She opened her eyes and swept her gaze over Barrington's shoulder to the little girl, the shackled man, and the bloodied bride. And behind them were countless more spirits in the fog. She had vowed never to use that power again, but she couldn't let herself and Barrington die here.

"One!"

The ghosts reached a hand to her. *Show you...*

This was many more spirits than she'd channeled before, and now that she could be possessed, there was no telling whether they would let her go. But as Barrington released her and spun around draped in black mist intent on ruin and death, Sera aimed her wand to the door. "Show me."

"*Fire!*"

The ghosts lunged.

Barrington pulled the door open.

Heat enveloped them, and blinding orbs of magic approached. The world around her vanished then, consumed by darkness, chaos, and the Barghest's sulfuric roar.

. . .

She crashed down onto a patch of grass, branches and rocks digging into her back. Gasping, she rolled onto her belly and clawed her fingers into the earth for stability, but the world still whirled wildly around her.

"Professor?" she croaked, her heart in her ears and her stomach lodged in her throat. She wiped her hair away from her face and crawled forward to find Barrington on his hands and knees, gagging, but he didn't throw up.

"What the bloody hell was that?" he groaned between ragged breaths. "Where are we?"

Relieved, Sera sagged back onto the grass to find Barrington's manor in the distance. "We're home. The Barghest transferred us out of the Aetherium; hence they'll be unable to track us."

The hellhound trotted beside her and laid down, resting his head on her lap, wholly pleased with himself.

She smiled. "Thank you. You're wonderful. And you need an equally brilliant name." She thought on it a moment. "How about Valiant?"

He turned his head away and huffed, clearly not fond of it.

Sera laughed. "Very well. We'll think of another."

She opened her palm and whirled an orb of magic into her hand. The Barghest whipped his forked tongue around it and sucked it into his mouth.

"Of course," Barrington muttered, now flat on the grass, his eyes closed. He'd taken off the Aetherium robe, and his white shirt clung to his sculpted chest and shoulders with sweat. "You two are bound."

Sera's eyes narrowed. "*Bound?*"

"When we use magic on an object continuously, tethering occurs between the item and the magician. It is the reason we're encouraged to change our wands as we mature, not just to allow more magic to travel through it but because tethering hinders growth in magic if it exists for too long. Later, when the magician wishes to move on to a new medium, they are unable to because the connection has been solidified and your magic will view this source as its only outlet."

Sera's brows rose. "Yes, I remember Mr. Armitage mention something similar the night of the Feast of Edification. There was a crystal ball there, and apparently the owner grew bound to it and it only shows images of the Underworld now."

"*The Underworld's Eye*," he murmured. "The tales vary, but essentially, yes. She grew magic bound to her crystal ball. It's as if you are each half of a whole. It takes years to establish that strong a bond, but it appears you and the Barghest have started. He has fed from your hand continuously for months now and refuses to feed from anyone else. He protects you as he would himself, the same way you will eventually be receptive to him should you maintain the connection. Your magic lives in him now, and the more he answers when your magic calls to him, the more you will grow coupled to him. You're magic bound."

"Magic bound," Sera repeated, testing the phrase on her lips. She pressed a hand to her heart, warmth blooming in her chest as she recalled the times he'd come to her aid: when the first ghost had possessed her in the orphanage, and when Gummy's thugs had nearly killed her at the smuggler's den.

Now he'd saved not only her but Barrington as well. And while Sera knew she had much to learn about this concept, she leaned back and smiled. Given the limited relationships in her life, she would cherish this one for as long as it lasted.

Barrington rose to his feet, snatched up his robe, and draped it over his shoulders. "I must go. Lucas was waiting near the Aetherium. I'll make sure he's all right, then we'll go to Rowe and bring home the carriage and horses."

Sera stood up, her legs still a bit wobbly. "Are you sure you're well enough to transfer? The Barghest can help."

"I can manage," he said, side-eying the hellhound beside her. Sera pursed her lips; transferring by horse was easy for him, but apparently traveling by Barghest was his undoing. Yet, when he snatched out his wand, her brow furrowed. For him to need his wand to transfer meant he was much too addled to hold the transfer coordinates in his mind. And sensing the dark humor now exuding from him, Sera neared him.

"Are you sure you're all right?" She tried to meet his eyes, but he wouldn't look at her. "Professor?"

He shook his head to himself, and his fingers tightened around the wand's holder. "I'm sorry about tonight. It was never my intention to put you in danger."

His shame at that moment stirred her soul, and she walked to him. "Danger is a part of our job. Besides, I requested to go."

"And I'm a wretched man for not having denied you. You have your exams, your career, your family to find. I've nothing but a name burdened by lies, toxic experiments that ruin lives, and revenge," he said before she could speak. "Mrs. York is right. There is no penance for me, and I don't deserve your trust."

Sera winced, the word *trust* like a blade to her heart. She shook her head, wishing she were brave enough to tell him about her possessions, regardless of his reaction. Instead, she settled for another truth. "I wish you knew just how brilliant you truly are. How you deserve better than withdrawals and the threat of arrest. More than people like Doctor Figgis and Gummy."

He looked to her at this, and a blush warmed her cheeks. Had she gone too far? Perhaps, but she met his stare, unwilling to take the words back. "If you saw yourself how Rosie and Lucas see you. How I see you…"

"I wouldn't dare," he said so quietly that if she hadn't seen his lips move, she would have doubted he spoke at all.

"Why?"

His jaw pulsed. "Because I might be tempted to believe them and hope for things I shouldn't… For good and pure things I don't deserve."

"Like what?

Walking to her, he cupped her cheek, drew close, and pressed a light kiss at her temple, his lips lingering there. "Please don't ask," he whispered against her ear, and then, like a breeze, he was gone.

For a long time after, Sera stood there in the dark. A torrent of butterflies fluttered madly in her belly at his unexpected affection, yet she touched her fingertips to her temple, the coolness of his lips alive on her skin, and her soul hurt at his confession. What good things did he think he didn't deserve? Peace? Happiness? Love?

She lowered her hand and stared down at his house and the moors. So many times she'd gazed upon these wild and savage lands and thought them a mirror image of their master. And after tonight, she believed it to be so once more.

Perhaps he'd unwittingly transferred his emotions onto this land, the only place vast enough for his miles and miles of sorrow. And maybe he and these moors were bound after his years of using magic here, where now the land and the man were one.

With this in mind, she thought of him and everything she yearned to tell him. Everything she wished he saw in himself. The torrent of emotions in her heart spurred her magic until her veins were filled with fire.

When she could no longer hold the fierce ache that pressed down on her chest, she laid her palms flush on the cool earth and transferred these emotions into the land, waves upon waves of admiration, gratitude, strength, and love.

And maybe, wherever he was, he would feel this, believe it, and hope.

12

shattered

Later the next day, Sera stood before her Aether exam proctor, once again grateful for the hellhound and their singular bond. Had she used death magic the previous night, there was no telling whether her reserves would be replenished for the test—that is, if she was alive.

But now, Sera bit her inner lip to stifle a satisfied smile. This was her last test and one her work with Barrington had left her more than adequately prepared for. She answered questions about the history of the Aetherium, the Pragmatic Crusades, and the Persecutions with ease, then gave detailed answers on the various kinds of scrying and necessary tools.

The proctor, Mrs. Underwood, now motioned to the array of scrying tools on the long table in the back of the room and walked toward it.

"Elementary scrying is a requirement to proceed into the School of Continuing Magic. As such, please select the tool you will use to scry for your subject. You will be graded on clarity of the subject and their location."

Sera surveyed the offered instruments. They all droned with magic, but she had to locate the one whose energy called to her. Unlike wands, which a magician chose and discarded at will when they'd outgrown them, scrying tools chose their user and time for their connection to remain. At Barrington's home, she'd bonded with her maps and crystals, but there was no map here. She started at the head of the table, where there was a bowl of water. She'd studied Hydromancy in attempts of locating Mary, but with no luck. Though it was probably the spells around Mary's location that kept the place a secret—much like Barrington's home. Sera moved past the bowl. No need to test her theory now.

She paused before a crystal ball, and her magic swirled faster, sensing the connection. The previous semester, she had successfully scryed using a similar orb after experiencing an instant bond. She lifted a hand to the cool crystal, but this time the attachment was much weaker. No, there was a stronger pull from another instrument somewhere down the table.

Lowering her fingers, she walked past a teacup, a round mirror—

She stopped, frozen as though the mirror had wrapped invisible fingers around her wrist to keep her fixed. She turned to the scrying glass, and her magic flared, a reply to the mirror's phantom beckon.

"The mirror," she said to the proctor, who then handed her a file.

"At this moment, your subject, an Academy matron, is at a designated location within the school. This is their information. Please scry for them."

She handed Sera a file. Flipping it open, Sera smiled at seeing Mrs. James's face. She read over details of her life, like how she had only one sister and had become a matron after a successful career as a governess to a previous archdeacon. She had to use these facts to scry for Mrs. James, but Sera rubbed her fingers together, knowing a better way to scry for the woman.

She touched the glass. Her magic rushed to her fingertips, and a deafening hum filled her head instantly but faded as the connection between her magic and the mirror stabilized. Vastness consumed her mind as her magic waded in this void, waiting for direction.

Focusing on her memory of Mrs. James and feelings of mourning, Sera fed more magic into the mirror.

Mrs. James. Lost a sister to consumption. Grief. Loss. Pain.

Cognizant of her own feelings of sorrow from losing Timothy and Mary, she honed in on Mrs. James's like sentiments. Smoke swirled over the glass. The mist thinned and darkened in spots until a shadowy outline appeared. But she was going to be graded on clarity. This was not enough. Sera pulsed her powers and allowed more of her emotions and magic into the connection. But however hard she tried, the image of Mrs. James wouldn't sharpen.

A pit formed in Sera's stomach. She should have been able to do this. Sera released the image of Mrs. James and feelings of sorrow in her mind, and a sheet of fog washed over the smoke. She attempted it again, but this time, Sera gasped. Various images whisked by the glass, of children and students in their Academy robes, one of which was Eliza Douglas. She noted Mrs. James as well.

Mrs. Underwood leaned into the glass, studied the hazy image, then wrote down some notes. "You may call your magic back now."

Sera tried releasing the connection, but stark cold skittered down her body as though icy tentacles wrapped around her limbs. More and more faces washed through the glass, and with each passed reflection pressure built in Sera's head and the room grew bitingly frigid.

The images stopped on a gaunt woman in a black dress. Her face covered by a beaked plague mask, and her hair was stiff with frost. Sera winced, her connection with the mirror growing stronger, as was the pain in her head and the ice in her bones.

"Scrying for additional subjects will not improve your score, Miss Dovetail. Please call back your magic and sever the connection."

But Sera was frozen, and her fingers were affixed to the glass. She wanted to end the scrying, but the mirror refused to release her, and her headache spiked.

The woman in the mirror tilted her head, her neck *crack-crack-crackling* like ice. She flexed spindly fingers and lunged for Sera.

"No!" Sera's magic crested, and the mirror exploded. Crystal shards were ejected from the blast and scattered about the room.

Doctor Morgan ran to her. "Miss Dovetail, are you all right?"

Sera toured widened eyes between Doctor Morgan and the now-steel frame of what used to be a mirror. She shook her head, and with the exam now clearly over, she let Doctor Morgan guide her over the glassy rubble, out of the room, and down onto a bench.

"What happened, Miss Dovetail?" she asked, brushing the shards of glass from Sera's shoulders and hair.

"I was scrying for Mrs. James, but then… I think I saw ghosts. I'm not sure." She leaned forward onto her hands. "I feel like I'm going mad."

"You did brilliantly today," Doctor Morgan said. "You scryed for your subject, so you satisfied the requirements.

There might be point deductions for everything else, but I don't see why you wouldn't pass. But I am interested to know why the dead have been able to reach you so frequently. Your second sight is like a door that can be closed, but for some reason yours remains ajar. If you're up to it, I'd very much like to check your reserves."

"Yes, of course."

"Grand. This way," she said, leading them out into the gardens.

Barrington crossed the field, his robes billowing behind him like black wings. Those devastating gray eyes found her instantly, and he slowed down, always so cognizant of her pains and predicaments. No doubt the events she'd experienced during her Aether-level exam were imprinted on her face.

Sera knew she should look away, lest they draw any attention and suspicion, but remembering their nearness at the morgue, his forehead resting on hers and fingers anchored into her waist—and more, his warm kiss on her temple and the emotion she'd transferred into his lands— heat flushed through her. His stare softened, and the iciness that had lingered in her bones melted away.

Yet, his gaze swept to Doctor Morgan beside her, and though sunny, the day seemed to darken. Turning away, he stalked to the main building, pulled the door open, and vanished inside.

Doctor Morgan sighed but, shaking her head, continued across the lush field and to her room in the matron's hall.

"Are you and the professor…?" Sera trailed off, her heart pounding. There were more important topics to tackle, yet, with the memory of his embrace and kiss on her temple, she had to know. "Did you break his heart?"

Doctor Morgan's cheeks flushed, and, opening the door,

she nodded. "But not in the way you think, and he will hate me forever. But you must speak to him of it," she said gently before Sera could prod. "It isn't my place to discuss it. I'm sorry."

Sera nodded. Doctor Morgan had been nothing but kind, and this conversation filled her eyes with pain. She would have to ask Barrington.

They entered the apartment. Doctor Morgan's room was a boxed chamber that didn't leave enough space for furniture other than the essentials: a bed, a small dresser, a narrow wardrobe, and a table and two chairs pushed against the wall, by the only window in the room. Sera blinked. She'd always thought her tower room was the smallest accommodation in the entire school, save for the closets.

Motioning for Sera to sit, Doctor Morgan poured them both a glass of water, from which Sera drank readily. To allow someone to access her reserves this way after what Mary did stoked her pulse, but she had to do it. Armitage's wards might help with her ghosts, but what if there truly was an underlying problem? What if Noah hadn't just scarred her body but her magic? What had just happened at her Aether-level test could not happen again.

Besides, she'd just seen Barrington. Should Doctor Morgan have any ill will, he would know where to find her. And a slight relief rolled through Sera. She was magic bound to the Barghest. Surely, he'd come.

"There's no need to be nervous." Doctor Morgan sat across from Sera. "We will start slowly, and if at any point you feel uncomfortable or unable to go on, we can stop." She gave Sera a reassuring smile, drew her wand, and nodded once. "Whenever you're ready."

Sera dragged her damp palms against her skirt and swallowed past the knot in her throat. "Is there anything specific you're looking for? It might help calm me down if I can prepare myself for the worst. Perhaps what you read in your friend's notes?"

"I seek a few indicators, but seeing as you successfully used death magic, I am searching for *shattering*. Back before I knew of his horrible endeavors, my friend conducted heinous experiments into the limitations of seventhborns. His subjects engaged in other forms of death magic—namely, necromancy—and ultimately encountered what he called shattering, or broken reserves. After the seventhborns were forced to raise body after body, their reserves, in essence, cracked, creating a tear in the veil between our world and the realm of the dead. Spirits ultimately found their way through, leading to a number of seventh-born possessions."

"But wouldn't Mrs. Lange have voided my exam if there was something wrong with my reserves? I passed the evaluation."

Doctor Morgan shook her head. "Reserve checks merely evaluate the breadth and depth of your reserves and how quickly they deplete at various intensities of magic use. Furthermore, your reserves are vast, and for her to have been able to see any signs of shattering, they would have needed to be emptied, but she had no reason to suspect otherwise or to look for anything more."

Sera gulped. *Shattering*. Could her reserves really be... broken? It would explain her condition and the increase in ghosts, but... "What happened to his subjects?"

She was quiet for a moment. "We can discuss that later, once we know more—"

"I want to know now. Please."

Her lips pressed to a tight line. "A number of them perished."

All air left Sera in a rush, and she gripped the stool's

edge, her hands trembling and damp. *No...*

"But they were in fragile states," Doctor Morgan explained quickly. "Malnourished and sickly, kept in deplorable conditions and weakened further by continued use of necromancy and other death arts. You are much stronger."

"What of the others?" she asked, her voice weak. She wetted her lips. "The ones who didn't die. Did they recover?"

"Some did, yes, but I was much too hurt and disgusted by what I'd read and couldn't bring myself to finish. But let us first see if shattering is even the cause of your problems, and we will proceed from there."

Sera swallowed thickly and nodded, hoping to all magic that shattering was not the cause of her ghosts.

Doctor Morgan stood up and held her wand toward Sera. Sera mirrored her, their wands joined at the tip. Wisps of blue smoke twined about Doctor Morgan's wand and enveloped Sera's. A foreign, potent magic seeped into Sera's veins—a direct contrast to hers and closer to Barrington's in likeness, calm and cool, yet fierce and bold. Sera's magic flared and rushed up her body to fight against Doctor Morgan's invasion, but she yanked it back.

"No, release your magic," Doctor Morgan said, her voice tranquil. "Allow it to fight against me. I will be able to get a better reading and see whether the problem is in your reserves or something else within your magic."

Sera relinquished control. Vicious, hot fire slammed against Doctor Morgan's powers with so much force she stumbled back. Regaining her footing, she pushed back against Sera's abilities until they were caught in a stalemate of magic.

"Good, now hold your powers there," she instructed.

Sera allowed her magic to flow wildly against Doctor

Morgan's, which was now akin to a brick wall. Pressure gathered at her temples, Doctor Morgan's blockade spurring the flames within her. At her core, they rotated faster and harsher with each rotation. It hated the resistance, wished to create enough speed to ram down the wall. To devour it. Sera gripped her abilities.

"You must let it go; I can handle it," Doctor Morgan said measuredly.

She surrendered to the ravenous surge. Doctor Morgan's wall receded slightly against the rush of wildfire battering against it, an intoxicating, blinding, glorious flare of heat. The only other time Sera had experienced such raw power was when she'd burned down the forest during last semester's Solstice Dance. That fire had been a beast, angry and raw, and dormant for months now, it woke from its slumber.

A slice of pain cut behind her eyes, scattering like a web of lightning. Sera winced as intense cold radiated across her skull. Sera groaned and gripped her wand tighter. A tinkling rattle resounded as the furniture and trinkets around them trembled. The candles flared, and the shadows in the room danced in the new, agitated light.

"All right, I see it," Doctor Morgan said, her voice strained. "Draw your magic back."

The feel of Doctor Morgan's powers subsided within Sera, but her magic no longer cared and roiled with the rabid need for release, to wrap everything in flames. Fire lashed her joints and bones and muscles and rushed to her hands. Sera ground her teeth tight against the strain of keeping her powers confined, but there was no way she could draw this amount of magic back. She needed to spend it somewhere, and everywhere was too dangerous. This fire was cruel enough to burn down the school and everyone in it, herself included.

The Aetherium crest on the wall tumbled to the bed. The jug of water crashed onto the floor. All color drained from Doctor Morgan's face, her eyes widening. "It's too much magic to draw back safely," she realized aloud. She ran for a stick of chalk on the worktable. "A containment spell—no, it won't keep you safe." She dropped the chalk and pressed a hand to her forehead. Spun in a tight circle. Frantically looked about the room for somewhere Sera could unload her magic.

Warmth dribbled from Sera's nose and onto her upper lip: blood. A thin layer of fire rolled over her wand and crawled up her hands. She couldn't hold this magic for much longer.

"Go," she muttered through clenched teeth. "I will hold it back for as long as I can."

Doctor Morgan gasped, ran to her wardrobe, and yanked open the door. Pressing her index finger to her mouth, she nicked her skin with her teeth and scribbled a series of ciphers on the glass. She turned the mirror to Sera. "Release your magic and focus it here. The mirror will absorb it."

Sera met her stare, her breaths breaking in her chest and her entire body trembling. "Just...go. I don't want to... hurt you."

"Miss Dovetail, trust me." She moved behind the wardrobe door. "Go!"

Sera aimed her wand and relinquished. A bestial wave of fire roared from her hands, consuming her wand. The single fiery shaft crashed against the glass and through it, vanishing into whatever void existed on the other side. Sera expelled the flames, her magic churning and churning out fire until the numbness of spent reserves flooded her veins, and the fire waned.

Fatigue clamped its bite into her bones, and her knees

buckled. She collapsed back onto her chair. A headache pounded behind her eyes in tune with her frantic heartbeats, but at least her magic was settled now, a satiated animal sinking back into slumber.

Doctor Morgan rushed from behind the wardrobe door, breathless. "Are you all right?" She hurried across the room and sat before her. "I—I didn't expect your magic to react in such a way, though with your past, I should have known better, should have had an adequate outlet," she rambled. She cupped her mouth with trembling hands. Her skin was clammy, and Sera knew that though their battle had been a mental one, it had taken its toll on her reserves as well.

"The mirror was enough," Sera said, glancing at the glass that was now stained black. "Though it won't be of much good to you anymore."

Doctor Morgan blew out a breath and settled back, a slight sheen of sweat on her brow. "It's temporary. The darkness will vanish once the magic you poured into the glass fades. For the time being, it works as a scrying glass, should you need one. It's how they're made and strengthened, by continuously pouring magic into them."

Considering the blackening glass within the school, Sera's eyes narrowed. Could it be Meredith was attempting to turn whatever reflective surface she could find into a scrying glass in her desperate attempt to somehow find the children? Given her delicate mental state, Sera didn't doubt this. She'd seemed desperate enough at the smuggler's den. *A crisis of conscience, indeed*, Sera mused.

Doctor Morgan's mien dimmed. "And speaking of magic pouring into a vessel, I was able to see your reserves and your powers. Your magic is fine and impressively strong. Your reserves, however... I'm terribly sorry, Miss Dovetail, but it appears they're shattered."

All thought of Meredith vanished. As did Sera's pulse. And despite Doctor Morgan's previous warning, Sera shook her head. "I... I can't be." Her words faded, her throat thick and dry. "Maybe I'm tired. I've been through a lot. It might be trauma..."

"Miss Dovetail, the symptoms are all consistent—"

"The professor and I have been working a rather difficult case lately. And with exams, I'm overworking myself and perhaps it leaves me susceptible to the ghosts..."

Doctor Morgan set a hand over Sera's, her look one of pity and a silent *I'm sorry*. "I will do everything in my power—"

Sera slid her hand away and rose from her chair so quickly it toppled back. She didn't want anyone to touch or look at her. She didn't want to speak. To think. To breathe.

"I know this is hard, but shattering isn't an immediate thing; it takes continuous uses of black magic to fully break. So long as you don't use death magic, your condition shouldn't worsen. But using it again can cause severe conditions, so I beg of you to refrain and insist you take care. As a precaution, use magic only when necessary, and even then, try and limit its intensity as best you can. I will be going back home this weekend to look over my friend's research. We'll talk when I return and come up with a suitable plan of action."

She met Sera's stare, and though she was pale and weary, her gaze was firm and honest. "We will get through this, Miss Dovetail. You're not alone."

But Sera shook her head, pain and panic like fingers weaving their claws into her chest. She couldn't do this with Doctor Morgan. Not now. She didn't want plans and promises. She couldn't bear one more try at hope. How many times would her dream be built up, only to be snatched away? How many times did her heart have to break?

"I have to go," she breathed and stumbled to the door. With her reserves so low, she could barely walk straight. But with Doctor Morgan also weakened, she was unable to stop Sera from reaching the door.

"Miss Dovetail, please," she called, but Sera lurched into the hall. Closing the door behind her, she staggered out into the newly settled night.

This couldn't be happening. She couldn't be shattered, reduced to nothing but a vessel for ghosts to possess and commandeer at will. Worse, she'd been a fool to think she was done with Noah now that he was truly and fully dead. He'd marked her body with his evil, and because of him, her reserves were also hurt. How long would she have to suffer his influence on her life? Would she ever be free?

Leaning her head back, she took in a shuddering breath but paused. Light shone from within her tower room.

Meredith.

Sera's anger roiled. Driven by rage, sorrow and guilt, she moved toward the main building, through the corridors now a touch dimmer due to the blackened windows. Up, up, up she climbed to her tower room. Lucid or not, Meredith would answer for what she did to the children. And if they could be saved, Sera would force her to say where she could find them. Too long had monsters gone unchecked to inflict their cruelty upon the world, a viciousness that reverberated even when they were gone.

She pushed the door open and rushed inside, her wand raised. If Meredith thought she would escape again, she had another think coming.

She stopped short at the sight of Hadden Whittaker by the open wardrobe. Behind him, Meredith's carpetbag was open, her dresses spilling out the top.

He fixed a black gaze on Sera and gripped his hands at his side. "So, this is where you're keeping her? Right beneath our noses." Whittaker raised his wand. The writing desk and chair raked across the room. Sera jumped aside. They clambered over one another in a discordant rattle and blocked the door. "Tell me where she is, seventhborn. Where's Mary?"

Sera gripped her wand tighter. Her magic roiled within, a weak flame she doubted could do any real damage after having been spent with Doctor Morgan. But she bit her nails into the encasement. However little, it would have to be enough. "Don't do anything you'll regret."

"Or what? You'll set me on fire?" He bared his teeth, a feral animal in wait to strike. "Try it, witchling." He punched his chest with a fist, a hollow thump resounding. "Try to burn me like you've done before."

Sera clenched her jaw. This was impossible. She had to mind her magic, but the look of murder in his eyes told her now was not the time.

"Tell me where Mary is and Delacort might let you rot in a hovel with the rest of your kind." He glared at Sera. "The way Timothy is rotting in a grave."

"Is he why you're doing this? Timothy was your friend; he wouldn't want this."

"He was a fool! Soft and stupid and willing to give up everything for you."

Sera flinched. She'd known Timothy loved her—he'd told her numerous times, and they were his last words when he died. And yet, to hear it from Whittaker stirred what magic she had inside.

"But he promised me his father would get me into the Aetherium without a referral, and now he's dead, because of you! I will get what I was promised, witchling. If not from the son, then from the father. All I have to do is find Mary and kill you."

Sera clutched her wand tighter. The old Whittaker may not have, but this monster standing before her wearing the face of a man most certainly would. He was so desperate, Sera was sure there was little he wouldn't do.

He paced forward. Sera watched him closely as he spewed his venom, anticipating his next move the way Barrington had taught her.

You must always be one step ahead while calculating another.

His movements were slow, his stare keen on Sera with a black intensity, so acute it dwarfed the room and deepened the shadows. She moved diagonally away and toward the door, refusing to remain near him. So long as she dominated their distance, she was safe and could collect her magic until she could pool enough for a formidable defense when he attacked; she was not leaving here without a fight. If it were up to him, she wouldn't leave here at all. At least not alive.

Seeming to gauge her intentions, Whittaker raised his wand and brushed it aside. Her old bed shifted in Sera's direction. She jumped back to avoid getting hit and aimed her wand, but Whittaker had already speared another blast of magic at her. The burst rammed into her like a boulder and slammed her back against the wall, her spine cracking against a shelf. Sera cried out, her scream in time with the tolling bells, and she crumpled to the floor.

Pain radiated across her back, and a headache dug its vicious claws into her skull, made worse with each of her quickened heartbeats. Her magic roiled inside, a weak flame that dispersed under the blinding pain.

"You have some nerve coming back here, parading yourself like nothing happened—as though you did nothing to cause Timothy's death." His lips pulled back into a snarl. "You lured him to that church, and now he's dead. He was my friend, and you took him away!"

Anger soured Sera's stomach, and her scattered magic surged from the farthest reaches of her being and pieced itself together. A venomous wave of heat bloomed from her core, and she thrust a surge of magic in his direction in the form of white bands to restrain him. She didn't have enough in her for more.

He moved his wand in a swift arc motion and deflected the bands. The white strands veered right and wrapped around the Aetherium flagpole instead. He aimed his wand again and drove a continuous shaft of ravenous wind at Sera. Air manipulation was not her forte and it was clearly his inclination. Still, she gathered what magic she had and met his attack with a gust of fire.

His wind splintered her shaft of red flames and drew closer, but she had to hold him at bay until she thought of something—anything to give her a fighting chance. He would kill her otherwise.

She cried out; the pain in her head now wormed down into her body and numbed her limbs, her reserves dangerously low. There was no telling how long her magic would last…but if she used this small amount to summon the spirits, then perhaps she could defeat him with their help.

Doctor Morgan had warned her against using her magic, but she would never survive this fight. She focused her powers and opened her mind to spirits, but her reserves were much too spent and the sense of ghosts too far.

Fatigue became a rabid beast that devoured the last of her strength. Her knees buckled, and her shoulders gave way. Whittaker's blast crashed into her chest, one blow thrusting her back against the curio cabinet. Her ribs felt to shatter within like the cabinet's glass doors at her back. Pain crackled through her body like electric currents wishing to animate her limbs, but they simply wouldn't start.

Warmth spread beneath her. Sera glanced down. A shard of glass punctured her shoulder, and blood bloomed around her, staining her maroon gown a deeper shade of red. But things couldn't end this way. Maybe if she could gather what infinitesimal magic she had, she could heal herself.

She lifted a hand to tug out the glass. Her fingers tangled with Barrington's necklace instead.

A hiss resounded, and a sudden coolness swept over the room. Billows of smog spilled out from the glass panes at the window and the wardrobe mirror. The white smoke filled the room. Fear thickened Sera's throat; she wasn't doing this, and as Whittaker spun in a circle, she realized this wasn't her second sight. He could see this, too.

"You think this parlor trick is going to save you?" He turned to her, but his gaze drifted to the wardrobe mirror closest to him, and he froze.

Sera followed his gaze. Her throat dried. Reflected in the glass was the emaciated woman she'd seen during her Aether exam. Her face was downcast, but she glared at Whittaker through a part in her stringy black hair stiff with frost.

Rime crawled out from the mirror, spreading along the floor like icy vines and around Whittaker's feet. She reached for him, and closed her rotted fingers around his neck. He sucked in a gasp, and his eyes widened.

Thoughts sped past Sera's mind at an alarming speed, Meredith's words come to haunt her.

She could be watching. She's everywhere.

Awareness struck her. The Enchantress was real, and she had taken the children. Now Whittaker grew translucent, and within moments, he was gone.

Blunt cold stabbed into her leg. She glanced down. Frost crept up her skirts, which grew frigid and firm.

Sera kicked, but ice shot through her veins in a paralyzing rush, and the order never reached her limbs. Cold wormed around her chest and squeezed, then scuttled up her throat. The Enchantress turned to Sera, a sick fascination in her black eyes. She reached for her.

With the pendant clasped between her fingers and the last drops of magic she had, Sera focused on the cool metal, and everything faded to darkness.

The next moment, she crashed face-first onto a carpeted floor and cried out; the collision pushed the glass deeper into her shoulder, and a shock of pain ran down her arm like nails tearing at her skin. Frantic and shivering, she attempted to move, but ache gripped her and she sobbed again.

A door was thrust open before her. "Miss Dovetail?"

The world was a painful amalgamation of unstable shadows and light to her eyes, but she would recognize Barrington's voice anywhere.

Beside her in an instant, he curled an arm behind her back and knees and lifted her up against him. The next moment, she was laid back onto a soft and inviting surface…a bed. But something wasn't right. This place felt different than his home, cold and vacant, and it smelled sweet. Too sweet.

But these facts were thoughts her mind was too tired to process, and they faded away. There was just the ache in her skull and the pain radiating from her shoulder.

"She's real. The Enchantress…" she struggled to say, but her words were gurgled and hoarse.

Barrington took her face in his hands, grazing his thumb along her cheek. Frantic gray eyes took her in and locked on the glass shard in her shoulder. He met her stare. "I can't heal you unless I take it out. This is going to hurt. I'm sorry."

He yanked the glass out before she could agree.

White, blinding, and searing agony filled her head, and a scream tore through her throat. Barrington pressed a hand onto the wound as a flood of coolness washed down her body. Weak cries slipped from her lips, the ripple of his magic agitating the pain of her broken ribs.

He closed his other hand behind her neck and leaned forward, then touched his forehead to hers. "I'm so sorry," he said.

A jolt of his magic flushed her chest with cold and gripped her ribs. The ache too much to bear, Sera screamed into unconsciousness. But in that moment before the world faded black, it wasn't her cry she heard. Rather, Barrington's voice in her ear as he held her close and whispered, "I'm so sorry, *my love.*"

13

the boy i fell in love with

She blinked her eyes open but groaned and closed them again, the light in the strange room like needles to her pupils. Barrington ordered someone to turn down the lights, and then the mattress beside her dipped. His scent swept over her, a much-welcomed comfort over the tart odor in the room.

Sera sucked in a breath, his cool hands suddenly at her temples. "It's just me," he coaxed her. "You're safe now. I'm here."

Cold prickles of his magic crawled down her body and up into her head, and the pain subsided significantly. When it no longer seemed like her eyes would melt if she opened them, Sera lifted her lashes. The world morphed from indiscernible smears to Barrington towering over her. Her heart jerked with emotion, but her stomach readily sunk. Gummy stood just behind him, her full figure covered by a floral robe open precariously low. She slung a hand onto her waist, a frown on her lips. Her face was bare, missing her usual layer of heavy eye paints and rouge. It made her look younger and her skin supple, though given Barrington's product, that could all be an effect of Beauty.

Of course. The sweet smell. The cold and devoid atmosphere. Gummy's brothel.

It was Sera who frowned now. Of all the places for Barrington to be when she needed him, he had to be here. Worse, would he have really called her *my love* in front of Gummy? No, that had probably been the delusions of a broken body, a tired mind, and spent reserves.

Still, matters of the heart had to wait. Finding Meredith and the children was now doubly important after having seen the Enchantress.

Sera tried to lift onto her elbows, but Barrington eased her down. "What happened? Tell me everything."

The events of the night rushed out of her. "He was manic and blamed me for Timothy's death. He said Delacort tasked him with finding out where Mary is and then he was to kill me. That's when…the Enchantress took him."

Gummy snorted from her vanity across the room, where she pinned up her brown hair.

Barrington's brow dipped. "Miss Dovetail—"

"I know what I saw. There was smoke and a woman in the glass, but it wasn't Meredith. She had a plague mask, like the woman in Serena Shaw's picture. It makes sense—the mirrors and the disappearances. Meredith warned me the children were here and there. I thought it was the ships, but it's the glass. We have to warn Mrs. York. The school is in danger."

"I will go back to the school and see what's happened and will warn Mrs. York if needed," he said.

"You don't believe me? I felt her icy tentacles around me, watched Whittaker disappear."

"Your reserves were also spent, which is known to cause hallucinations. And after learning of Serena Shaw last night, dealing with your ghosts, the case, and a week of testing…

That's a lot of stress on your magic and your mind."

Her eyes widened, and a blush gathered at her cheeks. "I'm not mad!"

"I'm not saying you are, but we are stewards of facts and logic."

She opened her mouth to protest, but he said first, "I promise I will go with an open mind and alert Mrs. York regardless." Barrington's eyes darkened, his entire mood shifting to a man set on ruin and devastation. "Right now, I want to find Mr. Whittaker."

Panic gripped Sera by the throat. She flinched and dug her fingers into his arm. "Be careful."

He touched her chin. "Aren't I always?"

Furious warmth spread through Sera, and all pain, the bed, the room, and Gummy faded away.

Seeming to remember time and place, Barrington lowered his hand and cleared his throat. "I must go now. If any of the staff heard anything, they might report it and contaminate the scene. I will be back shortly."

She gripped the sheets. "You're leaving me here?"

"Rosie and Lucas are out, and I don't want you home alone in this state. You'll be safe here."

"This will cost you extra, Barry," Gummy said.

"Barrington," he corrected her. Standing, he turned a steely gaze to Gummy. "I will include the fee with the remaining amount I owe you once you find Armitage. The shipment I've just given you is more than enough to expedite the search. For the time being, guard Miss Dovetail with your life."

Gummy crossed her arms over her chest and pursed her lips, but she nodded.

A low humming resounded, and his appearance grew transparent with each second as he transferred. He exemplified perfect mastery over his magic, and a terrifying chill washed down Sera's spine. Whittaker might fare better with the Enchantress.

Still, worry gripped Sera's heart. She had seen the Enchantress, and nothing would make her doubt.

Gummy sighed. "Don't look so glum. He's not going to kill the boy...or maybe he is." She waved a hand airily, tightened the straps of her long, flowery robe, and turned back to the ornate vanity mirror. The room was lavish, the furniture an amalgamation of gold and beige pieces. Even the bedspread Sera clutched in her fingers was of the softest silk, stitched with small gold flowers.

Sera blinked, awareness flushing her cheeks with warmth. This was Gummy's private room.

Grunting, she set her jaw and struggled to stand, but pain radiated across her chest and she winced. But regardless of the ache, she tried to stand again. There was no way she could stay. Anywhere was better than here.

Gummy watched her struggle from under an arched brow. "I can call someone to help you, you know."

Sera gripped the nightstand and braced. It was going to hurt, but she could do this. "I can manage."

She hummed. "Suit yourself." Gummy opened a canister of ivory cream. Brushing a curl behind her ear, she dipped two fingers into the balm and applied it to her skin in graceful strokes. Sera swallowed. Did Barrington sit here and stare at her, pleasure coursing through his veins as he did so?

She shook away the thought. "Where are your transfer stations?"

Gummy laughed, a low, sinuous rumble in her chest. "And where do you think you're going?"

"Back home or to the Academy." *Anywhere that isn't here.*

She scoffed. "No, you're not. You're his pet, and if anything happens to you, it will be my neck. And"—she met Sera's stare in the reflection—"there is something I think we should discuss."

Sera hobbled to the door, a hand pressed to her side that pulsed with each step. "We have nothing to talk about." She gripped the glass doorknob.

"It's about your family."

Sera's fingers fell from the handle, the word "family" like a punch to the gut.

"Barry has been inquiring about memory chambers and binding spells and the like, and he has been quite unlucky."

Sera faced her. "And?"

"And I'm the person you're looking for, Miss Dovetail. I can help you unlock your memories."

"You?" Sera scoffed, unsure whether to laugh or burn the room down around Gummy, had she the magic to do so, of course. "What would you know about memory chambers?"

"Tsk, tsk. Barry's arrogance is rubbing off on you, girl. Do you really think liquor and sex are the only ways my girls gain information? Let me guess. You also thought Mr. Armitage was just a lowly thief? Though a bastard, he was a great teacher and taught me that sometimes the most valuable riches are found in a man's mind. He showed me the basics during my time with him, but enough to help you unlock some of the doors inside that head of yours."

She motioned to the settee opposite her with a finger, her nails bright red. "Hear me out, and if you don't like what I say, I will transfer you back to Barrington's home myself."

Crossing the room, Sera sat.

"I think we got off on the wrong foot, you and me. You see, in the end, we're not so different."

Sera bit back a sneer. "We are nothing alike."

"Aren't we, though?" She closed the canister of cream and turned to face Sera. Tilting her head to one shoulder, she dissected her as though she could see through her skin. "Yes, we're both too independent for our tumultuous times, full of fire and magic that few men can appreciate...save for Barry, of course. Prepared to do anything to get what we want and fight to the death when we're cornered."

"And I'm supposed to think you want to help me out of the goodness of your heart, because we're so similar? It's no secret you don't like me."

"And the feeling is mutual, I'm sure, but the sooner you regain your memories, the faster you'll be out of Barry's life. You think he hasn't been able to find a magician to break your spell chamber? He has, but no one will risk their lives for a schoolgirl, much less a seventhborn. Spell chambers are volatile and dangerous, and breaking them costs more than even our dear Barry can afford." She crossed one leg over the other, exposing her smooth alabaster skin. "Take the offer, witchling. I doubt you'll get another as good as this."

Sera blinked. She'd prepared for her and Barrington's imminent separation were she to pass her exams, but she never imagined it would be forever. But while the thought of no longer being in Barrington's life was painful, the mere possibility of leaving him to this place—*to her*—spurred her anger the most. "Why are you doing this? What do you want?"

"I want you gone. I thought he would have rid himself of you by now, but from what I've just seen, apparently I was wrong. Whatever his reasons for keeping you, seeing as he hasn't come to his senses yet, I will do the dirty work for him. Your memories in return for your exit from his life."

"You can have any man here at your beck and call. Why the professor? I'm sure he's not the only one capable of supplying you with blood magic."

She stroked a finger along her pouty lower lip. "Oh, Barry is a great manufacturer to be sure, but he is wonderful at so much more." Sera pursed her lips, but Gummy waved off her disgust. "Swear a blood oath to me that you will give him up, and I will help you unlock the memories in your pretty little head."

"You're mad if you think I believe you."

"Then let me give you a taste of what you can have if you accept my generous offer."

She touched Sera's hand. At once the world swayed nauseatingly around her. She closed her eyes at the sensation, and when she blinked them open, she gasped. They were no longer in Gummy's room, but rather the vestibule of stone within her spell chamber. Sera peeled back, a cold chill skittering down her spine. For months she'd attempted to find this place, even if only to stare at the doors and beg for them to open.

To release her memories. To make her whole.

She looked at Gummy. "How did you…?"

"Usually it takes time to find a magician's spell chamber, but blood magic heightens my abilities tenfold…" She trailed off, moving to the nearest wall. The space between the damp stones glittered blue like before, telling of magic, only now there were hairline cracks running the length of the wall. Shimmery drops streamed down the wall and pooled on the ground.

Gummy spun in a circle and arched a brow. "Seems like I propositioned you at the right time. Your spell chamber is falling apart."

Doctor Morgan's revelation whisked through Sera's mind, and her pulse quickened. The torchlights flanking the various doors rustled violently, and phantom wind wheezed through the cracks in the walls. Her reserves were broken, so it was logical that this place, built and sustained by her magic, would be broken, too. But…

"What happens if it breaks? Will my memories be free?"

"Quite the contrary. You will lose them forever."

Sera shook her head. "You're lying," she said. There was no way she could trust Gummy, yet the mere possibility that she could be right spurred Sera's panic, and pain crowded her heart. The hallway shook around them, the gates rattled on their hinges, and the doors shook in the frames.

"Relax," Gummy snipped. She spun to Sera and, gripping her shoulders, gave her a firm shake. "Relax, girl! Or else you'll trap us both in here."

Sera took in a deep breath and forced herself to calm. Her spell chamber was breaking, but it wasn't yet destroyed. She could still recover her memories.

I will find my family, she thought to herself like a mantra. *I will find where I belong.*

The walls stopped rattling until all went still and quiet, the only sound the droplets of magic falling onto the stone floor and the now-calm whooshing of the torches around them.

Gummy dropped her hands from Sera's shoulders, a frown creasing her forehead and her mouth clamped tight. "Come, I must inspect the chamber, but keep your emotions under control or this place will crash down around us, and Barry is no good to me if I'm dead."

They walked along the corridor of doors. In only her thin robe, Gummy trembled and stroked her arms as though to conjure heat. The bottom of her floral robe dragged on the stone and was now a darker shade of red.

"Can't you make it a little warmer?" she hissed, her teeth chattering.

Sera gazed around at the doors, to the torches offering little light and no heat. "I don't know how this chamber was constructed at all, much less how to make it warmer."

"Well, that's easy enough to find out." Gummy approached one of the illuminated doorways. Sera debated warning her against touching the locks; her first time in the spell chamber, she'd touched a padlock and singed her skin on the hot metal.

Before she could decide whether or not to issue caution, Gummy brushed her robe aside and snatched her wand out from her garter. The tip was filed to a sharp point, which she pushed into the lock and turned over. She hummed and moved aside for Sera to see.

Sera froze. "That can't be." Her own name was etched into the back of the lock.

"It can. You created your own spell chamber, and so you can make it warmer. Though, never mind that." She looked around the entryway. Drops of magic dripped from thin crevices. "This place is unstable as it is."

"But how could I create this spell?"

Gummy released the lock, a loud clang resounding as it fell back onto the gate. "Not a spell, but spells," she said, stressing the *S*. She abandoned the doorway and continued on down the hall. "A binding spell chamber is a series of spells built independently of one another and then brought together to form a hall such as this. Whenever a new spell is attached onto the existing, it results in a new door…but it takes a great deal of skill to build one properly."

She continued, "Our memories and abilities are, for all intents and purposes, countless different threads. When dealing with spell chambers, we must isolate the threads we wish to bind and form the spell around them. But it's a dangerous and unpredictable spell, old magic that must be wrestled into submission. If you don't put an end to the spell, it will devour all your memories, sucking everything in like a vortex until there is nothing left. Given the breadth of your chamber, I suspect that's what happened to you."

Sera's heart dimmed. Knowing how uncontrollable her magic had been, she deduced this to be the case; she'd somehow lost control and didn't put an end to the spell, and now all her memories were stuck behind doors.

"All right, I've seen enough. This trip was free, witchling, but if you want to open these doors, you know the price. And I suggest you accept my offer." She glanced around. "You're running out of time, and the moment this place crumbles, not even I would be able to help you."

The spell chamber vanished from around them, and they were back in Gummy's room.

Gummy crossed one leg over the other, her brown eyes glittering with triumph. "So, do we have a deal?" She held her wand out to Sera.

As she considered it, Sera's heart thundered. For a long time, her driving force had been her family and the desire to find them, and yet to consider accepting Gummy's offer hurt her in the fiercest of ways, a metal rod flaying her soul. The ghost of Barrington's kiss on her temple and the memory of his shame strummed her heart, and she swallowed tightly.

Never would she have thought she would delay her dream of finding her family for anyone, especially for a man. But Barrington was more than that, and giving him up would be trading one half of her heart for another.

"No. I'll find another way to unlock my memories. Your only concern should be finding Armitage."

A flash of anger crossed Gummy's features, but a slow smile worked onto her lips.

"Oh, I will find him. Of that you can be sure. I always get what I want." A dangerous look glimmered in her eyes, and Sera shivered, unsure whether turning Gummy down so soon had been the wisest choice.

Spent reserves assured a magician of one thing: a lengthy and deep sleep. Sera woke up to Rosie reading at her bedside, where she confirmed Sera had been asleep the entire weekend. Sera sat up; her bones popped and cracked, and, sore, they weighed her down with the stiffness of someone who hadn't moved for much longer.

"Worse than the severest of hangovers," Rosie said, a hand at each side of Sera's temples. "What kind of magic were you employing, child? Your reserves were so low, you wouldn't have been able to light a candle had you tried."

The memories of her encounter with Whittaker brushed through her mind, chased by images of the Enchantress and Gummy's bargain. A fierce ache spread through her chest, but a more dispiriting thought pushed the pain aside. Had Barrington found Whittaker? Worse, had he encountered the Enchantress?

Her heart pounded as she sat up. "Is the professor in?"

"Of course. Can't you tell?" Rosie nodded to the nightstand. Sera followed her gaze to find a book there and, beside it, Barrington's glasses. There was also an empty goblet, a notebook, and a pencil. "The wards keeping this manor a secret are powerful, to be sure, but if anyone truly wants to find him, all they need to do is follow his mess. I'm sure he'd still be here," Rosie went on, pouring Sera a glass of water, "had that boy not gone missing. He was in his office all evening with Mrs. York about it. Horrible news, and so close to the election. She was frantic—well, as agitated as someone like her could possibly get. Not to gossip, but I've often wondered—"

"Rosie," Sera cut in as Rosie handed her a glass of water.

"What boy is missing?"

"The Whittaker boy."

The room whirled around her in one great spin. She clutched the glass to keep it from falling, and the water shuddered within. "Whittaker? Are you sure?"

"Yes, and it's quite the mystery. Apparently, a number of students and staff have all just…disappeared."

Sera set the glass aside, her hands trembling. She had to see Barrington.

She dressed quickly with Rosie's help and hurried down to Barrington's office. Her movements were stiff, and her knees cracked for the first few steps. When down on the second floor, she marveled she'd made it there in one piece.

She walked into the hall, toward his office.

"There was no way I could have known," said a feminine voice that sounded very much like Doctor Morgan.

"Truly, Cressida," Barrington said, confirming Sera's suspicions.

Sera stopped cold; a fist lodged in her belly. She shouldn't be hearing this, and yet, her body refused to move from the door.

"You have some nerve coming into my home and asking favors of me after you left her, drained of her reserves!"

"Nik, please." Doctor Morgan's voice broke. "To think I would have left her to Mr. Whittaker's attack is—"

"Is what? Farfetched?" Barrington cut in. "Is it really that unbelievable? The Brotherhood tried to kill her twice, Mr. Delacort would love to see her dead, not to mention she's a seventhborn, and you thought no one might want to hurt her? I thought you smarter than that. But then again, I shouldn't be surprised. You do have a tendency to leave people in need. Thankfully Miss Dovetail is still alive. Too bad Filip can't say the same."

Sera's eyes widened. *Filip?*

"Of course. This venom is about more than Miss Dovetail, isn't it?" She chuckled, a humorless, bitter sound. "Go on, then, Nikolai. What is it you really want to tell me? I suppose you've kept it to yourself out of respect for Mama, but she isn't here, and I'm not some impressionable young schoolgirl anymore."

"He trusted you, and you turned your back on him like everyone else. And to think he was going to marry you. Whatever atrocities he and my father may have been accused of would have been nothing compared to you carrying the Barrington name."

Sera's mouth gaped. Doctor Morgan was Filip's fiancé, and turning her back on Filip was how she'd broken Barrington's heart. Why she believed he would hate her forever. Despite this, Sera's cheeks warmed at Barrington's toxic tone, her anger simmering on Doctor Morgan's behalf.

"I accept my responsibility in how things ended with Filip," Doctor Morgan said. "I live haunted by it every single day. That's why I didn't come back. To be around the places he frequented…to be around you. But this isn't about us. I only ask that you read what's in his journal and help me. I don't know black magic like you, and the calculations are either incomplete or fundamentally Purist and beyond my expertise."

Sera gasped. The friend conducting heinous experiments had been…*Filip*?

"If you think your pathetic tears will sway me, you've obviously confused me with my brother. All I am interested in knowing is about Miss Dovetail and her ghosts."

"I can't discuss that with you. She's my patient—"

"Then get the hell out of my house."

Sera flinched; Barrington's wrath was wholly unfamiliar.

But Doctor Morgan didn't deserve this venom. Sera twisted the doorknob and rushed into the room. The air was charged with old pains and violence, and a similar storm brewed over the moors, gray clouds flashing white in the distance.

Doctor Morgan stood by the fireplace, her face in one hand, a thick journal cradled in the other as she wept.

Barrington opened his mouth, but Sera held up a staying hand. "Professor, that's enough." She moved to Doctor Morgan and drew her into her arms.

"She doesn't deserve your kindness," he seethed, and lightning crackled over the moors, followed by a deafening boom of thunder. "Filip needed one person, just one person to believe him, to be there for him—"

"He needed you!" Doctor Morgan sobbed, her voice shaking with pain and rage. She turned in Sera's arms toward Barrington. "Nothing I did could have ever taken your place. He missed you terribly. I know why you left; your father's obsession was stifling, and it ruined him, Nik. He filled Filip's head with his theories and experiments. I watched him succumb to that darkness. Suffered as he slipped away. You weren't there, but I was, and I saw the change."

She took a deep breath, then continued. "It was gradual at first. We bonded over death, yes, but whereas I sought to understand it…he wanted to control it. That darkness consumed him, and the Brotherhood seduced him with that power over time. He didn't resist. They gave him what he wanted most—freedom to hurt at will. And that's how I failed him, Nikolai. How I failed everyone. By not turning him in. By not denouncing him sooner. By not coming to you for help. I loved him more than I've ever loved anyone, but he was a monster, and I never said a word." She wept desperately, and pain gripped Sera's heart as she recognized the cries of pains long denied. She carried them within her over Timothy and Mary, over her family.

She looked up at the portrait of Filip and Professor Barrington as children that hung over the fireplace. "You love your brother, the sweet and gentle boy you remember. The boy I fell in love with." She shook her head, and cried freely now. "That's not the man he became. Those whom he loved, he loved. Everyone else was a specimen to him. Mere things to cut apart, to inspect and discard. Your brother was a—"

"Don't you dare finish that sentence."

She sighed, tired. Defeated. "Whether or not I finish it, you must believe me."

"Why should I? Because you're telling me, the woman who abandoned him? Because the Aetherium says so, the same people who turned on him based on the claims of a wretched human like Vincent Delacort?"

"Because of me," Sera said.

His silvery stare cut to her, those same eyes that had regarded her with such warmth. His hands clenched to fists, the same hands he'd used to hold and comfort her. If she continued down this path, there was a chance he would regard her with scorn. Would be too disgusted to ever touch her again.

But Sera didn't let this fear dissuade her. She couldn't.

"She needs you to read his journal because my reserves are shattered."

He swallowed visibly, the intent to speak weighing down his brow, but though he opened his mouth, no words came out. Still, she heard the question, and knowing there was a chance he would be disgusted in her, this wasn't a discussion she wished to have. But, taking the leather journal from Doctor Morgan's hands, she asked for some privacy so they could speak.

"I will be at the Academy for a few more days, in case you need me." Doctor Morgan squeezed Sera's hands and walked out of the room.

But Barrington only looked at her, unmoving. Unblinking. Afraid.

She walked to him and set the leather book on his desk, this tome that could potentially save her. And she sat across from him, just as she'd done when he'd asked her to be his assistant. The moment that started their journey. She hoped this discussion didn't prove to be their end.

"After I summoned the spirits to kill Noah and started having my problem with ghosts, we believed it was just a side effect of the death magic and that Armitage's wards would have helped me, but then things worsened. Where I was once able to banish ghosts simply by telling them to go away, that didn't work anymore. Now they were able to reach me."

A line formed on his forehead. "Reach you?"

She swallowed thickly. "At first they could touch me… and then they possessed me."

He pressed fingertips to his desk as if to keep from crumbling, and Sera's soul ached. Never had she seen him this disarmed. But with her labor of truth started, she couldn't stop now. "The first time was at the orphanage. A ghost took me to that pond, and had the Barghest not saved me, I would have died. The second was at Father Warner's home."

"No," he said, his voice breaking. "You would have told me. Why didn't you tell me?"

"After all you've done for me, I couldn't burden you with this, too. And once Delacort announced his black magic initiative, I feared this would drive you to darker magic and put you in more danger. But most of all, I was scared that you would be disgusted and would hate me, and I couldn't bear the thought of it."

He looked at her, the whites of his eyes glinting, but he said nothing. If it wasn't for the rise and fall of his chest, she would have thought him a ghost. But only the truth mattered now, above broken and hurting hearts, and so she continued.

"After I discussed things with Doctor Morgan, she recalled reading of similar symptoms in Filip's work about a condition called *shattering* and thought there might be something in there about how to fix me. And I know what it is I am asking of you, for you to consider that…that the things in your brother's journal are true, and I do not take that lightly. I swear to you I don't. Were it asked of me, I would probably refuse and—"

"I will look."

Sera blinked, her coming words dead in her throat. Did he… Did he say…? "You will?"

He nodded, just barely. "I can't promise I will find what you seek, but if it'll help you, I will do anything."

A breath broke in her chest, and the first tear spilled from her eyes. Then another and many more.

Barrington moved around his desk and brought her up in his arms, his hold tight and desperate, as though, all by himself, he could mend her.

"I'm scared," she confessed against his heart. "I'm so scared."

Resting his head on hers, he held her tighter. And where she thought he'd assure her everything would be all right, that they would get through this together, he said, "Me, too."

degrees of mourning

They stood there for some time, their bodies adhered in this quiet intimacy, as though testing the fit and feel of their togetherness and fading boundaries, until there was a knock on the door. Barrington sighed weightily, and they released one another, though they didn't move far. Sera held herself now, cold in the void of his embrace.

"Come in," he murmured, his voice a low rumble in the silence.

The door opened, and Rosie entered, a large envelope in her hand. Three bands marked the cream-colored envelope just beside an Aetherium crest. "It's just come, sir. You said not to disturb you, but it was marked urgent."

Barrington moved across the room readily and took the parcel. "Thank you, Rosie."

Rosie gave Sera a concerned look, but Sera smiled and nodded, assuring her she was fine. Rosie left the room.

Tearing open the envelope, Barrington pulled out a note and read it quickly. "It's from Mrs. York. Mr. Whittaker's parents have officially reported him missing."

"I knew it," she breathed and walked to the chairs before Barrington's desk, then sat down. "It was the Enchantress. I know what I saw. He was there, that wraith reached for him from within the mirror, and then he was gone. If I hadn't used the coordinate necklace, it would have taken me, too. And the night I found Meredith, I felt a ghost touch me, and then she went missing. And all of the faces I saw in the mirror during my Aether exam… I think it's everyone she has taken. And think of the mirrors. Serena Shaw's spell signature is on every piece of evidence we've found. Surely she's the Enchantress."

"Or perhaps Meredith isn't as frail as we all think and was influenced by tales of the Enchantress. With a bit of imagination and ill intent, she has used black magic to conjure up something with which to inflict harm. Given that Miss Shaw's spell signature was found at the scene, I believe it is a blend of death magic and mirror magic."

"Those are advanced arts and surely not something known by an orphanage matron," she countered.

He lowered his eyes to the journal on his desk. "Yes, well, not everyone is as they seem."

Sera pressed her fingers together, the desire to walk around his desk and hold him overwhelming.

Sighing, he handed her Mrs. York's envelope. "Given the disappearances, Aetherium guards questioned both students and staff. She's enclosed a copy of their reports to see if we find any similarities or patterns they've missed, as well as duplicates of their spell samples."

Sera took the file from him. "I will get started on this and send the Barghest out right away."

He pulled the journal closer. "I will be here if you need me."

The memory of his embrace warmed her, but the thought of his fear and trepidation at the coming endeavor sent a chill down her spine. "Would you like some help sorting through it all?"

Barrington lowered his eyes, his previous pain manifesting once again. "I would prefer to do this alone, but thank you."

Sera wished to insist, to be there and hold him and keep his hurt at bay, the way he'd done with her. But she nodded and walked to the door, wishing Barrington knew out of all he'd ever done for her, above kisses and protection and employment, his willingness to help her that moment despite the pain it would bring him was the greatest gift of all.

Curled up on the settee in the library, Sera reached for one of the open books beside her. Countless were spread over the table and the floor, some pages marked and others folded. Barrington would be cross at the state of his books, but finally, progress! Her previous search for the Enchantress had garnered little information, save for what menial descriptions she could find. But in light of Serena Shaw's occupation, Sera's current pursuit of texts on scryists proved much more fruitful.

For hours she pored over tales about the aether-inclined witches chosen to serve the Purist regime. Their task was to scry for seventhborns in hiding during the Persecutions.

She read,

To evade mass terminations, seventhborns used safe houses along their journey to wherever they could find safety. Purists employed their strongest scryists to track them down, but because seventhborns rarely owned any possessions or wands that could be used to trace them, scryists were instead trained to search for large clusters of negative emotion. Fear, sorrow, mourning, and feelings of the sort most likely experienced by seventhborns. It proved successful and led to thousands of executions.

Sera set the book down and picked up another. As she read on, her heart ached for both scryist and seventhborns alike.

Whereas modern scrying requires a magician to focus on a mix of mental images and an array of emotions, Purists were brutal in their approach. Taken in as children, these scryists were isolated, tortured, starved, and hunted, giving them firsthand experience with the emotions they would soon scry for.

Sera looked at the pictures on the page—Purist bastards in their plague masks standing with their hunting dogs, and sitting before them were young scryists covered in mud, leaves, and blood.

Mastering her anger and pity, she glanced down at the files Mrs. York had sent them of the missing students and staff. After hours of attempting to find similarities, Sera hadn't found any pattern to the vanishings, save for that they happened at the Academy during the past week.

But she pulled the files close now, using her newfound knowledge of scryists and emotions as a guide. Within minutes, she sat up straight, a pattern having emerged.

One student had lost her father. A maid had been abandoned by her fiancé. Mrs. James had lost her sister. Eliza had failed her exam. And, however much Whittaker wished to pretend Timothy's death didn't affect him, the Enchantress took him because he grieved his friend.

Following this trail of evidence, Sera thought on Meredith and the children. Meredith feared her charges had been taken and grieved their loss. The children, all seventhborns, no doubt lived haunted by feelings of abandonment and sorrow. And once they started to vanish one by one, they grew fearful.

"They were all in varying degrees of mourning," she whispered and looked at the Barghest, but the hound was fast asleep. He had spent the better part of the day tracking the magic samples Mrs. York provided them from the missing students and staff, but of course he'd uncovered nothing. Taken into the mirror world, they would never be found.

And the disappearances all took place at night, when a scryist's power is at its strongest.

But, Sera mused, how had the Enchantress found her way into the orphanage's mirrors and soon after the school's? Meredith was the only link between both places. Had she summoned her?

Sera groaned, the questions multiplying in her mind.

Gathering up her findings, she hurried out of the library and down the hall. She had to theorize with Barrington. She stopped at his office. It was empty and the journal gone. She walked to the workroom; he wasn't in the main space, but his private laboratory door was ajar. She should have left him to his discoveries, but the agony she'd sensed in the containment chamber spilled out from the part in the door, thrummed her heart, and drew her into the room.

She walked inside. His blood magic experiments rumbled lowly in the silence, and thunder rattled the windows, but Barrington was not there.

She moved past the tables of his product and paused. The door to the storeroom where he kept his father's and brother's things was partly open, Barrington visible through the seam.

He sat on the floor within the circular room, notebooks

and papers scattered around him. In his hands was Filip's leather-bound journal. He focused straight ahead, his gaze far and unblinking and his eyes glinting with unshed tears.

She entered the room and knelt before him. "Professor?"

He looked at her, and Sera's chest tightened. Though present in body, he gazed at her with the distant stare of lost faith, a broken heart, and an unmoored soul. The dangerous look of a man seconds away from sinking. She pressed her palm to his cheek, hoping to draw him back from this dark and barren place his mind wandered.

She glanced down to the journal he held and gently pried it from his hands. Setting it on her lap, she opened the soft skin cover and surveyed the contents. Her breath died in her lungs.

Crude diagrams of dissected bodies filled the book, horrid sketches bordered with measurements, required tools, and instructions. On others were scribbled notes of horrifying procedures in rushed and frantic handwriting, accompanied by the heinous results. Pages upon pages of unspeakable evils stained with smears of blood and all signed with the Barrington name.

Upon reaching the end, Sera paused. Stuffed between the last page and the back cover was a photograph of two men. One looked like an older version of Barrington, his skin weathered, hair silver, and his brow more pronounced. The other was identical to Barrington, only younger. But his stare was cold and unfeeling, like looking into a pit of ice. They both wore black robes with a raven crest on the breast. And tucked beneath their arms were black plague masks.

Barrington's father and Filip, in the Brotherhood garb.

And if there was any doubt, their names were scripted on the back.

All air left Sera in a painful gust.

"I thought they were delusions," he said, focused on the openness before him. "When I read some of Filip's notes long ago, none of it made sense. But this journal changes everything. He speaks of it, Sera," he said, his voice breaking on her name. "In these pages of madness, he speaks of shattering and the toll of the ghosts on a seventhborn's magic. The *deterioration of their souls.*" He gripped his hair and squeezed as if to keep the pain away. "How else would he know this?" He looked at her. "How else would he know?"

Sera shook her head. "I'm so sorry."

Standing, he paced slowly out of the storeroom and into the laboratory's main space, quiet. But outside the winds wailed and thunder rolled over the moors, shaking the windows on their frames.

He stared at the various tables filled with the brewing blood magic. The air in the room thickened with violence, and the candles in the room pulsed as if scared.

"To think of the things I've done for them." Lightning flashed, thunder echoed again, and with it, the deafening hush of rain. "I did this all…for them."

Sera made to walk to him, but he held out a hand, a pleading look in his stare. "Please, stay there."

He motioned aside with a finger; a protection spell burned into existence on the threshold. But what would she need protection from?

Before she could ask, he moved to the nearest table, gripped the edge of the desk, and flipped it over. Sera gasped, but the winds outside screamed and a crash of lightning overpowered her sound. He cleared the tables of his toxic experiments in one swipe, others he thrust aside. Books flew from the shelves, materials whisked out from within curios. A growl built in his chest, and, clenching his hands, he unleashed the roar, and everything burst into white flames.

Safe within the storeroom, Sera felt her magic spin wildly with a desperate desire to save him from this maelstrom of rage. But she could only watch blood-filled flutes crash and spill everywhere as he purged his soul of pain. Beauty, Knowledge, and Strength reduced to crimson smears on the walls, the floor. Him. Fire licking away evidence of the black magic he'd undertaken to clear his father's and brother's names only to realize they could never be cleansed.

The storm outside stopped, and the flames withered. Barrington stood in the middle of the chaotic chamber, his frame heaving and his hands covered in blood as burned pages from books floated down like phantoms around him. Defeated, he stumbled back over glass shards until he bumped against the wall. His knees folded, and he slid slowly to the floor, surrounded by all the things that shamed him and consumed him, the things he did to avenge a father and brother whose innocence turned out to be a lie.

"Do you think…" He swallowed tightly and clenched his jaw, but nothing could keep the tears from his eyes. "Do you think their cruelty is in my blood?"

"Oh, Nik." Sera waved a hand across gently and conjured a whispering breeze; the last licks of fire were extinguished, and the glass rubble whisked to the corners of the room. The blood remained. Still, she cut through the crimson stained floor to Barrington and sat beside him. "You are nothing like them. You are a kind and honest man with a good heart. What they did was their choice, and the blood they shed is on them, not on you."

He glanced down at his palms as though to make sure this was true, then dropped them onto his lap, hopeless. Sera touched his shoulder, and, as though he needed to be held with the same ardor with which she wished to hold him, he let her bring him down into her arms.

And they stayed like this, with blood and glass fanned all around them.

Sera pushed up to sitting and paused. She was in her room. Memories flooded her then, and warmth filled her chest. She and Barrington had remained embraced for hours until he had fallen into a grief-induced sleep. She didn't remember walking here, much less releasing him, which she'd never do. So, she must have fallen asleep also, and after he'd woken, he'd brought her to her room.

As she hugged herself, Sera's heart soared and equally broke. His grief that night had been a torment, and it pained her to see him hurt in such a way. But he'd needed her to hold him and accompany him in his agony. Not Rosie or Gummy. But her.

She dressed quickly, then walked downstairs. Would she once again find him in anguish? Or would his mood have shifted to denial, then anger, like hers had after Timothy's death?

Humming resounded from the inner workroom, and Sera's brow dipped. She rounded the corner. "Rosie?"

The stout woman spun to Sera, a bright look in her blue eyes. Behind her, the windows were open wide, the ivy cleared away, allowing for fresh air and shafts of golden sunlight. "Good morning, dear. I didn't sense you arrive, but you and the master feel so similar, it's sometimes hard to tell you apart."

Sera's blood warmed at Rosie's words. She often felt she and Barrington communicated on a different plane than everyone else, and that summer, consumed by their experiments, cases, and studies, it was as though they existed in another world. "I never left; I was asleep upstairs."

Rosie propped her broom against the wall. "So, you were here when…" She inclined her head toward Filip's journal on the table and, beside it, a retort hung over a small burner.

Sera nodded but inched closer to the new experiment. Black liquid bubbled within the glass flute, but while she wasn't sure what he brewed, she breathed freer at knowing it wasn't blood magic.

Rosie pressed her lips to a tight line. "I'm glad of it," she said, though hints of pain marred her stare. "No one should have to experience a truth like that alone."

"Are you all right? I know you cared for them both since they were children."

Rosie slid a chair back into place by the table. Gripping the wooden top rail, she cleared her throat, her nose and cheeks red. "As hard as it was to hear and see it, I think a part of me always knew. I just hoped against it. They were so different, you see. The master has always been a restless soul like his mother, ever since he was born. He constantly moved from one thing to the next before finishing the first. But Filip… He was never quite satisfied in this world. He had a keen and obsessive curiosity, an unquenchable thirst to know how things worked, very much like their father. When he stumbled upon black magic and death sciences…" She shivered.

Picking up her broom, she continued sweeping, as if to brush away the thoughts with each stroke. "It consumed him. He grew angry and cruel. At times, it scared me to know exactly what he was doing when I'd find blood on his shirts. I thought blood magic, but when rumors started to spread about murders and missing witches, deep down I knew. I had no proof, surely, just a nudging intuition. And it was all true."

She cleared her throat and wiped at the bottoms of her eyes. But, slinging a hand on her hip, she surveyed the immaculate laboratory, free of glass and blood, of heinous black magic and other dark arts. "Looks much better now, doesn't it? But it could use some flowers."

Sera smiled and, draping her arm over Rosie, gave her a half hug. "It's perfect, Rosie. You're a wonder for having cleaned it all so fast."

"Oh, it wasn't only me, surely. The master removed the larger things, and I tended to the rest. Besides, I imagined what was in here, and it always tore me apart to see him enter. I will clean this room a hundred times over, glad that it's all finally gone."

Sera was certain she would do the same. "Is he in?"

Rosie set an empty glass vase in the middle of the table, no doubt for the imminent flora she desired. "No, dear. He left early this morning and has yet to return."

A blush thorned Sera's cheeks within as a hollow ache reverberated in her chest. He must have left to see Gummy after he'd taken her back to her room. Perhaps to tell her he'd ruined their product and he'd be unable to fulfill her orders? Or did he seek comfort from someone who could soothe him in amorous ways beyond a simple embrace?

Her mind was cruel and conjured up memories of the previous night, of a grieving Barrington in her arms. Of his hands anchored into her as he wept and rid his soul of pain. She pressed a hand to her chest, the air suddenly too thin to breathe.

"Miss Dovetail? Are you all right?" Rosie asked.

Sera forced a smile, though inside her soul was slowly breaking. "I think I'll go for a walk. Let me know if he returns."

"Yes, of course." She glanced out the window. "It's a lovely day; best enjoy it now before winter comes to take it all away. Oh, perhaps you can find some nice flowers."

Sera nodded and left the room quickly, before she broke apart.

Downstairs, she pushed the double doors open and rushed out into the sunlit moors, farther and farther away from the manor. It did nothing for the pain that weaved around her bones and embedded into her soul. Still, she trudged forward against the combative breeze, toward the sea in the distance. Wild rolling fields spread all around her, steep hills and shallow caves full of secrets, just like their master. A patch of heather covered a large expanse of land. Sera ventured toward it with Rosie's request in mind.

Her own heartache aside, Rosie was right—some good had come of that night. Barrington now knew the truth, and it seemed he was done with blood magic. All that was left now was learning to live with the pain and, as Barrington once told her, make a life with what remained.

She stopped. A ghost knelt in the distance and plucked at the flowers, though her hands moved right through them. She clasped the invisible buds to her chest and inhaled as though they were a real fragrant bouquet. Sera spun away, lest she see her staring and wish to share her pain. Her next breath was a weak whisper.

Barrington emerged from over a slope but didn't see her. A breeze brushed his hair over his forehead, and his cloak billowed around him like wings. Dressed in a white shirt with no cravat, tan pants, and mud-speckled riding boots, he looked borne of his surroundings, a wild beauty, tamed by no one and shaped by the wind.

Her place of comfort and peace. Her home.

Behind him was the cemetery where he'd buried Filip, and Sera's chest ached. Had he just come from visiting his brother, or had the pain been so much that he never made it in? Whatever the case, should she stay, or had she intruded in his desire to be alone? And if she stayed, what would she say? Was "good morning" too careless a phrase? Was "I'm sorry" too little?

He lifted his head, his gaze fell upon her, and all her thoughts faded away. A small smile touched his lips, though it did nothing for the sadness in his stare. He stopped before her, and for a moment, neither said a word. The silence was filled by a cool breeze that tugged at her skirt and pulled at his cloak and filled the air with the scent of the ocean.

"You look surprised," he said then. "I take it we're not alone…"

"I… I didn't expect to see you here," she said, not wanting to discuss the ghost who still picked phantom flowers in her peripheral vision.

"No?" His eyebrows quirked, and he glanced around the moors. "I was under the impression I live here, but I've been known to be wrong…rarely."

A blush pricked her cheeks within. "I mean, I thought you'd be…anywhere but here."

He looked down to the swells of heather at their feet. "I thought about it, but the truth will never change, regardless of how far I go."

"No, I suppose it won't."

Silence.

"I should go," she said, though every fiber within her wished to stay with him and, if she was not able to soothe his pain, to at least travel it with him. "You probably want to be alone."

He shook his head, just barely, and held a hand to her. "Will you walk with me?"

Anywhere, her heart screamed, but she merely nodded and slid her fingers into his. He helped her down a patch of rocky terrain, attentive to her footing. But when down on leveled ground, he didn't let her go. She made no attempts to draw her hand away, either. They walked in a comfortable silence, testing the fit and feel of their entwined fingers, a delicate affection where their hands seemed to talk, asking one another, *Is this all right? Shall I let go, or can I hold you a little longer?*

Sera's heart thundered, her mind wondering if it was all a dream. A violent gust whisked past as if to blow away the thoughts.

"I read through Filip's work," he said. "His methods are definitely Purist and the calculations archaic, and I'm having trouble understanding them. If I had the texts he based his research on, I could figure it all out, but Purist writings are hard to come by. There's the library Timothy showed you; I'll have to double my efforts to get inside. In the meantime, I have something for you."

He reached into his inner pocket and handed her a vial filled with a black substance. The same she saw brewing in the workroom.

"Apparently, shattering is a black magic injury associated with seventhborns. Your reserves broke when you used death magic. Every possession after that is a blow to your reserves. The more ghosts that come through, the bigger the wound grows. Filip mentioned an elixir of black tourmaline and obsidian helped stabilize his...patients," he said, struggling with the last word. "I know the tourmaline in the wards I installed here has been ineffective, but that was because it only solved half of the problem. I didn't target what attracted the ghosts."

"And what is that?"

"You. Those who die knowing they are loved rarely return, but those who passed under excruciating circumstances are desperate to share their pain with someone who will understand. Your past made you a beacon. With your reserves shattered, they were able to slip through and possess you. The tourmaline in the wards clears negative energy from a space, but the obsidian cleanses those feelings from your aura, which in turn makes you less visible to the ghosts, or at least that's what he deduced."

He handed her the vial. She took it from him and gazed down at the tincture.

"Unfortunately, the dosage wasn't provided, and neither was the exact formula, but given what I know about both tourmaline and obsidian, the amount I've used in this potion isn't dangerous. It won't make the ghosts go away or heal your reserves, but it should make it so they can't see you. I'm not sure how long it will last, but with prolonged use, the tonic begins to lose potency, so Armitage's wards are the ideal solution until we're able to get into the library to translate the rest of Filip's work. So long as you don't use black magic again, the shatter shouldn't worsen, but still, be mindful of your reserves."

Sera blew out a breath, and, plucking out the cork, she put the vial to her lips and spilled the contents back into her throat. Partial relief was better than nothing. And if the ghosts couldn't see her, then at least she couldn't get possessed.

Bitter sweetness filled her mouth. She pressed her lips together to keep from throwing up, and forced the tonic down. Barrington gripped her shoulders, held her steady, and watched her closely, as though he could see the potion course through the map of her veins. Warmth washed through her in a single wave, but then everything went bitingly cold, and she hugged herself, shivering.

Barrington slid off his cloak and draped it over her shoulders.

"Thank you, Professor."

"Nikolai."

Sera lifted her lashes and met his stare.

"Unless, of course, you prefer to call me otherwise, like 'fool' or 'buffoon.'"

Despite their dark night and present uncertainty, a laugh bubbled in her throat. "I think I prefer Nikolai."

"Yes, I think I like that one, too."

"Sera."

He nodded. "Sera."

Lifting a hand, he untucked her hair from beneath the cloak's collar, chestnut strands that instantly whisked across her face in the savage breeze. Barrington caressed them down, his touch a whisper against her skin.

"I'm sorry about all of this," Sera said. "For Filip, for my shattering, for the journal... But thank you for considering it to be true, even if just to help me."

"You asked me once about a time I was most afraid. Last semester, when Mrs. York told me you were missing, that they suspected Noah Sinclair had taken you and they didn't know where. The thought that I had lost you, that you had moved on to a realm where I couldn't feel you, see you, hear you... There's not magic dark enough for what went through my mind."

He shook his head to himself, his brows drawn together as if the mere thought brought him physical pain. "I am a Pragmatic, Sera. Reason, certainties, and measurements are the core of my being, but I would shun every book and fact and search for the power over time just to bring you back to me. You are my greatest fear. My knowledge, my beauty, my strength. You're my religion, and for you, I'll believe in anything."

Tears filled her eyes, and though she forbade them to

fall, they spilled onto her cheeks anyway.

He took her face into his hands. "And I swear to you, Sera. I've failed you in everything else, but not in this. Whatever it takes, whatever the cost, we will find a cure. The ghosts can't have you."

She cried openly now. His words were sweeter than she'd ever imagined them, even if they'd been spoken here, amid his nightmare. Maybe she'd gone mad and this was all a dream borne of her grief and guilt, but she leaned her face into his touch; she would chase this madness anywhere.

Barrington didn't deny her. He skimmed his knuckles along her jaw, his look full of sorrow, yes, but also another emotion. One that searched her gaze openly and made everything grow hazy and warm. After Noah, she never imagined she'd want to be this close to a man, much less desire his hands upon her. That part of her had died, snuffed out and buried beneath every scar Noah had inflicted upon her flesh. And yet, she moved closer to Barrington, alive again.

His brow dipped, a look of pained restraint, of holding back before jumping wholly into oblivion. Cradling her neck in his hands, he rested his forehead against hers, the tips of their noses touching in contemplation. "May I kiss you?"

Sera's heart soared. Here, on the edge of her greatest fear and desire, he once again asked for her choice. "Yes."

He leaned closer, slowly, and pressed a tender kiss on one cheek. He waited, his breath a tremulous fog against her skin. When she didn't deny him, he kissed her other cheek. She didn't fight this, either.

His hands tensed on her shoulders, his composure clearly frayed and his eyes black with desire. "All in magic, Sera, tell me when to stop. I will go only as far as you wish for me to go."

A watery laugh escaped her. "I know."

His look changed then, as though longing were a starved spirit he had leashed. Now, unbound, he wound an arm around her waist and a hand behind her neck, and, drawing her against him, he kissed her.

The brush of his lips was gentle, his taste an intoxicating blend of black tea, sea air, and heather. But she craved more of this and parted her lips to welcome him further. To fill her until she could barely breathe. Barrington understood the unspoken request and groaned into their kiss, which grew deeper. Their bodies angled and aligned until they were flush against each other, yet she felt him entirely too far. He held her closer as though cognizant of the same, their hands anchored onto each other like souls clutching tightly to sanity. To life. To magic. To home.

Breaking away, he trailed kisses along her jaw and, brushing her hair over her shoulder, he journeyed his lips along her neck. Warmth flooded Sera at the feel of his mouth against the delicate skin there, and she arched into him, wholly disarmed.

This was what it was supposed to be like, what it was meant to feel like all along. To be kissed and held and wanted this way. To give freely of herself, without an edge of fear. Wholly happy. Wholly safe. Cared for and wanted. Free to simply be.

She weaved her fingers into his hair, wanting more of him. All of him. To know the full extent of passion free of pain and regret.

The winds changed direction, sweeping over the field toward the ocean, odorous of damp earth, moss, and…sulfur?

Something nudged her leg. Sera yelped and stumbled away from Barrington, breaking their kiss. The Barghest hovered beside them, his ruby eyes bright within the black cloud. He grumbled, and a letter dropped at their feet, covered in drool.

"Rosie must have sent him when she couldn't find either of us," she said as Barrington knelt to pick up the note. Holding it between his fingers, he tore it open and slid the cream-colored page from inside. He read it quickly and bristled as he scanned the page.

"What does it say?" she asked, mindful of the change in him.

"It's from Gummy. They've found Armitage."

15

mirror bound

The mood had instantly shifted, and there had been no time for etiquette…whatever decorum was appropriate after a kiss and confessions like theirs, Sera mused as she tied on her kit belt and picked up her cloak from her bed. The moment the Barghest had vanished, Barrington transferred them back to the workroom, where she revealed everything she'd learned about scryists and their purpose, as well as the connection of sorrow and mourning between the missing students and staff. She sensed a measure of doubt in him, but, as promised, he kept an open mind, and they agreed to meet once they were ready.

Picking up her veiled hat, Sera wavered at the door. How were they to act now that the real world had reasserted itself and she was once again his assistant? Or after his confession, was she now more? She pulled open the door and walked down to Barrington's office. These were things they would have to tackle later, despite the knot of nauseating uncertainty lodged in her stomach. Tonight, they would question Armitage, obtain her wards, and learn the entire truth about Meredith, her mirror magic abilities, and the scryist Serena Shaw.

She entered the room to Barrington sheathing his wand, though it was clear he had no intention of using it. Not with his aura dark and murderous as it was. He met her gaze; all his previous passion was gone, replaced by the cool and collected Barrington, the one angry enough to forgo magic, only finding pleasure in violence and blood. Dressed in all black, he was no longer an angel of tenderness but rather a harbinger of death.

"We leave for Gummy's at once," he said. "She says they found him at the ports just north of the Aetherium. He must have been seeking passage across. This also tells me he's on the run. I don't think it's a coincidence he goes underground the moment his sister vanishes and wreaks havoc on the Academy. Whether she is responsible for the mirror magic or has somehow conjured up a wraith that is, I believe this is why Armitage was so desperate to find her, and now that he can't, he's running away."

Remembering the Sister of Mercy, sourness settled in Sera's gut, the word *Delacort* surfacing from the far reaches of her mind. Surely he was involved somehow.

Barrington put on his top hat, then held a hand to Sera. Her pulse quickened, but, straightening, she walked around the desk and slid her hand into his. He brought her close, and a furious heat swept up her body. They'd done this hundreds of times, the need to transfer together vital for their work, and yet her mind whirled with other things they'd done together. Did he think of this, too?

Barrington touched his fingers to her cheek and answered the silent question. She looked up at him, his eyes darkened with a raging desire that made her knees a little weak. "Are you all right?"

Warmth flooded her cheeks, and she nodded. "Yes, very. You?"

"Yes, very." He took her hand and pressed a light kiss on her knuckles. "Perhaps we can discuss things a bit more later?" Though his look promised more than words, and Sera's blush deepened.

"I should like that very much."

He hummed, a low rumble in his chest. "Me, too."

And with mirroring smiles between them, they plunged into darkness.

They landed on a black marble platform lined with golden transfer wheels. Slow, hazy music came from outside the cream double doors bordered in ornate gold. And through there, Gummy's brothel. An older man who Sera recognized as Gummy's butler, Barnaby, approached them, wearing his usual uninterested expression.

"Good evening, Professor, Miss Dovetail," he said with a small bow. "Miss Mills is expecting you. This way, please."

He led them over the blue Persian carpet spread over polished wood floors and pulled open the doors. Laughter and music spilled into the room. Barrington reached beside him and, lacing his fingers with Sera's, pulled her close.

Barnaby guided them upstairs and into a circular parlor scented heavily of vanilla and lavender. Sera's stomach clenched, the fragrance thick in her throat. Various candelabras were stationed along the red-wallpapered room crowded with crimson settees and burgundy wingback chairs.

Gummy's girls were lounged along the couches, a dreamy look in their stares. One smiled at Sera; blood was smeared on her teeth. Another woman sat on a man's lap at a nearby table. She buried her fingers into his hair and yanked his head back. The man opened his mouth, and she poured a vial of blood magic down his throat. She proceeded to kiss him.

Sera tightened her hold on Barrington's hand. Like hell she would leave him to this place. If it were up to her, she would burn it all down.

They rounded a corner to a staircase and stopped. Gummy stood at the head of the landing, a hand slung on her hip. Dressed in a royal blue gown with a form-fitting, low-cut bodice and ruffled bustle, she sauntered down the steps. Her gaze flicked to Sera's hand in Barrington's, and a smile curled her lips. Despite their present situation, Sera's heart stuttered. Gummy was his lover, but what would happen now?

Gummy stopped before them but never acknowledged Sera standing there. "This isn't good for business, Barry. Friday nights are our busiest, and you're holding up one of my rooms."

"I will make it worth your time and inconvenience," he said.

Her brown eyes brightened, and she leaned into him, her ruby red lips pulled to a smile. Barrington reached into his inner pocket with his free hand and withdrew a velvet bag. "There's enough Beauty there to pay for rooming. I suggest you use it wisely; it is the last batch."

"For how long?"

"Forever."

A mix of shock and disbelief flashed over her eyes framed in black and purple eye-paint, but, setting her jaw, she handed the bag to Barnaby without checking the contents, then trailed a finger along Barrington's lapel. "Is that all I'm getting?"

Sera's stomach knotted, and her magic roiled within her. She clenched her free hand to keep from slapping Gummy's finger away from Barrington, but it wasn't her place; this was for him to turn her down.

He removed Gummy's hands gently and met her stare. "It's all I can give you."

Gummy's face hardened, a sudden darkness swathing over her features. She glanced at Sera and smirked, but her gaze held something much darker. "We'll see about that."

Unease filled Sera at the words and the black determination that made Gummy's eyes sparkle.

"Where is Armitage?" Barrington asked.

"Follow me." She led them down the hall, her walk graceful and sensuous, and all Sera could think of was a snake slithering toward her prey. She stopped at a drawing room, pushed the doors open, and strutted inside.

Armitage sat at an armchair before the unlit fireplace, but where Sera imagined him to be disheveled and apprehended in some way as other suspects had been when Gummy detained them in the past, he was dressed in an immaculate blue suit, unbound, and smoking a cigarette. Except for his palpable nervousness, Sera wouldn't have thought him a captive at all.

Gummy sauntered past him, slid a hand onto his shoulder.

At Gummy's touch, Armitage lifted his gaze. Upon seeing them standing there, he bolted to his feet. "Did you find my sister? Is she here?" he asked, breathless, through a plume of rose-scented smoke.

Barrington released Sera's hand and approached him. The fireplace behind Armitage roared to life, the flames white. "Sit down, Mr. Armitage. I will be the one asking questions here, and you will answer me truthfully or you will burn."

Gummy slid her hands onto Armitage's shoulders and encouraged him down into his seat; her hungry black gaze remained on Barrington.

"Now, now, Barry. We're all friends, here to do a bit of

business," Gummy said and glanced to Sera.

Concern crept into Sera's belly, but she pursed her lips and moved into the room. Sitting down at a blue tufted settee nearest Armitage, she drew out her notepad. She had no time for Gummy, not now, when there were answers to be had and monsters to be found.

"We have reason to believe your sister has used a combination of mirror magic and death magic, which has led to the disappearance of the children at her orphanage," Barrington said.

Armitage's blue eyes widened, and he flinched back. "No, you're mistaken. That's impossible."

Barrington went on, "She has now moved on to infect a school with her evil endeavors, and we seek to stop her."

He shook his head, strands of his disheveled black hair clinging to his forehead with sweat. "No, you don't know what you're saying. Meredith couldn't have done those things; she isn't trained."

"We have evidence," Sera said. "So how about we start again, with the truth this time? Spell signatures found on the orphanage mirrors and the school belong to a dead scryist, and your sister is the connection to both locations."

"I said it wasn't her," he growled, his blue eyes frigid and his face contorted with violence. Sera's magic rushed to her fingertips, but Barrington lifted a hand. Fiery bands of magic slammed into Armitage's chest and bound him to the chair. Thin, silver ropes twined tightly around his torso and feet, and thinner strands of magic were wrapped around his mouth. Droplets of blood trickled down from where they dug into his skin. Sera shook her head; gone was the man who looked borne of shadows. With his eyes wide and screams muffled through his gag, it seemed as if even they had abandoned him to Barrington.

"I would be mindful of how you answer our next questions." He brushed a hand aside, and the binds on Armitage's mouth vanished with a hiss. "Tell us what you know about your sister's abilities."

Armitage gasped in a deep breath but winced; reedy burn marks cut across his face from where the binds had singed his skin. "It wasn't her. I told her it was harmless." His gaze grew distant with the look of a man seeing all the events that led to his present situation play out in front of him, and with each moment, terror filled his eyes. "What have I done?"

"I don't know, Mr. Armitage," Barrington murmured. "What have you done?"

He swallowed tightly. Droplets of sweat streamed down his face, commingled with blood, and dotted his white shirt. "Last month, Vincent Delacort asked me to find the tomb of an old Purist scryist. He gave me the file of her information. I asked Meredith to research it for me; I always like to know what I'm being asked to steal, to make sure I'm charging an adequate price. She was frantic when she found out what scryists did, especially with her caring after seventhborns. She begged me not to take the job, but I didn't listen."

"Why was she so wary?" Sera asked.

"The woman I was asked to find was the Aetherium's strongest scryist during the Persecutions. She alone is credited with over a thousand deaths."

"What was her name?"

"Serena Shaw," he said, sniffling. "But in her reports, her commanding officers called her the Enchantress."

Barrington's jaw tightened, and the flames at the hearth flared. "Don't waste my time, Mr. Armitage. The Enchantress is a children's tale."

Yet, Sera's pulse quickened. Folktales often derived from

truth like the Scrolls of the Dead...

"She was real. I swear it," Armitage said. "I found her tomb; you can go and see for yourself. Her body is still there. Delacort only wanted the mirror."

Sera stopped mid-script. "Mirror? What mirror?"

"Mr. Delacort said she only used one scrying mirror throughout her entire career and she had it when she was buried alive. I promised Meredith she only had to keep it for a short time, while I asked for more money from Delacort. He said we could talk the night of the Feast of Edification. But by then, Meredith was gone, and so was the mirror. That's all I know, I promise. He wanted a strong scrying glass, and I wanted my money."

"What did this mirror look like?" Barrington asked.

"A hand mirror with a black glass and a floral pattern on the handle."

No...

The pieces of this devastating puzzle came together in her mind, and she set her notebook down, feeling utterly sick.

"That still doesn't explain the disappearances," Barrington said.

"Yes, it does," Sera breathed, understanding. "Serena Shaw used only one scrying glass for her entire career, feeding it magic continuously for years. She was mirror bound. So even when she passed away, her magic and soul never truly died. They live on in the mirror. While it was buried, it was unable to hunt, but then he stole it and gave it to Meredith to keep at the orphanage where the Enchantress took the children. When the children disappeared, Meredith fled but took the mirror."

Sera remembered her encounter with Claire, the seventhborn at the smuggler's den.

Many have been so desperate, they've just disappeared,

even after paying their fee. Left their belongings behind and everything.

"The mirror continued to hunt there. And after saving Meredith, I took her back with me to…the Academy."

"Where she continues to search for souls in fear and mourning, negative emotions, just as she was trained to do," Barrington said, awareness growing in his gaze. "Only now she drags them into the mirror world. But what on earth could Delacort want such a strong scrying glass for?" Barrington asked.

Sera's stomach knotted, the floor seeming to vanish from beneath her. "Mary. It was why Whittaker attacked me. He said Delacort wants her found."

Yet, Sera's suspicions flared. For months she'd wondered when the Brotherhood would come for her, to draw Timothy's spell from her brain by whatever method necessary. For her protection, Barrington assured her the investigative file mentioned Mary had been present during Timothy's death and Sera was held hostage too far to have heard their conversation. Mr. Delacort knew Timothy was the Keeper and died from revealing his spell. Did he then seek Mary to make her pay for luring his son to the Brotherhood, or did he seek to obtain the seventh spell himself?

A new wave of determination swept over Barrington. "We must secure the mirror and warn Mrs. York to evacuate the school and reinforce Miss Tenant's location."

"What of my sister?" Armitage said. "Is she safe?"

"Your sister was safe, before you gave her that blasted mirror. Now she is in the mirror along with her seventhborn charges, and we must find a way to get them out. But as promised, we found her, and now you owe us," Barrington said. "What are the wards needed to deter ghosts?"

He opened his mouth to speak, but the words tangled

in his throat. He tried again but sputtered nonsense and broken sounds.

Sera's pulse quickened, and the fires at the hearth withered as Barrington grew cognizant of the same.

"Unfortunately, he can't tell you," Gummy said, confirming Sera's fear. She stroked Armitage's hair away from his face and rested his head back onto her breasts. "At first I thought to kill him so that he could take the wards to his grave, but you're a necromancer, Barry. It wouldn't take long for you to raise his soul."

"What did you do?" he asked, his voice terse.

"In exchange for his life, he swore me an oath."

The floor swayed beneath Sera, and her stomach plunged. *I always get what I want...*

"What the hell have you done?" Barrington rasped, louder than Sera had ever heard him. A loud and dry crack chased his words, the windows all around them shattering.

"You paid me to find him, and I did. You never said I couldn't make a bargain of my own." She looked at Sera and smiled, despite Barrington's venomous glare. "When you're ready to make a deal about your spell chamber or your wards, you know where to find me. I have it locked away in here," she said, tapping a red-polished nail to her temple. "You know the cost."

Sera's magic roiled. Her breaths came in fast and raw. Around them, the trinkets rattled and the windows vibrated on their frames. "Move away from her," she ordered Barrington, the blunt of her magic coiled tightly in her belly.

"Sera, your reserves," he warned over his shoulder, but, trembling, Sera didn't care. There was just the fire rushing up her veins and the desire to see Gummy burn.

Barrington released Gummy and spun to Sera. "Look at me, Sera." Cupping her cheek, he encouraged her face to his. But rage built within her, and a plume of ravenous fire exploded over the walls. Flames shaded them in amber, but he brought his forehead to hers and held her closer in the gathering smoke.

"I will deal with this," he spoke against her lips. "If you kill her with the spell locked in her mind, I can raise her, but I won't be able to obtain the wards."

She knew this, but she couldn't see beyond her rage. How could she be so close to freedom from her ghosts only to lose to Gummy?

Barrington kissed her temple and then neared her ear. "I promise what I've reserved for her is far worse than whatever magic we can wield. I just need you to trust me."

He straightened and met her stare. His gaze was eerily calm, despite the orange firelight reflected there. There was not one ounce of doubt in his plan, whatever it was. With every desire to wrap flames around Gummy's throat and watch the life leave her eyes, Sera nodded, and the flames extinguished.

"Oh, how tender," Gummy said. Coming from around Armitage, she slid a hand onto her hips, haloed by billowing smoke. "So, Barry, are you ready to talk business? Seeing as there's no more blood magic, perhaps we can discuss alternate forms of payment. Though..." She looked at Sera. "I'm sure you don't want her here for that...*discussion*."

Sera curled her fingers to fists, her magic yearning to burn Gummy until there was nothing left but bones. "You're a monster."

Gummy shrugged a shoulder. "Aren't we all?"

Barrington bristled, and the temperature in the room dipped significantly, his rage thinly veiled. But, squeezing Sera's hand, he guided them from the room.

"You'll be back, Barry," Gummy warned. "You always are."

He closed the door behind them.

"What do you mean to do?" Sera asked once they reached the transfer wheels.

"I'm going to make a deal with the enemy," he said, "but first we need to secure the mirror."

His stare was shuttered, but their months together had taught her to see beyond this facade he often wore when in the throes of his withdrawals, a steady and confident gaze of ice and steel, while sweat dampened his skin and his hands shook. And though it wasn't his addiction now, whatever he was set to do was tearing him apart.

The transfer rings spun until the coordinates for the Academy were displayed. The ciphers illuminated, filled with Barrington's magic. Sera braced, but the transfer wheel extinguished, and they hadn't moved. The magic powering the spell whirled away in strands of smoke.

"Is everything all right, sir?" the attendant asked before Sera was able to.

Barrington attempted the spell again. The first few ciphers pooled in golden light, but the last ones never illuminated, and the entire spell faded to tendrils of smoke once more.

He tried and tried again.

The last set of coordinates changed incrementally as he adjusted where they would land at the Academy, but none of it took.

He cursed. "The coordinates for province and town work, but not any of the ones for the Academy."

Sera unsheathed her wand and pointed to the rings. The last few wheels turned to adjust the coordinates to her tower room. Warmth coursed through her as she fed her magic into the wheel. The sequence of coordinates glimmered, except for the final symbols.

"It's not working for me, either."

He met her stare. "Either we've both been banned or something's happened at the school. Given the mirror, I'm thinking the latter."

She made to try again, but Barrington touched her hand and stayed her. "No, you must save your magic. I'm not sure how quickly your body will metabolize the elixir, and using large amounts of magic usually hastens the process." He brought her hand to his mouth and pressed a kiss on her knuckles. "But thank you."

She nodded her "you're welcome," her mind a little foggy from his affection.

The coordinates to his home locked into position. The floor vanished beneath them, a flash of black, and they landed neatly in the workroom.

"Rosie!" Barrington called out, moving swiftly toward his laboratory. He whirled a hand, and the black door swung open. "Rosie!"

He vanished into the laboratory just as Rosie hurried into the room.

"Oh, thank goodness," she said, flushed. "I didn't know where you'd gone. I sent Lucas out to find you. So horrible what's happened. I dislike Mr. Delacort, but goodness, first his son and now his wife."

"Rosie, what's occurred?"

"Inspector Lewis was here earlier and said Mrs. York requests your presence right away, whatever the hour. All travel to the Academy has been banned on account of Mrs. Delacort's disappearance. Mrs. Delacort's magic was last traced to the school. Apparently, she had a meeting with the headmistress and never made it back home. The transfer room attendant claims she arrived but never left. The school has been locked down as Aetherium guards search for her."

Barrington surfaced from the laboratory. "We can't wait until they're done."

"What of the Barghest?" Sera asked.

Barrington stiffened, no doubt remembering their last Barghest transfer. "Even if we could, there are warding spells against them at the Academy; he cannot enter. I enacted them after our first encounter with the beast. I'd feared he would find you and seek his vengeance. It's most likely the reason he didn't appear when Mr. Whittaker hurt you."

Sera's heart stirred. Under influence of the Brotherhood, the Barghest had tried to kill her when they'd first met. To save herself and Barrington, she'd bound him in magical ropes, determined to destroy him. Had Barrington not talked her down, she would have.

"Mrs. York should be able to provide us with a way in," he said through her thoughts. "The school might be inaccessible to everyone, but officials are still able to transfer there using provisional coordinates. We leave right away. Rosie, tell Lucas to empty our stores and take all the vats of blood magic to Gummy. All of it. It is imperative not one vial remain in this house or any place associated with my name. He's to have Rowe help him, then both must stay away from Gummy's establishments for the foreseeable future."

"It would be my pleasure, sir," Rosie said and walked out.

Sera touched a hand to his arm, worry fluttering in her belly. "I want the wards, but not if it causes you to deal in blood magic again. We will figure out a way to reach the secret library to better understand Filip's research."

"We will," Barrington said, smoothing the back of his knuckles across her cheek, those silver eyes fixed on hers. "And this guarantees we will have access. Now let us go to Mrs. York about the provisional coordinates."

She nodded, ready though wholly curious about the

logistics of his plan. But she trusted him, and that was enough.

Darkness enveloped them, and, the next moment, they landed on a beige-and-white checkered floor, each tile marked with the symbol of one of the seven elements. Sera and Barrington separated just as a butler appeared at the top of a grand staircase in the lavish entryway lined with tapestries edged in gold. Gilt chandeliers had been turned down and cast long shadows that made monsters out of numerous pillars lining the entrance hall. A large portrait of the chancellor hung at the top of the stairs, his stern face and biting blue eyes so unlike the frail man with unfocused expression he'd been rendered into.

The butler approached them and inclined his head to them both. "The chancellor and Mrs. York await you in the library. This way, please."

The staircase split in two, one landing headed to either side of the house. They followed him up the left stairs and to the second level and entered a wide hallway with a bloodred carpet running the length of the corridor. Along the walls were paintings depicting various events in the Aetherium's history, but the majority was of the folklore surrounding the seven guardians of magic, from beautiful watercolor renderings of the sisters to grotesque depictions of the seventh sister being locked behind the gate. A chill skittered down Sera's spine at the macabre portraits, wrongness settling in her belly. Who would ever want to be surrounded by images of this kind?

The butler stopped before massive double doors at the end of the hall. Turning the brass handles, he pushed them open and led them into a three-story library. The long room was separated by three spiral staircases. Rows and rows of black book shelves lined the dark wood-paneled walls. Mrs. York sat on a black settee in the middle of the room, her face downcast. The chancellor was beside her in a wicker bath chair, his gaze ages away.

"Abby?" Barrington approached Mrs. York. She rose to meet him, and he embraced her.

"Nikolai, what's happening?" They parted. "Is Cressida in danger? I was unable to warn her before transferring was barred."

"Cressida is smart as she is strong. I'm certain she's fine. When did the school closing occur?" Barrington asked.

"Sometime yesterday evening, though we've only heard word of it now. Mrs. Delacort was at the Academy to approve the location of an observatory they're having built and dedicated to their son. She never made it back home. All transferring in and out of the school has been banned."

"It explains why you weren't able to transfer in," he told Sera. "The newer spell superseded the exemption I placed on your tower room."

"All in magic, Nikolai. Do we have a murderer on our hands?" Mrs. York asked, her brown eyes keen. "This Meredith girl you told me about, is she responsible for the disappearances?"

"I'm not sure. There have been no bodies, yet the other vanishings follow the same modus operandi. We've only just discovered the connection and were on our way back to the school to confirm our theory."

"Tell me what it is."

Barrington hesitated. "A scrying glass that we believe is hexed has found its way into the school."

Sera's cheeks warmed, and she met his stare, thankful he'd withheld the whole truth, that she had been the one to introduce it into the Academy.

Barrington explained all that Armitage had told them. "The magic samples recovered from the various mirrors found at different scenes all belonged to a Miss Serena Shaw, a scryist from the Persecution. At first, I believed it was Meredith employing a blend of mirror magic and death magic, but it appears Miss Shaw was mirror bound and still roams the mirror world. Given recent events, it appears she is only able to spread to the mirrors within her general vicinity, though that might change as she grows in power."

"You think *The Enchantress* is responsible for the disappearances?" Mrs. York asked, incredulous.

"I saw her," Sera said. "When she took Mr. Whittaker. Furthermore, based on the files you sent of her victims, they're all emotionally compromised in some way. Whittaker mourned Timothy, Mrs. James lamented her sister, Mrs. Delacort grieves her son. The children at the orphanage were seventhborns; that is a pain all on its own. And the spell signatures all belonged to her."

The chancellor's mouth moved with whispery words, and he grew agitated.

"And the mirror is still at the school?" Mrs. York asked, rubbing small circles on his back.

"Yes, and we need the provisional coordinates to secure it or else all the guards there are in danger," Barrington said.

"Inspector Lewis has gone on ahead to request them and find Cressida, but he has yet to return. I will inform you once I know anything. For now, I must settle Duncan." She embraced them both. "I will be in touch soon."

Sera and Barrington clasped hands. Mrs. York nodded once, and the floor gave way beneath them.

They landed back in Barrington's home. Sera made to move, but Barrington didn't release her, and they instantly transferred to the stables. Darkness swathed the stone building, the dimness cut by the light of a full moon filtering in through a window above the stalls.

"Lucas isn't back," Sera noted, and the Barghest was also nowhere to be seen.

"We aren't here for Lucas. We will get to the school ourselves." He slid off his coat and hooked it on a nearby tack. "I will transfer us as close as I can to the Academy. Provisional coordinates often spread a few miles wider than needed as a buffer, so we will have to travel the rest of the way on foot…or horse."

Barrington moved to the first stand and looked through the bars on the wooden door, to a black horse with a white stripe shaped like an elongated crescent down its face.

"Hello, Moon."

Moon nickered and turned to face Barrington. He pulled the door open and entered the stall; Sera waited at the threshold and watched Moon bring its head close to Barrington and nuzzle his shoulder and neck with its muzzle. Barrington patted the horse, who Sera quickly learned was a mare, and spoke endearments against her shiny coat, encouraging words of speed and bravery in a low and stable tone.

Despite their night and her memory of transferring with a horse, Sera smiled at the mount's dewy gaze and the shared affection between horse and master.

"She's not the fastest, but she's my bravest," he explained in the same timbre as he guided Moon out of her stall and to a clearing where he secured her to a post. Rolling up his sleeves, he then seized a brush. Without Lucas there, he was forced to ready Moon himself.

After grooming Moon and picking her hooves, Barrington washed his hands and ran wet fingers along his hair to push the strands back. Putting on his coat, he held a hand out to Sera, and her pulse quickened. But, forcing their imminent journey to the forefront of her mind, she tangled her fingers with his and joined him by the mare.

He drew close, silvery eyes fixed on hers. "I'm going to help you up now."

Though he'd warned her, Sera sucked in a quiet breath as his hands splayed on her waist, firm yet gentle. Her fingers alighted on his shoulders in readiness, but their gazes locked, and for a sliver of a moment, time seemed to still. They stood there in the dim stable, shrouded by shadows and weak streams of amber firelight.

His fingers anchored into her, and heat flooded Sera's veins. His gaze dropped to her lips, and her magic roiled in her belly. The lamps nearby pulsed wildly, but in feeling Barrington's hands tremble ever so slightly upon her, Sera was unsure whether it was her magic or his stoking the flames. But the trivial thought didn't matter, and as Barrington's face drew closer, all traces of reason, heartbreak, and fear fled to the darkest reaches of her mind. There was just their slow breathing, flushed bodies, and then the warmth of his kiss.

Breaking away, he lifted her up onto the horse, then swung up in front of her. Despite Barrington guiding her arms around him and the memory of his kiss alive on her lips, Sera tensed at the height from the ground, the movement of the horse beneath her, and the sheer power it exuded. Her pulse quickened and magic churned. Moon's ears pricked upright, and her back grew rigid. Barrington spent the next few moments urging both Sera and Moon to settle down.

When they'd both relaxed, he clucked, and they took off on a steady trot out of the stables and down the lane, toward the iron gates towering in the distance.

Barrington coiled the reins shorter. "I will bring her to full speed, then conjure the transfer spell. Whatever you feel, try to remain calm and hold on tight. I'm right here." He gazed at her from over his shoulder. "I'll always be here."

Sera glanced up at him. His words were a dream, and she held him tighter, knowing this was another promise he would keep.

He turned his attention back to the openness of the field, clucked, and hugged his legs against the mare. Moon's pace quickened to a canter. He squeezed again, tighter, and Moon bolted down the path.

The moors sped past in shadowy smears of green and black. Sera's heart crashed against her ribs, the steady hoofbeats upon the earth spurring her pulse. But fear would not master her. She focused on Moon's power beneath her and the cool breeze of their quickening speed. On the feel of Barrington in her arms and his heartbeat against her ear. On his scent of sweat and sandalwood mingling with traces of heather, horse, and night. On the taste of his kiss...

The coolness of his magic cloaked them, a steady hum that skimmed Sera's skin.

"Go!" he yelled. Moon galloped harder, faster. Sera's lungs constricted, but she forced her eyes to remain open and watch whirls of blue smoke materialize in the distance, faster and faster until a ring of ciphers burst in the gathering mist like an explosion of starlight.

Barrington drove them inside.

Blackness enveloped them, and Sera's stomach plummeted, but, holding tightly to Barrington, she relished their fall.

Moon's frantic hoofbeats thundered again, this time against the damp Academy countryside.

"Easy!" Barrington commanded, and Moon's speed slowed to a canter, then a trot.

Barrington loosened his grip on the reins and heaved a sigh. "Are you all right?"

She nodded but stiffened at the orbs of red light dashing

into the air over the Academy spires in the distance like bloody shooting stars. "The Aetherium call for aid."

Barrington spun them around as the crimson hue illuminated their surroundings and the bodies of dead Aetherium guards strewn along the ground, rings of fire burned into their chests.

Sera's heart tightened. "This wasn't the Enchantress."

"You're right," Barrington said, staring down at the dead body beside them wearing a Brotherhood robe and beaked plague mask.

16

the enchantress

Barrington and Sera kept their wands tight at their sides, their footsteps light and movements quick as they dashed among the shadowy trees and wild brush of the Academy forest. Bodies of dead Aetherium guards and Brotherhood members marked the bloody path toward the school.

Barrington stopped and whipped Sera behind a tree. He lifted a finger over his lips, his silvery gaze fixed beyond her shoulder. She peered around the corner, and her anger surged at the gathering of Brotherhood keeping watch in the distance.

"How are they already here?" she whispered.

"Gummy could have told someone of our discussion, or maybe Armitage told Delacort. Aside from Mrs. York, they're the only ones who know about the mirror, which I'm certain they're here for. Whatever the case, we must avoid any large displays of magic to prevent detection for as long as possible." He took her hand and guided them parallel to the Academy.

Within minutes, they encountered an old graveyard. The headstones were unkempt, and foliage had grown savage, overtaking the crumbled statues and blocking all traces of names.

Barrington guided them to a flat headstone marker and touched his wand to the gray stone. The slab moved aside to reveal a staircase leading down into darkness.

"What is this place?" she breathed.

"Purists used this tunnel to smuggle seventhborns in and out of the dungeons. I encountered it when attempting to clear my father's name. It will be safe; I made it so only my magic allows for entry on either side. Follow it—it will lead you to the servant halls in the basement. From there you can take the service stairs up to your old room."

She would still need to go through the library to reach the landing that led up to the tower, but it was still her best chance to remain undetected.

Yet, Sera paused. "You're not coming?"

"I must locate the charms providing the provisional coordinates. They are often arranged around the place they're meant to block or hide. If I can manage to find and destroy one, the natural coordinates will be reinstated so you can transfer out the moment you have the mirror and the Aetherium can send reinforcements."

"Surely the Brotherhood thought of the same. They'll have the talismans heavily guarded."

He brushed his knuckles along her cheek, and her words faded. "Will you always worry about me?" he asked.

"Someone has to."

A branch snapped, and footsteps approached.

"Get the mirror, transfer back to the house, and secure it within the containment room." Barrington gripped her fingers and helped her down into the tunnel. "I will meet you there."

She met his gaze. "Be careful."

Leaning forward, he caught her lips in a kiss. "I always am."

Their hands parted. The stone slab slid in between them and thrust her into darkness.

Her pulse quickened, and worry grew to a tight fist lodged in her chest. But she lifted her wand, sparked a flame on its tip, and turned to the long stretch of road ahead of her. This case wasn't going to solve itself, and if the Brotherhood thought they would win this one, she would prove them wrong.

A mile or so later, Sera's torchlight bounced off the back of a door. She eased closer and inclined her ear. Satisfied at the lack of sound, she extinguished her fire, twisted the knob, and pulled the door open a crack. The hinges creaked, and she winced but breathed freer to find herself within a broom closet. From the outside, the tunnel entrance looked like a plain wall.

She stepped over leaning brushes and stacked buckets and moved to the main door. Again, she opened it slightly but paused at the shuffling of feet. Two Brotherhood members ran down the hall. Sera's anger spiked, but she dug her nails into the metal encasement on her wand and stifled the need for revenge.

Securing the mirror came first, and then these men would pay.

When they were out of sight and the sound of their steps faded, Sera exited the closet and gathered her bearings. She moved quickly toward the alcove that would leave her within the Ethical Magic section of the library, where she would cross over to the Astral Studies aisle and gain access to the stairs leading to the tower room.

She neared the door. "Right above all else," she

whispered. The wall clicked. Sweat sprouted along her skin. Anything could be waiting on the other side. She allowed her magic to fill her wand and slipped into the library.

The coast was clear, and yet, dread seized her. The dim library was frigid, her breath a pulsing cloud of smoke. Screams resounded outside. Some yelled for help. Others shouted to run.

Her pulse quickened, fear a thick fist in her throat. She gripped her wand tighter and moved farther into the library, down the nearest aisle. She ducked into the shadows and peered around the bookcase. A Brotherhood member ran into the library and shut the doors behind him. Punches and screams for him to open resounded against the wood. Blasts of magic exploded outside, chased by bloodcurdling screams. The knocks stopped.

The Brother stumbled back, his panting breaths muffled beneath his raven mask. His gaze remained focused on the door, where slivers of smoke slithered through the seams, followed by a web of ice. Sera's eyes widened. *What on earth...*

Movement in her peripheral vision caught Sera's attention. Smoke billowed out from the windows and a decorative mirror whose glass was black. The fog rolled and pulsed like a heartbeat and covered its surroundings in ice.

The Brother whimpered and thrust off his beaked mask. He aimed his wand at the door, unaware of the mist that approached him from behind and the feminine figure manifesting in the smoke. Grayish blue hands gripped the Brother's shoulder. He screamed, but ice crawled up his limbs and into his mouth, and the cry died in his throat. The mist covered him, throbbed once, and he was gone.

Sera clapped a hand over her mouth to stop a scream. Reason told her to run, but paralyzing terror rooted her to the ground.

A tendril of fog slithered around the corner, and the temperatures plummeted so fast the books beside Sera crunched, suddenly covered in ice. A shuddering, muffled breath rattled nearby. The Enchantress drifted into view before Sera, the floor beneath her crackling and overcome by frost. Sera stiffened, and her magic rushed to her fingertips and filled her aimed wand, but the Enchantress turned away and vanished into the receding mist, which then rolled back into the surrounding glass.

Sera gulped. The fog had gone, but she didn't move for a moment. It hadn't seen her. If her logic was right, it had sensed her fear, but she'd been invisible to its eyes.

Barrington's elixir, she realized with a relief that weakened her knees. So long as it was in her system, the Enchantress could perceive her fear but was unable to see her.

A curdling scream outside pulled her from her contemplations. She had to hurry. Barrington said the effects were temporary, and she wasn't going to test its brevity now.

She hurried to the Astral Studies section and neared the bookcase. "By the stars," she whispered, and the bookcase swung open. She rushed inside and up the stairs. Frantic servants dashed past her, uncaring of who she was and why she was there. She glanced up from whence they came, and her chest caved. A plume of fog bowled out from intermittent windows and down the landing like a tidal wave, the upper tower indiscernible through the smoke. The Enchantress moved within the smog and seized a Brother, who sought to run away. He tried to fight, but rime climbed over him and quickly absorbed him into the mist. A servant girl was next, followed by another who froze mid-step, her hands stretched out for help. Fog covered her, and she too was gone.

Sera gripped her wand tighter, her knuckles white. She

set one foot on the stair and climbed up. She had to get that mirror or else everything was truly lost.

The higher she scaled, the colder it got, but she stayed focused on the next step until she made it to her tower room. Thrusting open her wardrobe, she yanked out Meredith's carpetbag and pushed aside a bundle of clothes to reveal the scrying glass.

All in magic…

The black glass was no longer broken, and the oxidized handle was polished and gleaming. Myriad faces rushed across the glass, as the Enchantress no doubt traveled the mirrors of the school consuming those in fear or mourning. Sera aimed her wand at the mirror but paused. Perhaps breaking it would stop the spread of the Enchantress's evil, but if she did, were the spirits within lost forever?

No, she would take it back to Barrington's containment room the way they'd planned. With the mirror tight in her hands, she aimed her wand to the ground. Surely Barrington had located and removed the provisional coordinates by now. With the ciphers to his home fixed in her mind, she braced and whispered, "Ignite."

The floor vanished beneath her, and she crashed down into Barrington's office. He wasn't there, but she dashed to the workroom; she had to secure the scrying glass behind the containment room's protection spells. She pushed the door to the secret laboratory open, hurried across the room, yanked the gate open, and slid the mirror inside.

Slamming the door shut, Sera leaned back against the wall, her heartbeat thundering in her ears. If the past was any indication, with the mirror now away from the school, the Enchantress was gone from there, too. And locked behind these spells, she shouldn't be able to infect Barrington's home. Still, she ran out of the room and into the hall, where a few mirrors hung intermittently between the artwork on the walls.

He would be against it, wholly confident in his magic and ability to protect his home, but she wouldn't risk it. At once, she took to removing the mirrors.

"Miss?" Rosie said at the head of the stairs, Barrington's cloak in her hands. "Is everything all right?"

She looked at the clock; goodness, an hour had passed since she'd arrived, but, absorbed in collecting the mirrors, shuttering curtains, and securing all the reflective surfaces in the home, she hadn't even noticed.

"Yes, I'm fine," she said, breathless and relieved at the sight of Barrington's garment. She climbed up the stairs and met Rosie on the second level and quickly explained all that had happened. "Every mirror needs to come down immediately, and be sure not to draw the curtains. I've put some mirrors outside; have Lucas take them as far as he can. I'm not sure how quickly it takes for the Enchantress to infect the mirrors."

"Yes, Miss."

She started up the landing toward the workroom and Barrington's office. "Thank you, Rosie. Is the professor in his office?"

Rosie's brow furrowed. "Ma'am?"

Sera motioned to his cape in her hands. "That's his cloak from today?"

"Oh, no. He'd left this one draped over his chair." She sighed. "The master and his messes."

Sera swallowed through a thickened throat "So, he… he isn't here?"

"No, dear. The last I saw him, he was with you."

Numbness rushed to Sera's legs, and she gripped the banister to remain upright. Memory of the Brotherhood and the Enchantress whisked through her mind, of the Brothers and servants consumed by the mirror-bound wraith.

But no. Barrington was strong and brave, a master magician of the white and dark arts. If someone was capable of fighting against the Enchantress and defeating the Brotherhood, it was him. Besides, he was only supposed to find the provisional coordinates, which he'd done. Then he was supposed to meet her here.

But if so, why wasn't he home?

She drew her wand, but her hands trembled, and her magic scattered within. There was no way she could mentally hold the transfer spell to the school, much less gather the magic needed to get there safely.

"Rosie," she said, her voice unsteady. "Can you transfer me back to the Academy, please?"

The stout woman unsheathed her wand and aimed it at Sera's feet but paused, her eyes wide. "Miss, where is the master?"

"Please, Rosie. I'm sure he's fine. We ran into a bit of trouble, but I will find him and bring him home. Transfer me to the school and remember to tell Lucas about the mirrors, immediately."

Rosie gulped and nodded, though her watery stare told Sera she already mourned.

A moment later, Sera landed within her tower room. With her wand tight in her hands, she inched to the door and pulled it open slightly. Satisfied at the lack of movement and fog, she descended the stairs. Barrington had told her to take the servant stairway up to her room. If he'd come to find her, which he shouldn't have, that's the way he would have gone.

She rounded the corner, entered the broom closet under the landing, and, moving the brooms aside, she neared the wall. "Safe passage."

The outline of a door glittered blue, and the stone faded to reveal an entryway. With her wand aimed before her, Sera walked inside. Quiet swathed the staircase. For the next few minutes, Sera stepped through puddles and dropped wands, beaked masks and cleaning supplies. Unconscious or dead Brotherhood members, Aetherium guards, and servants.

But none was Barrington.

Some of the staff emerged from the various floors, all wearing frightened and dazed expressions, and their question the same: What on earth is going on?

Sera searched their faces, too, but she reached the ground floor and had yet to find him. She ventured outside, to where Aetherium guards swept the surrounding lands and inspectors listened to those well enough to talk.

None of them was Barrington.

Where was Barrington?

The world blurred to a smeared mess around her. But damn it all, she couldn't cry. How could she ever find him if she couldn't discern his face?

"Miss Dovetail?"

Sera spun to Doctor Morgan, who pulled her into her arms. "Thank all magic he found you." She peeled back, her hair frazzled and her dress cold and wet. "Nikolai was so worried. We both were."

"You...saw him?" Sera asked, breathless. "When?"

"Earlier in the night. He helped Inspector Lewis carry a few injured into the forest, but a maid claimed she saw you in the library, and they ran back inside."

The world swayed, and Sera's knees weakened.

"Miss Dovetail!" Doctor Morgan gripped Sera's arms and guided her to the damp ground.

"I'm fine," she whispered and attempted to stand, but raw and blinding pain clawed her insides with cold, and her body trembled violently, as if each tremor sought to embed the truth deep into her soul.

He used black magic for her.

Weathered accusations and jail for her.

Confronted his greatest fear and accepted Filip was a murderer, all to find a cure for her.

Had run into a ghost-infested school for her.

Had bled and killed for her.

Had kissed her.

But surely, he couldn't have died for her.

Desperate, she scratched at her neckline and yanked his pendant out from inside her dress. She clasped it tightly in her hands and closed her eyes. "Nikolai."

A moment passed, and she lifted her lashes. Nothing had changed, except for Inspector Lewis approaching, a solemn look on his face.

Sera shook her head. "No."

No.

No.

No.

But Inspector Lewis stopped before her. In his eyes was all the pain in the world.

And in his hands was Barrington's wand.

17

gone

Sera sat in a black wingback chair before a worktable within Barrington's training room, the Barghest curled at her side. She held Barrington's cloak draped against her chest and her nose buried in the fabric. Just as she'd been all morning. And for two weeks prior. Stacks of books surrounded her, tomes on folktales and urban legends, others on black magic, mirror magic in particular. Aside from the heinous tales of mourners gone missing, there was nothing in any of them on how to summon the Enchantress, much less on how to defeat her and recover the missing souls.

Missing, Sera repeated to herself, *not gone*.

So long as Barrington was missing, he could be found. She just had to work harder to figure out how.

Sera hauled in a deep breath of Barrington's musk clinging to the cloak, and her heart ached, but regardless of the sorrow that stifled her magic and color and taste, the Enchantress hadn't come, despite the hours Sera had spent removing all of Barrington's deterrents along and around his home. It had been a tedious affair. The spells were protected against magic and she was forced to use her hands. Bruises and cuts now covered her fingers and arms, commingled with her scars. Still, not even the ghosts had returned, and she was once again left with nothing but books and the memories of a missing man waiting to be found.

And mirrors.

Though she still possessed the Enchantress's mirror, which she'd told Mrs. York and Inspector Lewis had been lost that night, other mirrors of all sizes and designs now lined the training room walls like a patchwork of glass. Having almost run out of space, she propped them against every surface that could support them. Each one was a doorway, and she would give Barrington the best chances to come home.

She held the cloak tighter and breathed in his smell of sandalwood and traces of old books, coffee, and ink. Yes, he would come home because he was missing, not gone. Someone like him didn't vanish forever. The etiquettes of ordinary life didn't apply to him. He defied expectations and magic, shunned rules and proprieties. In his words, he was unorthodox, and at any moment he would appear in one of the mirrors, and together they would solve this mystery, like they did every other.

Together, they would defeat the Enchantress and free him and the others, after which he would take her lips in a kiss, brush a hand gently against her cheek, and call her *my love*.

A fierce ache spread in her chest, but she clawed her fingers into the cloak and mastered the pain. She would not grieve him.

He was alive.

Alive.

Alive.

Alive.

She whispered this to herself like a mantra until numbness once again wormed into her chest and the pain there froze. It didn't leave or grow but merely remained as a fist in her throat.

A low knock resounded, and Rosie entered. She wore a black dress and a lace cap and a somber expression that she sought to hide behind a small smile. Her bloodshot eyes betrayed her. Sera turned away toward the window, where a single shaft of light cut through a crack in the curtain and across the dark wood floors. They were being ridiculous, all of them, wearing black as if…as if…

She blew out a shuddering breath. Let them keep their dreary clothes. They would feel positively foolish once Barrington returned. No doubt he'd say something clever about everyone underestimating his strength. Everyone except Sera.

"Doctor Morgan is here to see you, dear."

Sera plucked a nail on the clasp on Barrington's cloak, and it gave under her finger and now hung on by a strand of thread. Goodness, she'd nearly pulled it right off. She folded the cloak and held it out to Rosie. "The clasp on this needs mending. I'd do it, but I never learned. I'm sure the professor will want his cloak once he returns. The nights have been getting rather chilly."

Rosie's nose reddened, and she pressed her lips together, though they still trembled. "Yes, miss. And what of Doctor Morgan? She called on you yesterday, but…" Rosie cleared her throat.

Yesterday had been rather difficult, with the nightmares that had plagued Sera whenever she dozed off and caused her to set various rooms in the house on fire. She was certain Rosie and Lucas would either kick her out or abandon her to her flames and sorrow, but they claimed they never would.

Sera hoped they wouldn't. Barrington would appear in one of the mirrors at any moment now. She would figure out a way to rescue him, and things would go back to how they were.

"I will tell her you're indisposed," Rosie said, tearing Sera from thought.

"What for? Have her pass."

"Are you sure? Would you perhaps like a new dress?"

Sera rose from the chair and smoothed down the blue gown she'd worn for three days prior. Not black. Never black, not anymore. She chased her fingers through her hair and bound the uncombed and frizzy strands into a quick braid. "No need. Have her pass."

Rosie nodded and walked down the hall to the grand stairs in the middle of the corridor. Doctor Morgan appeared at the top of the stairs and followed Rosie into the training room, a file clasped in her hands. As always, she was regal in a black mourning gown, though she looked rather pale. She brushed across the room as though to embrace Sera, but Sera turned toward the worktable, and she was forced to stop mere inches away. She set the file she held on the bench and smiled at Sera, but it never reached her reddened eyes. "My dear, how are you?"

Sera gave her a quick arch of her lips. "I'm well, thank you." Grabbing her notebook, she walked along the room, documenting the various temperature readings of the numerous mirrors. She'd taken to monitoring the temperature fluctuations just in case Barrington was better able to make a connection on one mirror versus another. A dip in temperature would tell her when he or the Enchantress sought to make contact.

And when that time came, she would be ready.

Lucas appeared in the doorway, rolling a crate before him. Dark circles cradled his eyes, matching his midnight-black attire. He stopped short. "Oh, forgive me, miss. I'll come back."

"Nonsense. You've met Doctor Morgan." The two exchanged a quick hello, then Sera waved Lucas forward and grabbed a page from the worktable. "Come, set the mirrors down and take this list. I found these types of mirrors are often mentioned in the tomes. Surely there must be a reason for their popularity. Can you seek out a vendor and place an order? Two of each will do, please."

Doctor Morgan and Lucas exchanged glances, and even the Barghest whined, but Lucas deposited the newly delivered crate and took the offered list. "Yes, miss. Should I hang these up for you?"

"I can manage. Thank you, Lucas."

"Yes, miss." He bowed his head at Doctor Morgan and, turning, he walked away. He passed a mirror, and Sera noticed he wiped tears from his cheeks, but, grabbing a crowbar, she moved to the crate. He would be better soon enough.

She shoved the bar in and, gripping the iron rod tightly, pushed down.

"Here, let me." Doctor Morgan set her hand on the crate, and the nails all loosened. One tug, and the crate was opened. Sera nodded her thanks and moved the straw within aside to reveal a mirror with a golden-wreathed frame.

"You're not using magic?"

"I have to save my strength," Sera said, lifting the narrow mirror out of the crate. "Since I don't know when he will reach out, my reserves must be at their optimal capacity in case he needs me."

Sera surveyed the surrounding mirrors. Noting a space wide enough for the new mirror between two frames, she grabbed a nail from beside her stack of books and hooked the hammer into her kit belt. She moved across the room, pulled a rolling ladder beneath the empty spot, and climbed up to reach it.

"Mama sends her love. She wanted to come herself, but there's much work to be done now that the election has been lost."

Sera paused mid-step. "Lost? The elections aren't for another month."

Doctor Morgan laughed humorlessly. "With the Academy closure and magicians still unaccounted for, including Mrs. Delacort, and lack of evidence or an explanation, public support has swayed unanimously in Mr. Delacort's favor. The margin is too great; Duncan will never recover."

"That's…terrible," she said, but, numb, she climbed the rest of the way, unable to feel the crushing disappointment. Unable to feel anything at all.

"Indeed. A great deal of change is coming, and it appears we are on the losing side. But as Mama always says, we shouldn't ever tire of fighting for our lives."

Sera's grip tightened on the hammer. *Fighting for our lives…*

The memory of Inspector Lewis's account of how Barrington was consumed by the Enchantress's cloud filled her head, chased by the horrible questions that had plagued her since. Had Barrington fought for his life? Had he used every ounce of his magic to evade the Enchantress? Or had his grief over Filip been so strong that, wearied and brokenhearted, he'd allowed himself to be caught?

Pressure mounted in Sera's chest, a ravenous ache building there, joining her existing pain for Timothy and Mary. But she let it hurt and struck the first spike into the wall. The Enchantress would feel her pain and come, and then she could save Barrington using white magic, death magic—whatever it took to get him back into her arms.

Doctor Morgan joined her, standing beside the ladder as Sera hammered the second nail. "You know, when Filip… passed, I thought perhaps I'd dreamt it all," she said, hugging herself as if remembering Filip's embrace. "I was so certain of it that I refused to sleep for fear I'd dream of it all over again. I pored over work and books and lessons, and I drank countless tonics and elixirs in order to stay awake. But day after day, he didn't come back."

Sera descended and, after retrieving the mirror, climbed back up as Doctor Morgan went on. "So then, I slept. I thought if he didn't come while I was awake, then perhaps I could survive off the nightmares until he returned. But he still didn't come back."

Sera secured the mirror against the wall, climbed down, and walked to the crate to retrieve another.

"As the days went on, I realized that no matter what I did, whether awake or asleep, the pain remained. So, I let it hurt. I burned and broke things and screamed and cried. I loathed him and hated myself for a very long time. But then, the interval between my tears lengthened, and one day, I didn't cry. One day, I got dressed. One day, I ventured outside. I emerged from sorrow to find the world kept moving and I had survived. Surely that had to stand for something. I didn't know what at the time, but then, one day I met you and I understood why. I was needed. You needed me." She walked to the workbench and slid the Aetherium folder across toward Sera. "And now others need you, desperately."

Sera gripped the edge of the crate, the sudden ache in her chest a rival to the wood splinters digging into her palms. "I appreciate your words, truly, but my work here…" Her heart clenched; a harsh wind blustered past, and the candles were extinguished with a whoosh. "He isn't gone."

"Perhaps." Doctor Morgan snapped, and the candles ignited. "But the world is moving, and those in need are calling."

Sera glanced at the dossier, the Aetherium crest on the front. Her chest caved, but she stifled the throb and turned back to the crate, where she brushed more straw aside to reach two smaller mirrors there. These she would put in the corners, facing them toward the center of the room so she could see them when she sat to continue her research. "I really ought to get back to my work now. Thank you for your visit, but I can assure you, it was wholly unnecessary."

Doctor Morgan pressed her lips together, the whites of her eyes glistening. "It was my pleasure. Besides, Mama always thinks good news should be delivered in person." She walked to the door. "Take care of yourself, Sera. And congratulations. Whether or not you heed the call, we're all so very proud of you."

She walked out and closed the door behind her with a click.

Sera blew out a breath and glanced at the file, but, grabbing a mirror, she turned away and continued on with her work instead. Others might be calling for her, but there was a man who needed her most.

Once he returned, they would answer the call together.

Later that night, a thunderstorm poured blankets of rain over the moors. The Barghest slept beside the window as if thunder were monsters and he sought to keep them away. Sera closed her most recently finished book of folktales and stroked a hand along the cool leather cover. Imprinted into the black hide was the mythical gate in the Underworld, the six sisters before it and the seventh locked inside.

She set it down. Her eyes caught on the Aetherium file, still where Doctor Morgan had left it. She pressed her fingers together. Doctor Morgan had all but told her she'd been accepted, but never had she imagined it would be this bittersweet. And despite how hard she'd worked for it—bled and nearly died to achieve it—it wasn't any less surreal. Blowing out a long breath to bolster herself, she reached for the file, flipped it open, and read the admissions letter on top.

Dear Ms. Dovetail,

On behalf of everyone at the Aetherium School of Continuing Magic, I am pleased to congratulate you on our acceptance of your application. We were very impressed by your academic history, entrance exam scores, and glowing referral, and feel that you would make an excellent addition to the Aetherium alumni.

Please find all the necessary enrollment forms enclosed with this letter. We appreciate your filling them out and returning them to us when you come for your scheduled entrance interview September 30th at 10 in the morning in order to ensure your enrollment and facilitate the acceptance process for our winter program.

Sincerely Yours,

Director Victoria Thorne

Sera clutched the letter tighter, brought the page to her nose to take in the scent, then stroked it against her cheek.

She drew it back down again and stared at the scripted letters.

It was real. She'd done it. Years of blood, sweat, and tears. Of magic and death and betrayal, and she'd passed the bloody test. Sparks of joy broke through her sorrow and tugged a quivering smile onto her lips. Yet, her gaze swept to the file on the table, to a sheet peeking out from underneath the enrollment forms, and her previous mirth died.

She would recognize that horrid penmanship anywhere.

She pushed the other paperwork aside to reveal Barrington's referral. A laugh mixed with a sob escaped her; though still rather sloppy, his handwriting was slightly more legible. He must have toiled over the letter all night.

Reason told her she wasn't ready to read its contents. But, hauling in a breath, she picked it up and read.

Dear Aetherium Admissions Board,

My name is Professor Nikolai Anton Barrington, Professor of Alchemy at the Aetherium's Wizard and Witchling Academy, entrusted with the care of fledging wizards. My referral, however, is not for a wizard, but rather one of the most talented magicians who has graced the Academy halls. I speak not as her teacher, but as a steward to the Aetherium, bound by the duty my Invocation ring placed upon me to forever act in a way that will serve the Aetherium and all under its law.

It is for this reason that I recommend Miss Seraphina Dovetail to the Aetherium School of Continuing Magic. Her grades and reserve levels are enclosed and, while impressive, are not the basis of my referral, and so I will not discuss them.

As illustrated by the black marking on her application, Miss Dovetail is a seventhborn, and as such, she has met discrimination, cruelty, unfairness, disdain, and a plethora of prejudices much too heavy for any one person to bear, regardless of age or gender or station in life—all three of which have also given Miss Dovetail a disadvantage at competing with her peers.

At times she has retaliated and has suffered punishment for her offense, as you can note in her file—penalties that at times have been harsher than needed. Despite this, she has accepted those reprimands with grace and maintains her desire to enroll in the Aetherium School of Continuing Magic, to serve the very society which has so willingly ostracized her and her kind. Her strength and dedication are not only indications that she has the impetus, tenacity, and loyalty needed to serve the Aetherium, but that she represents everything our current empire is built upon.

I sign this recommendation with the wholehearted belief that accepting Miss Seraphina Dovetail into your program would benefit the school immensely and eventually the Aetherium, once she is appointed detective inspector. She has my highest endorsement, and I believe there will be no limit to her growth and achievements in the program and beyond, something I look forward to witnessing.

Sincerely yours with every truth,
Professor Nikolai Anton Barrington

One tear spilled onto the letter, and then another, and smeared the ink as Barrington's words echoed in her mind, bouncing off one another in discordant, vicious waves. Sera clutched her chest and hauled in a breath, but her lungs locked and refused all air. Her magic roiled at this sudden panic, rattled like a wild beast desperate to chew through the bars she'd placed upon it.

Barrington wasn't gone.

She believed this. Surely she did, and yet the floor beneath her tremored. The tables shuddered, and books tumbled down from their piles. The lights quivered, casting frantic shadows about the room.

The Barghest whined and nudged her hand, but Sera shook her head and held herself tightly against a rush of manic hot and cold that smothered her from within, blaring a truth she'd refused for days. But she couldn't accept it.

Barrington wasn't gone.

He'd written that he looked forward to witnessing her growth. Had told her he would be careful and that he'd meet her at home. Had kissed her and whispered *I'll always be here.*

How could he be gone? A gentleman, a man of his word?

But she shivered, and her tears flowed unchecked as sorrow crawled from the furthest reaches of her soul. Pain gripped her like sharpened teeth biting through her skin and into her bones, a feral ache that fueled her magic and filled her head with a blinding desire to cry, to bleed, to burn.

Sera screamed, a soul-wrenching roar that did little to the truth now haunting her mind.

Barrington was gone.

Emptied of all air, she gasped in another desperate breath and screamed again. Her tightly coiled magic broke free, and plumes of fire exploded all around her, burning the walls, her books, the curtains, the rug.

The Barghest whipped around the room, devouring the magic and extinguishing the flames, but nothing could douse Sera's pain except for the one thing she couldn't have.

Standing, she stumbled through the twines of smoke and lingering embers and collapsed before a mirror. She stared at herself, her eyes bloodshot and cradled by black half-moons. Her hair disheveled and her dress three days old. Grieving.

And it was all his fault.

"You bastard," she cried. "You promised you'd be careful,

and you weren't. You said you would meet me at home, and you didn't. You told me you would always be here, but you're not. If you're still alive, then I need you to come back to me. But if you're not…"

A sob tore through her, and her body was racked with her cries. "If you're not alive, then at least have the decency to haunt me. Possess me if you must, if only to feel you one last time. To let you know that I love you." She pressed her hands against the glass and, leaning her forehead against it, she closed her eyes as she felt her heart crumble within. "You're a liar and a fool, but you're mine, and I love you."

A cool breeze whisked past the room, and goose bumps sprouted along Sera's body. A whispery crackle resounded, and a sheet of rime crawled over the mirrors like spilled ink. She shifted back, and her breath cut short. Faces watched her from within the many mirrors on the wall, each one like a prison. Trapped magicians pressed their pale hands against the glass, their features contorted in agony, and cried, *Help me! Is anyone there? I'm so alone.*

Sera looked back to her mirror and gasped at Barrington's reflection. He was surrounded by thick fog; his black hair was icy, his skin gray and lips blue.

"Nikolai!" Sera said and pressed a hand to the glass.

Biting cold clamped down on her bones, and she closed her eyes, stiffening at the blinding ache cutting through her person. It was gone at once, and she blinked her eyes open. She paused.

The warmth of the August day was replaced by a bitter cold that encrusted the edges of the frames in ice. All the warm colors in the room were now grays and blacks. Awareness cut through Sera, and she glanced outside. The sun was a black orb in the sky, its muted dark blue rays streaming across black moors.

The mirror world.

"Hello, my love."

Sera startled and spun to the doorway, to Barrington leaning against the training room doorframe. He stared down at a black apple in his hand, and his feet were crossed at the ankles. He lifted his gaze, and Sera gasped. His face looked the same, but his eyes were made of black glass.

18

my love

Sera snatched out her wand, her magic hot and churning at her core.

Barrington brought the apple to his lips and took a bite, staring at her as he did the first time she had entered his home for their initial case. Countless faces flashed across his dark stare, the images of all the persons the mirror had consumed.

He chewed with a slow precision, then pushed off the doorway and entered the room. His elegance was paramount, identical to Barrington's confident ease. Sera moved back at his approach, and he stopped. A smile spread on his lips, cruel and slow. "What's wrong, Sera? I thought you loved me?"

The souls trapped in the mirror echoed his words.

Loved me. Loved me. Loved me.

"Will you let me die, too?"

Die. Die. Die.

Too. Too. Too.

Around her, some of the mirrors depicted her memories of that horrible night when she'd been forced to battle Noah. In one, she held a dead Timothy in her arms. The mirror beside it was a reflection of her, but this version of her pointed at Timothy's dead body and laughed, her black eyes glittering like onyx stars.

He laughed then, as did the trapped souls, though they themselves wore hurt expressions.

"Release him," Sera said, her magic churning wildly at her core.

"Or what?" he asked, using the same words she'd instigated Barrington with. "Will you get angry? Lose your temper and fight me? That never seems to work out well for you, does it?"

Images of her countless mishaps at the Academy flashed through the mirrors, while some portrayed the night she'd set Barrington's office on fire around him. Clearly it was privy to her memories yet chose her worst ones. Her mind worked quickly, piecing the clues together. So far it had shown her moments meant to elicit feelings of agony, hurt, shame. Scryists were forced to focus on negative emotions to scry, feeding the mirrors with sorrow and fear. This was its aim. To scare her and hurt her and make her feel alone, all the while wearing Barrington's face for the maximum infliction of pain.

Cognizant this was its nourishment, Sera stifled the flames that wished to engulf him and drive this evil out. More, she suppressed the fear of what would happen if she never got out of this fog, lost forever in this void. She couldn't give in to this dread or all would be lost.

Barrington walked past her to a black birdcage that hadn't been there before. Within the enclosure was a small black bird huddled in a corner. Anger pricked Sera's scars, and Barrington grinned. The images along the glass changed, now portraying her moments with Noah, from the day he'd first rescued her on that ship, to the first time he'd taught her to use her magic. To those rare moments of tenderness before he drained her reserves. Cold flushed through her, the sensation of his touch and kisses alive on her skin. The song he always sang after he took her magic echoed through the room, made doubly cruel coming from Barrington's mouth.

Sera, Sera in a cage
Sera, Sera wants to fly
But her pretty wings are broken
See her fall from the sky...

Barrington set his apple down and reached in gingerly to get the frightened bird. The closest mirror replayed the memory where she'd huddled the same way in the corner of the bed, sobbing and begging Noah not to drain her.

"Tell me, do the scars still hurt?" He opened his palms and released the bird into the air, but its wing was broken and it crashed down to the floor. It twitched and fluttered, but within moments, it stopped.

Sera gripped her wand tighter, wells of heartache wanting to burst open within. "I won't fall for your trick, no matter how hard you try to hurt me."

Barrington leaned back against the edge of the workbench, his arms crossed over his chest, and chuckled. "Oh, I'm not trying, believe me. If I wanted to hurt you, I'd show you this."

He nodded to a mirror opposite them. Sera followed his gaze, and a stab of pain twisted her heart at the reflection of Barrington bringing a vial of blood magic to his lips and tipping the contents back. Of his veins turning black as the poisonous tonic coursed through him. Of him writhing in pain within the containment room, the shackles burning into his wrists as he fought against them, desperate for blood and death.

"Or I'd show you this."

The reflections changed to Barrington and Gummy entwined.

Sera turned away, but there were mirrors everywhere and they all showed her the same. Barrington loving another woman who wasn't her.

"No, no. I have just the one." He pushed off the desk and walked around her slowly, his steps echoing in the deep silence. "You see, I'm privy to many things here: unfulfilled dreams and regrets, fears and sorrows, but I must say truth is the best one yet. That's how I would hurt you, *darling*. With the truth. This truth."

The Enchantress burst into a cloud of shattered glass, then re-formed into a woman who looked like an older version of Sera, only with lighter hair and eyes. Her nose was upturned at the tip, just like Sera's. For a moment, Sera thought it to be her in the future, but when she noted the lack of a seventhborn tattoo and the woman's swollen belly, her heart pounded.

It wasn't her but her mother.

"What do you think she would say if she saw you now? *My daughter, the fool. After all I did, this is how you repay my sacrifice?* No, wait. I didn't get her voice quite right."

"Stop," Sera begged, the image of this woman clawing at her soul. It wasn't real. It wasn't. Yet, while there was always the possibility she would find her father and siblings, this was the one face she would never see. The one person she would never meet. Her mother. The woman whose death she'd caused. But Sera gripped her hair. It wasn't real. She had to remember it wasn't real.

"Don't you want to know what she sounds like?" the

Enchantress asked. "She spoke a lot to you while in the womb, you know."

"You're a liar," Sera rasped. "My memories are bound."

"True, but these first memories cannot be locked away or destroyed, dear. They were made while you were being made. You carry them inside every fiber of your being. They make you who you are."

Sera shook her head. She couldn't bear this. Not this...

The sound of a steady heartbeat echoed all around them. The Enchantress smiled and, turning her face down, stroked a hand along her pregnant belly. "Be strong, my darling. You will change the world."

The sound of her mother's heartbeat and voice slammed into Sera, and pain webbed beneath her skin. She screamed the lifetime of guilt and yearning she carried in her soul. The cries vacated her as black smoke that was absorbed into the Enchantress

"Such pain, such sorrow."

The Enchantress raised a hand. Black orbs of magic blasted into Sera and thrust her back into a mirror. She cried out; glass stabbed her back, and pain radiated through her. She collapsed into a heap on the floor, surrounded by crystal shards.

The Enchantress walked to her, now a mirror image of Sera. The chamber around her also changed to reflect Sera's room at the Academy. Between the mirrors on the walls were burn marks from the times Sera lost her temper, and around her was the broken furniture from when she'd kick or burn something out of frustration.

"Poor, poor Sera. Look at this mess you've made. Not just here, but in everything. Mary betrayed you. Timothy and your mother died for you. Nikolai abandoned you, and now you're in here with no chance of ever getting out. Of ever finding your family."

Exhausted, Sera collapsed down onto her hands. This was too much. Was this truly what her life had become?

The Enchantress knelt beside her. "Look at yourself." Gripping Sera's hair, she yanked her head up and forced her to look at herself in the broken shards of glass. "Abomination. Curse. Murderer. This is who you are. Did you really think you could ever belong? That you could truly be loved?"

Sera caught sight of herself in the reflection. Bloody and beaten and so very sad. And yet, she had been here before. Broken by Noah. Broken by the Brotherhood. Broken by life, but she'd survived. She looked all around her, to the most painful fragments of her life playing over as though they were present devastations. From Mary's betrayal and Timothy's death. To Barrington imprisoned in a mirror, his hair growing white as the Enchantress fed on his agony and greatest regrets. To her mother cradling her belly as her mouth moved with words Sera couldn't hear. A trembling smile touched Sera's lips, and a surge of warm magic spread through her.

The Enchantress's brow dipped, black eyes gleaming. "Why are you smiling?"

"Because you're right. This is who I am." A low rumbling shook the room around them, but Sera went on. "Mary lied and delivered me to the Brotherhood after she'd done all she could to keep me safe."

The Enchantress hissed in pain, and she released Sera. The hand she'd held Sera with was now burned.

Sera pushed back onto her knees, glass shards stabbed into the palms of her hand. "When Timothy broke his blood oath and died, it was to protect me."

The mirrors around the room vibrated and rattled against the walls. The Enchantress gasped and shuffled back, looking frantically around the room. "What are you doing?"

Sera struggled to her feet. "Barrington might have once been Gummy's, but now he loves me. And my mother… She died so I could live."

The Enchantress screamed and thrust a cluster of black magic at Sera, its sound a harmony of sorrowful cries. Sera raised her hand and met this hatred with her own power, a shaft of white magic filled with everything she was: someone who belonged. Someone who was loved.

A loud snap resounded at the clash of their white and black magic, and all the mirrors burst into clouds of pulverized glass. Freed from their prisons, the spirits within dissolved, twines of glittering light that quickly vanished.

The Enchantress's eyes widened at their disappearance, and she screamed. Reinforced by her hatred and desperation, her magic strengthened and pulsed closer to Sera, but Sera didn't fear her.

She focused only on Timothy's kindness and sacrifice.

On Mary's friendship and smile.

On Barrington's strength and loyalty.

Glass floated up from the ground and spun around them, faster and faster, akin to Sera's magic churning wildly at her core. The Enchantress screamed again. This time, her sound was an amalgamation of all the sorrow and sadness contained in her mirror world. The deafening shrieks stabbed at Sera's eardrums, and the Enchantress's magic drew closer. Sera ground her teeth together and pushed back with what strength she had left, but her reserves ran low, and the Enchantress was strong, powered by centuries of fear and mourning.

All the screams filled Sera's head and her hold on her memories. She closed her eyes, hoping to focus on Barrington and Timothy and Mary, on Doctor Morgan and Lucas and

Rosie, on everyone who had ever shown her a slight bit of kindness, but the shrieks were everywhere, as was the ice radiating from their battle, a frigid breeze that chilled her bones in this vortex of glass. The thoughts grew fragile and burst into clouds of smoke.

But here at the very end of her strength, Sera remembered her mother's heartbeat and voice.

Be strong, my darling. You will change the world.

A rush of magic, hot and burning, surged from the deepest part of her soul. Blinding and searing white fire swathed down her arms and burst from her hand. It cut straight through the Enchantress's magic and to her core. The Enchantress arched back, her facade cracked, and the white light of Sera's magic burst from the seams. She screeched, an inhuman roar, and exploded into sparks of magic and ice. A cold ring of frost burst outward, a blast of power so strong it thrust Sera back.

She slammed onto the training room floor, once again in the realm of the living. The Enchantress's mirror was beside her, its glass broken. All the mirrors on the walls were also shattered, their remains scattered about the rug like diamonds. A formless black cloud glittered in the middle of the chamber, twisting and twining into itself; all the pure black magic contained within the Enchantress's mirror, now without a vessel to call home. It spun, no doubt searching for a new mirror, but finding only broken frames and shattered glass, it issued a vicious cry that whipped against Sera as a harsh, cold gale. It lunged toward Sera, but the Barghest materialized before her, opened its wide jowls with a vicious growl, and swallowed up the black cloud.

He turned to her, his red eyes pooled with worry, and nudged her foot as though asking if she was all right.

Sera nodded and wrapped her arms around him, despite

the smell of sulfur. His magic crackled like red lightning beneath his skin. "Thank you for saving me, again…Storm."

He inclined his head and extended one paw, clearly pleased with the name.

A loud thud resounded down the hall.

Storm whipped into a cloud and dashed to the sound. Sera groped the wall and struggled to her feet. She ran out of the training room just as Barrington stumbled out of his office, his arm pressed against the doorframe for support. His clothes were wet, his skin pale, and his hair white.

A breath rattled in Sera's lungs. Was he real, or was this his ghost come to haunt her? Or, worse, when he looked at her, would she find his eyes were black glass? *Please be here*, she begged. *Please, please be you.*

Footsteps clambered down the stairs. Rosie appeared at the foot of the landing and screamed. "Master!"

Barrington lifted his eyes. They were gray. "Sera?"

A cry broke in Sera's chest, and though spent, she picked up her wet skirts and ran to him. Barrington stumbled forward onto his knees, but Sera caught him and helped him to the ground. And she held him and kissed him and felt him.

Alive. Here. Safe.

His cool hand came upon her face, his gaze weary and disoriented. "Are you really here?"

She nodded and held him closer. "I'm here, my love."

EPILOGUE

A pinkish sky spread over Barrington's land as the sun set on the moors. The hue added a warm glow to the field, softening the jagged peaks and rocky edges. Sitting on the patio overlooking the heaths, the light also covered Barrington, yet he still trembled. And though humidity made the air thick, his skin remained pale and lips blue. Beside him, Inspector Lewis and Lucas chatted, but Barrington was silent, his gaze fixed on the hills.

"How has he been since our last visit?" Mrs. York asked from beside Doctor Morgan. With them sitting side by side, Sera mused how she hadn't seen the resemblance earlier.

"Better, but not much." She poured them each a glass of lemonade. "When not asleep, he's sitting in the sun or before a fire, wrapped in a blanket or cloak, and drinking warm tonics, but nothing has rid him of the cold."

Doctor Morgan took a sip and set down her glass. "Based on what I've gathered from those freed from the mirror, the Enchantress functioned the same as a warlock. It drained its victims of magic to sustain itself and its mirror world. And just like with constant draining, Nikolai's magic has been stunted, and it has affected his ability to produce warmth. It will take time to improve his rate of replenishing, and his magic must be coaxed and treated gently, but with rest he will do well."

Sera looked back to Barrington, and her heart wrenched. That was easier said than done. After she'd escaped Noah's clutches, she too had been seized by vicious tremors, and it had taken almost a year for the shakes to go away. But Barrington was a man of magic and power; he would not rest until his powers were restored. Just that morning, she'd woken to find him in his workroom. A spell book was opened before him to a page for an elixir to induce warmth. However, unable to light a fire with his magic or steady his hands enough to use a match, he'd fallen asleep in the dark.

"But it might help him to know he's doing much better than any of the others who made it out of the mirror. His hair is an indication he's improving."

Indeed, the black coloring had returned, though parts of it were still streaked white.

"Some are having difficulty with their memories, while others have shown no improvement at all. Mrs. James, Miss Douglas, and Mr. Whittaker have yet to regain consciousness."

Sera's heart stuttered. "What of the children?"

"They too remain asleep, I'm afraid. But I'm confident they will recover. Whereas our reserves only respond to healing magic of our inclination once we've reached adolescence, their reserves are still developing and respond to treatment in every element. They should be awake soon and will be safe…for now. I daresay with Mr. Delacort's win, no one feels safe."

"Indeed," Mrs. York lamented, fanning herself against

the heat. She wore all black, and Sera wondered if, given the state of things, her choice of attire was figurative. "While everyone believed our story, that a student's spell went horribly wrong during the examination, it has given Delacort more public sympathy. And after this morning's arrests, we won't ever recover."

"What arrests?" Sera asked.

"You haven't heard? I'd imagine Nikolai would have gotten word first, though he has been under the weather. A number of brothels across the Aetherium were raided this morning. They were Miss Mills's establishments. They're crediting Mr. Delacort's blood magic initiative; apparently her store of product was immense. She's since gone into hiding. I'm sure she has people of power under her influence who have helped, but her empire of blood magic is in ruin." She sighed. "Yes, I suppose he got the blood he needed; I'm glad it wasn't Nikolai's. Sadly, this is a blow."

Sera looked at Barrington in the distance, his gaze still far away. Had this been the deal with the enemy he'd spoken of that would hurt Gummy more than their magic combined? Delacort was indeed the enemy, and the raids on Gummy's brothels destroyed what she loved most: her power.

Patting Sera's hands, Mrs. York pulled her from her thoughts. "But there is still work to be done. So long as the Brotherhood persists, so will we. Is that the mirror?"

She nodded at the metal chest on a side table beside Sera. The box was riddled with containment and protection spells, though a thorough check of the glass revealed none of its magic remained. The mirror, however, was still black and functioned as a powerful scrying glass.

"What is left of it, yes." She handed Mrs. York the box as Barrington and Inspector Lewis joined them. Lucas ventured down the path toward Storm. After devouring the Enchantress, the Barghest had fallen ill at the pure black magic he had consumed, but with a hearty dose of Sera's white magic, his health had improved, and their bond was strengthened.

"Are you certain it will be safe?" Barrington asked. "The Brotherhood was at the school, so someone told them about it. There's a chance Miss Mills told someone and they shared it with the Brotherhood, or Armitage told Mr. Delacort and he's still associated with them. But we also cannot overlook the possibility that there may be a mole in your home."

"It will be kept in my personal vault." She handed Inspector Lewis the box. "And we are having everyone on our staff thoroughly assessed."

"What of Mary?" Sera asked. "Did you manage to alert the Sisters of Mercy? With Delacort as chancellor, it will be harder to keep her safe as he will oversee all information. If he went to these lengths to find her, I fear what he will do once he's assumed control."

"She's safe. I told the Sisters, and they've changed her location. They evaded the Brotherhood for ages; they will protect her."

The bells tolled the hour. Noon.

Mrs. York snapped her black laced fan shut. "We must go. I want to be out of the capital before Delacort's acceptance speech tomorrow morning. I don't think Duncan will survive it, to hear the cheers for that man."

"Was concession truly the right choice?" Barrington asked as they all rose to leave.

"It was our only choice if we wished to keep what good favor we have from the council by not dragging them through a vote. We may come to need it."

With their goodbyes said, the three of them transferred out.

Sera sat next to Barrington, their silence a deafening and heavy thing between them. Given Rosie's constant fussing and visits from Mrs. York and Doctor Morgan to check on his progress, their time alone had suffered. And amid his long bouts of sleep and solemn moods, so had their conversations and affections. But here, their eyes met, and despite his shivering, desire and unsaid words crowded the air like starved, uninvited guests seeking someone to feed them.

Their hands moved to each other's, but Sera hissed at his touch, and he drew his hand away.

"Sorry," he murmured.

"It's all right. Headmistress Reed once said I had a peculiar fire that needed to be quelled and had me stand in the cold for hours with no shoes or cloak. I think I can handle it." She smiled.

He returned the gesture, but it vanished quickly as he retreated into his thoughts once more.

She moved close to him, hoping her presence gave him some comfort. "I heard about Gummy's brothels," she ventured. "Am I right to think that was you?"

His jaw pulsed, but he nodded. "We needed access to the secret library, and he needed a prominent arrest to secure his reputation as a strong leader. It was clear Duncan wasn't going to win, but Delacort is blinded by his desire for popularity and power; I knew he wouldn't refuse."

Despite the cold, she slid her hand over his and gave it a squeeze. "Thank you. When do you intend to go?"

"I thought after your Aetherium interview tomorrow. I'd go alone, but given this wretchedness I've become, it may not be the wisest choice."

Sera winced at the bitterness in his words. "It will get better, I promise," she said, hoping he could withstand it. He hadn't turned to blood magic, evident by the lack of change in his condition, but surely the thought lingered close. His brooding deepened with each passing day, and Sera hoped he was strong enough to resist it.

"Hopefully sooner rather than later. The fact the Brotherhood emerged means they not only knew about the mirror, they wanted it. I suspect that, like Delacort, they sought it to aid them in finding Mary, and with it, the spell Timothy died to reveal. They will not stop looking for it, and neither will we stop hunting them. But with Mrs. York vacating the Aetherium, Mr. Delacort in power, and Miss Mills gone, we will have to do this on our own."

She moved close to him and rested her head on his shoulder. "I wouldn't want it any other way."

He tilted her head up to his and kissed her softly, a gentle glide of his cool lips, then together they watched the last of the sun die over the horizon and darkness claim the land, the same way the Brotherhood sought to infect the world with their evil.

Never again.

Together, she and Barrington would hunt the Brotherhood and bring them to justice, just as they would do to all other monsters, whether human or phantom.

Sera tugged on the high collar of her new Aetherium gown, the official dress required by all Continuing Studies students. Though wearing it had been a dream, the scratchy burgundy material was a downright nightmare. The neckline seam of her waist-high cape chafed the bottom of her jaw, and the seven decorative buttons of each element on her dress nicked at her collarbone. Her legs weren't used to these new leather boots; her others had all been hand-me-downs from Mary, already softened from use.

But she pressed a hand to her chest, to Barrington's coordinate necklace hidden beneath the fabric, and gazed to the opulent room around her. To the chandelier above, each crystal fashioned into a wand that caught the sunlight and spread small rainbows along the waiting room. To the wooden floor stamped with golden protection circles, to artwork along the walls in gilt frames. More, her gaze drifted beyond the open turquoise curtains to the Aetherium visible in the distance. However rough her dress and aching her feet, these discomforts were trivial compared to the hell she'd already endured to get here.

Warmth spread through her. She had witnessed its beauty at night, but no pamphlet or impression could ever capture the beauty and strength exuded from the seven Aetherium towers encircling the glittering bay. Sera leaned forward and peeked up. Unlike the soot found elsewhere in the city, the constant ocean breeze here pushed the grime and darkness away to reveal a vibrant blue sky. No, nothing could have prepared her for the sight of this place, and tears filled her eyes.

The cherrywood door groaned open, and a secretary in an elbow-length crimson cape stepped out. "Miss Seraphina Dovetail."

Sera rose and walked to the open door, her heart a knot in her throat. She'd already been accepted, but this was the final test. The magicians behind that door would either admit her as a Fire-level apprentice, where she could pursue her degree in Investigative Arts to learn defense and all that was needed to protect the Aetherium, or they would recommend another option that was not a recommendation at all, not if she wished to remain in the Aetherium.

With a final glance at the towers, she walked inside. A crimson runner of a flourish design led the way into the dim, wood-paneled chamber, where a long table mastered the back of the room. Seven magicians in robes representing their elements sat behind it with their hands clasped on top. They all watched her, their gazes shuttered and cold and expressions stoic. Still, Sera held her chin a touch higher and moved down the aisle.

She deserved to be here.

For the next hour, each of the magicians questioned her on her qualifications until the Fire-levels interviewer, Commander Olson, stood and paced around the table, her boots echoing in the quiet room.

Tap. Tap. Tap.

Sera gulped. All Aetherium defense, from the inspectors and guards to the military, served under the Fire branch, and this woman in an ankle-length robe would eventually become her direct superior, should she be accepted as a Fire-level student.

She was tall and full-bodied, her warm golden skin marked with freckles. Her pin-straight hair was cut to her chin, perfectly even and not one hair out of place. She turned brown eyes to Sera, her mouth pressed into a tight line. "It says in your file you wish to become an inspector."

"Yes, ma'am."

"Our Investigative concentration is one of the most rigorous pursuits in the school, second only to our military program, a portion of which you will have to undertake during your time here. You will need to be knowledgeable in all of magic in order to properly defend it, especially Fire, Metal, and Wood levels. Wisdom, defense, and a thorough knowledge of law are essential, and they are not easy to attain, more so for someone of your…condition. Would you not be better suited for a profession as a Seer? It is a suitable option for your kind. You've recently developed the sight, yes?"

Sera nodded. In the past, she never would have admitted it, but seeing as she was no longer an Academy student, they couldn't force her to become a Seer. "Yes, ma'am. But, with all due respect, I have no desire to see evidence and impressions of crimes and be powerless to do anything about it."

"Fair enough. But why an inspector? You could still effect a great deal of change in another field of study, without the added hardship of a Fire-level education."

Sera's heart pounded. A personal statement. She'd read this was one of the most important questions and was encouraged to work on an answer, though she hadn't gotten the chance with the madness consuming her life.

But, bolstered by the memory of Barrington, Mrs. James, the children, and everyone else who'd been trapped in the mirror, she drew in a breath.

And, focused on all other seventhborns now scared for their lives under Mr. Delacort's imminent rule, she said, "Because I am a seventhborn, ma'am. I am what is thought of as a weaker sex and cursed birthright. I have been on the edge of death and have seen beyond it. Have witnessed the rage of men and bear the proof of it on my skin. I have come across monsters of all sorts, suffered through my own, all because of this mark upon my wrist."

She paused. "And do you know the worst part? There are so many others like me, who are invisible, even when they're seen. Who are ignored, even when they scream at the horrors done to them. But I have also seen kindness. Not much, but enough to know it's worth fighting for. Just as one person gave me a chance, I want to be that for someone else. I will see them and hear them, those in this life and beyond. I will find and fight their monsters and let them know they're not alone."

The commander's face remained stoic, her mouth pressed to a severe line. She closed Sera's file and walked around the table. Sera's stomach tightened; surely she had heard enough, had noticed how short and utterly unprepared her statement had been.

Commander Olson stopped beside Sera's chair. "On your feet, apprentice."

Sera stood, though her knees were numb and wholly unstable.

"Your wand."

Sera's pulse quickened, but she did as she was told. Whatever happened next, this wouldn't be her end. If she was assigned to any other program, she would merely be the best student in that endeavor and prove to them she was better suited elsewhere. She would fight. She would always fight.

Commander Olson touched her wand to Sera's. "It is my honor to welcome you to the Aetherium School of Continuing Magic as a Fire-level apprentice, with a pursuit in the Investigative Arts. Do you vow to work ardently in support of the Aetherium and all under its law?"

The words "Investigative Arts" gripped her heart, and her legs weakened beneath her, but Sera forced herself to remain upright. "Yes, Commander."

"Then please state the oath."

"I do solemnly, sincerely, and truly declare and affirm that I will never betray my wand, my honor, my character, or the Aetherium's trust. I will perform my duties with fairness, integrity, diligence, and impartiality. On my magic and my life, I will uphold fundamental human rights and accord equal respect to the Aetherium and all under its law."

Their respective magic filled the other's wand, her Aetherium oath now made. Commander Olson lowered her wand and nodded once. "You're dismissed."

"Thank you, Commander," Sera said and, with a small bob, walked to the door.

"And Miss Dovetail?"

Sera paused and turned.

"I look forward to hunting these monsters together."

"Yes, ma'am," Sera said. The hunt was underway.

Closing the door behind her, she pressed trembling fingers to her mouth as tears smeared the world around her. Where once she'd been ostracized and cast aside, she now had a home and a place to belong. Despite Noah's scars and Mary's betrayal, she had real friendships and Barrington's love. And though she had been expelled from the Witchling Academy, she sheathed her wand, now a proper Fire-level apprentice in the Aetherium's Investigative Arts.

One step closer to becoming an inspector. To finding her family.

She shut her eyes. Though she could not remember them, she focused on the phantom faces she'd imagined as those of her siblings and father.

And while they were blurs, one part of her family was clear. Her mother's voice, which she carried now deep in her heart.

Be strong, darling. You will change the world.

Sera smiled and pushed off the door, her head held high. As the first seventhborn in the Investigative program, she already had.

She'd only just begun.

ACKNOWLEDGMENTS

First and foremost, I give all thanks to God for the gift of words. For guiding and providing and sustaining and just being all. I'd be nothing without His mercy and grace.

To Cliff, my love. Thank you for your selflessness, gentleness, and constant encouragement. I love you, always.

To my little darlings, you three have changed my world for the better and continue to do that each and every day. Stay focused on the Lord and keep shining your light; the world so desperately needs it.

To my family. Your unending support is everything. I love you all so much. So, so much.

Alice, there are not enough thank-yous and will never be enough thank-yous for your friendship and support. Still, I love you and thank you, thank you, thank you.

Cathy Holst, thank you for your help and words of encouragement on this story and all the others I've sent your way. It means more than you'll ever know. You're such a blessing, and I am so very thankful.

To my Wattpad4 girls: Leah Crichton, Rebecca Sky, Erin Latimer, Lindsey Summers, and Fallon DeMornay. I am so proud of what we've accomplished and continue to accomplish. Every writer needs a tribe, and I'm so glad to have found mine.

To the Wattpad staff, thank you for giving us writers a safe place to explore and grow our craft. Finding Wattpad changed my life and I will be forever grateful.

To my dear readers, thank you for letting me share Sera and Barrington's story with you. This book was hard to write for many reasons, so the fact you're reading it makes it a hundred times more special. Thank you.

Turn the page to start reading the romantic,
mysterious new book from Kelsey Sutton

SMOKE

AND

KEY

CHAPTER ONE

A voice penetrates the silence.

At first, it's just a string of syllables without meaning. I float in the unending darkness, disoriented and drowsy. The voice calls to me again. Frowning, I try to concentrate. When it comes a third time, I finally understand some of what it's saying. *Wake up.*

My eyes fly open.

Darkness surrounds me. The voice reaches out a fourth time, still muffled but easier to comprehend now. *Please wake up,* it's pleading. At last I try to answer; the only sound that emerges from my throat is an odd grunt. The beginnings of hysteria stir within me. *All right,* I think. *Be logical. Find out where you are.*

Slowly, I work out that I'm lying down. Whatever is against my back and shoulders is plush and foul smelling. I lift my hands, blinking, and touch a smooth ceiling. What is this place? How did I come to be here?

I strain to hear the voice, but it's gone. Now confusion gives way to fear and my hands become fists. I shove at the ceiling—it doesn't move. A frenzy overtakes me as I begin hitting it. The grunt has progressed to a hoarse shout. Wherever I am is so quiet, so still that I know I'm alone.

Panic burns through my veins and I attempt to roll over in the tiny space, kicking and clawing. Then someone screams, *"Let me out!"*

It takes a moment to recognize that it's my own voice, weak and rough. Suddenly a new sound vibrates through the stillness, a thundering *crack*.

Then I'm falling.

Air rushes past me. Acting on instinct, I spread my limbs out in a wild attempt to save myself, but there's nothing to latch onto. Faint lights shine below. I blink, too shocked to scream again. The ground—or whatever awaits at the bottom—approaches rapidly. I glance backward and see long hair and a skirt flapping like a sheet in the wind.

There's no time to notice anything else; I'm seconds away from the ground. Somehow I think through the panic and curl up into a ball to brace for impact. I do so just in time, and as I crash down, the entire world trembles. Earth billows up around me, and a shock goes through my limbs. There's not as much pain as there should be, though, only a slight disturbance on the skin and bones I landed on.

Trembling, I open one eye and watch the dust settle. A thousand questions churn in my mind as I uncurl and look around.

"Hello? Is s-someone there?" I manage to whisper. The words shake so badly even I can hardly understand them. I'm sitting in what appears to be a narrow alley. Everything is dirt, even the walls on either side. Lit torches appear sporadically, giving this frightening place an orange tint. The small flames sputter every few seconds, and it's the only sound I detect around me. A faint musty smell fills my nose. I push myself up on unsteady legs and turn in a circle, searching for anything familiar or living. I cup my elbows to protect myself from terror rather than cold.

"Hello?" I call again, louder this time.

There's movement out of the corner of my eye and I spin toward it. A face peers around the edge of the doorway. One of the torches is directly above it, casting flickering shadows over the little girl's face. I recoil instinctively, gasping, and the girl vanishes back into the house-like structure made entirely of earth.

But it's too late. I saw her. I saw the way her eye dangled from its socket and how her skin was half withered away.

I retreat until my back hits the wall behind me. *This is a dream,* I think faintly. So I squeeze my eyes shut and will myself to wake up. Nothing changes, though. Intending to run from this place and the appalling girl, I slide away from the wall and into the path.

"She won't hurt you. Doll's afraid of her own shadow," a voice drones.

I let out a small cry and stagger back yet again. This time my heel catches on something and I land hard on my bottom. I frantically search for the speaker. The words came from another doorway, one opposite where I spotted the young girl. No one else appears, though, and it takes several attempts to speak again. "Who's there?" I squeak.

Seconds pass. Then the same voice answers, "No one."

His tone is so reasonable, so indifferent, that I'm able to gather my thoughts. Perhaps this person can help me? Swallowing, I strain to see in the gloom. "If n-no one's there, then how are you talking to me?" I challenge, finding a bit of courage.

"Perhaps you're talking to yourself."

Instead of responding, I get to my feet. I dare to step closer, and when nothing leaps out or attacks, I take another. There *is* someone beyond the threshold—the light is just enough that I can make out the details of his appearance. It's a boy.

He sits in a wooden chair, bent forward, wrists dangling atop his knees. Between two of his fingers is a single, unlit cigar. The holder containing it is lovely, shining white like a pearl, the edges adorned with carvings. As for the boy himself, his features are hidden, but I can see a shock of blue-black hair against the back of his neck and curling over his ear. His profile is lithe and…sad, somehow.

"Who are you?" I whisper, stopping again.

The boy doesn't react. "Weren't you listening?" he asks without glancing up, as though he's carrying on a conversation with the dirt. His accent is distinctly American. "I'm no one. We're all no one."

"I'm someone," I say without thinking. It doesn't make any sense, because of course I am, but suddenly I need to prove it's true.

An odd sound escapes him, something that is more bark than laugh. The edges of it are sharp and mocking. "Oh, really? Then what's your name?" Now his head tilts slightly in my direction, though not completely.

Curious, in spite of the alarming strangeness all around me, I fiddle with my skirts and resist the temptation to move even closer. "It's…" I begin, then trail off. This shouldn't be a difficult question. Yet I don't remember. It's a sensation similar to fumbling in the dark, reaching for an item that should've been there, and finding empty air. How can I not know my own name? Everything has a name. I can tell him what the oceans and continents of the world are called, so why can't I recall that one word that defines the entirety of my being?

The boy lets me struggle for a few seconds. "See?" He doesn't sound smug, just resigned. He still doesn't turn. I want him to *see* me, to say that this is a terrible nightmare.

There's a bleak feeling spreading through my chest, a sinking sensation, because there can't possibly be any good answers to the question I'm about to ask.

"Where are we?"

The torch closest to us is dying. It makes a pathetic sound, and I'm so distracted by the dwindling flames that I almost don't hear the boy. "…one of those, are you? Need to have everything said out loud." I wait for him to go on, refusing to rise to the bait, and he sighs. He puts the cigar to his nose and takes a long inhale. "You're dead, darlin'. This isn't hell, but it's the next best thing."

"You're lying," I manage, frozen despite everything inside me urging me to *run*.

His shoulders lift in a careless shrug. "Wish I was."

"I think I would remember dying."

"Not in this place, you wouldn't. No one remembers anything here. Also, why don't you try finding a heartbeat? Go on. I'll wait."

My hands rise of their own volition. The skin they flatten against is cold. *Too cold*, I think numbly. I stand there, waiting, praying to sense that steady *thump, thump, thump*.

Nothing.

It feels like my lungs are swelling, horror trapping all the air and protests. In that instant, I realize I'm not breathing. The corset; it must be too tight. Disregarding rules of propriety, I reach behind me to undo the strings. The dress hinders every effort, but I stubbornly keep at it. When the stillness lingers too long, the boy finally looks at me. "You don't need to breathe…" he starts to say, impatience coloring the words. Our gazes clash.

Every thought I have vanishes. I nearly bolt again. The boy is pale…too pale for someone living. His eyes are a too-light shade of blue and his lips are nearly white. His shirt is buttoned up the front but open at the collar, revealing the raised tissue across his throat and the line of stitches closing it up.

No one would survive a wound like that.

A sound of terror escapes me as I retreat. The boy studies my face, and now there's obvious interest in his expression.

"Wait—" he starts.

I flee.

He says something else, but his words are overpowered by the roaring in my ears. There's no sign of the little girl as I burst out of the alleyway and into another. There are more doorways, more torches, more moving things in the darkness. It's a maze.

Mindless with terror, I sob and stumble along. "Help! Please, help! Anybody—"

My face slams into a wall.

No, not a wall. "What we 'ave 'ere?" a new, deep voice rumbles above my head. The brogue of someone who works in fields and has calluses on his hands. Fingers catch hold of me, huge and rough, and I scream as I try to yank free. The grip on my arms tightens as though I'm no stronger than a child. The man pins me with one hand and explores my face with his other—I'm so shocked that the next scream catches in my throat. An acrid smell assails every sense. Before I can look up or demand release, he continues. "Aye, dis is a new bake. Boys, come greet our latest arrival! Gracious, you're a juicy lassie."

Indignation shines through the terror fogging my mind. "Let *go* of me!" I finally snap, flattening my fists against the man's chest to put distance between us. I kick at his shins, and he chuckles. Torches approach from every side, held aloft by hands of all shapes and sizes. My gaze flicks over the people surrounding us, and colored spots mar my vision when I see the various states of decay they're in. Exposed tissue and gaping teeth and flapping skin.

I shriek yet again, a high and piercing sound. Then I happen to catch a glimpse of my captor's face, and I go mute with horror.

He might have been a man, once. But what I see now is purely a monster. His skin is charred and peeling, his scalp red and shining. The tips of his fingers and ears and nose are missing, and he has no eyes. Empty sockets leer down at me.

I open my mouth to scream again.

"Let her go, Splinter."

Through my terror, I recognize that voice—it's the boy with the unlit cigar. Several moments go by as I search for him in the crowd. Eventually I see his silhouette leaning against one of the dirt buildings close by, hands shoved in his pockets. That cigar dangles from his lips.

"An' if I don't?" the hideous Irishman snaps. Seconds tick by, thick with tension. The boy doesn't say a word; he just stares. Slowly, the steel grip around my middle relents. The man spits on the ground next to my foot. Or, at least, he tries to—nothing leaves his mouth. "Was just a bit o' fun. Not much else to do round 'ere." He stomps off.

Some of the creatures still eye me with curiosity. So much pale skin. So many dark eyes. My stomach quakes when I realize there's nowhere to run.

After another moment, the boy shoves off the wall, pocketing his cigar. The moment he approaches, the crowd begins to disperse, taking their torches with them. Like black iron, they meld with the darkness. One of them hesitates, though, and glances back at me. A man in rags who's less rotten than the others. The hair at his temples is a distinguished gray and there's a slight limp to his step. Our gazes meet for an instant, and then he's gone.

The boy reaches my side and touches my elbow. "Are you all right?"

It's too soon after being assaulted by that monster. I jerk away. "Don't touch me!"

He eases back and puts some distance between us. "Are you all right?" he repeats carefully.

I push my hair out of my face, shaking so badly that there's no way to hide it. "Yes, I'm fine. Just fine." No matter how many times I say the words, they don't become true. He waits, giving me a chance to regain my composure. Eventually I can think again, and the need for answers intensifies. "You said this is hell?" I whisper, keeping my focus on the direction the creatures disappeared.

Now I believe it.

I can feel the boy looking at me as he answers. "Well, we call it Under."

At this, I frown. "Why—"

"Look up."

Obeying, I arch my neck back. Instead of sky, there's a ceiling, of sorts. More dirt and what appear to be tree roots. Scattered among these roots are splotches of shadow, though it's too far away to tell their purpose or origin. "What are those?"

"Those are the holes each of us fell through. Our graves are right over them."

The word *graves* jars something within me, and suddenly everything makes sense. Opening my eyes in that dark, soft space. The closeness of those smooth walls, the muffled noises above. Something cracking beneath me. Then soaring through open air and hitting the ground.

It was a grave. *My* grave.

He's telling the truth.

If I had any food in my stomach, it would be surging up right now.

Tearing away from the sight of those holes, I face the boy. I know I should thank him for saving me from Splinter, but there are too many questions to ask. "So this is it? This is the afterlife?" My voice is faint. I want him to lie to me. I want him to tell me there's something more, something better. Whoever I was in life must have spent time in a church, because I find the thought of wooden pews and stained-glass windows comforting.

But he only shrugs again. "For some, I suppose. Judging from the size of the graveyard and the number of holes above us, there are many who don't fall."

"If that's true, why did we?"

"Who knows? Maybe it's unfinished business. Or it only takes a particularly loud noise. Or we're just too stupid to stay dead." He begins to walk, and after a brief hesitation, I hurry to follow. Splinter might come back, or some other creature from a nightmare, and this boy has proven to be an excellent protector. His long-legged strides make me break into a run to keep up. The space is so narrow that our arms brush.

Neither of us attempts conversation, and I realize this place isn't as quiet as it seemed in the beginning. There are sounds echoing through the giant cavern. A laugh, a hiss, a whisper. A reminder there are monsters here. How can I know that this boy isn't one of them? *He did save you,* a tiny voice reminds me.

Glancing at him sidelong, I find his profile is appealing. His eyelashes are long and dark. He has a generous mouth. Upon our first meeting, I remember with some shame, I'd been too horrified by the wound across his throat to notice anything else. "What's your name?" I blurt. He raises a thick brow at me, and I bite my lip. "I mean, what do they call you here?"

After a long moment, he murmurs, "Smoke."

I'm about to reply when I recognize where we are. We've reached the location where I fell; the indent my body made is in the dirt. There are the doorways where Doll peered out and I first encountered Smoke.

Now that I'm not running from something, there's more time to absorb this place. In every direction, there are crude houses of dirt with no spaces between them, as if the occupants were trying to create a city. There are no cobblestones or carriages, no trees or signs. Just passages that end in darkness and these earthen homes. But if I squint just so, it's easy to imagine a sky beyond the line of roofs, the faint colors of dawn.

Eventually I realize not all of the structures are the same—some of them have square openings next to the doorways, crude imitations of windows. Of course there's no glass, though. There must be torches inside a few of the dwellings, because shadows dance on the ground, cast by gentle flickers from within. In a way, it's almost comforting.

While I examine our surroundings, my eyes feeling so huge they might as well swallow the rest of my face, Smoke watches me. "You'll have to pick one of your own, you know," he says. "A name, I mean. Usually we just use whatever we fell into Under with. Splinter, Smoke, Doll."

Something we fell into Under with? Unconsciously, I run my hands over my stomach and sides and thighs, searching for any kind of pocket. His eyes track the movements, an odd tightness to his mouth. My hands halt and I wonder if it's possible for the dead to blush. But now I know there's nothing else on my person besides the dress.

No, wait.

For the first time, I notice a weight against my skin, near the center of my chest. I reach for it…and my fingers collide with something curved and hard. It hangs from a chain around my neck and glints gold in the firelight.

Smoke smiles, a ghost of what a smile should be. "Nice to meet you, Key. Welcome to Under."

IF YOU ENJOYED THIS EXCERPT, GRAB

SMOKE AND KEY

WHEREVER BOOKS ARE SOLD

A lush, unique new fantasy trilogy about a girl tasked with stealing the prince's heart... literally. From New York Times *bestselling author Sara Wolf.*

BRING ME THEIR HEARTS

Zera is a Heartless—the immortal, unaging soldier of a witch. Bound to the witch Nightsinger, Zera longs for freedom from the woods they hide in. With her heart in a jar under Nightsinger's control, she serves the witch unquestioningly.

Until Nightsinger asks Zera for a prince's heart in exchange for her own, with one addendum: if she's discovered infiltrating the court, Nightsinger will destroy Zera's heart rather than see her tortured by the witch-hating nobles.

Crown Prince Lucien d'Malvane hates the royal court as much as it loves him—every tutor too afraid to correct him and every girl jockeying for a place at his darkly handsome side. No one can challenge him—until the arrival of Lady Zera. She's inelegant, smart-mouthed, carefree, and out for his blood. The prince's honor has him quickly aiming for her throat.

So begins a game of cat and mouse between a girl with nothing to lose and a boy who has it all.

From Lindsey Duga, author of Kiss of the Royal comes another fast-paced, unique, romantic read for fans of Holly Black and Meg Kassel.

Glow
OF THE
Fireflies

Briony never planned to go back to the place she lost everything.

Firefly Valley, nestled deep within the Smoky Mountains, is better kept in her past. After an unexplained fire gave Briony amnesia, her mother disappeared and her dad moved them to Knoxville.

But now her grandmother needs a caretaker and Briony's dad volunteers her to help. The moment she returns, her whole world shifts. She feels a magical connection to this valley, as if it's literally part of her somehow.

And when she meets a hot guy who claims he was her childhood friend but now mysteriously keeps his distance, Briony starts piecing together her missing past…and discovers her mother didn't leave to start a new life somewhere. She's trapped in the hidden world within the valley.

Now, Briony will do whatever it takes to rescue her, even if it means standing up against dangerously powerful nature spirits. Even if it means giving up her first love.

Let's be friends!

@EntangledTeen

@EntangledTeen

@EntangledTeen

bit.ly/TeenNewsletter